DISCOVERY ACTIVITIES FOR ELEMENTARY SCIENCE

Arthur A. Carin
Queens College

Robert B. Sund
University of Northern Colorado

Charles E. Merrill Publishing Company
A Bell & Howell Company
Columbus   Toronto   London   Sydney

Published by Charles E. Merrill Publishing Co.
A Bell & Howell Company
Columbus, Ohio 43216

This book was set in Times Roman.
Production Editor: Martha Morss
Cover Design Coordination: Will Chenoweth

Copyright © 1980, 1975, 1970, 1964, by Bell & Howell Company. All rights reserved. No part of this book may be reproduced in any form, electronic or mechanical, including photocopy, recording, or any information storage and retrieval system, without permission in writing from the publisher.

Library of Congress Catalog Card Number: 80-80615
International Standard Book Number: 0-675-08089-4

Printed in the United States of America
6 7 8 9 10—89 88 87

CONTENTS

	Introduction		1
SECTION 1	**Discovery Activities for Living Sciences**		6
	Animals—Anatomy and Physiology		
	How Many Different Types of Animals Do You Know?	(K–6)	6
	How Do Ants Live?	(K–6)	8
	What Do You Know About the Birds Around You?	(K–3)	10
	How Do Birds Differ from Mammals?	(4–8)	11
	What Is the Difference Between a Frog and a Lizard?	(3–6)	13
	How Does the Lack of Oxygen Affect Animals?	(3–6)	15
	Animals—Reproduction and Development		
	How Do Some Insects Develop from Egg to Adult?	(3–6)	16
	Why Do You Resemble Your Parents?	(4–8)	19
	How Does a Chicken Develop?	(4–8)	20
	Humans—Anatomy, Physiology, and Nutrition		
	How Does Our Skin Protect Us?	(3–6)	22
	What Are the Functions of Bones?	(4–6)	24
	How Do Organisms Respond To Stimulants?	(4–8)	27
	How Do Our Muscles Work?	(4–8)	28
	How Do Humans Breathe?	(4–8)	31
	How Does Blood Circulate?	(4–8)	35
	What Does the Heart Do?	(4–8)	37
	What Happens to Starch in the Food You Eat?	(4–8)	40
	What Makes a Good Diet?	(4–8)	43
	Play "Check the Label" Game	(4–8)	43
	Plants—Anatomy and Physiology		
	What Is a Seed?	(K–3)	45
	How Do Roots Grow?	(K–6)	46
	How Does Water Get into a Plant?	(K–6)	48
	What Are the Parts of a Plant?	(K–6)	49
	What Is the Purpose of a Stem?	(K–8)	52
	Why Do Some Parts of Plants Grow Upward?	(K–6)	53
	What Is Variation?	(K–6)	55
	How Can You Tell the Age of a Tree?	(K–6)	56
	What Is a Cell?	(4–8)	58
	How Do Leaves Breathe?	(3–8)	59
	How Do Bacteria Change Some Foods?	(K–8)	60
	How Does a Fungus Grow?	(4–8)	62
	How Can Food Be Preserved?	(3–8)	65
	Plants—Reproduction and Development		
	How Can You Get Two Plants from One?	(K–6)	67
	What Function Does a Flower Serve?	(4–8)	68
	Why Is There Plant and Animal Breeding?	(4–8)	71

Ecology

What Do Plants Need to Grow?	(K-6)	72
What Types of Life Can You Find in a Pond?	(K-6)	74
How Does the Environment Affect Life?	(4-8)	76
How Do Animals Affect Their Environments?	(3-8)	79
How Is Life Affected by Variations in Temperature?	(4-8)	81
How Do Earthworms Change the Soil?	(K-6)	82
How May the Unwise Use of Various Substances Endanger Your Health and Safety?	(K-6)	84

SECTION 2 Discovery Activities for Environmental Sciences 88

Meteorology—Weather

What Is a Barometer?	(K-6)	88
How Can Solar Energy Be Used?	(4-8)	89
How Can You Make a Cloud?	(3-8)	91
What Is a Hygrometer?	(4-8)	94
How Much Water Will Snow Make?	(K-6)	96

Geology

How Are Crystals Formed?	(K-6)	98
How Are Rocks Alike?	(K-6)	102
How Do Limestone, Marble, and Granite Differ?	(3-8)	103
How Does Erosion Affect the Soil?	(3-6)	104
What Is a Fault?	(4-8)	107
How Does a Geyser Work?	(2-8)	110
What Are Fossils and Fossil Beds?	(3-8)	111
How Can a Fossil Be Made?	(K-6)	113

Astronomy

What Is the Shape of the Earth?	(K-3)	115
Why Is There Day and Night?	(K-3)	116
How Do the Planets Move?	(4-8)	117
What Size is the Sun Compared to the Earth?	(K-3)	119
What Does the Sun Do for Us?	(K-3)	120
How Long Is a Year?	(3-6)	121
What Causes the Seasons?	(4-8)	124
Why Do Stars Appear Close or Far Apart?	(K-4)	126
What Causes Some Stars to Be Different Colors?	(4-8)	127
Why Does the Moon Shine?	(2-4)	129
Why Are There Phases of the Moon?	(3-8)	131
What Causes the Tides?	(4-8)	132
What Is an Eclipse?	(4-8)	134

SECTION 3 Discovery Activities for Physical Sciences 136

Structure of Matter

What Is Matter?	(K-3)	136
What Are Molecules?	(K-8)	137
What Are Water Molecules and How Do They Affect Each Other?	(K-8)	139
What Causes the Molecules of a Liquid to Move?	(4-8)	142
What Are Atoms?	(4-8)	144

Thermal Energy (Heat)

What Is Heat?	(K–8)	145
What Happens to Molecules of Solids When They Are Heated or Cooled?	(4–8)	148
What Happens to Molecules of Liquids When They Are Heated or Cooled?	(4–8)	150
What Happens to Molecules of Gases When They Are Heated or Cooled?	(K–8)	152
How Is Heat Transmitted by Conduction and Radiation?	(4–8)	153
What Is an Insulator?	(4–8)	156

Changes in States of Matter

How May Matter Be Changed?	(K–8)	158
What Effects Does Heat Have on the States of Matter?		
Part I—Solids	(K–6)	159
Part II—Liquids	(4–8)	160

Air Pressure

What Is Air?	(K–3)	163
What Shapes and Volumes May Air Occupy?	(K–6)	164
How Can Air Pressure Move Objects?	(K–8)	166
How Do the Effects of Moving Air Differ from Nonmoving Air?	(4–8)	168
How Big Should You Make a Parachute?	(K–8)	171

Sound

What Is Sound and How Is It Produced and Conducted?	(K–3)	173
How Does the Length of the Vibrating Body Affect Sound?	(3–6)	173
How Does a Violin or Cello Work?	(4–6)	175
How Does the Length of an Air Column Affect Sound?	(K–6)	176
What Causes Sound to Be Louder?	(4–6)	178
How Do Solids and Liquids Conduct Sounds?	(4–6)	178
How Can the Reflection of Sound Be Changed?	(3–6)	181

Mechanics

Why Use an Inclined Plane?	(K–8)	183
Why Use a Jack?	(4–8)	185
What Is the Advantage of Using a Wheel and Axle?	(K–8)	186
Why Use a Lever?	(4–8)	189
How Does a Second-Class Lever Work?	(4–6)	191
How Does a Third-Class Lever Work?	(4–8)	192
Why Use a Single Fixed Pulley?	(4–8)	194
Why Use a Movable Pulley?	(4–8)	196

Magnetism and Electricity

What Is a Magnet?	(K–6)	198
What Is a Magnetic Field?	(K–3)	200
How Does a Magnetic Field Appear to Look?	(3–8)	201
What Is Static Electricity?	(4–8)	203
How Can You Make Electricity by Magnetism?	(4–8)	207
How Can You Make an Electromagnet?	(4–8)	209
What Are Parallel and Series Circuits?	(4–8)	210

Light
How Does Light Appear to Travel?	(3–8)	212
How Is Light Changed When It Passes from Air to Water?	(3–8)	213
How Is Light Reflected?	(4–8)	215
What Does a Prism Do to Light?	(4–8)	217
How Do Convex and Concave Lenses Affect Light Passing Through Them?	(4–8)	219
Why Do You Need Two Eyes?	(2–6)	221

SECTION 4 Less Structured Discovery Activities — 223

Preschool
Rolling Things	223
Blocks	225
Wheels and Things That Roll	226
Water	226
Color	228

Preschool-Primary Grades
Making Things	229
Identifying Things	231
Tying Knots	232
Making Things with Animals	233
Maps	235
Doing Things with Plants	237

Grades 4–6
Water Drops	238
What Do Chicks Like to Eat?	240
Making Soap Films	240
Who Can Lift the Most with a Tongue Depressor?	240

Grades 6–8
Fun Practice Using Metrics	241
What Do Things Look Like Under Sun Lamps?	243
Flying Things	244
What Will Happen to Ice Cubes Placed in Alcohol and Water?	246
How Can You Make Something Move Up and Down without Touching It?	247
What Can You Find Out About Isopods?	247

SECTION 5 Piagetian Types of Discovery Activities — 248

Primary Grades
Class Inclusion: Do they know that subclasses are included in a major class? (Ages 6–7)	249
Spatial Relations (Ages 6–7)	249
Ordering: Placing objects in order (Ages 6–8)	250
Associativity: Realize that it doesn't matter how you arrange things. The number or area will remain the same. (Ages 6–8)	250
One-to-One Correspondence (Ages 6–8)	251
Coordinating Systems, Horizontal and Vertical (Ages 6–12)	252
Conservation of Length (Ages 7–8)	253
Conservation of Area (Ages 7–8)	254

Ascending a Class Hierarchy   (Ages 7-8)   255
Time—Understanding Sequence and Duration   (Ages 7-8)   255
Spatial Relations   (Ages 7-8)   256
Constructing a Set Containing a Single Element   (Ages 7-9)   257
Making *All* and *Some* Relationships   (Ages 7-9)   257
Reordering   (Ages 8-10)   258
Spatial Reasoning   (Age 9)   258
Unit Repetition or Iteration   (Ages 7-10)   259
Ordering by Weight   (Ages 9-10)   259
Concept of a Null Class   (Ages 9-11)   260
Descending a Classification Hierarchy   (Ages 9-11)   260
Conservation of Weight   (Ages 9-12)   261
Conservation of Displacement Volume   (Age 11 and up)   262
Law of Buoyance—Flotation   (Age 11 and up)   262
Conservation of Internal Volume   (Ages 10-12)   263
Spatial Relations   (Ages 11-12)   264
Continuous Divisibility   (Ages 11-12)   265
Spatial Relations   (Age 11 and up)   265

SECTION 6   Discovery Activities for "Special" Children   266

Sensory Handicapped Children   267
How Can Blind or Visually Impaired Children Learn about Magnets?   (K-8)   267
In What Ways Can the Blind or Visually Impaired Identify Objects?   (K-8)   267
What Are Some Ways for Blind or Visually Impaired Students to Find Out About Their Bodies?   (K-8)   268
How Can Blind Students "See" and Compare Varying Polluted Water?   (4-8)   269

Mentally Retarded Children
How Can Mentally Retarded Children Learn to Develop a Thermic Sense?   (K-8)   270
How Can Mentally Retarded Children Learn Sense of Weight?   (K-8)   271
How Can Mentally Retarded Children Learn to Discriminate Tastes?   (K-8)   272
How Can Mentally Retarded Children Learn to Recognize Common Odors?   (K-8)   273

Children with Visual Perception Problems
Observing Properties of Leaves   (K-3)   273
Comparing Properties of Shells or Buttons and Classifying Them   (K-3)   274
Using Plants to Teach Visual Sequencing   (K-3)   275
"Mr. O" and Relative Position and Motion   (K-6)   276
Outside-the-Classroom Walk to Develop Visual Scrutiny and Analysis   (K-6)   277

Emotionally Handicapped Children
Learning About Our Environment by Touching   278
Learning About Our Environment by Listening and Moving   279

Hearing-Handicapped Children   280

APPENDIX A   Supplies, Equipment, and Materials from Community Sources   282

APPENDIX B   Selected Sources of Scientific Equipment, Supplies, Models, Living Things, Kits, and Collections   284

APPENDIX C   Noncommercial Sources and Containers for Organisms   286

APPENDIX D   Requirements for Various Animals   287

INTRODUCTION

The Discovery Approach

No one method of teaching science is best for *all* children, *all* of the time, under *all* situations. Discovery teaching/learning, however, has a number of advantages: students learn how to learn; learning becomes self-rewarding; students are active participants; learning is more transferable; learning builds positive self-concepts; learning by discovery avoids rote memory; and discovery learning helps individuals become more responsible for their own learning and as a result, helps them become autonomous persons. In addition, discovery science teaching/learning incorporates the best of what we know about the processes and products of science, how children learn best, the goals and objectives of science, and the relationships among science, humanism, values, and our concerns about the environment.

Discovery teaching is not new. Socrates of ancient Greece, with his questioning style, in a sense used a discovery, nontelling approach of learning. More recently, John Dewey, the main spokesman for progressive education in the 1930s, advocated that children should "learn by doing," rather than be lectured to. Jean Piaget, Swiss psychologist, and Jerome Bruner, former Harvard psychologist, were responsible for a sharply increased interest in learning by discovery in the middle 1960s.

Discovery is the process by which the learner uses the mind in logical and mathematical ways to discover and internalize concepts and principles. For example, students may discover the existence of cells, that is, form a concept of cells or later they may discover the scientific principle that cells come only from other cells. In addition to learning science concepts, the student learns how to learn. The more students are actively involved in solving problems, the more likely they are to learn to generalize what they have learned into a style of discovery that will serve them well throughout their lives.

How to Use This Book

This book contains classroom-tested science activities in the discovery format for nursery or preschools, elementary schools, and middle or junior high schools. The lessons are designed so that your students discover concepts and principles for themselves through their own mental processes — observing, classifying, measuring, predicting, describing, and inferring. The activities cover the major areas of science: Living Sciences, Environmental Sciences, and Physical Sciences. Most of the activities in this text (Sections 1-3) are *guided*, or structured, discovery activities. If you and your students have not had experience in learning through discovery, you may need more structure, initially, in your lessons. These lessons, however, should not be followed like recipes. By modifying and adapting each lesson in the way that *you* think will work best, you will continually gain in your understanding of, appreciation for, and commitment to discovery learning. After you and your students have gained some experience in how to carry out discovery investigations, you will both be able to work on less structured activities (Section 4). The less structured, "quickie" discovery activities in Section 4 are not meant to be exhaustive, but are simply samples of what can be done informally in preschool or primary grades, open classroom situations, and for enrichment and fun in upper elementary and junior high school grades. The discovery activities presented in the less structured format lend themselves to creative modification for use in many different learning situations. As you become more experienced with this method of teaching science, you will develop your own discovery techniques and activity ideas.

In addition to the structured and less structured discovery activities, samples of two other kinds of science activities have been included in this text:

> Piagetian types of discovery activities which involve children in specific Piagetian operations (classification, conservation, and so on) (see Section 5).
>
> Discovery science activities for "special" children such as the blind or visually impaired, the deaf, and the physically, mentally, and emotionally handicapped (see Section 6).

Discovery Science Activities Format

All of the guided science activities (Sections 1-3) have been tested by teachers and children in preschools, elementary schools, and middle or junior high schools. The teachers testing them did not have any special preparation in science. In fact, science had not been part of their preparation for teaching or their curricula until these activities were introduced into their classrooms. Several teachers evaluated each activity; the activities were rewritten to conform to their suggestions and then retested. Although the activities were originally written for *teacher* demonstration, in most cases they have been modified to be used as *student* discovery activities.

Since the object of the discovery activities is to have students discover the concepts in the course of doing the activity, you should not *tell* your class the purpose of the activity or what can be expected to happen. Before you go into your classroom to present a particular activity, you should read it thoroughly, however, and go through the steps in the activity. Particular attention should be paid to the questions presented. These are meant to be guide questions only. *Remember*: although these activities have been tested in actual classroom situations, no teacher can be certain that his or her class will respond in a step-by-step manner throughout an activity. Nor do we expect that teachers will attempt to use the activities in that way. The activities are intended only as a *resource* to which teachers can go for ideas. You will obviously modify and alter the delivery of these activities to meet the needs, interests, and abilities of your individual class.

Discovery activities need not be taught in the order presented and are meant as *sample* activities only. To be of greatest value in *your* classroom, these discovery activities must be supplemented and integrated with many other curricular activities. After you have had experience in using several of the sample activities with your class, you will easily gain competence and confidence in designing others for your own science program.

Each discovery science laboratory activity in Sections 1-3 includes ten major parts described in the following sections.

1. Age-Level Range or Group

To help you quickly and easily select discovery activities that are most appropriate for your group, the activities are organized by these age ranges and groups:

Preschool
Primary or lower elementary grades (kindergarten to third grades)
Upper elementary grades (fourth to sixth grades)
Middle or junior high school (sixth to eighth grades)

Grade levels are usually written as ranges because many of the discovery activities have been tested in several grades and found to work reasonably well in all of them. It depends upon how much depth you want to probe and the level at which your students are working.

Reminder: These are age *ranges* only. Because of the uniqueness of each class, only *you* can make a professional judgment about the suitability of any particular discovery activity and how it has to be modified to fit your class.

2. Science Topics

The broad science topics of the discovery activities are those suggested by a national conference on elementary science education. The scientific concepts for each activity were taken from a list of scientific principles thought by scientists to be important for any person having a general education. The complete list of these scientific principles is available from the U.S. Office of Education.[1]

Important note: No effort has been made to cover *all* concepts and principles embodied in an elementary science curriculum, since such a project would require an entire book for the activities alone. The discovery activities are organized along these three main sciences only as an aid for teachers in quickly locating a particular science topic:

Living sciences
Physical sciences
Environmental sciences

3. Statement of Problem

The problem of each discovery activity is stated as a divergent question, for example, "What Causes the Seasons?" This helps you quickly select the *specific* area within one of the three sciences to present to your class.

4. What Do I Want Children to Discover?

The fourth question concerns the scientific principles and concepts children are to discover in doing the discovery activities outlined in each lesson. They are not exhaustive and others may be discovered by your students as a result of their backgrounds, your skill in guiding them, and other factors.

5. Science Processes

Scientific processes are listed at the left to show you the types of mental operations your students will be required to perform in each part of the discovery lesson.

---

1. E.W. Martin, "Major Principles of the Biological Sciences of Importance for General Education," Selected Science Services, Circular No. 308-IV, Division of Secondary Schools, U.S. Office of Education (Washington, D.C.: U.S. Government Printing Office). H.E. Wise, "Major Principles of Physics, Chemistry, and Geology of Importance for General Education," Department of Health, Education, and Welfare (Washington, D.C.: U.S. Government Printing Office).

6. What Will I Need?

The science supplies and equipment needed to perform the discovery activities are noted. Whenever possible, easily obtainable and nontechnical materials are suggested. For instance, instead of using a beaker (costly) for nonheating activity, a plastic tumbler may be suggested, or a pyrex baby nursing bottle may be suggested for a beaker that will be heated. Materials easily found in the immediate environment are stressed for two reasons:

> Most elementary schools do not have extensive science supplies or money to purchase them.
>
> It is important for children to see that the activities can be done with things easily available to *them*; hopefully, the children will replicate the activities at home. *Caution*: Please make it very clear that children should never use open flame or dangerous or unknown substances without adult supervision.

Important: Enlist your students' help in getting supplies and items needed for your discovery activities from *their* homes or environment. Besides saving you time, it will provide for greater involvement of the children in *their* discovery science activity.

7. What Will We Discuss?

Discussion questions are given for you to ask before your students start the discovery activities. The purpose of this section is to set the learning environment for the discovery activities that follow.

8. What Will Children Do?

The eighth question refers to the pupil discovery activities or investigations the children actively participate in, leading to their discovery of the concepts and principles listed under item 4 above.

9. How Will Children Use or Apply What They Discover?

Open-ended questions suggest to children additional investigations they might do to apply what they discover to new situations; for example, "On a cold day, why do you feel warm in the sunlight but very cold in the shade?" You should encourage students who are interested to attempt to answer these open-ended questions through further investigations. Many of the activities suggested by these questions can be done at home and need not take additional class time. These open-ended questions will also help children probe the values level of science as well as integrate other curricular subjects such as mathematics, social studies, and language arts.

10. What Must I Know?

Suggestions are given to you for guiding the children in their discoveries, and these things you must know to make the discoveries as meaningful as possible:

> *Teaching tips* to explain more complicated or involved parts of the discovery activity
> *Science content* (facts, concepts, principles, or theories) relevant to the discovery activity
> *Variables* in the discovery activity that can affect the outcomes, especially useful to you if "the experiment does not work"

Reminder: Some of the information in items 1 to 10 above is to be used by you and other parts by your students. Which ones are to be used and how can be determined only by *you*, the teacher. Some teachers using the discovery activities have duplicated these sections for children to use,

4 DISCOVERY SCIENCE RESOURCE ACTIVITIES

mostly in the upper elementary or middle/junior high school grades:

>Statement of Problem
>What Will Children Do?
>How Will Children Use or Apply What They Discover?

You have permission to reproduce those parts of the discovery activities that your students can use directly in your classroom. (*Caution*: They may *not* be further distributed or sold.) The rest of the above format you will find useful for your own background. In using it with primary grades (where a student may not read or read well enough) or in upper grades (where a student may not read well enough), you can read the appropriate sections to the students. Some teachers have even put the directions on cassette audiotapes for students to use by themselves.

The most important element in these discovery activities is for children to discover concepts through actual physical and mental participation in the activities. Do not tell the children beforehand what they should expect to find. This robs them of the joy of discovery.

SECTION 1

Discovery Activities for
LIVING SCIENCES

ANIMALS: ANATOMY AND PHYSIOLOGY

How Many Different Types of Animals Do You Know? (K–6)

What Do I Want Children to Discover?

Each animal lives in a place (environment) that best suits it.
The way the animal is built depends on where and how it lives.
Animals that live on dry land breathe through lungs.
Animals that usually live in water breathe through gills.
Land animals usually move by legs and may run, hop, or crawl.
Many land animals have claws and sharp teeth.
Animals live in water, on land, in the air, and on both land and water.
Animals that fly have wings and light bones.

What Will I Need?

Fish to be dissected (this may be obtained from the local fish market)
Aquarium with large goldfish
Frog or chicken leg to be dissected
Aquarium with a frog (live)
Cutaway model of a human chest cavity showing the lungs
As many models of stuffed animals as can be obtained
Dry bones from a chicken, cow, and any other animal that may be available
Claws, beaks, and teeth from as many animals as possible
Animal's lung in alcohol
Live animals that take a minimal amount of care (such as salamanders, goldfish, crayfish, and white mice)
Set of scales for weighing the bones
Dissecting kit
Pictures (Set I): common animals, birds, fish, and reptiles
Pictures (Set II): rare or unusual animals, birds, fish and reptiles
Paper towels
Pencil and paper

What Will We Discuss?

How can animals be classified?
How do animals breathe?
What does a gill look like, and how does it function?
What kinds of animals use gills for breathing?
What does a lung look like, and how does it function?
What kinds of animals use lungs for breathing?
How does an animal's body structure affect its locomotion?
How does its body structure affect its diet?

What Will Children Do?   PROCESSES

                                          PART I

Observing   1. Observe the fish in the aquarium. Note their breathing, locomotion, and feeding.
                                          2. Obtain a dead fish, dissecting kit, and paper towels. Carefully dissect a fish. Your teacher will demonstrate the proper method for you to follow.
Observing   3. Describe what you see in the area of the gills.
Inferring   What function do you think the various sections serve?

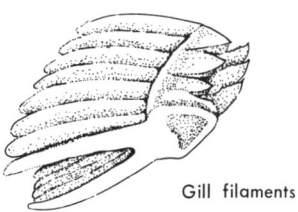

What Must I Know?   You may want to demonstrate the proper method for dissecting a fish. Have the children work in groups of four. Cut the fish along the ventral side from just below the anus to the throat. Cut up from this incision to the dorsal side (top) of the fish at both ends of the incision. Using the scissors in the dissection kit, cut the ribs and expose the air bladder. Also remove the operculum or gill cover on one side. This will expose the gill filaments. (See diagram.)

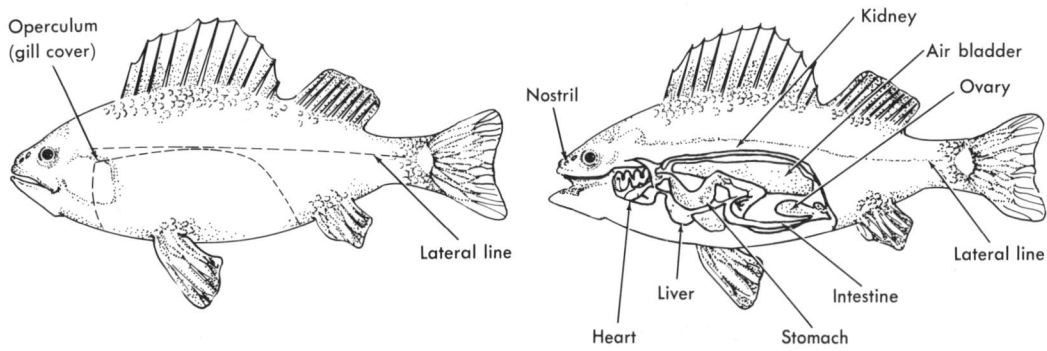

Inferring   In what ways does a fish use its fins and tail?
Inferring   How does their structure affect their use?
Inferring   In what manner does a fish ingest its food?
                                          Describe the bones of the fish.
Inferring   How do you think they affect its ability to swim?

                                          PART II
                                          1. Obtain a frog or chicken leg, two bones from a bird and a cow, and a scale.
                                             Carefully dissect and record your findings about the frog or chicken leg and how the leg affects the animal's locomotion.
Measuring   2. Measure and weigh two bones of equal length, one of a fowl and one of a cow.
Observing and inferring   3. Obtain and examine at least two sets of claws, beaks, and teeth and describe what you think the diet of each animal might be.

LIVING SCIENCES

Observing
Hypothesizing

Comparing
Hypothesizing

4. Obtain a cutaway model of a human chest cavity showing the lungs.
   Describe the lungs.
   What is their function?
   Name some animals that breathe with the use of lungs.
   How do human lungs differ from those of other animals?
   Why do land animals have lungs rather than gills?

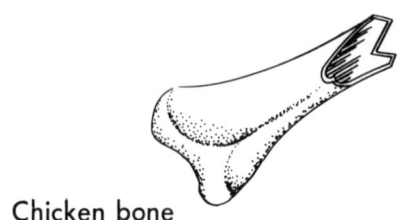
Chicken bone

Beef bone

PART III

1. Obtain a collection of pictures of animals and a pencil and piece of paper.

Classifying

2. Sort the pictures of animals into categories on the basis of the data you obtained from your previous investigations.
3. List the animals down the left-hand side of a sheet of paper by the categories you have determined. Leave two spaces between each entry. Rule your paper into three lengthwise columns. Title the columns as follows:
   a. How does the animal breathe?
   b. How does the animal move?
   c. What physical characteristics influence its diet?
4. Complete the columns for each entry as indicated.

How Will Children Use or Apply What They Discover?

1. How would you use balloons to show how a lung operates?
2. Using the data gathered in your experiments, how would you construct, illustrate, or give a written description of an imaginary animal that can live in water or on land, fly, crawl, and walk?

How Do Ants Live? (K–6)

What Do I Want Children to Discover?

Ants are social insects.
All insects have three parts to their bodies.
All insects have six legs.
Ants are beneficial because they help keep the forests and fields clean.
There are different kinds of ants in a colony.
These different ants do different kinds of work in the colony.

What Will I Need?

Large glass jar (commercial mayonnaise or pickle jar)
Soil to fill the jar two-thirds full
Sponge
Large pan
Sheet of black construction paper
Crumbs and bits of food: bread, cake, sugar, seeds, and so on
Colony of ants

8 DISCOVERY SCIENCE RESOURCE ACTIVITIES

What Will We Discuss?   What do the different kinds of ants look like?
In what ways are the ants different?
How does the body of a worker ant compare to that of a queen ant?
How many pairs of legs do ants have?
What are the antennae on the head used for?
What does the egg of an ant look like?
Where do ants make their homes?
How do ants move?
How could you keep ants from leaving a jar?

Ant eggs

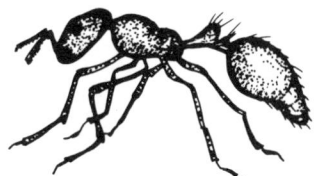
Mature ant

PROCESSES

What Must I Know?   This activity should be done as a large group activity.

What Will Children Do?   1. Obtain a large glass jar, soil to fill the jar two-thirds full, sponge, large pan, sheet of black construction paper, crumbs and bits of food (bread, cake, sugar, and seeds), a colony of ants, and water.

Designing an investigation
Hypothesizing

How could you arrange these materials to make a home for ants?

What effect will a sheet of black paper placed around the jar have on the ants?

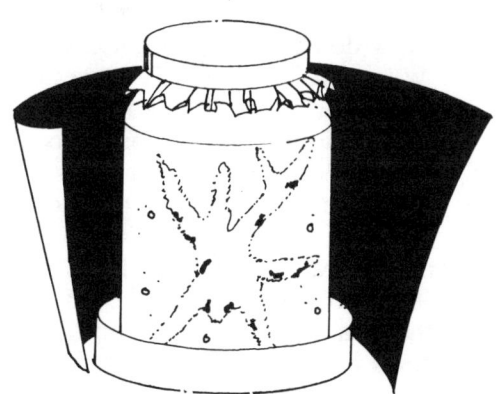

Observing
Observing
Hypothesizing

Hypothesizing

2. Observe and record what the ants do.
How do the ants connect their homes in the jar?
What would happen to the ants if they did not carry soil to the surface?
What do you think would happen if there were no queen in the ant colony?

LIVING SCIENCES

Comparing   What changes have been made by the ants since they were first placed in the jar?

How Will Children Use or Apply What They Discover?
1. In what ways are ants useful to man?
2. What are some other insects that live and work together?
3. What are some living things that are sometimes mistaken for insects?
4. What would happen if the ant colony were placed in a light, warm place?
5. How are ants different from spiders?
6. What would be a good description of social insects

What Do You Know about the Birds around You? (K–3)

What Do I Want Children to Discover?
Birds vary in color and size.
Birds sing different songs.
Birds make different kinds of nests.
Birds eat many different kinds of food.
The male may have a more colorful plumage than the female.
Some birds migrate.
Some birds change color with the season.
Birds care for their young.
Some birds prey on birds.

What Will I Need?
No special materials are necessary; however, the following may be helpful:
  Bird book (showing local birds)
  Pictures of birds—if birds cannot be observed in nature

What Will We Discuss?
Carefully record on the board the responses of the pupils to the following questions:
  What are the names of some birds?
  What do these birds look like?
  How do chickens and ducks differ?
  What are the main differences between a turkey and a robin?
  Where do some birds go in the winter?
  Where do baby birds come from?
  Where do birds lay their eggs?
  What kinds of food do birds eat?

What Must I Know?
If the natural environment lends itself to observation of birds, have the children observe birds on the way to and from school or take a field trip in the local area, park, or zoo. If this is not possible, you may provide pictures of different birds, nests, and eggs for the pupils to observe.

PROCESSES

What Will Children Do?
The pupils should report to the class the things they have observed about birds. After the children have made their observations, record their findings by asking and writing on the board their answers to the following questions:

Comparing   In what ways are birds alike?
Comparing   In what ways are birds different from each other?

10   DISCOVERY SCIENCE RESOURCE ACTIVITIES

How Will Children Use or Apply What They Discover?

1. What advantage is there of laying eggs in nests?
2. What could you do to find out more about birds?
3. On the bulletin board are the lists of the important things you have learned about birds. In the next few days, try to find out as many new things as you can to add to the lists.
4. What are the different ways birds build their nests?
5. How could you find out if there are more birds in the city or in the country?

What Must I Know?

The following types of questions can be asked about any of the local birds. These questions will have to be modified depending on the kinds of birds that are found in your region.

Redheaded Woodpecker. (1) Where does the woodpecker build his nest? (2) How does he build his nest? (3) What kind of food does the woodpecker eat?

Hummingbird. (1) How does the male hummingbird differ in color from the female? (2) Where do hummingbirds get their food? (3) Are hummingbirds as big as the cardinal or sparrow? (4) Why do you have difficulty finding their nests?

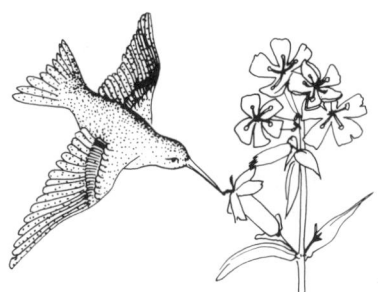

Starling. (1) Why do many other birds prefer not to live near starlings? (2) What color is the starling? (3) How does the starling vary in color compared to the hummingbird and woodpecker?

How Do Birds Differ from Mammals? (4–8)

What Do I Want Children to Discover?

Birds are the only animals that have feathers.
Both mammals and birds are warm-blooded.
Birds have two legs and two wings.

LIVING SCIENCES 11

The female mammal has glands for nourishing her young with milk.
Mammals are more or less covered with hair.
Birds do not vary as much in structure as mammals.
The bones of birds are somewhat hollow and light in weight. Mammal bones are not hollow and are proportionately heavier in weight.
Birds tend to eat approximately the amount of their weight in food each day.
Mammals do not eat as much per body weight as do birds.
Birds use considerable energy in flying and therefore need a great amount of food.
Female birds lay eggs.
Almost all female mammals give birth to live babies.
Only a few mammals, such as the platypus, lay eggs.

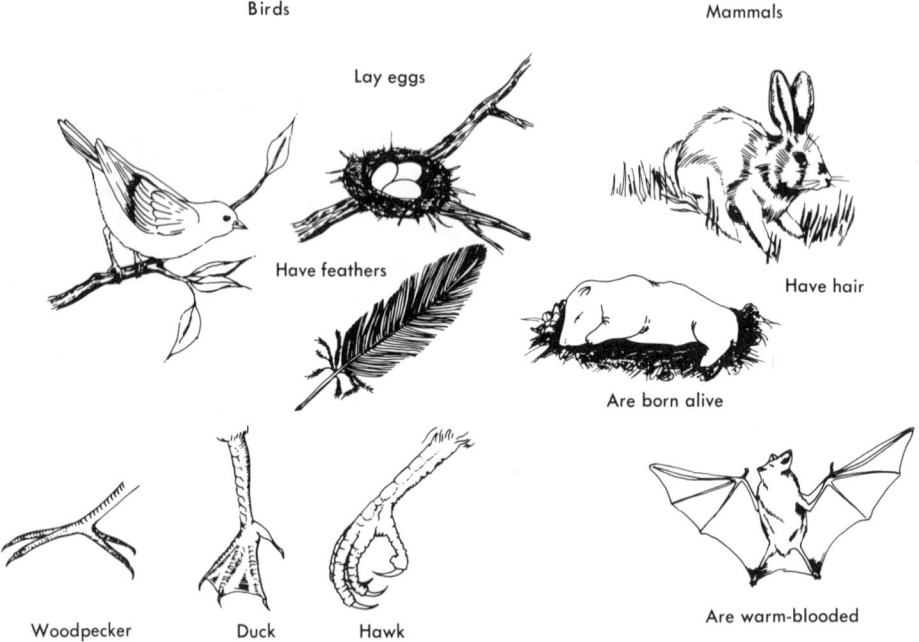

What Will I Need? Live or stuffed specimens of birds and mammals or pictures of them.
Beef and chicken bones (one of each for every two students). If possible, these should be cut in half.
Wing bones of chickens (or any other bird).

What Will We Discuss? Give as many characteristics as you can that *birds* have in common.
Give as many characteristics as you can that *mammals* have in common.
In what ways do birds differ from mammals?
What could you do to compare more closely the differences between birds and mammals?

What Must I Know? The teacher should record on the board the students' ideas on these questions. Or allow the students to divide into groups and discuss the questions. Each group could report their ideas to the class.

PROCESSES

What Will Children Do?

This activity should be done in groups of two or more students. Encourage children to bring specimens, alive or stuffed, to school. Perhaps a pet day or animal show might be arranged to make the most of this activity. The children should be allowed to help in furnishing any of the other supplies such as beef and chicken bones. Children should be encouraged to bring pictures of animals to class, and these can be placed on a bulletin board.

1. Obtain a cut chicken bone, a cut beef bone, and a wing bone of a chicken.

    Classifying — How did you know which bone was from a chicken and which was from a steer?

    Observing and Comparing — Examine the centers of the two bones and record how the structure of the beef bone differs from that of the chicken bone.

2. *Comparing* — Look at the chicken wing bone.
   How does its structure compare with the arm bones of man?

3. *Summarizing* — Make a list of all the characteristics in which birds and mammals differ.

4. *Comparing* — Compare your list with those made by other members in your class and make any corrections or additions to your list that you think should be made.

How Will Children Use or Apply What They Discover?

1. What are the main structural differences between birds and mammals?
2. How does the structure of the feather help a bird to fly?

What Is the Difference between a Frog and a Lizard? (3–6)

What Do I Want Children to Discover?

A frog is an amphibian.
Amphibians are animals that spend part of their life in water and part on land.
As tadpoles, amphibians live in water. They have a slippery skin, and late in their development they have toes without claws.
A lizard is a reptile.
Reptiles have skin covered with scales; there is no tadpole stage; toes, if present, have claws.
Reptiles produce eggs with shells because they must lay their eggs on land and depend on the sun for hatching them.

LIVING SCIENCES

What Must I Know?   This activity should be done in groups of five or more students. Commercial-sized mayonnaise jars may be used for terrariums.

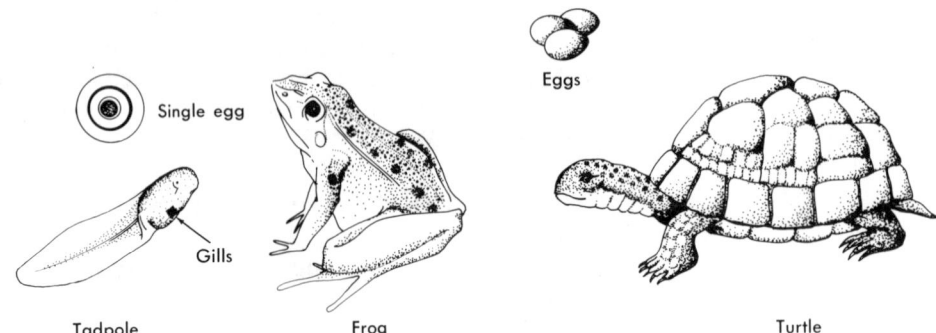

What Will I Need?   2 terrariums—1 equipped with water and aquatic plants for the frog; 1 equipped with sand and a rock for the lizard
Containers of water for the frogs
Frog for each group
Lizard for each group
Variety of insects for feeding both frog and lizard
Eggs or young of both the frog and the lizard

What Must I Know?   If it is not possible to obtain the developmental stages of the frog and lizard, get some pictures of the different stages.

What Will We Discuss?   To which group of animals do lizards belong?
To which group of animals do frogs belong?
What are the general characteristics of each of these groups?
How are these animals like or unlike each other?
How does a given environment affect each animal?

What Must I Know?   This activity should be done in groups of 5 or more students.
Commercial-sized mayonnaise jars may be used for terrariums.

What Will Children Do?   PROCESSES

Observing
Observing
Observing

1. Observe the frog and lizard in the 2 terrariums.
   How do they breathe?
   How do they move?
   Describe their physical characteristics.
   Do they have any young?

Observing
Observing
Comparing

   How do they react to their environment?
   What are the characteristics of the environment?
2. Compare your observations with those in the classroom reference books.
3. Note any additional differences as indicated in your reading.

Classifying

4. Using the data gathered in steps 1 and 2, list the characteristics of an amphibian in one column and the characteristics of a reptile in another column.

Inferring

5. List the names of some other amphibians and reptiles.

14   DISCOVERY SCIENCE RESOURCE ACTIVITIES

How Will Children Use or Apply What They Discover?	1. Obtain other amphibians and reptiles. Use the same procedure as in the previous activity to compare them. 2. How would you prepare an environment to grow salamanders?

How Does The Lack of Oxygen Affect Animals? (3–6)

What Do I Want Children to Discover	Animals need oxygen to live. Oxygen dissolves in water. Some animals need dissolved oxygen in water. A gas will dissolve better in a cool liquid than in a hot liquid. Fish breathe through gills.
What Will I Need?	2 pint bottles with caps 2 goldfish or any small freshwater fish in a small bottle Burner and a stand or electric hot plate on which to boil water Matches Pan large enough to boil a pint of water
What Will We Discuss?	What happens to the air dissolved in water when you boil it? What do you think would happen to fish if they were placed in water that had been boiled and then cooled? What would you do to find out?
What Must I Know?	This activity may be done in groups of two or more pupils.
What Will Children Do?	PROCESSES
Designing an investigation	1. Obtain the following materials: A jar with a fish, two pint-sized jars with caps, a burner or electric hot plate, and a large pan. How would you boil water? 2. Heat the water to boiling and let it boil for several minutes. 3. While the water is being heated, label one jar "Boiled Water." 4. After the water has boiled, turn off the burner. 5. Pour the boiled water into the jar labeled "Boiled Water," cap it, and allow it to cool to room temperature.
Hypothesizing	What will happen if you place a fish in tap water? Place a fish in a jar filled with tap water and cap it.
Observing *Hypothesizing*	6. Observe its movements. What will happen if you place a fish in the cooled boiled water and cap the jar?
Observing	7. Place a fish in the jar of boiled water and cap the jar. Observe its movements. (*Caution*: If the fish turns on its side, take it out of the jar quickly, shake it in the air by the tail for a second, and place it into a jar of regular unheated water.)
Comparing *Inferring*	How did the movements of the two fish vary? Why did the fish in the cooled boiled water seem to vary in its movements compared to the other fish?
What Must I Know?	When water is boiled, the air molecules dissolved in it move more rapidly and escape into the air. The water lacks air as a result. Fish get the oxygen they need from air dissolved in water. When the air passes over the gills, the oxygen is absorbed by the blood passing through the gills. Fish

LIVING SCIENCES 15

are not able to survive in the boiled water because it contains little oxygen for the gills to absorb.

Inferring
    Why did you first heat the water and then cool it?
8. If you have not already done so, take the fish out of the jar of boiled water, shake it for a second or two by the tail, and place it in a jar of plain water.

Inferring
    Why is it necessary to shake the fish in the air for a few seconds?

What Must I Know?
    The shaking of the fish causes the air to pass over the gills so the fish gets oxygen from the air; the shaking also stimulates the circulation of the blood in the fish.

Inferring
    What do animals in the sea need to live?
Inferring
    How do they get the oxygen they need?

What Must I Know?
    Explain to the class that air is composed of a mixture of gases and that it is the oxygen in the air that animals need to breathe.

How Will Children Use or Apply What They Discover?
1. What experiment would you do to determine whether other animals require air (oxygen) to live?

ANIMALS: REPRODUCTION AND DEVELOPMENT

How Do Some Insects Develop from Egg to Adult? (3–6)

What Do I Want Children to Discover?
Insects develop from eggs.
Insects change in body form until they become adults.
Some insects pass through stages (*metamorphosis*) at different rates.
Flies lay their eggs on filth or decaying food.

What Will I Need?
Quart jar
Pint Jar
Small hamburger patties
Flies
Plastic wrap
Paper towel

Dissecting needle
Caterpillars
Green leaves and twigs
Grasshoppers
Small box with moist soil

 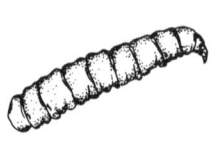  

    Eggs   Larva   Pupa   Adult

16   DISCOVERY SCIENCE RESOURCE ACTIVITIES

What Must I Know? This activity should be done in groups of five.

What Will Children Do? PROCESSES

PART I **Flies**
1. Make a small pattie of hamburger (about the size of a quarter). Place it in a pint jar.
2. Catch a fly and put it in the jar. Put a small piece of soaked paper in the jar. Keep the jar covered with plastic wrap and place it outside the room.

Hypothesizing
Observing
Inferring

   What effect will the moist paper towel have on the meat and air?
3. Observe the meat for several days.
   What causes the meat to change in appearance?
4. Obtain a dissecting needle and move the hamburger meat.

What Must I Know? By this time, the meat should start to decay due to the action of bacteria from the air and in the meat. The children should also be able to see the eggs the flies have laid.

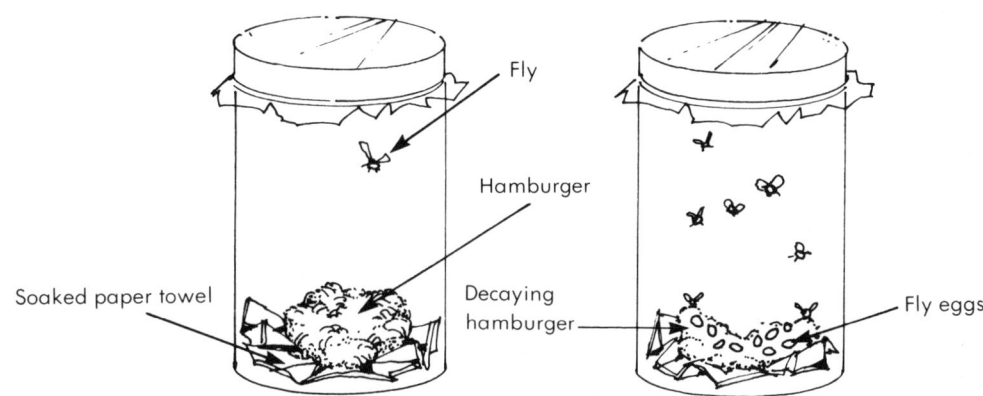

Observing

What do you see in the meat?
Cover the jar again with plastic wrap.
5. Observe the meat for several more days.

Observing
Inferring

What do you see?
Where did the white "things" come from?
6. Leave your jar undisturbed for several more days.
7. Record your observations each day.

Observing
Observing

What developed in the jars?
What effect does temperature have on the white things?

What Must I Know? A common name for the white thing is *maggot*. This is really the larva stage of fly metamorphosis.

Observing
Summarizing

What happened to the maggots that were in the meat?
8. Tell in your own words what happened from the time you put meat in the jar to the time the flies developed.

What Must I Know? Flies pass from eggs to larvae to pupae and finally to adults.

LIVING SCIENCES   17

PART II Moths

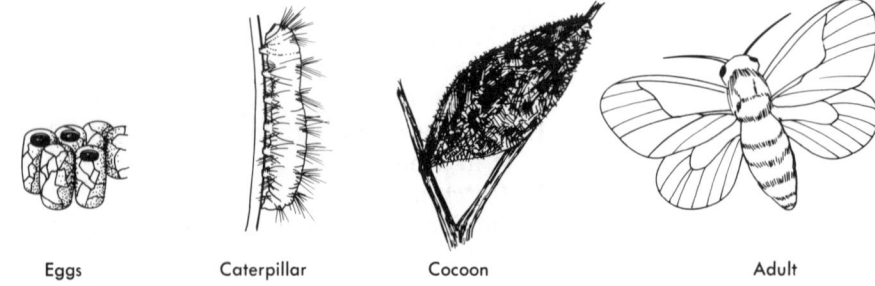

Eggs   Caterpillar   Cocoon   Adult

Developmental stages of moth

Hypothesizing

Observing

1. Obtain a quart jar with several fresh green leaves, a couple of twigs, and two caterpillars. Place a moist piece of cloth in the jar.
   Where do caterpillars come from?
2. Cover the jar with plastic wrap.
3. Observe the caterpillars over several days.
   What do they do?
4. Leave the caterpillars in the jar until they change.

What Must I Know?   Be sure the paper in the bottom of the jar is kept moist. Make sure the children loosen the plastic wrap every two or three days to allow fresh air to enter the jar.

Inferring

Summarizing

What would happen if you did not keep the air moist?
What is the last stage that you see called?
Describe in your own words the four stages of a moth.

PART III Grasshoppers

1. Obtain some grasshoppers.
2. Place the grasshoppers in a small box with moist soil and cover the box with plastic wrap.
   What might the female grasshopper do while in the box?

Hypothesizing
Observing
Inferring

3. Observe them over several days.
   What evidence do you have that some of the female grasshoppers did something?
4. Leave the box in the classroom, keeping the soil fairly moist but not soaking.
   Observe the box for several months.
   What happens to the grasshoppers?

Observing
Observing
Inferring

5. After several months, try to find some nymphs in the top of the soil.
   What are these nymphs?

What Must I Know?   The nymphs are young, developing grasshoppers.

Applying data   Where did these nymphs come from?

What Must I Know?   The nymphs came from the eggs the female grasshopper laid. If you do not want to take time for the children to observe the development of the grasshopper, you might show them some pictures of grasshopper development and ask the children to put them in their proper order of development.

18 DISCOVERY SCIENCE RESOURCE ACTIVITIES

How Will Children Use or Apply What They Discover?

1. What effect would the cutting of the outer layer of a cocoon have on what is inside the cocoon?
2. What effect would dry, rather than moist, air have on the fly eggs?
3. What would happen if you put shredded paper in the jar with the flies instead of meat?
4. After the flies have laid their eggs in the hamburger, what would happen to them if you place the jars in a refrigerator?

Why Do You Resemble Your Parents? (4–8)

What Do I Want Children to Discover?

Every living thing comes from another living thing of the same kind.
Heredity is the passing on of traits and characteristics from parents to offspring.
Food is necessary for growth.
At every stage of development, the individual is an integrated organism.
All cells, tissues, and organs are correlated and act together as a unit.

What Will I Need?

Day-old chick (or picture of one)
Hen (or picture of one)
Food
40-watt light bulb
Box or cage
Water
Growth chart (one per child)
Piece of cardboard for lid

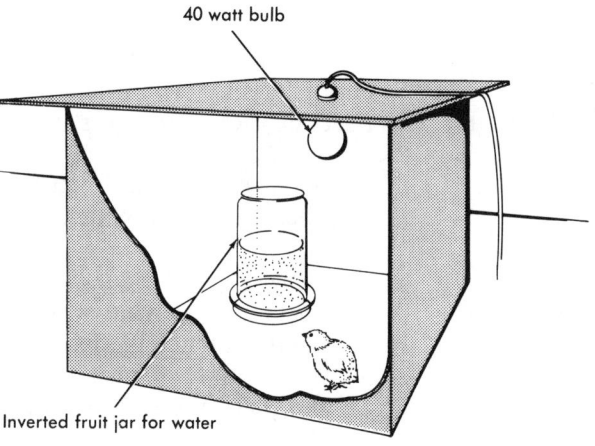

What Must I Know?

If you cannot get a hen, you can make a brooder to keep the chick warm by obtaining a small cardboard box about 18 x 18 inches and suspending an extension cord with a 40-watt bulb in it. (See the diagram.)

LIVING SCIENCES 19

PROCESSES

What Will Children Do? This activity is to be done by groups of 8 or more children.
1. Obtain an extension cord with a 40-watt bulb, a cardboard box, and a piece of cardboard to cover the box.
2. Insert a light socket with a 40-watt bulb into a piece of cardboard. This will be used to cover the top of a cardboard box about 18 x 18 inches.
3. Put the chick into the box. Place the hen in also if you have one.

What Must I Know? If a hen is not available, have the children refer to a picture of one.

Comparing How is the chick like the hen?
Comparing What are some other examples of living things that are like their parents?
Comparing In what ways are these animals alike?
Inferring Where did the chick come from?
Hypothesizing What would happen if you tried to get something living from something nonliving?
Imagining What would be the result of trying to get a chick from a horse or a cow?

What Must I Know? The children should decide that living things come only from living things that are alike.

Summarizing What can you say about the way living things look when they are born?
Comparing In what ways does the chick look different from the hen?
Observing 4. Keep a record of the growth of the chick for the next two weeks. Record everything you notice about the changes in growth of the chick.
Comparing In what ways do you resemble your parents?

What Must I Know? The children should decide that all organisms inherit traits and characteristics from their parents. They should see that the growth of the parts of the organism is balanced.

Designing an investigation What would you do to find out if you look anything like your parents when they were your age?

How Will Children Use or Apply What They Discover?
1. If some goose eggs were placed under a hen and side by side with the chicken eggs, what would be the result?
2. What evidence is there that a chicken egg needs or gets air?
3. What will happen if you take a needle and puncture a fertilized egg and place the egg in a warm box and wait for it to hatch?

How Does a Chicken Develop? (4–8)

What Do I Want Children to Discover?
When an animal grows, its cells divide.
When a chicken develops in the egg, it passes through different stages.
A chick embryo needs a constant temperature and moisture level to grow and develop.

A large part of the egg contains stored food for the young embryo to use in its growth.

What Will I Need?

Commercial incubator or gallon jar with lid
6–8 fertile eggs from a feed store
40-watt bulb and cord
Baby food jar or water dish
Binocular scope

Slides and cover slips
Stains for slides
Thermometer
Binocular microscope (if one is not available, a high power magnifying lens may be used)

What Must I Know?

This activity is to be done in groups of 5 pupils.
The pupils should have done some work using microscopes before doing this lesson.

PROCESSES

What Will Children Do?

1. Obtain a gallon jar and a 40-watt bulb; make an incubator for the fertile chicken eggs as shown in the activity, Why Do You Resemble Your Parents? The incubator should have a temperature of 37°C for the eggs to develop properly. Make sure the temperature can be kept constant over a period of days before placing the eggs in the incubator. A dish of water should be placed in the incubator. After the eggs have been placed in the incubator, they should be turned every other day.

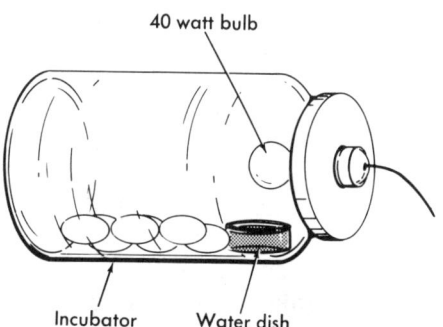

2. After 3 days, carefully crack open one egg.
Place the embryo under the binocular scope and focus under low power.

Observing

Describe what you see.

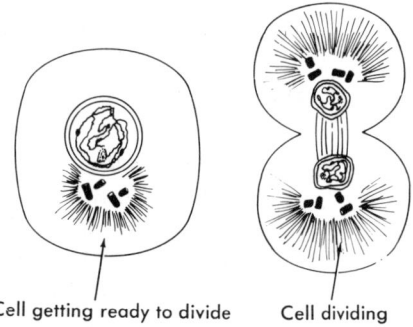

Inferring

What evidence is there that the developing chick embryo has a heart?

LIVING SCIENCES

Observing	3. After 12 days of incubation, take another egg and crack it open. Place the embryo under the scope. Make a drawing of the chick embryo.
	4. After 18 days, take another egg and compare its development with a 12-day embryo.
Comparing	How does the 18-day chick differ?
Observing	How is the chick able to escape from the egg?
How Will Children Use or Apply What They Discover?	1. How would you find out if the mother hen actually provides a temperature of 37°C when she sits on her eggs? 2. How do changes in the cell makeup of the chick explain how the chick grows in size?

HUMAN ANATOMY AND PHYSIOLOGY

How Does Our Skin Protect Us? (3-6)

What Do I Want Children to Discover?	The skin protects us from microorganisms that cause disease. A cut or wound in the skin can let microorganisms enter the body. Microorganisms sometimes cause infection and disease. A cut or wound in the skin should be properly treated immediately to prevent microorganisms from causing infection. Antiseptics kill microorganisms; thus they can be used for the treatment of cuts or wounds. Heat can kill microorganisms.
What Will I Need?	4 unblemished apples Book of matches Rotten apple 5 small pieces of cardboard for labels 3 sewing needles Candle Small sample of soil Alcohol
What Will We Discuss?	How is the covering of an apple or an orange like your skin? What are the advantages of the covering on apples, oranges, and other types of fruit? How does the covering of your body, the skin, protect you? What does a person mean when he says he wants to sterilize something? In what ways might you sterilize something?
What Must I Know?	This activity should be done in groups of 2 to 5 children. PROCESSES
What Will Children Do?	1. Obtain 5 pieces of cardboard for labels, a candle, a match, 3 needles, and 1 rotten and 4 unblemished apples. 2. Put labels A, B, C, and D with the four unblemished apples. 3. Sterilize three needles by heating them in the flame of a candle. 4. Puncture apple A with a sterile needle in three places. Apply alcohol over two of the punctures. 5. Push the second sterilized needle into the soil and then into apple B in three places.

6. Puncture apple C with the third sterile needle but do not apply any alcohol to the three punctures.

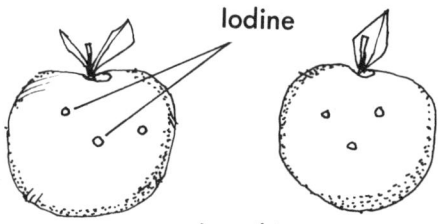   

(a) Three punctures with sterile needle; and iodine applied on two punctures
(b) Puncture with needle stuck in soil
(c) Puncture with needle but no iodine
(d) Control (no holes)
Rotten

7. Do nothing to apple D and the rotten apple.
8. Place all four labeled apples in a warm place for several days.
   Why was apple D not punctured?

What Must I Know?

If necessary, point out that this is the control in the experiment. Be sure the children understand the term *control*.

Hypothesizing — What do you think will happen if the apples stand for a few days?
Comparing — In what ways do you think they look alike?
Comparing — How will they be different? Why?
Observing
9. Observe the apples daily. Every other day make a diagram or illustration of the changes taking place. Discuss these with your lab group.

Observing — What has happened to some of the apples?
Comparing — How are the apples alike?
Comparing — How are they different?
Inferring — What do you think might have caused some of these changes?
Comparing — Which spots on the apples seem to be the most prominent? Why?
Comparing — Which other apple does apple C resemble most?
Observing — What has happened to apple D?
Inferring — What was apple D in your experiment?

10. Cut all five apples in half.
    Caution: Do not eat the apples because the alcohol is poisonous.

Comparing — Which apples seem to look most like a rotten apple?
Inferring — Why do you think so?
Inferring — Why did you apply alcohol over only *two* punctures on apple A?
Observing — What effect did the alcohol have? What about the third puncture?

What Must I Know?

Alcohol is an antiseptic. The alcohol probably destroyed any microorganisms present in the wound.

Inferring — What happened to all the microorganisms on the needles after they had been heated?
Comparing — The skin of an apple is similar to what part of your body?
Inferring — Why did the rotten spots seem to grow a little larger each day?

What Must I Know?

Microorganisms have a fantastic growth rate. As long as there is a substantial amount of food present and space enough for growth, they will continue to reproduce.

LIVING SCIENCES 23

Inferring
Hypothesizing

What do you think would happen if our skin were punctured?
What might a person do to a wound or puncture if he did not want to get an infection?

What Must I Know?

The wound should be cleaned, an antiseptic applied, and the wound covered with a sterile bandage.

How Will Children Use or Apply What They Discover?

1. How might you set up the above experiment using oranges instead of apples? What do you think would happen?
2. Conduct the same experiment, but this time place the apples in a *cool* place. What effect does temperature have on decay?
3. In what other ways does your skin protect you?

What Are the Functions of Bones? (4–6)

What Do I Want Children to Discover?

Bones are the framework of the body.
Bones are composed of calcium and phosphate salts.
Bones of an adult are different from the bones of a child.
Bones are classified as round, flat, long, and short.
The function of a bone is limited by its size and shape.
Bones may have defects.
Bones are made of organic and inorganic substances.
Calcium is necessary for the development of bones.
X rays pass through tissue and can be used to tell where a bone is broken.

What Will I Need?

Human skeleton (small model), skeletal chart, or good picture of a skeleton
5 chicken bones (legs or thighs are best)
Small tree twig
Small saw
2 X-ray pictures, one of a good bone and one of a broken bone
Vinegar
Medium-sized beaker or saucepan
½ pint of milk

What Will We Discuss?

How are the structure of a skyscraper and the structure of your body similar?
What is the framework of your body called?
What makes up the skeleton?
If you wanted to determine how bones function, what could you do to find out?

What Will Children Do?   PROCESSES

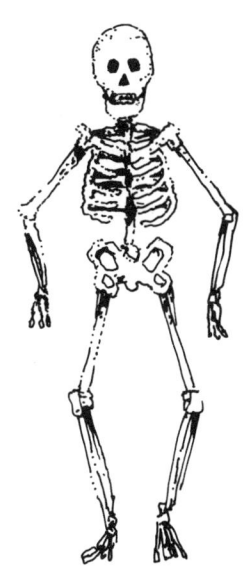

PART I
1. Obtain a model of a skeleton.

Observing — What are some functions of the skeleton or skeletal system?
Inferring — How do bones protect the softer parts of your body?
Name some places in your body where bones cover or protect important organs.
Point to some of these places on your body.

Observing — Where are some places that bones are joined together to allow you to move?
Point to some of these places on your body.

Observing — Which bones help you to stand up?
Point to some of these places on your body.

Observing — Feel the top of your head. Your head is really made up of several bones.

Inferring — How are they joined to each other?
Feel the jawbone. Open and close your mouth.

Observing — Does the bottom jawbone or the upper part of the jaw move?
Feel your spine.

Inferring — From feeling it, what can you say about the spine?
Observing — How many bones are in the spine?
Designing an investigation — How could you find out?

What is a fracture?
Classifying — What are the different types of fractures?

What Must I Know?   There are two types of fractures, simple and compound. A *simple fracture* occurs when the bone but not the skin is broken. A *compound fracture* is a bone fracture that produces a wound by puncturing soft tissues.

LIVING SCIENCES

PART II

Hypothesizing

1. Obtain two chicken bones.
   How could you fracture a chicken bone?
2. Fracture one of the chicken bones.

Describing

   Describe the appearance of the fracture you made.

What Must I Know?

You might have the children compare the fractured bones. Some of them will probably be simple and others compound. Give them the names for the appropriate fractures. (To observe properly a compound fracture, you will need a chicken leg or thigh with the skin and flesh still intact.)

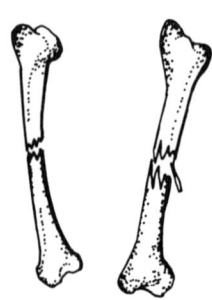

Describing
Inferring
Hypothesizing

3. Obtain a set of X rays and look at them.
   Describe what you see.
   How do X rays help a doctor treat a broken bone?
   What does a doctor do to correct or treat a broken bone?

Hypothesizing

4. Obtain a twig and the fractured bone.
   How would you use the twig to support the bone and keep it from moving?

Hypothesizing
Inferring
Designing an investigation

   What do you think a doctor does to keep the bone from moving?
   Older people fracture their bones more easily than do children.
   What can you do to find out why?

PART III

1. Obtain a bone, vinegar, and a beaker. Fill the beaker with vinegar.

Hypothesizing

   What do you think will happen to the bone if placed in the vinegar?
2. Take the bone out of the vinegar after a minimum of two days.

Observing
Inferring
Hypothesizing

   What effect did the vinegar have on the bone?
   How has the strength of the bone changed
   What could you do to find out?
   Compare an untreated bone to the treated bone.

Comparing
Inferring

   How do they differ?
   Which of these two types of bones do you think are similar to those of older people?

What Must I Know?

Older peoples' bones are more calcified than those of young people. As a result, they are more brittle.

Hypothesizing
Designing an investigation

What do you think bones are made of?
How could you find out?

26   DISCOVERY SCIENCE RESOURCE ACTIVITIES

What Must I Know?	Bones contain organic material and calcium and phosphate salts.
	PART IV
Observing	1. Obtain one-half pint of milk. Open the carton. Examine the milk. What do you notice about it?
What Must I Know?	The white material in the milk contains calcium minerals necessary for bones to grow.
Observing	2. Obtain a bone and a saw. Cut the bone in half. What do you notice about the inside of the bone and the dust material produced from sawing? What is the center of a bone called?
What Must I Know?	The center of the bone is called the *marrow*. It is important for making blood and for keeping the bone in good health.
	Name some foods you need to eat to keep your bones growing and in good health.
How Will Children Use or Apply What They Discovered?	1. What effect would the lack of milk over an extended period have on a person? 2. What are the steps a doctor goes through in setting a bone? 3. Why do some people need to have plates or rods attached or fitted to broken bones? 4. Why do a person's leg bones curve (or become bowlegged) if he or she has a disease called rickets? What can prevent rickets?

How Do Organisms Respond to Stimulants (4–8)

What Do I Want Children to Discover?	Nerves are sensitive to touch, to chemicals, and to electrical shock. Man is not sensitive to charges below 6 volts. A person should not handle electrical equipment with wet hands. For current to flow, there must be a complete circuit. Dry paper is a nonconductor of electricity.
What Will I Need?	1 or 2 earthworms Blunt metal object (tweezers) 2 ounces of vinegar (acid) Dry cell—1½ volt with wires connected to the electrodes 2 copper wires, each 8 inches Waxed paper (enough to wrap a worm in)
What Will We Discuss?	What happens when you touch a hot stove? Why do you jerk your hand away? How does this reaction help protect you?
What Will Children Do?	PROCESSES
What Must I Know?	This activity should be done in groups of two. (For further information, review the activity "How Does Blood Circulate?)

LIVING SCIENCES

Hypothesizing	1. Obtain a worm and place it on your desk and observe it without touching it. What do you think the worm will do if you touch it?
Observing	2. Touch the worm with a blunt metal object. What did it do? What do you think caused it to react?
Hypothesizing	3. Soak the tip of some paper in the vinegar. What do you think will happen if you touch the worm with this paper?
Observing	4. Touch the worm with the paper. How did the worm react?
	5. Hook the copper wire to each terminal on the dry cell. Be sure the ends of the wire have the insulation around them scraped off.
	6. Touch both wires of the dry cell yourself.

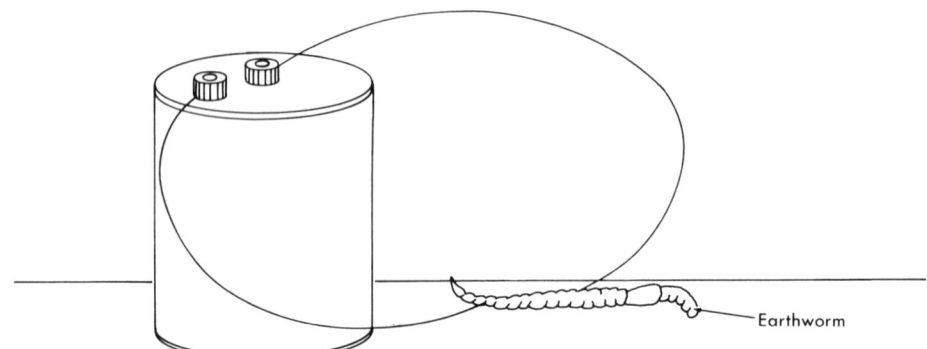

Observing	What did you feel?
Hypothesizing	What do you think will happen when you touch the worm with both wires?
Observing	7. Touch the worm first with one wire and note the reaction. Then touch it with both wires and see how it reacts.
Comparing	Which causes the most reaction, one wire or two? Why?
Comparing	Which causes the most reaction, the metal, acid, or electricity?
Hypothesizing	What do you think will happen if you wrap the worm in waxed paper and repeat the above tests?
	8. Wrap the worm in waxed paper and repeat step 7.
Observing	What is the reaction?
How Will Children Use or Apply What They Discover?	1. Why do you think too much electricity might kill you? 2. Why should you never pick up an electrical appliance or unscrew a light bulb when your hands are wet? 3. Why should you never touch an electrical piece of apparatus unless you know how it works? 4. Why is it a bad idea to have a radio plugged in near a bathtub or even in the bathroom?

How Do Our Muscles Work? (4–8)

What Do I Want Children to Discover?	Muscle cells make it possible to move parts of your body. There are two types of muscles: voluntary and involuntary.

Voluntary muscles are arranged in pairs and work on opposite sides of a bone.
There are three types of levers operated by voluntary muscles, causing the movement of various parts of the body.

What Will I Need? Uncooked chicken leg and wing, or frog leg, preferably with the feet attached to the legs
Forceps (to pull the skin off the leg)

What Will Children Do? PROCESSES

1. Where have you seen a muscle?
   Hold up an uncooked chicken leg and wing (a frog leg may be used).
Inferring
Observing
   How is the chicken able to move its legs or wings?
   What kind of tissue do you mainly see around the bones of the wing and leg?

What Must I Know? Most of the tissue seen and most of the meat you eat is muscle. The chicken has several hundred different muscles to move various parts of its body. Muscle tissue covers the body in sheets and bands that lie between the skin and skeleton.

What are the names of some of the voluntary muscles in the upper arm?

What Must I Know? You may have to explain that muscles that move bones are called *voluntary muscles*. The body also has *involuntary muscles* such as those that are in the wall of the intestines. The involuntary muscles move without a person's having to think about them. Some common voluntary muscles are *biceps* (located in the front of the upper arm), *triceps* (the large muscle at the back of the upper arm), and the *deltoid* (large, triangular muscle of the shoulder that raises the arm away from the side).

2. Obtain some forceps and pull the skin off the chicken leg.
   Point out several of the different bundles of muscles.
Applying
   Can anyone show me one of his muscles?

What Must I Know? The most common reaction to this is for someone to double up his fist and bring it up close to his shoulder. Have the class take a good grasp of their triceps (underside of the upper arm; see diagram below) and hold it while they raise their lower arms.

Observing
   What happens to the triceps when you raise your arm?
   Have the class lower their arms.
Observing
   What happens to the arm the second time?
Hypothesizing
   Why does the upper part of the arm get thicker when the arm is raised?

What Must I Know? To raise your arm, the muscle has to contract. As it contracts, it becomes shorter and thicker, forming a "bump." Have all the class flex their arms to show their biceps. Teach them the names of these upper arm muscles. The biceps are composed of two muscles connected to the bone by a tendon. The triceps consist of three muscles connected to the bone by one tendon. The triceps lie on the opposite side of the arm from the biceps.

LIVING SCIENCES 29

The chief characteristic of all muscles is that they can contract. This is because of the special function of the cells that form muscles. When one muscle contracts, the opposing muscle relaxes.

Hypothesizing

3. If a muscle can only contract how is it possible to return your arm to its original position?

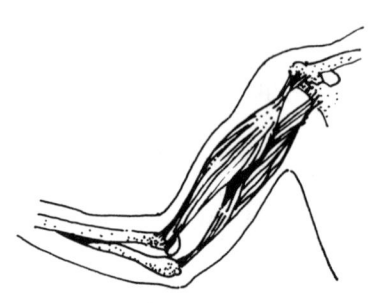

What Must I Know?

Muscles work in pairs. Biceps contract to raise the arms. To lower the arms, the triceps contract and the biceps relax. All bones are moved this way. Example: When you show someone how strong you are, you "make a muscle" by contracting your biceps, and your forearm is pulled up toward your shoulder. If you want to lower your arm, you relax your biceps and contract your triceps. As you bend your arm back and forth at the elbow, each of these muscles relaxes and contracts over and over. Draw the above diagram on the board to show how skeletal muscles work.

4. Show the lower part of the chicken bone to the class.
   Where can you see part of a tendon on the chicken leg?

Observing

What Must I Know?

If the foot of the bird has been cut off, only part of the shiny white tendon will be seen.

Inferring

5. How is a muscle fastened to the bone?

What Must I Know?

Some muscles are connected directly to the bone, whereas others are connected to a tough, nonstretchable cord, or tendon, which is connected to the bone. (Write *tendon* on the board.)

	Where can you feel a strong tendon in your own body?
What Must I Know?	If you reach down and grasp the back of your foot just above the heel, you can feel the strong tendon called the Achilles tendon that connects the muscle of your leg to your heel bone. (Write *Achilles* on the board.) Raise yourself on the ball of your foot. You can feel the calf muscles tighten and bulge as they contract and pull upward on your heel.
Hypothesizing	6. What is the correct way to lift an object so you do not strain your muscles? Have a child demonstrate by picking up a cardboard box as shown in the following diagram.

Incorrect (using arms only)   Correct (using legs)

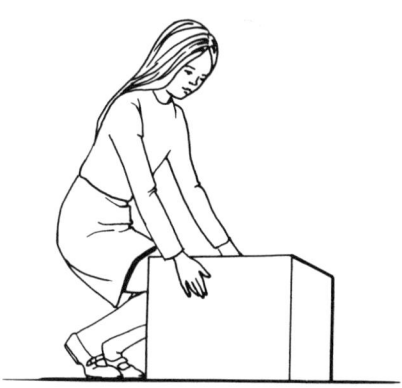

Hypothesizing	Why do you think one method of lifting objects is better than the other?
What Must I Know?	With the correct method, you use more of your skeleton and many more muscles than in the other, so there is less likelihood of straining any one muscle. Have all the members of the class practice the correct way to lift heavy objects.
Inferring	7. What kinds of machines make it possible for the body to lift more weight?
What Must I Know?	A lever is often used. A lever is a device consisting of a bar turning about a fixed point, the *fulcrum*, using power or force applied at a second point to lift or sustain a weight at a third point. Our body contains many levers. The joints act as the fulcrum, our muscles act as the force, and the weight is that part we lift.
How Will Children Use or Apply What They Discover?	1. What are some examples of levers? 2. Where are some levers in the human body? 3. Why are some weight lifters' biceps so large? Can you enlarge your biceps? How?

LIVING SCIENCES

How Do Humans Breathe? (4-8)

What Do I Want Children to Discover?

When a person exercises, breathing increases.
Breathing increases because more carbon dioxide is produced.
Carbon dioxide causes the diaphragm to work more rapidly.
When the diaphragm moves up in the rib cage, it forces air out of the lungs.
When the diaphragm moves down, air is pulled into the lungs.
Gases and water vapor are exhaled from the lungs.

What Will I Need?

Large rubber band
Stop watch
Tape measure
Glass tube or jar 6 inches in diameter and 10 inches tall with a hole in the bottom
Cork or rubber stopper with a hole in the center
Piece of pliable rubber or a part of a balloon (preferably 8 x 8 inches)
Balloon
Model of the chest cavity
Mirror
Paper cups or glasses
Straw or glass tube
½ cup or 100 cc. of limewater or calcium hydroxide (obtain in drugstore)
Water
Sealing wax
String

What Will We Discuss?

How many times a minute do you breathe?
How would you go about finding out?

What Will Children Do?

PROCESSES

What Must I Know?

This activity should be done in groups of two or three children. For exercise, the children may run in place.

PART I
1. Do the following with another student: Record the number of times he or she normally breathes by counting breaths on a mirror. Let the student also record the number of times you breathe.

	At Rest	After Exercise
One minute	_____	_____
Two minutes	_____	_____
Three minutes	_____	_____

Comparing What is the average number of times per minute a person breathes at rest?

Comparing What is the average number of times per minute a person breathes after exercise?

Have each child graph his or her rest and exercise record like the diagram.

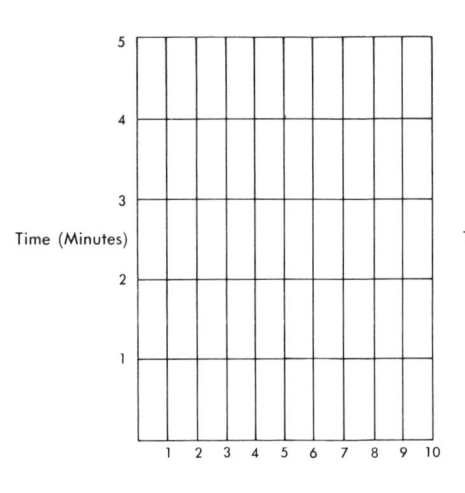

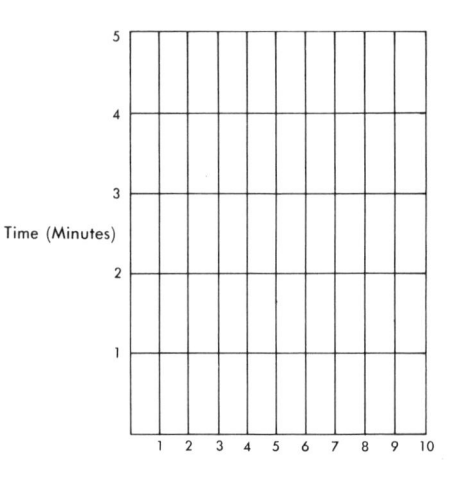

Time (Minutes)

Number
Breaths Rest

Time (Minutes)

Number
Breaths Exercise

Hypothesizing
Inferring

Hypothesizing
Hypothesizing
Designing an investigation
Designing an investigation

What makes a person breathe faster?
Why did you count the number of times a person breathes for several rather than for just one minute?
What gas do you need from the air?
What do you exhale?
How can you prove that you exhale water?

How can you prove that you exhale carbon dioxide?

What gas do you breathe from the air that your body does not use?

What Must I Know?

Explain that air contains about 80 percent nitrogen, 20 percent oxygen, 0.03 percent carbon dioxide, and small percentages of other gases. But the body does not use the nitrogen.

Designing an investigation

How does the size of your chest vary when you breathe?
How would you find out?
2. With the tape measure, check and record these measurements.

	Top of Chest	Lower Diaphragm
Inhale	_____	_____
Exhale	_____	_____

Interpreting data

3. Construct a graph to illustrate these variations.

PART II
1. Obtain a glass jar, glass tube, cork or rubber stopper, balloon, rubber sheet, string, and some sealing wax.
2. Fit the stopper into one end of the jar and insert the glass tube with the balloon tied on it through the hole in the stopper. Seal any holes around the tube with the sealing wax.

LIVING SCIENCES

3. Fix the rubber sheet onto the opened end of the jar with a large rubber band.

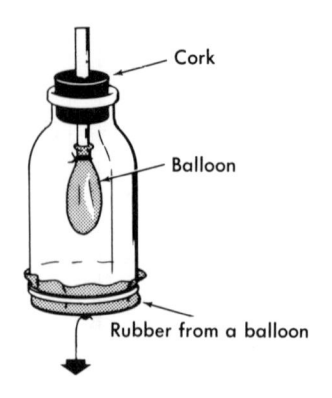

Hypothesizing — What do you think will happen to the balloon if you pull down on the rubber cover at the bottom of the jar?

4. Pull down on the rubber balloon.
   Record your observation.

Hypothesizing — What do you think will happen if you push up on the rubber cover?

5. Push up on the balloon.
   Record your observation.

Inferring — Why do you see these changes?

Inferring — Where in your body do you have something that works like this?

What Must I Know? — Introduce the word *diaphragm*. Use a model or a chart of the chest cavity for reference.

Observing — How do the diaphragm, lungs, and chest lie in relation to one another in the chest cavity?

6. Diagram and label the parts of the body used in breathing.

PART III **What do You Exhale?**
1. Obtain a mirror.

Hypothesizing — When you breathe, what leaves your mouth?

2. Take a mirror and exhale on it. Hold the mirror near your nose.

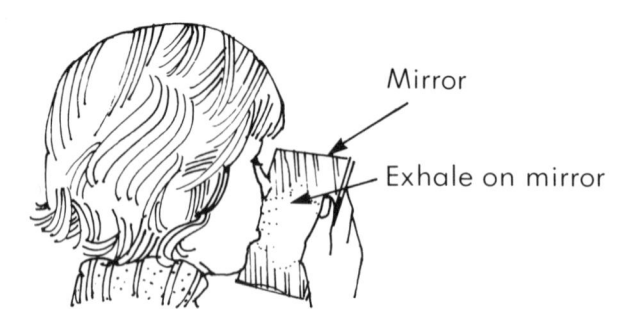

Observing — What do you see on the mirror?
Inferring — Why does moisture collect on the mirror?
Assuming — Where does the moisture come from?
Hypothesizing — What kinds of gases do you think you exhale?

34 DISCOVERY SCIENCE RESOURCE ACTIVITIES

What Must I Know? Explain that exhaled air contains about 80 percent nitrogen, 16 percent oxygen, 0.03 percent carbon dioxide, and small percentages of other gases.

Inferring What happens to the nitrogen you inhale?
Inferring What gas in air do you need?
Inferring What gas do you exhale more of than you inhale?

PART IV
1. Obtain a straw and 100 cc. of limewater (or some calcium hydroxide). Mix the limewater with water. Let it settle.
2. Blow through a straw or glass tube into the limewater.

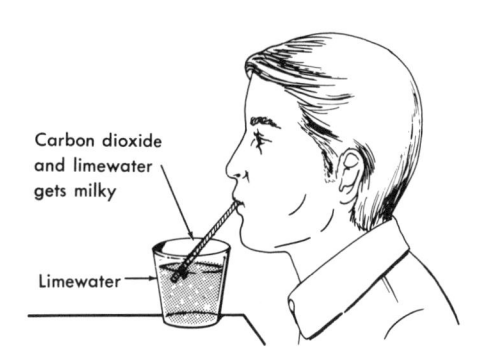

Observing What happens as you blow (exhale) into the limewater?
Inferring Why does it change color?

What Must I Know? When carbon dioxide is added to limewater, it changes to a milky color because the carbon dioxide combines with calcium hydroxide to form a white precipitate.

How Will Children Use or Apply What They Discover?
1. How does exercise cause the heart to beat faster?
2. Why does an increase in carbon dioxide in the blood cause the heart to beat faster?
3. Explain the hypothesis: "A person needing oxygen naturally breathes faster."

How Does Blood Circulate? (4–8)

What Do I Want Children to Discover?
The heart beats and pumps blood through the body.
Other animals have hearts.
Blood moves rapidly through the blood vessels.
Blood vessels are not all the same size.
Blood circulates
All animals have individual variations.
Some animals are warm-blooded; some are cold-blooded.

What Will I Need?
Several live earthworms   Paper cup
Paper towels   Ice water

LIVING SCIENCES   35

What Will We Discuss?	What is a warm-blooded animal?
	Snakes and turtles are cold-blooded animals. Would they be more active on a cold day or a warm day? Why?
	What advantages are there in being a warm-blooded animal?
	What evidence is there that an earthworm has blood vessels?
	How can you find out if blood moves in the worm's blood vessels?
	What evidence is there that the worm has a heart?
	How many times per minute does the earthworm's heart beat?
	How could you find out?
What Must I Know?	This activity should be done in groups of two or three. (For further information, review the activity "How Do Organisms Respond to Stimulants?")
What Will Children Do?	PROCESSES
	PART I
	1. Obtain an earthworm and a paper towel.
	2. Place the worm on the paper towel.
	3. Observe the worm to see if you can find any blood vessels.
What Must I Know?	There is an obvious blood vessel on the back of the worm.
Observing	Where do you find the blood vessel on the worm?
Observing	How does the vessel seem to vary in color?
Inferring	What is going through the blood vessel to give it that color?
Inferring	What makes you think the earthworm has a heart?
Observing	4. Observe and record how many times the heart beats a minute.
Collecting data	5. Determine the average heartbeat by using your figures and those of your classmates.
	What does *average* mean?
Inferring	Why do you average these figures to get the number of times the heart beats for a worm?
What Must I Know?	Each worm is a little different. The individuals counting the heartbeat might also have made a mistake. By taking the average, the mistakes are evened out.
Designing an investigation	What would you do to find out whether the earthworm is a warm-blooded animal or a cold-blooded animal?

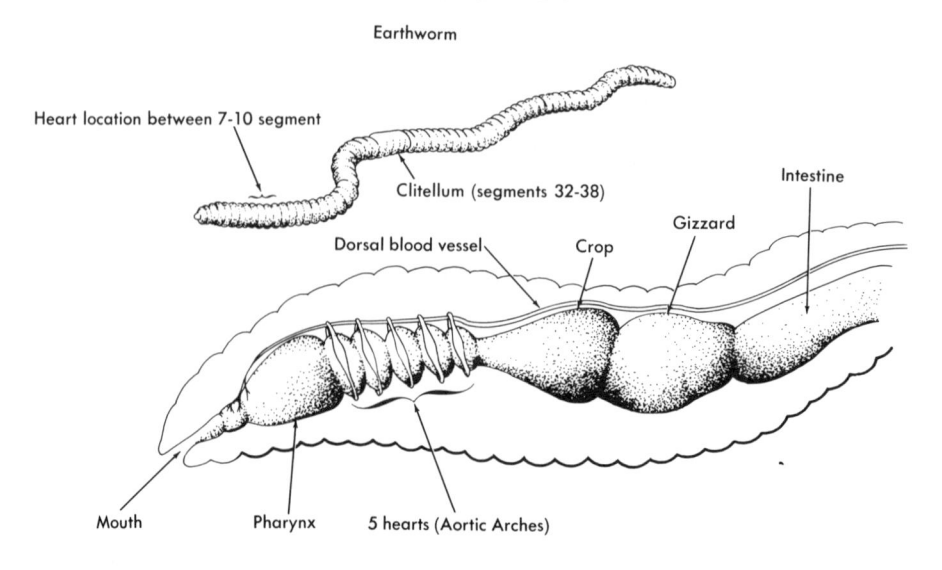

Earthworm

Heart location between 7-10 segment
Clitellum (segments 32-38)
Intestine
Gizzard
Dorsal blood vessel
Crop
Mouth
Pharynx
5 hearts (Aortic Arches)

PART II
1. Obtain a paper cup with ice water in it and an earthworm.
2. Place the worm in the ice water.

Observing 3. Observe and record the actions of the worm.
4. After the worm has been in the water 5 minutes, remove it.

Observing 5. Count and record how many times the heart beats.
Collecting data 6. Determine the average.
Inferring

How does the heartbeat of the worm vary after it has been placed in cold water?

What Must I Know? A worm is a cold-blooded animal. This means its body temperature is the same as the temperature of the environment. The colder the conditions, the slower the worm's body functions. The heart, therefore, beats slowly in a cold environment.

7. Graph your findings in Parts I and II.

How Will Children Use or Apply What They Discover?
1. How many hearts does the earthworm have?
2. How do the hearts function?
3. How does the earthworm ingest and digest?

What Does the Heart Do? (4-8)

What Do I Want Children to Discover?
The heart pumps the blood through the body.
The heart beats many times per minute.
When you exercise, the heart beats faster.
The heart has four chambers.
Blood moves in an orderly fashion through the body.

What Will I Need?
2 balloons
Live goldfish
Dish with wet cotton
Microscope or microprojector
Funnel
Rubber tubes
Y-shaped glass tubes or a small funnel
Model of heart obtained from the Heart Association, or purchase a calf or sheep heart (may be stored in alcohol)

What Will We Discuss? How large is your heart?

What Must I Know? Have the children make a fist. This is approximately the size of the heart. The heart of an adult is about 5 inches long, 3½ inches wide, and 2½ inches thick.

What does a heart look like?

What Must I Know? This activity should be done in groups of four children.

What Will Children Do? PROCESSES

PART I
1. Obtain a model of the heart, Y-shaped tube, a funnel, and 2 rubber tubes.

Observing How many compartments do you see in the model of the heart?

LIVING SCIENCES 37

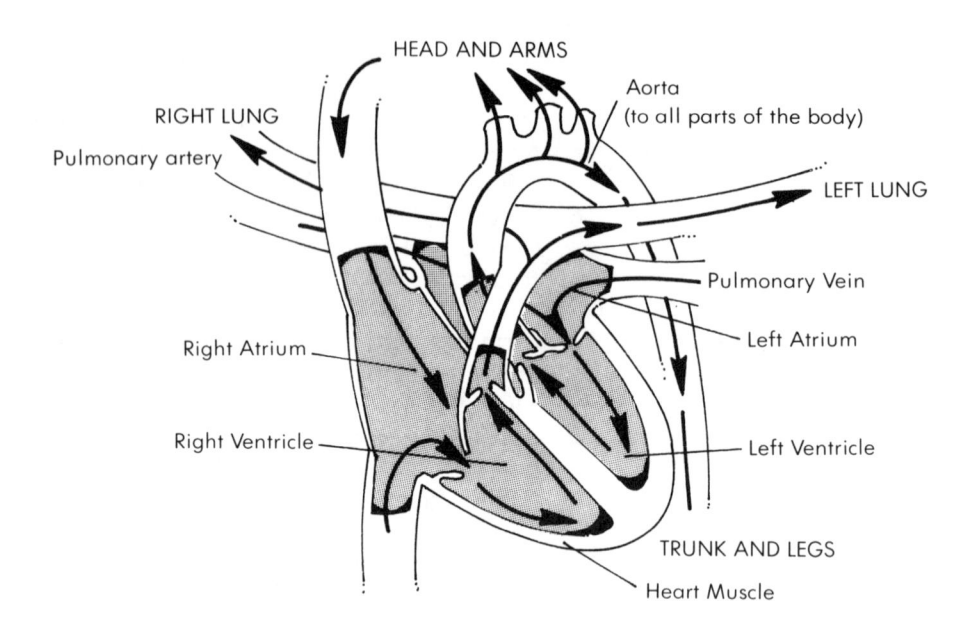

Diagram of the heart with labels: HEAD AND ARMS, Aorta (to all parts of the body), RIGHT LUNG, Pulmonary artery, LEFT LUNG, Pulmonary Vein, Right Atrium, Left Atrium, Right Ventricle, Left Ventricle, TRUNK AND LEGS, Heart Muscle

Observing	2. Observe how these compartments are arranged and their similarities and differences.
Observing	Where is the heart located in your body?
	3. Place your hand at the center of the rib cage, near the lower edge.
Observing	What do you feel?
Designing an investigation	4. Make a stethoscope by attaching rubber tubes to the three ends of a Y-shaped glass tube. Attach a funnel to the tail of the "Y" tube.
What Must I Know?	A small funnel with one rubber tube can be substituted if a "Y" tube is not available.
	5. Place the funnel on the chest of a friend.
	6. Place the other two ends in your ears.
	Caution: Use extreme care when placing the tubes in your ears so you do not harm the eardrums.
Observing	What do you hear?
Hypothesizing	Why do you think the heart sounds something like a drum?
Inferring	What makes the drum noise?
What Must I Know?	At this point, display a large chart or model. Identify the various parts of the heart and their functions. Trace the route of blood through the heart.

PART II
1. Obtain a balloon. Have your partner fill the balloon half full of water.

Designing an investigation
Inferring
Hypothesizing

How can the balloon be used to demonstrate how the heart pumps blood?
What does the water in the balloon represent?
What do you think would happen if you released the end of the balloon and pushed on the side of the balloon a little?

2. Gently push some of the liquid out of the balloon.

Inferring

How do you think the heart moves blood out of its chambers?

What Must I Know?

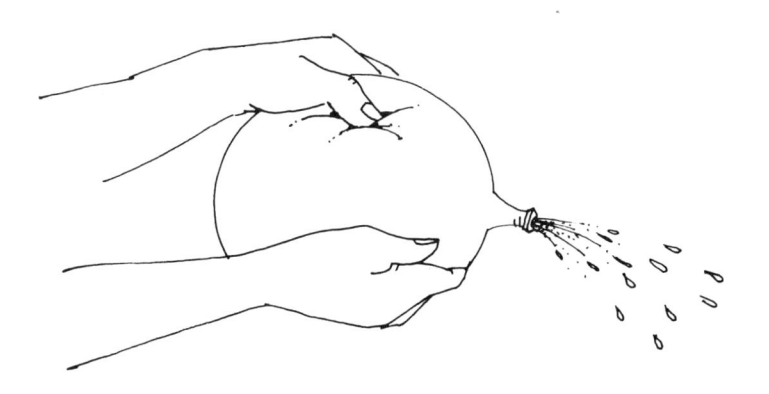

The heart is similar to the balloon in that it has liquid in it, but the heart actually has two pumps, one on the left side and one on the right side. The sound the students hear is due to the pumping of the heart.

Observing
Inferring

3. Feel your pulse as shown in the diagram.
   What do you feel?
   What causes the beats you feel?

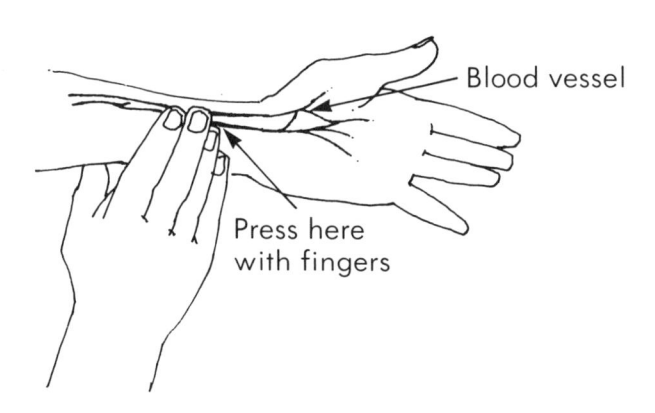

What Must I Know?

The pulse is caused by the surge of blood that passes through the blood vessels each time the heart pumps.

4. Listen to your partner's heart and record the number of its beats per minute. Then have your partner jump up and down 60 times. Record the number of heartbeats after the exercise.
   What happens to the rate of the heartbeat after the exercise?
   Why does the heart beat faster?

Observing
Inferring

What Must I Know?

When you exercise, your muscles use more oxygen and food energy. Your heart is stimulated because of this activity, and it pumps faster, sending more blood to all parts of the body.

Describing
Designing an investigation

How does the blood move through the body?
What could you do with a goldfish to see how the blood moves through its body?

LIVING SCIENCES 39

How Will Children Use or Apply What They Discover?

1. Why is it necessary for the blood to continue moving through the body?
2. What does the blood do with waste materials picked up from the cells in the muscles?
3. What causes the heart to beat faster after exercise?
4. What effect would the temperature of the water have on the flow of blood in a goldfish?

What Happens to Starch in the Food You Eat? (4-8)

What Do I Want Children to Discover?

Large food particles must be broken down into smaller molecules before they can be absorbed.
The breaking down of food by chemical means is called *digestion*.
Food must be dissolved before it can be used by the body.
Starch is a food.
Starch must be changed to dissolved sugar for it to pass through the lining of the small intestine.

What Will I Need?

Cornstarch (one teaspoon)
Sugar (one teaspoon)
Iodine (a small bottle with an eye dropper)
Spoon
3 glasses
Cracker
2 jars with covers
Funnel
3 paper towels
3 test tubes
Scale
Beaker
Rubber band
Flour (one gram)
4 cubes of sugar
100 cc. graduate

What Will We Discuss?

Look at the cracker.
How is the cracker going to help my body when I eat it?
What is going to happen to the cracker?
When will the cracker be ready to be used by the cells?
How is the body going to prepare this cracker for use?
If the body does not use every bit of the cracker, what is going to happen to that which is not used?
Where is the body going to digest this cracker?
What substances does the body contain to break down the cracker into usable substances?

PROCESSES

Water and sugar   Water and cornstarch

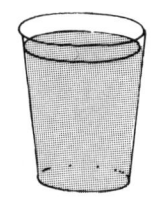

What Will Children Do?

Observing
Observing
Inferring
Hypothesizing

Inferring

Observing

Comparing

Observing

What Must I Know?

Summarizing

Observing
Hypothesizing

Observing
Inferring
Hypothesizing

1. Obtain a teaspoon of cornstarch, 2 glasses of water, and a teaspoon of sugar. Put the cornstarch into one glass of water and the sugar into the other. Stir each glass with a spoon.
   How does the starchy water appear?
   How does the sugar water appear?
   Which has dissolved?
   What do you think would happen if you let the glasses stand for a day?
   How would this experiment help to explain why starch has to be changed so your body can use it?
2. Stir the starch and water again until the starch is mixed with the water. Take a teaspoon of the starch and water mixture and put a drop of iodine into it.
   What color does the mixture turn?
3. Repeat the above step, substituting sugar water for the starch and water mixture.
   How does the result differ?
   Put a drop of iodine on your cracker.
   What is the result?

Iodine is used to test for starch. Starch in the presence of iodine turns blue-black.

How would you summarize this test in terms of the results you have observed?

4. Obtain a funnel, line it with a piece of paper towel, and set it in an empty glass. Stir the starch in the glass of water again. Slowly pour some of the starch water into the funnel.
   After the water has run through, look at the inside of the paper.
   Is there any starch left inside the funnel?
   How could you test the water to find out if any starch went through with the water?
5. Perform this test for starch.
   What color did the mixture turn?
   Is there starch present?
   What do you think will happen if sugar water is poured through filter paper?

LIVING SCIENCES   41

Hypothesizing	How can you tell if there is sugar in the water *before* and *after* you pour it into the funnel?
Inferring	Which do you think could go through the wall of your intestine better —starch or sugar? Why?

6. Make a 1 percent starch solution by taking one gram of flour and adding it to 100 cc. of water. (The 100 cc. measurement can be determined by using a graduate.) Stir the solution thoroughly in a beaker.

Measuring — Obtain three test tubes. Collect 20 cc. of saliva from your mouth in one test tube. Pour one-half of the saliva into the second test tube so there are 10 cc. in each tube. Label one of the saliva test tubes the CONTROL. (Put a rubber band around it.) Add 10 cc. of starch solution to the other saliva test tube and 10 cc. of starch solution to the empty third test tube. Now put equal amounts of iodine (1 to 2 drops) into each of the three test tubes. Label the test tubes as shown in the following example:

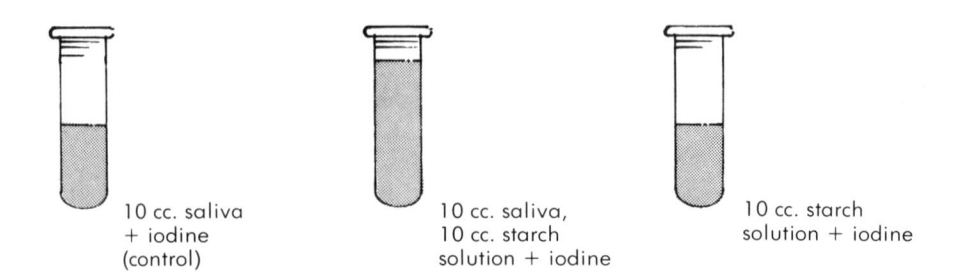

10 cc. saliva + iodine (control)

10 cc. saliva, 10 cc. starch solution + iodine

10 cc. starch solution + iodine

7. Allow the test tubes to stand for several hours.

Observing	Observe and record your results.
Observing	Which test tubes turn blue?
Inferring	Why?
Observing	Which test tube does not turn blue?
Inferring	Why?
Inferring	Why do you think you added saliva to test tube II?
Observing	After the tubes have stood for an hour, what tube changes color?
Inferring	Why?
Inferring	What effect does saliva produce on the starch in your mouth?
Applying	Why do you think you should chew your food well?

8. Obtain two jars with covers. Pour equal amounts of water into each of the two jars. Place two cubes of sugar into each jar and screw the covers on tightly. Place one jar aside and let it stand still. Shake the other jar vigorously.

Comparing — Compare the results occurring in the two jars.

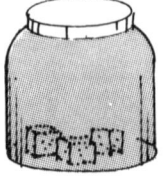

No shaking

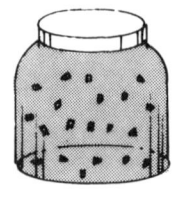

Shaking

Inferring — Why did the sugar dissolve faster in one jar?

42   DISCOVERY SCIENCE RESOURCE ACTIVITIES

Applying	What does this activity tell us about chewing your food before swallowing it?
What Must I Know?	The more the children chew their food, the more enzymes will mix with the food to break it down chemically. Chewing also helps to break the food down into smaller particles so more of it comes in contact with the enzymes.
How Will Children Use or Apply What They Discover?	1. How does saliva affect other foods such as poultry, fruits, and vegetables? 2. Why should diabetics not eat starchy foods? 3. Test other foods for starch content.

What Makes a Good Diet? (4–8)

What Do I Want Children to Discover?	The need to consider their diet.
What Will I Need?	Textbook, or some other source listing the "basic four" and other information about nutrition
What Will We Discuss?	How good is your diet?
What Will Children Do?	Write down what you think would be a good diet for (1) breakfast, (2) lunch, and (3) dinner.
How Will Children Use or Apply What They Discover?	PROCESSES
Inferring	How many different types of minerals would you get? Now check your text section on the "basic four."
Observation	What foods did you leave out?
Inferring	How many different types of vitamins would you be likely to eat?
Inferring	What foods do you generally eat that might be called "junk foods"?
Hypothesizing	Since you should *not* eat "junk" food, what would be good to eat instead?
What Must I Know?	Children should have a good, balanced diet. If they eat from the "basic four" categories of foods, this should help to insure that they get the right diet. However, they should be cautioned not to eat too many fatty foods such as meat, cheese, and ice cream, and not to eat too much sugar.

Play "Check the Label" Game (4–8)

What Do I Want Children to Discover?	Many foods have lots of sugar.
What Will I Need?	Empty packages, cans, and bottles with labels.

LIVING SCIENCES

What Will We Discuss? The contents of food in packages and cans must be labeled.
The contents are labeled in order by amount.
The first thing on the label is the greatest amount.
Often you can be fooled by how much sugar a food has.

What Must I Know? You have to know that there are many names for the different types of sugars. For example, all of the following are names for different sugar foods:

Sugar	Sucrose
Syrup	Lactose
Corn Syrup	Fructose
Dextrose	Corn sweetener
Maltose	Molasses
Glucose	

What Will Children Do? Look at the labels on these foods.
Write the name of each of the foods below: Under each one write the kinds of sugar it contains. Use the above list to help you.

Food Name _____   Food Name _____
Sugars   Sugars
Food Name _____   Food Name _____
Sugars   Sugars
Food Name _____
Sugars

How Will Children Use or Apply What They Discover?

PROCESSES

Inferring What did you find out about these foods? Which food had the most sugar?
Which food had the most vitamins? Which food had the most preservatives? How would you find out?

Valuing What will you do in the future so as not to eat too much sugar?

What Must I Know? A lot of packaged foods have preservatives in them.

What to Do FOLLOW-UP ACTIVITY
Look at the list below. Write on a piece of paper your guess of how much sugar each food contains:

	No. of Parts out of 10		No. of Parts out of 10
Canned peaches	_____	Chocolate ice cream	_____
Canned corn	_____	Catsup	_____
Peanut butter	_____	Italian salad dressing	_____
Yogurt	_____	Russian salad dressing	_____
Cereal naturally sweetened with honey	_____	Dessert type whipped toppings	_____
Chocolate bar	_____	Cracker wafer	_____
Cake	_____	Nondiary coffee creamer	_____
Flavored gelatin	_____		

Which food do you think has the most sugar? _____
Which is next? _____
Which is next? _____
Now look below and compare your answers.

Food	Approximate Parts out of 10
Canned peaches	2
Canned corn	1
Peanut butter	1
Yogurt	1
Cereal naturally sweetened with honey	2.5
Chocolate bar	5
Cake	3.5
Flavored gelatin	8
Chocolate ice cream	2
Catsup	3
Russian salad dressing	3
Italian salad dressing	1
Dessert type whipped toppings	2
Cracker wafer	1
Nondiary creamer for coffee	6.5

What Did You Learn? Which food had the most sugar? _____
Which other foods had a lot of sugar? _____

Using What You Learned What foods should you avoid eating too much of? _____
What foods do you think have little sugar? _____
How would you find out? _____

TOO MUCH SUGAR IS NOT GOOD

Sugar is an important food. Normally, you can get all the sugar you need from fruits and vegetables. Too much sugar from additional sources, however, is not good for your health. It may cause your teeth to decay. Sugar also doesn't have vitamins and minerals. If you eat too much of it, you are less likely to eat other foods that have vitamins and minerals. All parts of your body need these. If you do not get enough of them, all parts of your body suffer. You may then be more likely to get sick. Some people say sugar is "empty" or "trash" food. Why do you think they say this?

PLANTS: ANATOMY AND PHYSIOLOGY

What Is a Seed? (K-3)

What Do I Want Children to Discover? Seeds store food.
A seed has a young, undeveloped baby plant in it called an *embryo*.
Seeds usually sprout faster when it is warm.
The embryo obtains the food it needs to grow from the storage area of the seed.

LIVING SCIENCES 45

What Will I Need? Bean and radish seeds Magnifying glass
Paper towels Potting soil
Plastic wrap Plastic cups
Small dish or jar lid

What Will We Discuss? Sometimes farmers have to replant their crops. Why?
What would you do to prepare the best conditions for seeds to sprout?

What Must I Know? There are many variables; therefore, many suggestions can result. Evaluate and discuss the ideas and then allow pupils to perform acceptable experiments in addition to the activities that follow.

What Will Children Do? PROCESSES

PART I **How Does Temperature Affect the Sprouting of Seeds?**
1. Obtain 4 bean seeds, 4 radish seeds, and some plastic wrap. Place the seeds on well-soaked paper towels.
2. Wrap the seeds and towel material in plastic wrap.
3. Repeat the above procedure and place one plastic wrap near a heater and another in a cool place, preferably the refrigerator in the cafeteria or teacher's room.

Hypothesizing How do you think the difference in temperatures will affect the sprouting seeds?

Collecting data 4. Observe your wrapped seeds each day for one week and record your observations.
5. At the end of the week, compare the seeds in each plastic wrap.

Comparing What differences do you note?
Inferring Why do you think these differences occur?

Bean seed    Radish seed

PART II **What Are the Parts of a Seed?**
1. Obtain 12 bean seeds and plastic wrap. Place them on wet paper towels in a dish or jar lid.
Cover with plastic wrap. After several days the seeds should be swollen. Break 6 bean seeds open and look carefully at the parts using one of the magnifying glasses.

Observing 2. Describe what you see.
The baby plant you see is called the *embryo*.
Inferring Where do you think it got its food while it was growing?

What Must I Know? The stored food is called *cotyledon*.

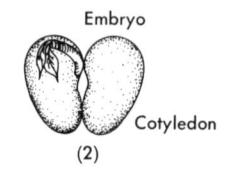

Embryo
Cotyledon
(2)

46   DISCOVERY SCIENCE RESOURCE ACTIVITIES

Hypothesizing

Designing an investigation

What do you think would happen to the embryo if you removed it from the seed and planted it?
How could you find out?

3. Plant the 6 beans *with embryos removed* in soil in a plastic cup.
4. Plant the other 6 bean seeds *with embryos* in soil in a plastic cup. Observe each day, and in a short time you should see what is illustrated in the diagram.

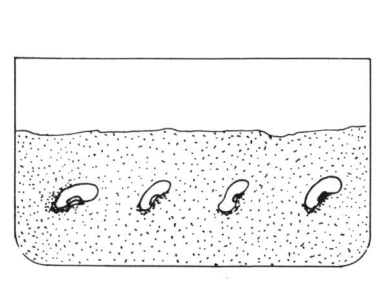

Bean seeds—embryos removed

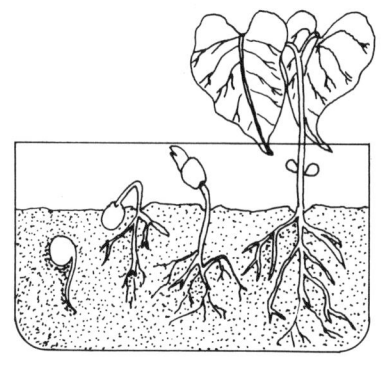

Bean seed with embryo

How Will Children Use or Apply What They Discover?

1. Why do seeds die after they have sprouted if they are not planted in the ground?
2. How long will sprouts live if not planted?
3. Do some kinds of sprouts live longer than others?
4. What happens to seeds if they remain wet for a long time?
5. Why do seeds not germinate if embryos are removed?
6. Why will seeds die if cotyledons are removed?

How Do Roots Grow? (K–6)

What Do I Want Children to Discover?	Roots move around objects in the soil. Seeds need water to grow. Roots grow downward.
What Will I Need?	Sprouted bean plant Bean seeds Small milk carton cut in half lengthwise 4 paper towels Plastic wrap 2 pieces of glass or thick plastic to place seeds between 2 tongue depressors or applicator sticks
What Will We Discuss?	What do you think would happen to roots if they were placed so they were growing up instead of down?
What Will Children Do?	PROCESSES
What Must I Know?	In the primary grades, this activity will have to be done as a demonstration because of the difficulty children have in manipulating the equipment. This activity should be done in groups of 4 students.

LIVING SCIENCES 47

Hypothesizing

1. Obtain 4 bean seeds, plastic wrap, a paper towel, a milk carton cut in half, and a cup of water.
   Place the paper towel in the bottom of a milk carton, and press it down. Soak the towel with water from your paper cup. Place 4 bean seeds on the paper towel. Cover the top of the milk carton with plastic wrap.
   What are the reasons for preparing the seeds this way?

Hypothesizing

2. When the seeds sprout, place them on several layers of paper towels, between two pieces of glass so the roots point up. Put applicator sticks or tongue depressors between the pieces of glass.
   What is the reason for putting the tongue depressors between the pieces of glass?
3. Stand the glass so the roots point up and the stems down.

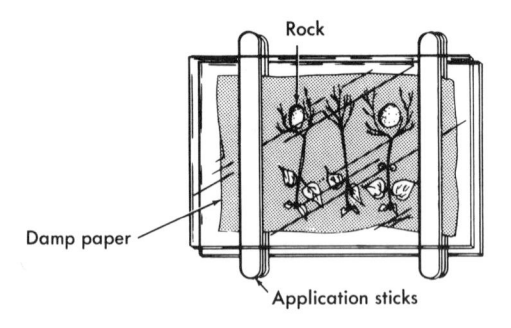

Hypothesizing

What do you think will happen to the growth of stem and roots?

4. Observe the plant growth for several days and record your observations.

Inferring
Designing an investigation

Was your hypothesis true or false, or does it need to be modified?
If you were going to do this activity again, how would you change it to make it better or more interesting?

How Will Children Use or Apply What They Discover?

1. How would the roots react if objects like cotton, a piece of wood, or a rock were placed in their way?
2. What would happen to the roots if the glass were rotated 90° in the same direction every day?

How Does Water Get into a Plant? (K-6)

What Do I Want Children to Discover?

Roots absorb water through small root hairs.
Root hairs are damaged when a plant is transplanted or pulled.

48 DISCOVERY SCIENCE RESOURCE ACTIVITIES

What Will I Need?	Radish seeds Pan or dish Paper towels	Plastic wrap Water Hand lens

What Will We Discuss?   What could you do to determine what a root does (its function) for a plant?

          PROCESSES

What Will Children Do?

1. Obtain a paper towel, several radish seeds, and some plastic wrap. Soak the towel so it drips with water. Place the towel in a dish or pan. Place several radish seeds on the towel and cover the pan with plastic wrap.

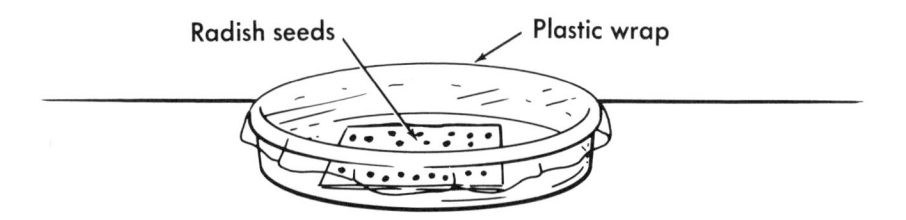

2. Observe for several days and record your observations.

Observing — What do you notice about the roots? Use hand lens.
What are the small fuzzylike projections from each root called?
Inferring — Why do you think the root has root hairs?
Hypothesizing — What happens to the roots of a plant when it is transplanted?
Hypothesizing — Why is some transplanting unsuccessful?
Designing an investigation — What would you do to determine the function of the root and root hairs?
Hypothesizing — What do you think will happen if you remove the root hairs from the root?
Hypothesizing — What do you think will happen if you expose the root hairs to air and sun?

How Will Children Use or Apply What They Discover?

1. Why are roots different shapes?
2. Why are some roots comparatively shallow and others deep?
3. How does man use the roots of plants?
4. What are the functions of the root other than to absorb food materials?

What Are the Parts of a Plant? (K–3)

What Do I Want Children to Discover?

Plants have leaves, roots, stems, and flowers.
Not all plants have the above four parts.
Leaves are able to make food.
The stems carry minerals and water from the roots to the leaves and flowers.
Flowers make seeds that can produce more of the same type of plant.
Some roots store food.

LIVING SCIENCES

What Will I Need? Complete plant such as daisy, geranium, or petunia for entire class
Carrot, radish, turnip, parsnip, and/or sugar beet
Several small, potted geraniums or coleus plants
Stems from assorted plants
Flowers from assorted plants
Milk cartons
Soil
Measuring stick—preferably metric

What Must I Know? Pull up a complete plant for all the children to see. How do you think roots are useful to this plant? Expect and accept various ideas. Allow the children opportunities to propose and examine their ideas.

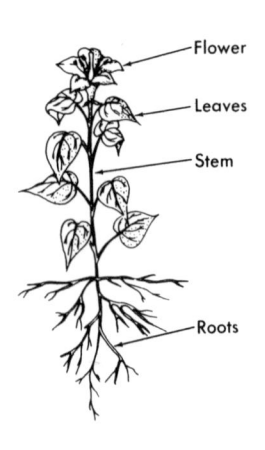

What Will Children Do? PROCESSES

PART I **How Are Roots Useful?**

1. Obtain 2 petunia plants and remove all the roots from one petunia. Obtain some soil and fill the bottom half of 2 milk cartons. Place the petunia without roots with its stem down, on top of the soil.
   What do you notice about the plant when you let go?
   How do you think roots might have helped this plant?

Observing
Inferring

2. Turn the stem right side up and push it to a depth of almost two inches into the soil. Water the plant daily. Allow it to set for 4 or 5 days. Set up the other petunia with roots as control as shown.

Hypothesizing
Observing
Summarizing

What do you think will happen to the plant?

3. After 4 or 5 days, record what happens.
   How do you think roots might have helped the plant?

50 DISCOVERY SCIENCE RESOURCE ACTIVITIES

What Must I Know?

Some plants develop roots in this situation. If they do, remove the plant and develop the lesson around the function of the newly developed roots.

PART II Why Are Stems Important to Plants?

Comparing
Observing
Hypothesizing

1. Obtain three stems different from those provided by your teacher.
   In what ways are they different?
   Which parts of the plant are attached to the stem?
   How do you think water and minerals get from the roots to the leaves and flowers?
2. Break open several of your stems.
3. Feel the inside of the stem.

Observing
Inferring

   What evidence do you have that stems contain water?
   Why do you think stems contain water?

PART III How Do Roots from Different Types of Plants Vary?

Comparing
Comparing
Applying

1. Obtain and compare a carrot, beet, turnip, or parsnip.
   How do their roots vary?
   How are they alike?
   Why do you think you eat these roots?

PART IV Why Are Leaves Important?

Hypothesizing

What do you think would happen to a plant if you removed all the leaves from it?

1. Obtain two potted plants and remove the leaves from one. Do not remove the leaves from the other. Water both plants regularly for 4 days.
2. Place the plants where they can obtain sunlight.
3. Measure the growth of these plants for a week and record your results.

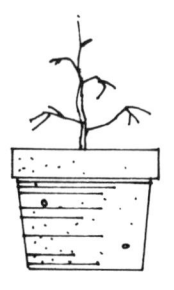

With leaves   Without leaves

Inferring
Inferring

Why do you think your results vary?
In what ways do you think leaves are important to plants?

How Will Children Use or Apply What They Discover?

1. How do plants vary in the number of leaves they have?
2. What plants do not have roots?
3. How are some plants able to survive without roots?

LIVING SCIENCES 51

What Is the Purpose of a Stem? (K-8)

What Do I Want Children to Discover?

Water must move from the roots to the leaves if a plant is to make food and live.
One of the main purposes of the stem of a plant is to carry water from the roots to the leaves.
There are small tubes inside the stem that carry water to the leaves.
Water moves up the stem.

What Will I Need?

Geranium or coleus stem
Red food coloring or ink
Drinking glass
Blotter paper
Water

What Will We Discuss?

How does the water get from the roots to the leaves?
How do you think a florist obtains a blue carnation?
If you wanted to change a white carnation into a blue carnation, what would you do?
How could you find out if your idea was correct?

What Will Children Do?

PROCESSES

1. Obtain a geranium or coleus stem with leaves on it, food coloring or red ink, water, and a drinking glass. Put some water in the drinking glass and color it with the food coloring or ink.

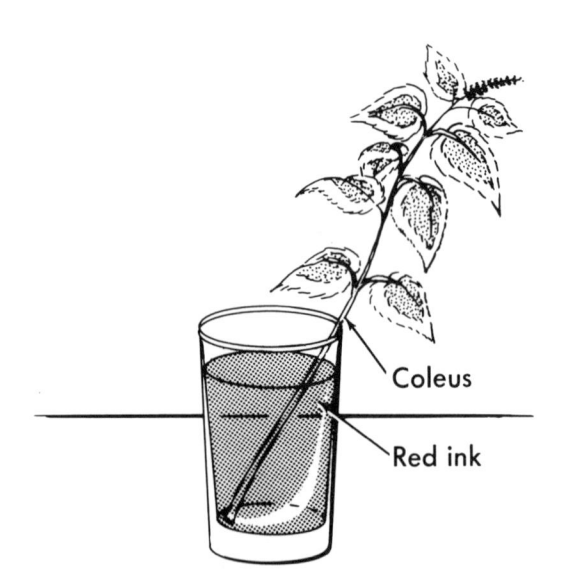

Hypothesizing

Why do you think you have added coloring to the water?

2. Cut a small slice from the bottom of the stalk of your stem and set it into the glass of colored water. Allow it to set in a sunny area for two hours.
3. At the end of this period, cut open the stem.

Observing — What has happened to some of the colored water?
Observing — What parts of the stem appear to contain the colored water? Describe these parts.
Inferring — What can you conclude about how a stem functions from this activity?

How Will Children Use or Apply What They Discover?

1. What effects might different temperatures have on how rapidly a solution moves up a stem?
2. What do you think will happen if you put half of a split stem in one color of water and the other half in another color of water?

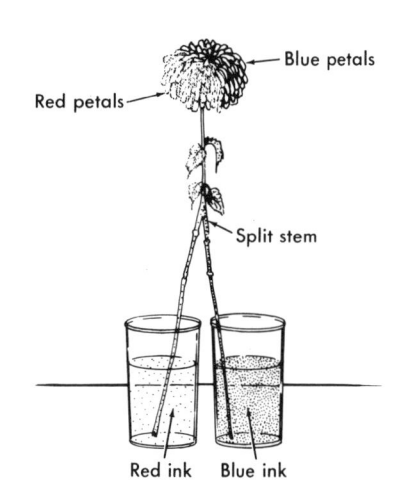

Blue petals — Red petals — Split stem — Red ink — Blue ink

3. What happens to the upward movement of water in a stem when it is dark?
   How could you find out?

Why Do Some Parts of Plants Grow Upward? (4-8)

What Do I Want Children to Discover?

Light and gravity play a role in determining how plants grow.
Roots respond to gravity.
Stems are affected by light.

What Will I Need?

Flat glass or plastic wrap about 4 inches square
2 glasses
Geranium or coleus plant
3 or 4 bean seeds
Tape
Light source
Paper towels
Cup of dirt
Ruler

What Will We Discuss?

What do you think will happen to a plant if its roots are placed in a glass of water?

What do you think will happen if the plant is inverted and the stem is placed in the water?

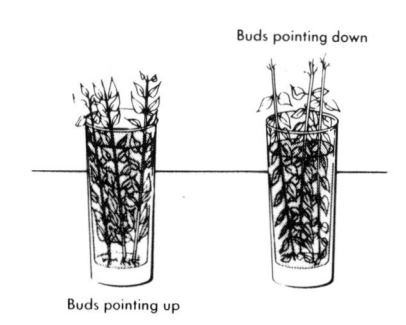

Buds pointing down — Buds pointing up

LIVING SCIENCES 53

What affect does light have on the way a plant grows?
What would happen to the way a plant grows if it were placed near a window?
What effect does gravity have on the parts of sprouting seeds?
What could you do to find out?

What Must I Know? The children should suggest the arranging of the sprouting seeds and apparatus as shown below.

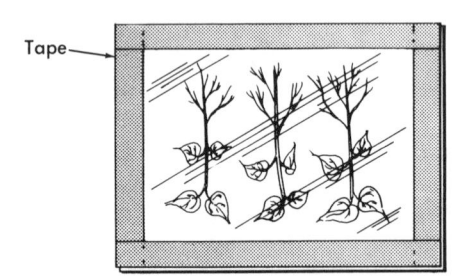

Seeds on soaked paper covered by glass or plastic wrap

What do you think would happen to the growth of seeds if they were left on the top of some moist dirt for a few days?

What Will Children Do? PROCESSES

1. Obtain a geranium or coleus plant, 2 glasses, a flat piece of glass, 4 bean seeds, tape, a paper towel, a cup of dirt, and a ruler.
2. Carefully outline the procedure you will follow for investigating the above questions. After your teacher has checked your outline, proceed with the investigations.

What Must I Know? The children could make several cuttings of geraniums or coleus or other plants that will root easily in water. Several of these cuttings should be placed right side up and others should be inverted. The inverted ones will not grow roots. To check for the effect of light on plants, the children could take a plotted plant and place it on its side near a window. The plant will turn toward the light source.

Observing

3. On a sheet of paper, carefully record any important changes in plant growth during your day-to-day observations.

Inferring 4. Graph your findings.
Inferring   *Hint*: How could you use your ruler in your observations?
Hypothesizing   What can you conclude from your data?
   What would you expect other plants and seeds to do under similar conditions?
Hypothesizing   What results would you expect if you used different light sources?
Applying   Of what value is this experiment to you?

How Will Children Use or Apply What They Discover?

1. What other living things are affected by light and gravity?
2. What are some other factors that affect the growth of plants?
3. Design an experiment to test some of these factors.
4. If you were to do this activity again, how would you change it to make it better?
5. What do you think would happen if you were to scatter mixed parakeet seed on a wet plastic sponge kept in a pan with a little water?
6. What do you think would happen if you obtained two milk cartons filled with soil and planted a handful of seed in one and only 4 seeds in the other?
Which plants would grow better? Why?

What Is Variation? (K-6)

What Do I Want Children to Discover?

There is tremendous variation in nature.

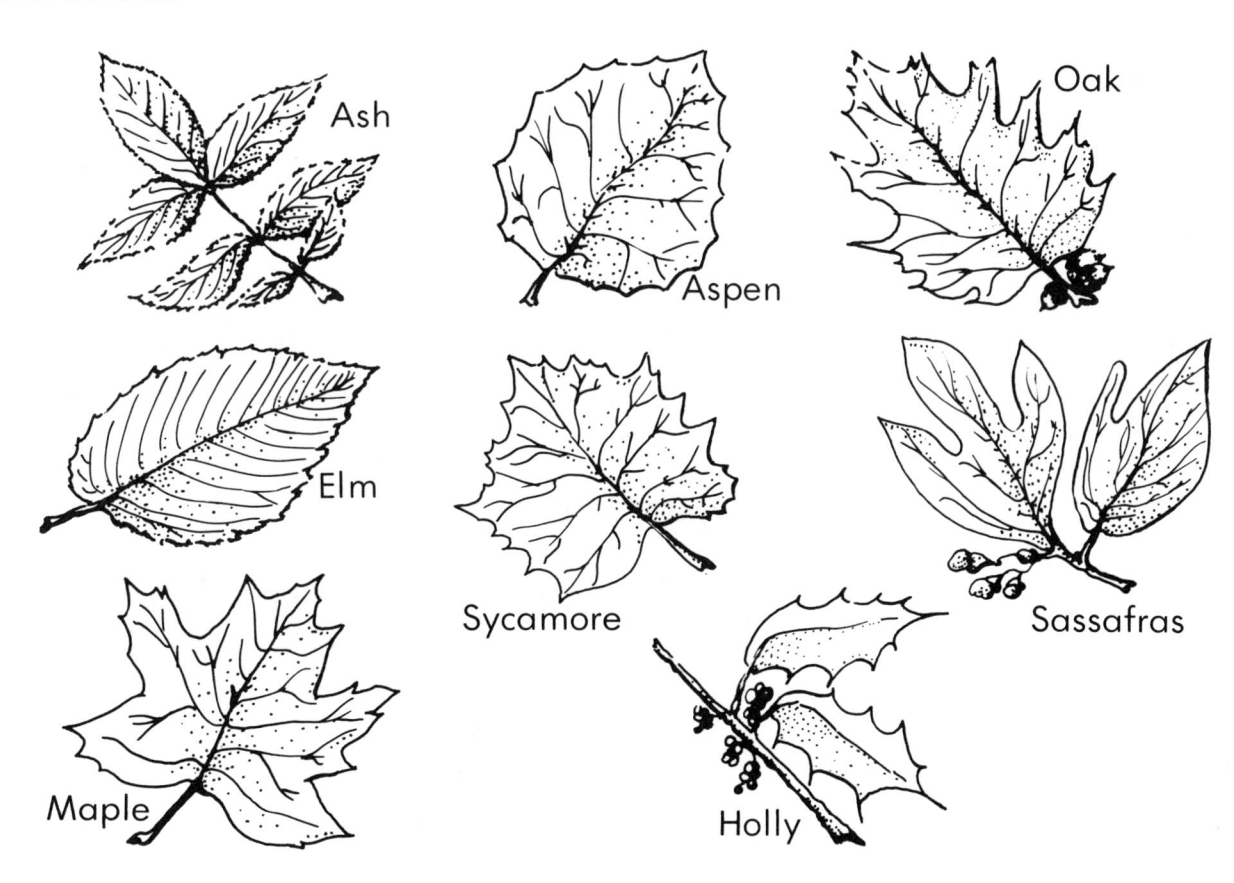

LIVING SCIENCES 55

What Will I Need?   Fallen leaves collected from your yard at home or at school to show variation
Twigs, stones, and shells to show variation also

What Will We Discuss?   How do leaves vary?
How could you find out?

What Will Children Do? PROCESSES

1. Collect different kinds of leaves and obtain a ruler.
2. Place them on your desk and compare them.
   What can you say about the shapes of the leaves?
   Inferring
   Comparing   How do they differ in size?
   Classifying
3. Place the leaves in groups according to color.
   How many groups did you get?
   Inferring   Why do you think leaves vary?

What Must I Know?   Leaves may vary because of inheritance, or because of the environment in which they live. For example, the leaves of a particular species may be large if the environment in which the plant grew richly supplied the needs of the plant.

Summarizing   Summarize how leaves vary.

How Will Children Use or Apply What They Discover?
1. What other things in nature vary?
2. How do humans vary?
3. How do dogs vary?

How Can You Tell the Age of a Tree? (K–6)

What Do I Want Children to Discover?
The age of a tree may be determined by counting the number of growth rings.
A tree grows from the outer edge of the wood to the inner bark.
Trees will have thicker growth rings during wet years.

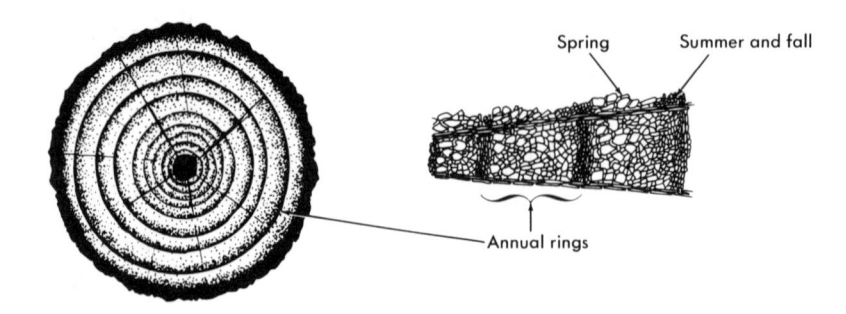

What Will I Need?   Limb cross sections of various sizes
Tree cross sections of various sizes

56 DISCOVERY SCIENCE RESOURCE ACTIVITIES

What Must I Know?	Each child should have access to a cross section. You should have, preferably, several sections from trees grown under different conditions, such as low or high rainfall regions. Sometime before the conclusion of this activity, an arrangement might be made with resource people such as forest rangers to speak on core sampling and other growth ring studies.
What Will We Discuss?	How can you tell the age of a tree? Why are some rings thick and others thin? Where does growth take place in a tree? How can you tell the climate of an area from the growth rings of trees? How can you tell the age of a living tree without cutting it down?

PROCESSES

What Must I Know?	In grades K-3, it is suggested that the children learn only that there are annual rings and that these rings vary from year to year.
What Will Children Do?	1. Obtain some cut pieces (cross sections) of a limb and a trunk of a tree.
What Must I Know?	If possible, have samples of cross sections of trees grown in areas with ample rainfall and in areas deficient in rainfall.
Observing *Comparing*	What do you notice about each section? How are the limb and trunk sections alike or different? 2. Compare your sections with those your teacher has.
Comparing	What do you notice about the rings of the trees grown in different areas?
Inferring *Inferring*	Why are some rings thick and others thin? How old do you think your cross section is?
What Must I Know?	Each year, just beneath the bark, a new ring is added on to the thickness of the tree. If the ring is thick, this indicates that the cells had ample water, grew larger, and produced more cells during the year. The thicker the ring, the more rain there was during the growing season.
Inferring *Inferring*	Why did you count the rings? Why do you think there is a ring for each year? Describe the area of the ring you think developed during the summer. Describe the area of the ring you think developed during spring.
Summarizing	3. Draw a diagram of your cross section and label the areas of spring and summer growth.
What Must I Know?	The inner part of each ring was produced in the spring.
How Will Children Use or Apply What They Discover?	1. What effect do you think fertilizer would have on the size of the rings? 2. What do you think the amount of sunlight would do to the size of the annual rings? 3. How do you think it is possible to make a mistake in counting the number of rings in the cross section of the tree? 4. If a tree were grown under the same conditions all the time, how would the annual rings appear? 5. What do you think disease in a tree would do to the appearance of its cross section?

LIVING SCIENCES 57

What Is a Cell? (4–8)

What Do I Want Children to Discover?
The smallest unit of life capable of existing independently is the cell.
The cell consists of many parts.
Each part functions in a special way.
There are many types of cells.
All living things are made of cells.

What Will I Need?
Onion
Eye dropper
Water
Small paper cup
Glass slide

Iodine, ink, or methylene blue stain
Glass cover slip
Knife
Toothpick
Microscope

What Will We Discuss?
How does a rock differ from a plant?
What do you think living things are made of?
How would you find out?

What Will Children Do?

PROCESSES

Observing
1. Obtain an onion and a knife. Cut the onion in half.
   What do you notice about its structure?
2. Obtain an eye dropper, a cup of water, a glass slide, iodine, and a glass cover slip. Peel off an inside ring of the onion.
   From this ring, pull off the outer layer of tissue. This layer should be as thin as tissue paper. Place this tissue in a drop of water on a glass slide.

Hypothesizing
   What do you think will happen if you place a drop of iodine on the tissue?

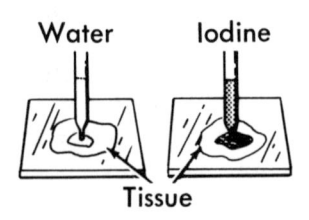

Observing
Inferring
3. Place a drop of iodine on the tissue.
   What effect does iodine have on the onion tissue?
   How will this help you to see the tissue?

Observing
4. Observe the tissue through the microscope.
   Record your observations.
   The small things you see are called cells.

Observing
   How are these cells arranged?

58 DISCOVERY SCIENCE RESOURCE ACTIVITIES

What Must I Know? The children should see what is illustrated in the diagram.

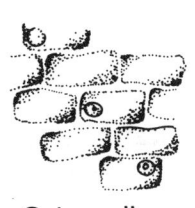

Onion cell (low power)   Onion cell (high power)   Cell membrane

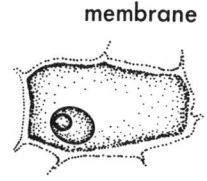

Hypothesizing   What do you think you see if you look through the high power?
5. Try the high power.
Observing   What do you see?
Designing an investigation   How could you find out what the parts of cells are called?
Designing an investigation   How could you find out about the functions of these parts?
Inferring   How do you think human tissue is similar to plant tissue?
Designing an investigation   How would you find out?
6. Obtain a toothpick, a knife, a glass slide, and a cover slip. Gently scrape the inside of your cheek or lip with the toothpick. With a knife, scrape some of the white material on the toothpick into a drop of water on a glass slide. Then add a drop of iodine.
7. Spread the material out in the water and place a glass cover slip over it. Examine the material with your microscope under high power.
Observing   What do you see?
Comparing   How are the cells similar to those you saw in the onion tissue?
Inferring   From what you have observed, what could you say about living matter?

How Will Children Use or Apply What They Discover?
1. What are some similarities and some differences of all living tissue?
2. How long can living tissues exist without water?
   How would you go about finding out?
3. How could you find out what effect prolonged darkness will have on living tissue?

How Do Leaves Breathe? (3–8)

What Do I Want Children to Discover?
Leaves have air in them.
Gas will expand when heated.
Because gases are lighter than water, they will go up through the water and escape.
Leaves have little openings (called stomata) through which air enters or leaves the leaf.

What Will I Need?
Elm, coleus, or geranium leaves
Beaker, dish, or saucepan
Lamp or sunlight
Cold and warm water
Hand lens

LIVING SCIENCES 59

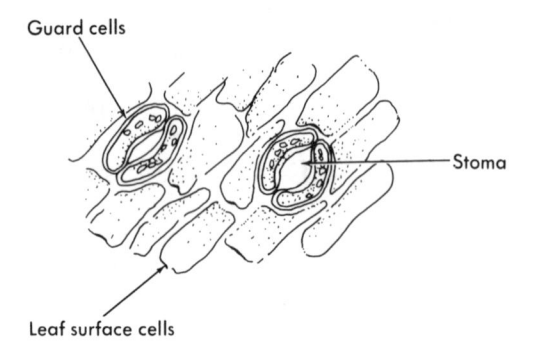

What Will We Discuss?	What happens when your head is under water and you let some air out of your mouth? What do you see? What do you think might happen to a leaf if it were placed under water? How would you find out?
What Will Children Do?	PROCESSES 1. Obtain a leaf, a lamp, and a beaker or pan filled with cold water. 2. Place the leaf in the water with the under side up. 3. Place a lamp so its light shines on the leaf. 4. Observe the surface of the leaf for 5 minutes.
Observing *Comparing*	What appears on the under side? How does the appearance of the top and bottom of the leaf vary? Use hand lens.
Inferring	Why?

What Must I Know?	Leaves generally have more pores on the lower than on the upper surface.
Hypothesizing	What do you think would happen to the leaf if you used warmer water in the above activity?
Inferring	What does this indicate about the surface of the leaf?
Inferring	If these bubbles are escaping from inside the leaf, how are they able to move to the surface?
What Must I Know?	Leaves have small pores called *stomata* through which air enters and gases escape.
How Will Children Use or Apply What They Discover?	1. What could you do to improve this investigation? 2. What could you do in addition to the above activity to prove that the surface of a leaf contains holes?

How Do Bacteria Change Some Foods? (K–8)

What Do I Want Children to Discover?	Milk may be soured by the action of bacteria. Apple juice can be turned to vinegar by the action of bacteria. Bacteria multiply slowly in a cold environment.
What Will I Need?	¼ cup of milk ¼ cup of apple juice 2 pint-sized jars Red and blue litmus paper

What Must I Know?	This activity can be done in groups.
What Will We Discuss?	What happens to apple juice or milk if it is kept at room temperature for several days? What could you do to find out?
What Will Children Do?	PROCESSES 1. Obtain one-fourth cup of milk, one-fourth cup of apple juice, and two pint-sized jars. 2. Pour the milk and apple juice into two separate jars. 3. Place your jars where directed by your teacher. 4. After two days, look at the milk and juice.
Observing	What changes do you notice?

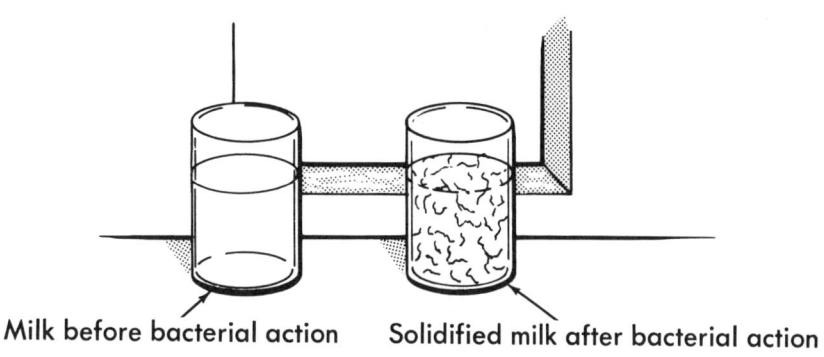

![Milk before bacterial action / Solidified milk after bacterial action]

Observing *Observing* *Hypothesizing*	What do you notice about the smell? How has the milk changed in appearance? What do you think the milk will taste like? 5. Taste the milk.
Inferring *Designing an investigation* *Applying data*	Why do you think the milk soured? How could you find out? How could you test the sour milk to see if it is acid or base?
What Must I Know?	Use red and blue litmus paper. This can be obtained from a scientific supply company, high school science teacher, or the local pharmacy. Red litmus paper turns blue in the presence of a base. Blue litmus paper turns pink in the presence of an acid.
Designing an investigation	How could you find out if the fresh milk was an acid or a base?
Inferring *Hypothesizing*	6. Test fresh milk and your milk sample to see if they are acid or base. What causes the milk to change? How do you think you could have prevented the milk from souring so fast?
What Must I Know?	Explain to the children that there are bacteria in the air that cause the change in the milk.
Inferring *Inferring* *Hypothesizing*	Why do you think you cannot see bacteria? How do you know bacteria are present in the air? What do you think bacteria would do to apple juice?

LIVING SCIENCES

Designing an investigation

How could you find out?

How Will Children Use or Apply What They Discover?

1. If you were a farmer and had to keep milk for two days before the milk truck could come for it, what would you do?
2. What would you do to milk to make it sour faster?
3. How do people use sour milk in their daily lives?
4. What does it mean to get a "yogurt starter culture"?
5. How can we make yogurt in class?

How Does a Fungus Grow? (4–8)

What Do I Want Children to Discover?

Fungi are plants.
Fungi are sometimes parasites.
Fungi reproduce by spores.
Mildew is one type of fungus.
Mold is another type of fungus.
Fungi need warmth, moisture, and usually darkness to grow well.

What Will I Need?

Orange
Bread (at least four pieces)
2 dishes or plates
Small pieces of various kinds of cloth (such as wool, rayon, and cotton)
String
Tripod lens
Microscope or microprojector
Plastic bags
Hand lens

What Will We Discuss?

What would happen to a piece of moist orange peeling if it were put in a dark place and left there for several days? Why?
How could you find out?

What Will Children Do?

PROCESSES

PART I
1. Obtain an orange and a plastic bag.
    What can you do with the orange peeling to make sure it remains moist?
    Where should you store the orange peeling for several days? Why?

Designing an investigation
Hypothesizing

What Must I Know?

If the children do not suggest anything, have them peel the orange, wet the peeling, place the peeling in a plastic bag, and put it in a dark place.

Observing
Inferring

2. After several days, look at the peeling.
    What do you think the green material on the peeling is?

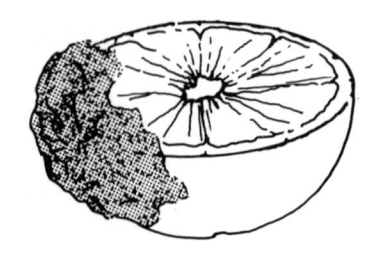

62 DISCOVERY SCIENCE RESOURCE ACTIVITIES

What Must I Know?

This will probably be one of the green penicillin molds which grows well on orange peelings.

PART II

What effect does light have on mold?
What effect does the lack of moisture have on mold?

Hypothesizing
Hypothesizing

Designing an investigation

1. Obtain four pieces of bread, two plastic bags, and two plates or dishes. What can you do with the bread to see if light and lack of moisture have any effect on mold?

What Must I Know?

The children might do any of the following: Wet one piece of bread and place it in a sealed plastic bag in the dark. Wet another piece and place it in a sealed bag where it will receive a lot of light. Wet another and place it on a dish where it will dry out. Place a fourth piece on a plate. (Do not wet it.)

Collecting data
Inferring

Observing
Inferring
Designing an investigation

2. Keep a record of what happens to the bread over a four-day period.
Did all of your bread tests change in the same way?
Why?
What is on some of the bread? Use hand lens.
Do you think it is growing? Why?
How could you find out if the mold is growing?

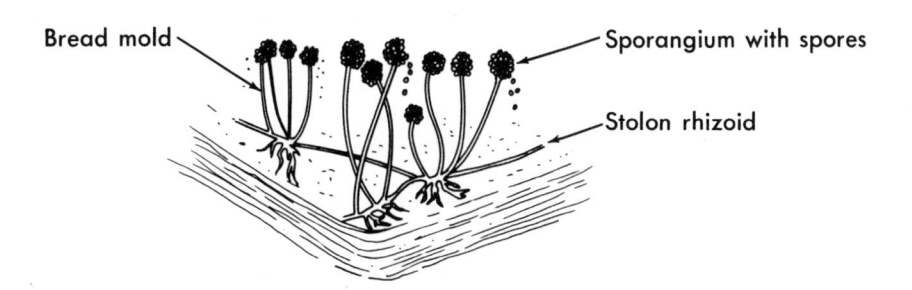

Bread mold — Sporangium with spores
Stolon rhizoid

What Must I Know?

The children should leave the bread in the bag for two more days to see if the mold growth increases in size. If it does become larger, it is logical to conclude that it is growing. The idea of measuring the size of the colonies accurately might also be introduced.

Inferring

Why did the bread placed in the sunlight not become very moldy?

LIVING SCIENCES 63

Summarizing	What conclusions could you make about mold and its need for light?
Inferring	Why did the mold *not* grow well on the dry plate?
Summarizing	What conclusions can you make about mold and its need for water?

PART III

Hypothesizing
What would happen to damp clothing left in a dark place?
Why?

1. Obtain a small piece of cloth, a string, and a plastic bag from your teacher.

Designing an investigation
With these things how could you prove that moisture and lack of light affect cloth?

What Must I Know? Each student should have a small plastic bag and a small piece of cloth such as wool, cotton, or rayon. All but two of the students should dampen the cloth. Place the dampened cloth in a plastic bag, and tie the bag closed. Two students should put a piece of dry cloth in bags and prepare the bags in the same manner. Two or three students should place their bags containing dampened cloth in sunlight. One student should place a bag containing cloth that has not been dampened in sunlight. The rest of the class should place their bags in the dark.

Hypothesizing
What do you think will happen to the cloth in each bag?
Why?

Hypothesizing
Which pieces of cloth will change the most? Why?

2. Observe the cloth in the bags each day for several days.

Observing What do you observe?
Inferring Why do some of the pieces of cloth appear the way they do?
Observing In which bags did the spots appear first? Why?
Inferring Why do some of the pieces of cloth have black spots on them?

Mildew

Inferring
What evidence is there that something is growing on the cloth? Use hand lens.

Designing an investigation
How could you prove whether something is growing on the cloth?

What Must I Know? Allow the bags to remain in the room and have the students compare the size and number of spots.

What is this type of fungus called?

What Must I Know? This type of fungus is called a mildew.

Inferring
Why is it a good idea to hang your clothes up to dry when they are wet rather than waiting several hours before you hang them?

Hypothesizing
In what way does mildew affect cloth besides discoloring it?

Designing an investigation
How could you find out?

64   DISCOVERY SCIENCE RESOURCE ACTIVITIES

What Must I Know?	Take some of the cloth out of the bag and test its strength by tearing it. How easily does it rip compared to cloth that has not been infected with mildew.
Summarizing	What does mildew do to clothing?
What Must I Know?	Mildew is a fungus that weakens cloth by producing substances that change the chemicals in the fiber of the cloth.
How Will Children Use or Apply What They Discover?	1. How does the amount of moisture present affect the growth of a fungus? 2. At which temperature does mildew grow the fastest? 3. Why will bread stay better and longer in a freezer than a refrigerator? 4. What is a dehumidifier? Why are they used in basements?

How Can Food Be Preserved? (3–8)

What Do I Want Children to Discover?	Spoiling of food is caused by bacteria and molds. Food can be preserved by canning, salting, drying, refrigerating, and by chemical means. Bacteria do not live well in an acid solution. Bacteria do not reproduce rapidly in a cold environment. Bacteria will not multiply without moisture. Sterilization and immediate sealing will prevent spoilage.

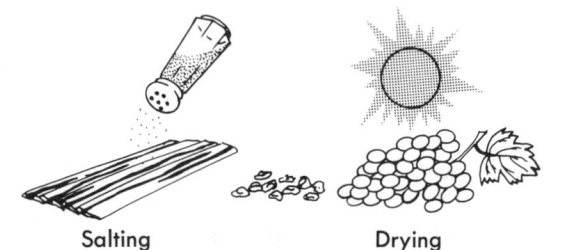

Canning   Salting   Drying   Refrigeration   Chemical
Ways to preserve food

What Will I Need?	Package of frozen peas 6 small jars, ½ pint or smaller (milk carton can be substituted for all but one of these jars) Hot plate Small saucepan Enough vinegar to cover the peas in the bottle Tablespoon of salt Paper towel
What Will We Discuss?	What causes food to spoil? How can you prevent food from spoiling? How could you find out the best way to preserve food?

LIVING SCIENCES

What Will Children Do? PROCESSES

What Must I Know?

This activity should be done in groups.

PART I
1. Obtain 6 small jars, enough frozen peas to fill all the jars one-fourth full.
2. After numbering the 6 jars, 1 through 6, fill them one-fourth full with defrosted frozen peas.

Vinegar and peas | Sealed after 15 minutes boiling | Unsealed in sun | Refrigerated | Water and salt | Control (at room temperature)

What Must I Know?

In the following activity, the children are encouraged to devise tests. After the class has written down their tests, discuss their proposals and have them carry them out. Refer to the diagram above for suggestions.

Hypothesizing — What are some possible ways to keep the peas from spoiling?
Hypothesizing — What are the best ways to preserve the peas using the materials you have?
Designing an investigation — How could you test vinegar, a weak acid, to see if it will prevent the peas from spoiling?
Designing an investigation — How could you test to see what effect sunlight has on the peas?

What Must I Know?

The children would have the best results if they spread the peas out on paper to dry.

Hypothesizing — What effect would boiling the peas for 10 minutes have?
Caution: Do not boil a sealed jar with peas. Why?
Designing an investigation — What could you do with peas to test the effect of a low temperature on them?
Designing an investigation — What could you do with peas to determine what effect salt and water would have on them?
Hypothesizing — What would happen to peas if nothing were added to them?
Designing an investigation — How could you find out?

PART II

Hypothesizing — How long do you think it will take for bacteria and mold to spoil the peas?
Collecting data — How should you record your data so others can see the results easily?
Observing — 1. Observe and record what happened to the peas in the jar with the acid (vinegar).
Hypothesizing — Why was the acid added to the peas?
Inferring — How do bacteria and fungi grow in acid?
Hypothesizing — Why did you boil the jar and lid before sealing it?
Hypothesizing — Why did you seal the jar after boiling it?
Observing — What happened to the peas you placed in the sunlight?
Inferring — Why do they look this way?
Inferring — Why haven't the mold or bacteria grown well?

66 DISCOVERY SCIENCE RESOURCE ACTIVITIES

Observing	What effect did a cold temperature have on the peas?
Inferring	Why haven't the mold or bacteria grown well in the refrigerator?
Observing	What has happened to the peas in the jar with salt water?
Inferring	How can salt water help preserve the peas?
Observing	What has happened to the jar to which you added only the peas?
Inferring	What conditions contributed to the growth of bacteria and mold in this jar?

How Will Children Use or Apply What They Discover?

1. What could you do to preserve peaches?
2. How are foods preserved? Make a list of common foods and methods of preservation, for example:

Food	*Preservation*
Milk	Pasteurizing-refrigeration
Meat	_____
Bread	_____
Grain	_____
Tuna	_____
Eggs	_____
Peanut butter	_____

PLANTS—REPRODUCTION AND DEVELOPMENT

How Can You Get Two Plants from One? (K–6)

What Do I Want Children to Discover?

Some plants can be grown from stems by using a method called *slipping*.

What Will I Need?

Freshly cut stems 2 to 4 inches long from any of the following plants: coleus, geranium, begonia, philodendron, wandering jew (trades-cantia), or ivy
Pint jar or 250 ml. beaker   6 inch ruler
Pint of soil (optional)   Hand lens
Water

What Will We Discuss?

If you had a geranium plant and wanted to produce another one like it, what would you do?

What Will Children Do?

PROCESSES

What Must I Know?

You will probably have to provide the stems for the children.

1. Obtain some stems provided by your teacher.
2. Make a slip by cutting or breaking about 5 inches off the tip. Cut this slip at a point on the stem just below where leaves or other stems are attached. The point where leaves or branches arise from a stem is called a *node*.
Remove some of the leaves (not all) from the lower part of the slip and place the slip in the jar filled with water.

LIVING SCIENCES

Break here and make slips

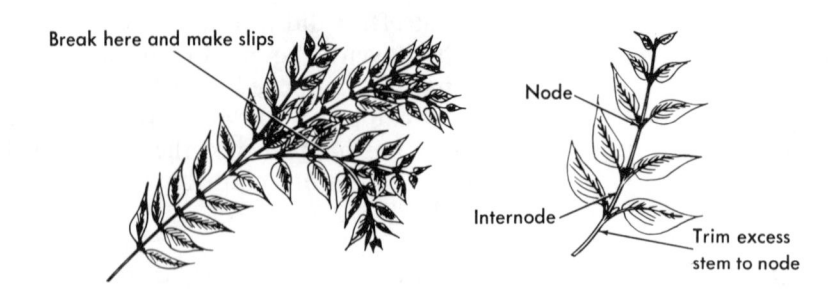

Node
Internode
Trim excess stem to node

What Must I Know?	The slip may be planted in soil provided the soil is kept moist.
	3. Place the jar containing the slip in a place where it can be kept for several weeks and will receive light from the sun.
	4. Add water to the jar as necessary to keep it nearly full at all times.
Hypothesizing	What changes do you think will take place on the slip?
Hypothesizing	Where do you think the water in the jar goes?
Observing	5. Make daily observations of your plant. Record what changes you see each day. Measure how much the plant grows each week.
Observing	What happens to the rate of growth after roots appear?
	6. Compare your observations with those of others in the class to see if you can find answers to the following questions:
Inferring	How does the number of leaves affect the growth of the new plant?
Inferring	How do you think the amount of sunlight affects the growth of the new plant?
Hypothesizing	What do you think would happen if the slip had no leaves?
Designing an investigation	What are other factors that might affect the growth of the new plant? How could you find out?
How Will Children Use or Apply What They Discover?	1. What would happen if you grew slips in soil instead of water?
	2. What do you think would happen if you tried to grow willow or apple trees by slipping?
	3. What types of plants might be difficult to slip? Why?
	4. What function does *root hormone* play in growing roots on slips?

What Function Does a Flower Serve? (4–8)

What Do I Want Children to Discover?	The chief parts of most plants are the stem, leaves, flowers, and roots. All seed-producing plants form either flowers or cones. The flower contains the reproductive parts of the plant. The flower is the seed-making structure of the plant. Animals help pollinate plants. Pollination is the process of pollen falling on the pistil of a flower. Fertilization occurs when part of the pollen enters the ovule or egg of the plant.
What Will I Need?	2 flowers or male cones 7 microscope slides 3 microscopes, magnifying lenses, or microprojectors Sheets of white paper Single-edged razor blades
What Will We Discuss?	How many of you have ever taken a flower apart? What if any purpose does the flower serve for the plant?

68 DISCOVERY SCIENCE RESOURCE ACTIVITIES

What Must I Know?　　Explain to the class that flowers serve as a reproductive part of the plant and that reproduction is a process of making more of something. Every flower has a material called *pollen*. The pollen is found on the part of the flower called a *stamen*.

What Will Children Do?　　PROCESSES

1. Obtain a flower, a sheet of paper, a single-edged razor blade, a glass slide, and a magnifying glass, microscope, or microprojector.
2. Shake the flower over the sheet of paper.

Observing　　3. Observe the material on the paper.
Analyzing　　　What is the material you see?
Inferring　　　Where did it come from?
Inferring　　　What purpose or function does this material have in the flower?
Hypothesizing　　Why is it necessary for a plant to produce flowers?

4. Place some pollen on the microscope slide.

Observing　　5. Observe the slide under the microscope, microprojector, or magnifying glass.

Observing　　6. Describe and draw a diagram of what you see.
7. Separate your flower into its different parts.
8. Place each part into a separate pile.
9. How many piles do you have?

Comparing　　　Refer to the diagram below and try to find similar parts on your flower.

Observing　　　Name as many parts of the flower as you can.

10. Place one of each of these parts on the piece of white paper and write the name of it next to the part.

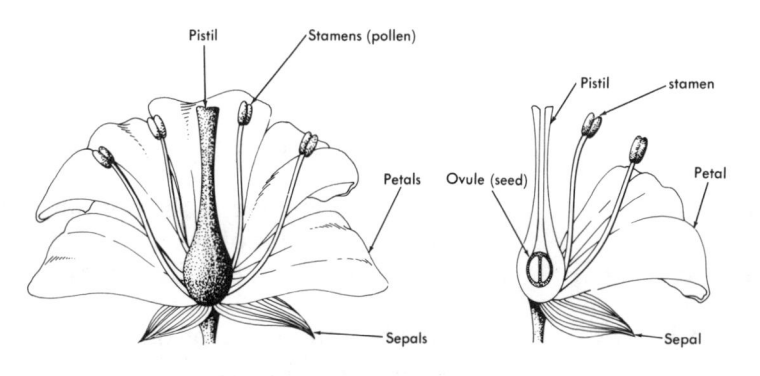

Observing　　11. From what part of the flower did the pollen come?

What Must I Know?　　Be sure to inform the class that each flower may have more than one stamen.

Observing　　　How many stamens does your flower have?
Inferring　　　What is the function of the stamen?

What Must I Know?　　Explain that the stamen is the male part of the flower and that the pollen is found there.

Observing　　12. Find the pistil.
13. Feel the tip of the pistil.
Describing　　　How does it feel?
Inferring　　　What purpose do you think it serves?

LIVING SCIENCES　69

What Must I Know? The pistil is the female part of the flower. The tip of the pistil is sticky. When pollen lands on it, it therefore sticks to it.

Inferring How do you think pollen gets from one flower to another?

What Must I Know? Certain animals such as the bee can help spread pollen from plant to plant so it comes in contact with the pistil. Wind may also help the spreading of pollen. Brightly colored flowers are pollinated by insects and birds. Flowers, such as grains, that are not brightly colored usually are pollinated by the wind.

Hypothesizing What do you think the process of pollen landing on the pistil is called?

What Must I Know? Explain that *pollination* is a process whereby the pollen from the stamen falls on the pistil.

Inferring What parts of a flower are necessary for the process of pollination?
Inferring What do you think happens during the process of pollination? (Refer to the diagram below.)

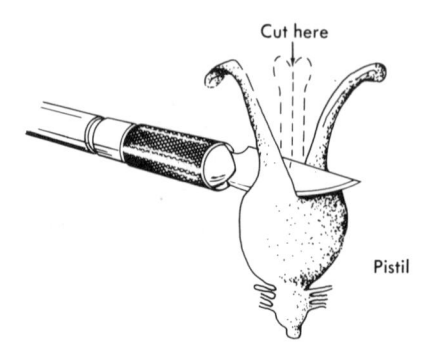

14. Carefully cut the pistil of your flower lengthwise, as shown in the diagram.

Observing What do you see at the bottom of the pistil?
Observing Draw a picture of what you see in the pistil and label it.
Hypothesizing What do you think the ovules will become?

What Must I Know? At the bottom of the pistil, tiny ovules are located. When a pollen grain and an ovule join together, a seed eventually is formed. This is fertilization. Explain that fertilization is the process of the male pollen joining with the female ovule to form a seed. Every seed that results contains a baby plant with a food supply to nourish it until it is able to make its own food when planted in the ground.

Summarizing Why is pollen necessary for the formation of a seed?
Summarizing Why are ovules necessary for the formation of a seed?
Summarizing Where do you think the seed is formed?

What Must I Know? Reemphasize that each part of the flower serves a purpose in the reproductive cycle. When the various parts have fulfilled their purposes, they are no longer necessary and therefore will fall from the flower.

Inferring What do you think is the purpose of the sepal?

What Must I Know?	The sepals help to protect the flower before it opens. Look at the diagram on page 70 and your flowers and also think of the flower before it opens.
Inferring	What do you think is the purpose of the petals?
Inferring	What do you think will happen to the petal and stamen once the seed is formed?
What Must I Know?	Petals and stamens usually drop off after fertilization, and the seeds develop inside the lower part of the pistil.
Inferring	Why do you think this occurs?
How Will Children Use or Apply What They Discover?	1. What would happen if there were no flowers? 2. What animals can help pollinate flowers? 3. What do you think would happen if the process of pollination did not occur? 4. How does a plant reproduce without flowers?

Why Is There Plant and Animal Breeding? (4–8)

What Do I Want Children to Discover?	The offspring produced by plants or animals tend to inherit characteristics from their parents. Some characteristics may be good, and some may be undesirable.
What Will I Need?	Small potato (type does not matter) Large potato Tape measure
What Will Children Do?	PROCESSES
What Must I Know?	This activity may be done in groups of two or more pupils.
	1. Obtain two potatoes and place them side by side on the table
Comparing	How are they alike?
Comparing	How do they differ?
	Mark one potato A and the other B and complete the information below.

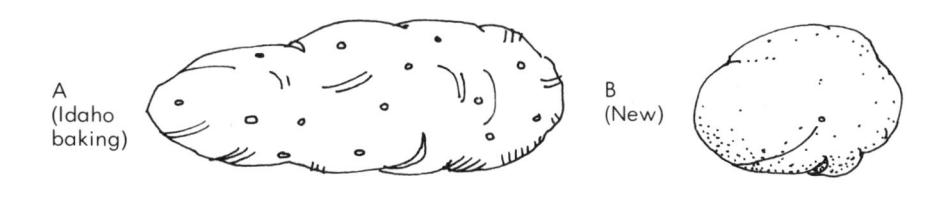

A (Idaho baking)   B (New)

	Size (roughly in inches)	Color	Type of Skin (texture)
Potato A			
Potato B			

LIVING SCIENCES

What Must I Know? When a potato or any part of a potato containing an "eye" is planted in the soil, it will grow and produce a potato plant, which will in turn produce potatoes.

   2. A farmer wants to grow potatoes on his farm. His neighbor who has two potato patches has offered to let him choose some potatoes to start his own patch. Every day the neighbor's wife tends the two potato patches, which she started from two different potato types. The two "starter" potatoes were different in size. Potato patch #1 was started with a small potato and potato patch #2 was started with a much larger potato.
   3. Suppose the larger potato on the table in front of you came from patch #1.

Inferring   What factor(s) do you suppose influenced its size?

Inferring   4. If the neighbor's wife had taken equal care of both patches and the larger potato had come from patch #2, what factor(s) do you suppose would have influenced its size?

Hypothesizing   5. What would you expect to happen if the larger potatoes were used in your potato patch?

Inferring   If larger potatoes were desired, from which potato patch would it be best to select the starter potatoes?

Inferring   If the potatoes planted came out large, and the soil, water, and temperature conditions were the same, from which patch do you suppose the potatoes came?

Inferring   6. What do you think *heredity* is?
   Look the work up in the dictionary.

Comparing   How did your definition differ from the meaning given in the dictionary?

Inferring   7. What characteristics do you think potatoes "A" and "B" inherited?

How Will Children Use or Apply What They Discover?
   1. Look at two other working partners in your class.
      How do they differ and how are they alike in the following ways: (a) height, (b) skin color, (c) hair, (d) eye color?
   2. From whom do you inherit your characteristics?
      From whom did your parents inherit their characteristics?
   3. From the potato example above, what are some factors influencing plant breeding?
   4. How can these factors be applied to animal breeding?
   5. Given two red hibiscus or carnation plants (one large and one small), which flower would you select to obtain seeds if you wanted a large red hibiscus or carnation?
      How would you test to see which flower produces large offspring?

ECOLOGY

What Do Plants Need to Grow? (K–6)

What Do I Want Children to Discover?
Plants need food to grow.
Plants need water to grow.
Plants need light to grow.
Too much water may kill some plants.

72   DISCOVERY SCIENCE RESOURCE ACTIVITIES

What Will I Need?	Seeds (pea, bean, or lima) 8 small milk cartons Topsoil
What Will We Discuss?	From previous activities with plants, state what plants need to grow. If you were going to raise some plants from seeds, what could you do? If you wanted to find out how light affects plants, what could you do? If you wanted to find out how water affects plants, what could you do?
What Must I Know?	PROCESSES In the primary grades, it is suggested that the class be divided into groups. Each group should be assigned to test the effect of only one of the variables listed below, such as water or light.

What Will Children Do?

1. Obtain 8 small milk cartons, topsoil, and bean seeds.
2. Punch 4 small holes in the bottom of 6 of the cartons to allow for drainage. Leave 2 cartons intact.
3. Fill all 8 cartons with topsoil.
4. Plant 3 seeds in each carton one inch deep.

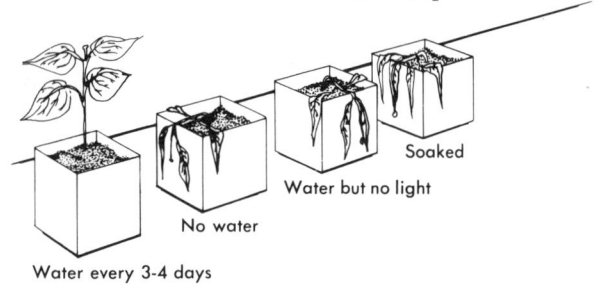

[Illustration of four cartons labeled: Water every 3-4 days, No water, Water but no light, Soaked]

   Cover the seeds with soil and pack the soil down with your hand.
5. Water all cartons so soil is damp but not soaking and continue to water them every 2 or 3 days until plants are a few inches high.
6. After the seeds sprout, keep the 2 cartons left intact filled with water so the soil is always soaked.
7. After the plants sprout, stop watering 2 of your 6 cartons.
8. Water regularly 2 other cartons, but place them in a dark place where they get no light.
9. Keep the other 2 cartons in a well-lighted place, and water regularly. This is your control.
10. Observe and record your observations daily.

Hypothesizing	What do you think will happen to the plants being soaked?
Hypothesizing	What do you think will happen to the plants not being watered?
Hypothesizing	What do you think will happen to the plants that are in the dark?
Hypothesizing	What do you think will happen to the plants kept in a lighted room and watered regularly?
	Why were there 2 cartons of each condition?
	Two weeks later, answer the following:
Comparing	Which plants appear to be the most healthy?
Observing	What happened to the plants that were kept soaked?
Collecting and organizing data	What happened to the plants you did not water?
Observing	What happened to the plants kept in a dark place and not exposed to light?
Observing	What happened to the plants kept in a lighted room and watered regularly?
Inferring	What do plants need to grow well?

LIVING SCIENCES

How Will Children Use or Apply What They Discover?

1. Why are cut flowers placed in water?
2. What would happen if they were not placed in water?

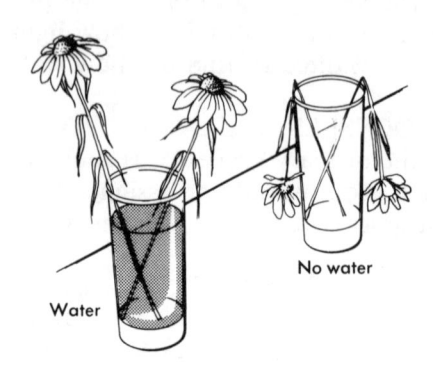

3. Do all plants need soil, air and water? Explain.
4. Of what importance are plants to man?
5. Under what conditions do plants grow best in your house?
6. What other factors influence healthy plant life?

What Types of Life Can You Find in a Pond? (K–6)

What Do I Want Children to Discover?

The color in animals or plants usually helps to conceal, disguise, or advertise their presence.
Every living organism has some body parts that are adapted for the life it leads.
Each species adapts to live where it does.
A pond is a small body of water containing many forms of life.
Some forms of life are very small and can be seen only under a microscope.
If a pond is not disturbed, its life forms will remain in balance.

What Will I Need?

Pond that pupils may observe
2 quart jars with lids
Thermometers
Microscope or microprojector and slides
Dip net (may use nylon stocking and hanger)
Mangifying glass
Pencil and notebook

74 DISCOVERY SCIENCE RESOURCE ACTIVITIES

What Will Children Do?

What Must I Know?

PROCESSES

This activity should be done in groups of 3 or 4 children. When the class collects materials, it would be desirable to have one or two other teachers or parents as chaperones. Since this lesson is designed as a field trip, you may want to collect other specimens for later study. Instruct the children to be on the lookout for cocoons, old bird nests, leaves, and so on. Respect environment. Do not strip trees or bushes.

1. Obtain the following materials: 2 quart jars with lids, magnifying lens, thermometer, dip net, pencil, and notebook.

Observing
2. As you approach the pond, notice the different kinds of plant life in the area.
How were you able to tell you were approaching a pond?

Inferring
Observing
Classifying
Inferring
Summarizing
Observing
Measuring
Observing
3. Look carefully for living things.
Count the different kinds of organisms you see.
Why was it hard to see some of these things?
How many different kinds of insects did you see?
What kinds of things did you find under the water?
4. Determine the temperature of the water at different depths.
How does the temperature change with the depth of the water?

Hypothesizing
Hypothesizing

How is the temperature of the water important to the life in a pond?
What might be living in the water that is so small you cannot see it?

What Must I Know?

There probably are microscopic plants and animals in the water.

5. Fill a jar with pond water and take it back to school.

Inferring
6. Find an insect (or other animal) that you think could live only near a pond.

Observing
Designing an investigation
What is there about this animal that helps it to live where it does?
How could you find out if this animal could live only near a pond?

7. Take this specimen back to school to find out whether it can live in a classroom. Some animals eat both plants and animals, and other animals eat only animals.

Hypothesizing
What do you think would happen if a farmer killed all the plants around a pond?

LIVING SCIENCES

8. Collect any other specimens to study at home or in school.

What Must I Know? If the children have had no experience with a microscope, it might be necessary to demonstrate the proper technique before doing the following part of the lesson. A microprojector works well for projecting a microorganism's image on a screen for all to see.

Applying

9. When back in school, have your teacher help you set up a microscope, and look at the water you obtained from the pond.
What looks like it might be alive in the water under the microscope? What makes you think it is alive?

How Will Children Use or Apply What They Discover?

1. How many different kinds of insects can you name that live near a pond?
2. You may have been lucky enough to have seen some single-celled animals called *protozoa* under the microscope. You may want to read about them.
How many different kinds can you find in the pond you studied?
3. How do different temperatures affect protozoa?
4. How could you kill protozoa?
5. Could the plants that live under water in a pond live above water?
6. How do animals that do not live near ponds adapt to their environments?

How Does the Environment Affect Life? (4–8)

What Do I Want Children to Discover?

Certain environmental factors determine community types.
Some types of communities are on land and some are in water.
Land communities can be subdivided into forests, bogs, swamps, deserts, and others.
A community is a collection of living organisms having mutual relationships among themselves and with their environment.
All living things have certain requirements that must be met by their surroundings.
Habitat is a place where an animal or plant naturally lives or grows.
Different environments are needed to sustain different types of life.

What Will I Need?

3 large, commercial-sized mayonnaise jars; 2 of them with lids in good condition
Cup of coarse-grained gravel
4 cups of beach sand
5 small aquatic plants (approximately 3 to 4 inches in height)
Freshwater fantailed guppy
2 water snails
5 inch square of fine-mesh screening material

Soda bottle cap
2 small cactus plants (approximately 3 to 4 inches in height)
Chameleon, lizard, skink, horned toad, or colored lizard
2 small dried twigs (no longer than three-fourths of the length of the mayonnaise jars)
Small water turtle or frog
Several small ferns, mosses, lichens, liverworts

What Will We Discuss?

What does environment mean to you?
What are some things that live around you?
Name some environments that you know about.

76 DISCOVERY SCIENCE RESOURCE ACTIVITIES

What Will Children Do?   PROCESSES

What Must I Know?   This activity is to be done in groups of 4 or 5 children. Each group might be responsible for only one of the habitats.

PART I   Aquarium
1. Obtain the materials listed above.
2. Clean the mayonnaise jar thoroughly with soap and water and rinse it well.
3. Wash 2 cups of sand to be placed in the jar. Spread this over the bottom of the jar.
4. Fill the jar with water and let it stand for several days before adding plants and fish.
5. Place the aquatic plants as suggested by the pet shop owner.
6. Place the guppy and snails in the jar.
7. Now cover the jar with the screening material.

Aquarium

Inferring	Why do you think it is necessary to clean the jar before using it?
Inferring	Why should the sand and gravel be washed before putting them in the jar?
Inferring	What would dirty water do to the gills of the fish?
Inferring	Why must the gills of the fish be kept clean?
Inferring	How do fish breathe?
Inferring	Why do you think the water was allowed to stand for several days before the fish were placed in the aquarium?
Inferring	What does our health department add to water that might be injurious to fish?
Inferring	Why were the snails added to the water?
What Must I Know?	The snails will eat the small green algae (the slimy plants that collect on the side of the tank).
Hypothesizing	Will the snails always be able to keep the tank clear?
Inferring	What does this imply that you as a group have as a responsibility?
What Must I Know?	The children from time to time will probably have to clean the aquarium.
Inferring	Why were plants added to the aquarium?
Inferring	What would the fish eat in nature?
Inferring	Would your guppy live if it did not feed on anything? Why?
Inferring	What do plants make that the fish can use?
Inferring	What does the fish make that the plant can use?

LIVING SCIENCES   77

What Must I Know? Plants make oxygen and food, and the fish produce carbon dioxide and waste products. The aquarium is not balanced so food must be added from time to time for the fish.

PART II Terrarium (desert)
1. Obtain one of the large, commercial-sized mayonnaise jars.
2. Clean the mayonnaise jar with soap and water and rinse it well. Wash and rinse the lid also.
3. Dry off the jar and screw the lid on.
4. With the jar on the floor, pound holes into the lid by hitting a nail with a hammer through the lid.
5. Place the jar on its side.
6. Spread the remaining two cups of sand onto the bottom of the jar.
7. Place the small bottle cap filled with water, the cactus, and one twig into the jar.
8. Place a lizard, skink, chameleon, or horned toad into the jar.
9. Cover the jar with the punctured lid.
10. Water the terrarium once every two weeks. Place the jar in a sunny area.

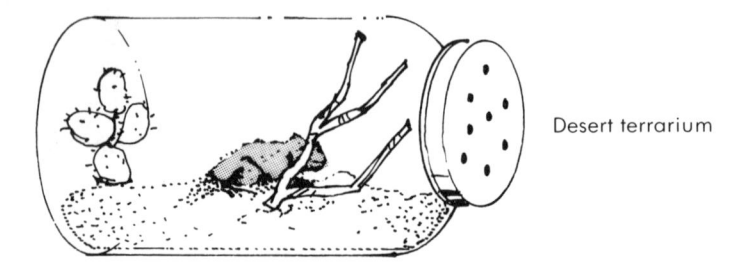

Desert terrarium

11. Feed the animals live mealworms. These can be obtained from a local pet shop.
12. Keep the bottle cap filled with water.

PART III Terrarium (bog)
1. Clean one of the mayonnaise jars with soap and water and rinse it well. Wash and rinse the lid.
2. Dry off the jar and screw the lid on.
3. With the jar on the floor, pound holes into the lid by driving a nail with a hammer through the lid.
4. Place the jar on its side and tape wood strips as shown to keep the jar from rolling.

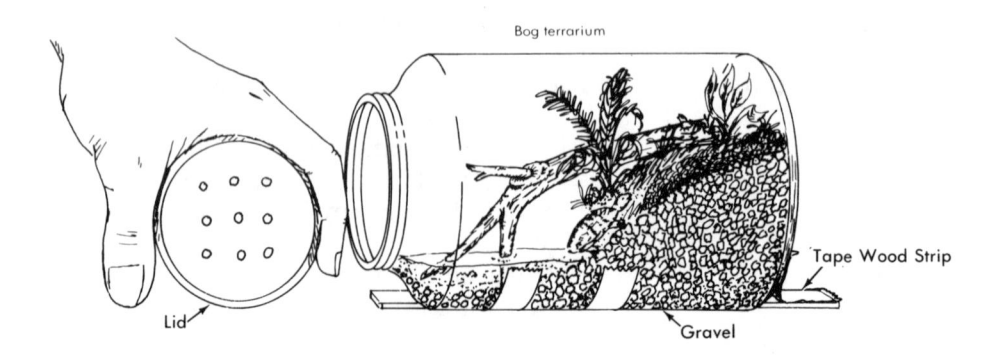

Bog terrarium — Lid, Gravel, Tape Wood Strip

78 DISCOVERY SCIENCE RESOURCE ACTIVITIES

5. Spread the gravel out on the bottom of the jar so it will be concentrated toward the back of the jar as in the diagram.
6. Place the ferns, mosses, lichens and liverworts over the gravel.
7. Pour some water in (do not put in so much that it covers the back portion of the arrangement).
8. Place a dried twig in the jar.
9. Place a small turtle or frog in the jar.
10. Feed the turtle or frog insects or turtle food every other day.
11. Cover the jar with the punctured lid.
12. Place the terrarium in an area where light is weak.

Comparing and observing
Classifying

Observing
Observing
Hypothesizing

How does the life found in the aquarium differ from that found in the desert and/or bog terrariums?
What kinds of conditions do the fish, turtle, frog, or lizard have to have to survive in their particular habitats?
What kinds of conditions do the bog plants require to grow well?
What kinds of food do the fish, the lizards, or the turtle eat?
What do you think would happen to the turtle if you left it in the desert habitat, or to the lizard if you put it in the bog habitat?

How Will Children Use or Apply What They Discover?

1. What experiment would you do to find out what happens to plants when grown under different environmental conditions?
2. What other kinds of surroundings or environments could you make through the use of mayonnaise jars?
3. What does the "environment" have to do with the kinds of organisms found in it?
4. Can you name some organisms that are able to live in many different surroundings?
5. What would happen to a fern plant if it were transplanted to a desert region?
6. What would happen to a penguin if it were taken to live in a desert?
7. What would happen to a primitive human being if he were suddenly brought to a large city?
8. What statements can you make about the effect of environment on a living thing?

How Do Animals Affect Their Environments? (3–8)

What Do I Want Children to Discover?

Living things are dependent upon one another for food.
In general, the smaller the animal, the greater the number present in a community.
Larger animals may consume many small animals to satisfy their need for food.
The stronger, better-adapted animals survive.
When the supply of food does not equal the demand in an environment, a change of some kind must occur in the numbers and/or types of organisms present in it.
Water plants are important to an aquatic community.

LIVING SCIENCES

What Will I Need?   Aquarium   2 or more Daphnia
Water from a swamp or lake   Rocks
Green algae   2-6 small fish
2-6 snails

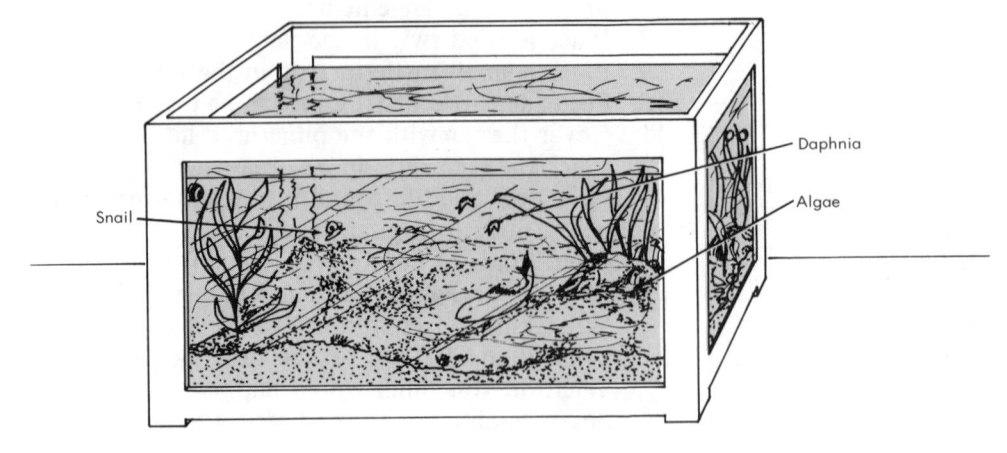

Stagnant-water aquarium

What Will Children Do?   PROCESSES

1. Obtain an aquarium containing some water from a swamp or lake, green algae, snails, Daphnia, rocks, and a small fish. Assemble the material as indicated in the diagram.
   You now have a *microcosm,* a small world environment.
   You are not to add anything to the microcosm.

Hypothesizing   What function do you think the plants serve in it?
Hypothesizing   What changes would you expect to take place tomorrow? in a week? in a month?

Observing   2. Observe and record what the animals eat.
Inferring   What does the plant do for the animals in the aquarium?
Inferring   Where does the plant get its food?
Hypothesizing   What might cause the fish to die?

What Must I Know?   The fish may die if there is not sufficient oxygen dissolved in the water or a sufficient food supply. If one of the fish dies, allow it to remain in the aquarium.

Observing   3. Observe carefully what happens to the fish after it is dead.
Inferring   What effect did the dead fish have on the number of small animals in the aquarium?
Inferring   What evidence do you have from the microcosm that one animal may be dependent on another for food?
Inferring   Why did the number of organisms start to decrease just after you set up the microcosm?
Inferring   Why did they later increase?
Inferring   What effect can the death of an animal have on the microcosm?
Inferring   Why is it usually true that the bigger the animal, the fewer of them there are in a particular area?

How Will Children Use or Apply What They Discover?
1. What would you do to make a microcosm using a land environment instead of a water environment?
2. Why is it important for the numbers of wildlife to be kept in balance?

How Is Life Affected by Variations in Temperature? (4–8)

What Do I Want Children to Discover?

A warm temperature is more beneficial to life than a cold temperature.
There are maximum and minimum temperatures that living things can stand.
Most animals tend to be more active when the temperature is warm.
Some animals are cold-blooded, and others are warm-blooded.
Fish and frogs are cold-blooded animals. Their body temperature is about the same as the environment around them.

What Will I Need?

4 quart jars   Paper towels
Thermometer   Candle
Ice cubes   Match
Polliwogs or goldfish   Tripod
Jar of ants   Plastic wrap
Bean seeds

What Will We Discuss?

What do you think would happen if you were to place goldfish in cold water?
What could you do to find out?

What Will Children Do?

PROCESSES

PART I **Goldfish or Polliwogs**
1. Obtain two jars of water, several ice cubes, two goldfish or polliwogs, and a thermometer.
2. Place the ice cubes in one of the jars of water.
   Keep the other at room temperature.

Observing
3. Place one goldfish or polliwog in each jar and observe the activity.

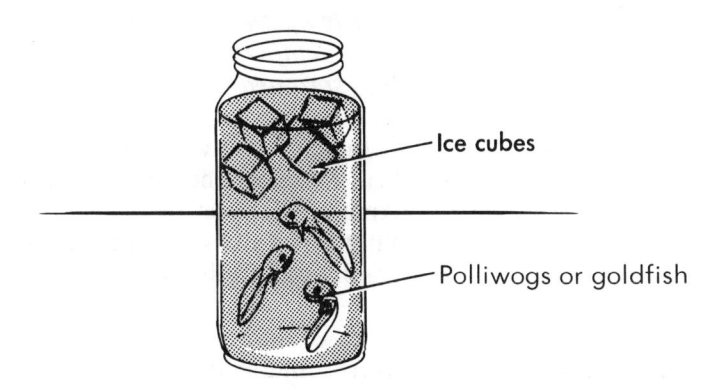

Collecting data
Observing
Comparing
Hypothesizing
Designing an investigation

4. After 15 minutes, note the temperature of each container and record it.
5. Note the activity of the goldfish or polliwog in each jar.
   Explain what you see and compare it with your first observation.
   What types of animals are more active in warm environments?
   What could you do to find out?

PART II **Ants**
1. Obtain ants, a candle, tripod, a match, and 2 jars. Place some ants in each jar. Place one jar in a refrigerator and keep the other at room temperature.

Observing
2. After one-half hour, observe the activity of the ants in each jar.

LIVING SCIENCES

Hypothesizing   What do you think would happen if a jar with some ants in it were heated *gently* with a candle?
3. Place a jar of ants on a tripod over a lighted candle.

Inferring   What effect does a change in temperature have on ants?

What Must I Know?   Do not leave ants over candle more than a few minutes.

PART III **Plant Seeds**

Hypothesizing   1. What do you think would be the effect of different temperatures on plants?
What could you do to find out?

Designing an investigation

2. Obtain two jars. Place water-soaked paper towels in the bottom of the two jars. Add bean seeds to each jar. Cover with plastic wrap.
3. Place one of the jars in a refrigerator and leave the other at room temperature.

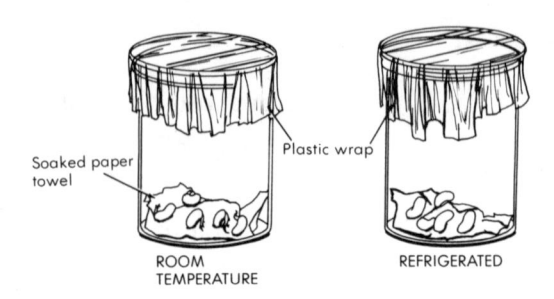

Observe   4. Each day check on what is happening in the experiment and record your observations as indicated below:
Date you wet them:_____
Cold temperature environment:_____
Room temperature:_____
Date sprouted:_____
Rate of growth:_____

Comparing   5. At the end of a week, remove the seeds from the jars and measure them to determine which group grew faster.

Observing   Explain what you see.
Inferring   What effect does a change in temperature have on the sprouting seeds?
6. Graph your findings.

How Will Children Use or Apply What They Discover?
1. What would happen in winter if you placed a plant outside?
2. Lizards and snakes are cold-blooded animals.
How active do you think they would be on a cold day?
3. Why do you think some people grow plants in a greenhouse?
4. How fast do you think plants would grow in a temperature of 200°F?
5. What other experiments can you think of to do with plants or animals that might show the effects of temperature?

How Do Earthworms Change the Soil? (K–6)

What Do I Want Children to Discover?
Earthworms loosen soil so it is more easily aerated.
Earthworms loosen the soil, helping to conserve water.

Earthworms are active in the dark and avoid light.
Earthworms eat the organic materials in the soil.

What Will I Need? 3 jars with lids Loamy soil
Can of sand Lamp
Box of cornmeal Black paper
Earthworms

What Will We Discuss? Why are earthworms important?
Where do earthworms live?
How do earthworms affect the soil?
How do you think earthworms react to light?
What can you do to find out the answers to some of these questions?

What Will Children Do? PROCESSES

1. Obtain three jars with lids and fill each two-thirds full with loose, loamy soil.
2. Add some earthworms to *two* of the jars.
3. To all three jars add about one inch of sand and on top of this about one-half inch of cornmeal. Cover with lids with holes.
4. Place one of the jars with worms near a window.
   Place a lamp near it that can be turned on at night.
5. Place the other two jars in the dark or wrap with black paper.
6. Add a small amount of water at room temperature to the jars every other day.

Observing 7. Observe the jars each day to note if any changes have taken place. Record in your notebook what happens.

Comparing 8. After 4 days, compare the jars and determine what is different about the can you kept in the light compared with the two you kept in the dark.

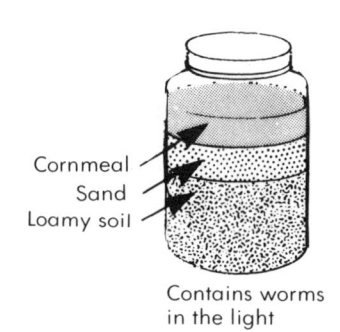

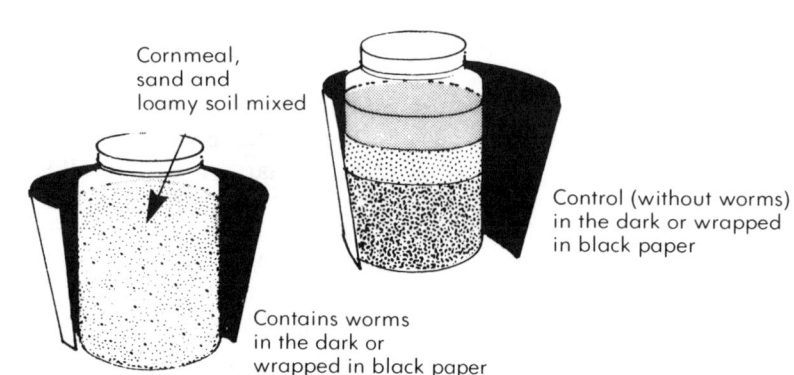

Inferring What was the purpose of the can without worms?
Inferring Why do you think the soil was moistened with water?
Inferring What conclusions can you make about the sensitivity of worms to light and dark?
Inferring Which of the cans seems to hold water better?
Inferring Why do you think they do?
Inferring What do you think happens to the water in the soil containing the worms?
Inferring How do you think worms help conserve water in soil?
Summarizing How do worms condition the soil?

LIVING SCIENCES

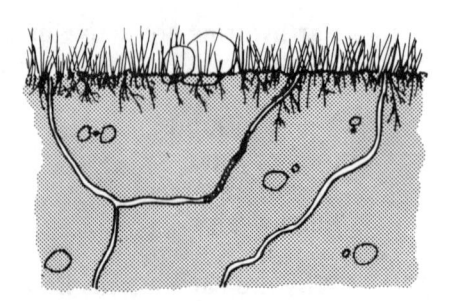

Earthworms help to mix air with the soil.

How Will Children Use or Apply What They Discover?

1. Why do you not see many worms on the lawns during the daytime?
2. Why do you think the cornmeal was placed on top of the soil?
3. How do you think worms help to conserve our soil?
4. Why was there less moisture in the soil without worms?
5. What caused the soil with the cornmeal to change in appearance?
6. What would you do to raise worms to sell to fishermen?
7. What can you do to determine the kind of soil in which worms will grow best?

How May the Unwise Use of Various Substances Endanger Your Health and Safety? (K–6)

What Do I Want Children to Discover?

Sink and toilet cleaners contain strong chemical materials that may injure the skin severely if used carelessly.
Some dry cleaning compounds are flammable (burn) and may give off dangerous fumes.
Most germ killers are extremely dangerous if taken internally.
Many insect sprays are poisonous to humans as well as to insects.
Paint removers often burn or give off dangerous fumes.
Household ammonia is poisonous and should be kept in a safe place, not in the medicine cabinet.
The poison label is a skull (skeleton head) with cross bones.
Bleaches should be used in the home with extreme caution.
All poisons should be kept "out of reach" of children. They can be used by adults, but with caution.

What Will I Need?

Empty containers with poison or warning labels on them:

Bleach bottle
Aspirin bottle
Medicine bottles
Gasoline can
Iodine bottle
Ammonia bottle

Sink and toilet cleaner cans
Paint remover can
Can of insect spray
Jar of insects
Piece of cloth

What Will We Discuss?

What is the symbol placed on bottles to indicate they contain poisons?

84 DISCOVERY SCIENCE RESOURCE ACTIVITIES

Poison

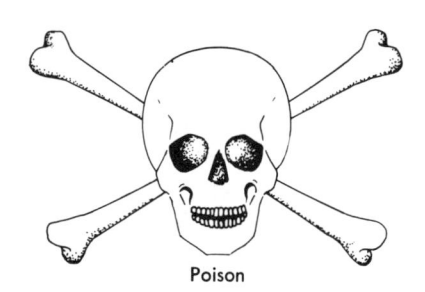

What Must I Know?   Display an enlarged picture of skull and crossbones or draw it on the board. A colored skull and crossbones would be very effective. Also place many of the containers suggested under "What Will I Need" on your desk.

Where should the word *poison* be placed on the board?
Why do you think these bottles were placed on the desk?

What Must I Know?   Point to the poison label on the bottles. Explain the reasons for each label. Some poison labels will also have antidotes listed on them. Discuss the purpose of the antidote with the class. Discuss the terms *flammable, antiseptic, bleach, ammonia,* and *medicine.*

What Will Children Do?   PROCESSES

PART I
Caution: Do this activity *outdoors* and discuss why it is important not to breathe the insect spray.

Hypothesizing
Observing
Inferring

1. Obtain a jar of insects and a can of insect spray.
   What do you think will happen to the insects when they are sprayed?
2. Spray the insects and observe.
   What do you think the spray would do to you?
   Where should these sprays be kept?

LIVING SCIENCES   85

PART II

Hypothesizing

1. Pour some bleach on a piece of cloth. Allow it to stand for several hours.
   What do you think will happen to the material on which the bleach is poured?

Observing
Inferring

2. After two days, have the children note results.
   What does this tell you about bleaches and other chemicals used around the house?

PART III

1. Place iodine on a leaf or skin of a fruit and allow it to stand for several hours.

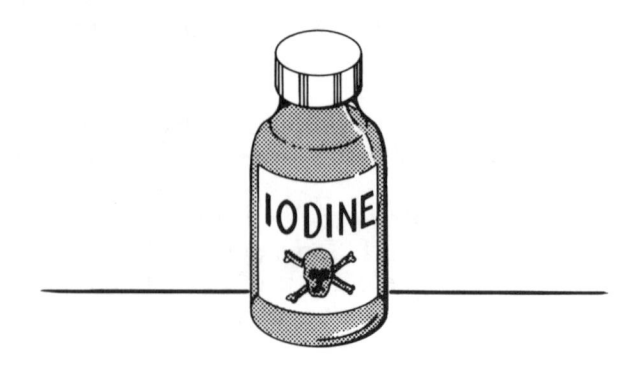

Hypothesizing

What do you think the iodine will do to the leaf?

2. Examine it after several hours.

Observing

What happened?

What Must I Know?

Point out that iodine is a medicine, but it may be harmful to the skin if used for too long on the same spot. Iodine also is very poisonous.

Inferring

What rule or rules would you make to follow in regard to medicines and the places they should be kept in the hours?

What Must I Know?

Explain that chemicals and medicines kept in the medicine cabinets may be dangerous if not used properly, and children should not use any medicines unless their parents are there to help them.

PART IV

Observing

1. Display the following cans: paint thinner, gasoline, kerosene, and cigarette lighter fluid.

What Must I Know?

It may be a good idea to have the children describe the smells these materials give off.

Comparing

What do all of these have in common?

2. Write the word *flammable* on the board and ask the children to explain what it means.
   What rule can you make in regard to the use and storage of flammable chemicals?

86 DISCOVERY SCIENCE RESOURCE ACTIVITIES

What Must I Know?   Point out they should never be used near fires. Gasoline should particularly never be used to start a fire. It is extremely dangerous to pour gasoline from a container onto a fire because the fire will travel right up the gasoline being poured to the container itself and may cause an explosion and burning.

Inferring   Why should you not play with chemicals you know nothing about?
Inferring   From what you observed with the insect spray, why should your parents wash their hands after using an insect spray?
Inferring   Why should you not get things from the medicine cabinet in the dark?
Inferring   Why is gasoline very dangerous?
Hypothesizing   How can you protect babies and small children from the dangers of medicines and chemicals?
Hypothesizing   What can you do to protect your family from the dangers of these various substances and make your home a safer place?

How Will Children Use or Apply What They Discover?
1. What do you think bleach would do to leather or skin?
2. Why is it dangerous to sniff glue, aerosol sprays, and so on?

SECTION 2

Discovery Activities for
ENVIRONMENTAL SCIENCES

METEOROLOGY—WEATHER

What Is a Barometer? (K–6)

What Do I Want Children to Discover?	Air Exerts Pressure. Air Pressure Changes. Air pressure may indicate the type of weather. Low air pressure usually indicates rainy or cloudy weather. High air pressure usually indicates fair weather.
What Will I Need?	Coffee can with plastic snap top Large balloon Straw Glue Straight pin Card
What Will We Discuss?	Have each child blow up a balloon and ask: What is in the balloon? How do you know there is pressure exerted in the balloon? How can you discover whether or not air has the same pressure at all times and at all places? What is a barometer? What is it used for? How might location affect the readings of the barometer?
What Must I Know?	The room temperature will affect the barometer the children will make in this activity. It does not, therefore, only measure air pressure differences. It might be desirable to have some students keep their barometers outside class and compare their readings with those in class.
What Will Children Do?	PROCESSES 1. Obtain a coffee can with a plastic snap top, straw, glue, straight pin, and a card. 2. Cover the coffee can with the plastic snap top making certain the can is sealed completely. 3. Place a small amount of glue in the center of the drum and attach a straw as shown in the diagram. Place another drop of glue on the end of the straw and attach the pin. 4. Mark a card with some lines that are the same distance apart. Tack it on the wall as shown in the diagram.

Coffee can with plastic snap top — Straw — Pin

Hypothesizing	What will happen to the plastic snap top if the air pressure on it increases?
Hypothesizing	What will happen to the plastic snap top if the air pressure decreases?
What Must I Know?	When air pressure increases, it pushes down on the plastic snap top, causing the straw to give a high reading. When the air pressure is low, the opposite will happen. A falling barometer may indicate that a storm is approaching.
Comparing *Comparing* *Inferring*	5. Record the readings of the barometer three times a day for a week. How do the readings of the barometer differ during the day? How do the readings differ from day to day? What causes the readings to vary?
Inferring *Inferring*	6. Record the type of weather existing at the time the barometer readings were made. What kind of air pressure generally exists during fair weather? What kind of air pressure exists during stormy weather?
Inferring *Applying*	7. Compare the readings of barometers in different locations. What reasons can you give for the readings? By using the readings of the barometer, predict what the weather will be.
How Will Children Use or Apply What They Discover?	1. Does air travel from an area of high pressure to an area of low pressure or from an area of low pressure to an area of high pressure? Why? 2. What would you do to improve the barometer? 3. What other materials could you use to make a barometer?

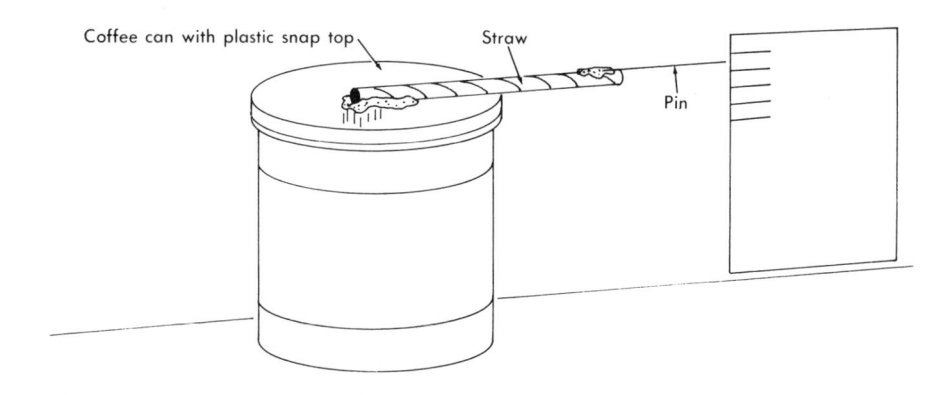

How Can Solar Energy Be Used? (4–8)

What Do I Want Children to Discover?	Water in a salt solution absorbs the sun's energy and evaporates, leaving the salt behind. Water vapor when cooled is condensed and changed into water.
What Will I Need?	Salt 2 dishes Water Plastic bag Ring stand (See diagram.) Ring clamps Spoon

ENVIRONMENTAL SCIENCES

What Will We Discuss?   What ways can you make the sun do work for you?

What Must I Know?   This activity should be done in groups of five.

What Will Children Do?   PROCESSES

PART I
1. Obtain 2 small dishes and some salt.
2. Pour a spoonful of salt into one dish, add water, and stir with a spoon until all the salt is dissolved.
3. Cover both dishes with a plastic bag, setting up the equipment as shown in the diagram.

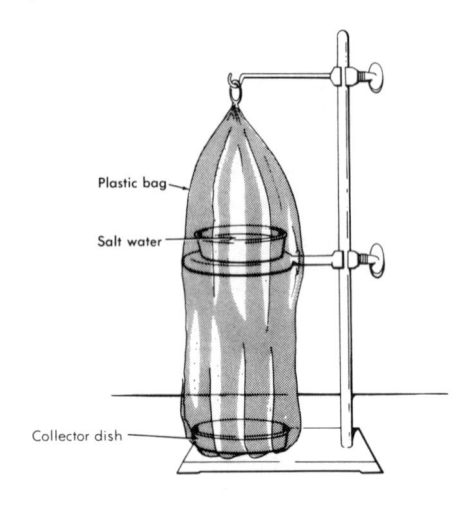

Plastic bag
Salt water
Collector dish

Hypothesizing
Hypothesizing

Observing

4. Place your equipment in the sunlight.
   What do you think will happen to the salt water?
   Why do you think you were told to cover the salt water with a plastic bag?
5. Record your observations every day.

What Must I Know?   When there is only salt remaining in the top dish and the water is in the bottom dish, the following steps should be done by the group:

PART II
   Taste the water in the bottom dish.

Comparing   How does the water taste?
Inferring   Where did the water in the bottom dish come from?
Inferring   What happened to your salt solution?
Inferring   Where did the water go?
Inferring   Why did the water disappear?
Applying   How does the sun's energy (solar energy) benefit man?
Applying   How could this method be helpful to people who live near the ocean but do not have enough drinking water?

How Will Children Use or Apply What They Discover?
1. What are some other uses for this method *of obtaining drinking water?*
2. What are some other ways in which the sun's energy (solar energy) can be used to help people?
3. Explain how this solar water heater works:

90   DISCOVERY SCIENCE RESOURCE ACTIVITIES

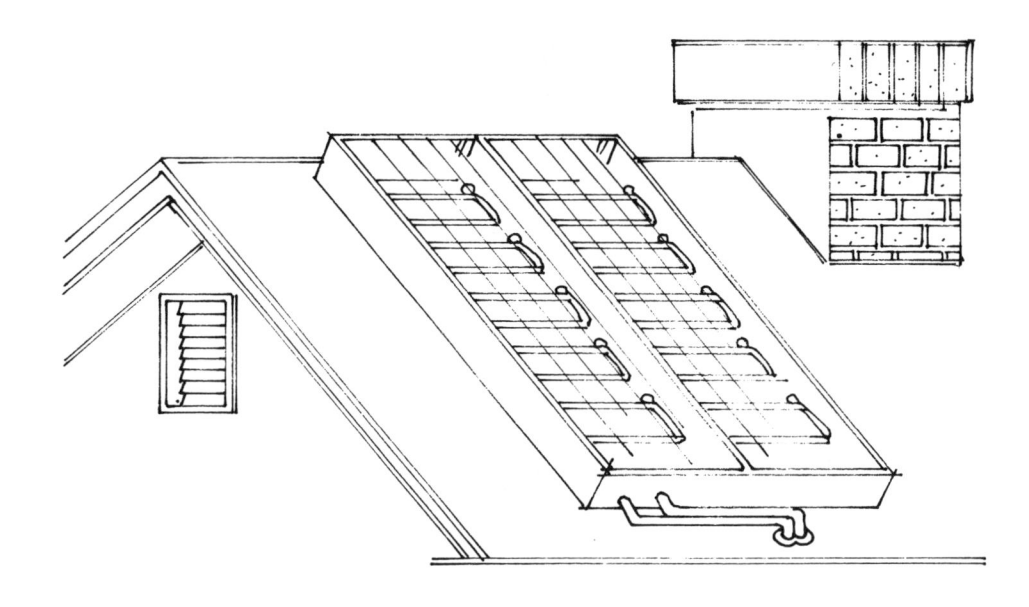

How Can You Make a Cloud? (3–8)

What Do I Want Children to Discover?
Water needs to have dust or other small particles for it to condense easily.
The decreased air pressure causes the temperature of air to drop.
The higher you go in the lower atmosphere, the more the temperature drops.
There is more rain and snow in mountain regions than in the lowland regions.
When the air is cooled, the water condenses.
Many fluids vaporize.

What Will I Need?
Gallon jug
Matches
Ice cubes
2 flasks
Source of heat (alcohol burner/or hot plate)

What Will We Discuss?
What is the name scientists give to the smallest particle of a substance?
What are the three states of matter?
What are the characteristics of each state?
How do you change a liquid to a gas?
How do you change a gas to a liquid?
What state of matter is rain?
What does rain come from?

ENVIRONMENTAL SCIENCES

What is a cloud made of?
What causes a cloud to form?
What types of air pressure do you know about?

What Will Children Do? PROCESSES

What Must I Know? This activity should be preceded by those on air pressure and molecules.

PART I
1. Obtain a gallon jug with about an inch of water in it and a match. Light the match, and drop it in the jug. Try to let it burn for a few seconds.
   As soon as it goes out, blow hard into the jug and then pull it away from your mouth quickly.

Assuming What does the jug contain?
Inferring What happens in the jug?
Inferring Where does the water come from that makes the cloud in the jug?

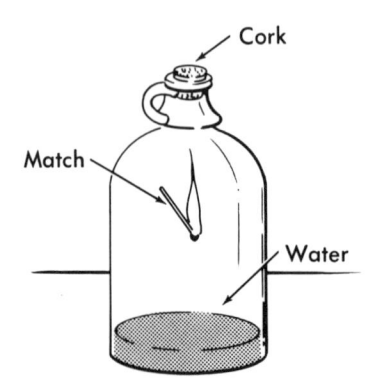

2. Try this activity again, but this time do not use the match.
Observing 3. Record your results.
Inferring Why do you use the match?
Applying What kind of air pressure exists in the jug while you are blowing into it?
Inferring What happens to the air pressure in the jug when you pull the jug away from your mouth?
Inferring Why does the water condense?
Summarizing What must happen for a cloud to form?

What Must I Know? In the jug activity, the match is necessary because it gives off tiny smoke particles that the water uses as a nucleus on which to condense. The sudden release of pressure in the moist air in the jug causes the temperature in the jug to drop, and the water then condenses.

PART II
1. Obtain two flasks. Fill them about one-quarter full with water. Heat one of the flasks. After it is fairly warm, remove it from the burner and place an ice cube on the top of it.

What Must I Know? Caution students about the dangers of boiling water.

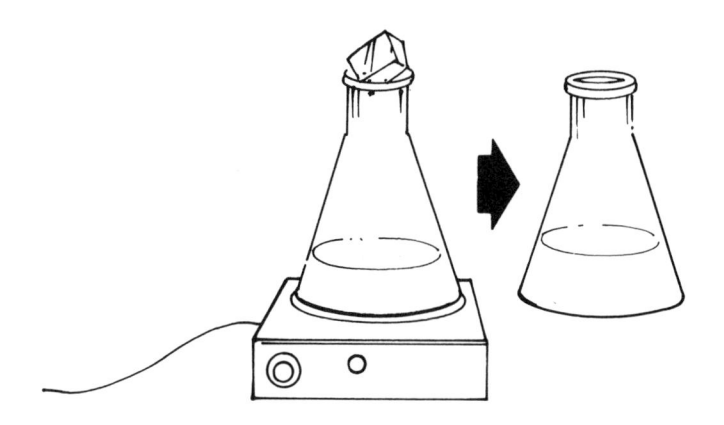

Comparing	2. Record what happens.
Inferring	3. Compare this flask with the other one.
Inferring	Why does a cloud form in one flask and not in the other?
Applying	What does the ice do to the water in the air?
	When air rises it cools. From what you have learned in this experiment, can you explain why there is more rain and snow in the mountains?
Imagining	What has to be done to air to see water in it?
Applying	Why does the air over heated water have more moisture?
Inferring	What happens to the moisture in the air when it cools?
Summarizing	How are clouds made?

What Must I Know?

In this activity, the air in the flask is saturated with moisture. The ice cube cools the air and causes the water to condense. Emphasize to the class that the higher you go in the lower atmosphere, the more the temperature drops. This causes condensation and helps to explain why there is more rain and snow in mountain regions.

Clouds can also be made with alcohol and an air pump. This can be done to show that many fluids vaporize.

How Will Children Use or Apply What They Discover?

1. What substances other than water can you use to make a cloud?
2. How could you make a cloud quickly?
3. What other factors could be involved in the formation of a cloud?
4. Identify these different clouds:

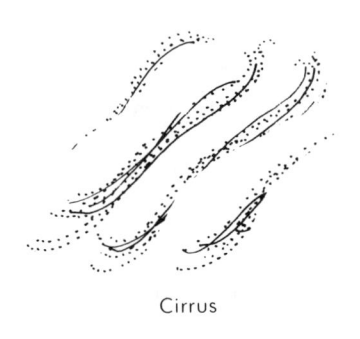

Cirrus

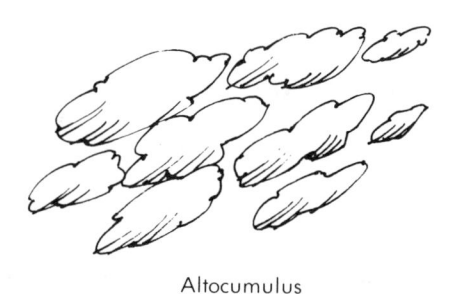

Altocumulus

ENVIRONMENTAL SCIENCES

Stratus   Cumulus

What Is a Hygrometer? (4–8)

What Do I Want Children to Discover?
Air contains moisture.
Pressure and temperature affect the amount of moisture air can hold at any given time.
Relative humidity is the amount of water vapor actually contained in the atmosphere divided by the amount that could be contained in the same atmosphere.
Relative humidity can be measured.

What Will I Need?
2 thermometers
Wide cotton shoelace
Small bottle or dish
Empty milk carton
Thread

What Will We Discuss?
What instrument is used to measure the amount of water or humidity in the atmosphere?
How does it work?

PROCESSES

What Will Children Do?
1. Obtain an empty milk container, two thermometers, a cotton shoelace, and some thread.

94   DISCOVERY SCIENCE RESOURCE ACTIVITIES

2. Cut a four-inch section from the cotton shoelace and slip it over the bulb of one of the thermometers. Tie it with thread above and below the bulb to hold it in place. Put the other end of the shoelace in a small bottle or dish inside the milk carton.
3. Attach both thermometers to the milk carton as in the diagram.

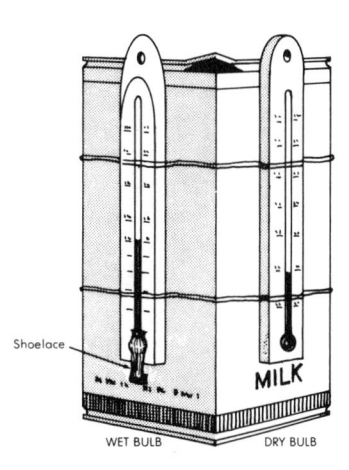

You now have a hygrometer—an instrument for measuring the relative humidity in the atmosphere.

Caution: The two thermometers should register very clearly the same temperatures when placed side by side before the shoelace is placed over one of them, or the difference must be considered a constant that is part of all computations.

4. When the shoelace is wet, fan it with a piece of cardboard for one minute.

Hypothesizing — What do you think will happen to the thermometer with the shoelace? Why do you think so?

Observation
Hypothesizing
5. Check the temperature readings of the two thermometers.
How do you account for the difference between the thermometer with the shoelace (called the "wet-bulb") and the one without the shoelace (called the "dry-bulb")?

What Must I Know?

When the shoelace is wet, the evaporation of the water will result in a cooling of the "wet-bulb" thermometer while the "dry-bulb" thermometer will continue to read the temperature of the air around it.

6. Compute the relative humidity by recording the temperature of the "dry-bulb" thermometer, the difference between the readings of the two thermometers, and applying these to the table on page 96.

Observation
7. Take readings on your hygrometer every day for two weeks and record your findings. Also try readings in different places.

Inferring — What reasons can you give for different readings?

Applying — Using your hygrometer, can you predict which days are better for drying clothes outside?

ENVIRONMENTAL SCIENCES 95

FINDING RELATIVE HUMIDITY IN PERCENT
Difference in Degrees between Wet-Bulb and Dry-Bulb Thermometers

Air Temp (°F)	1	2	3	4	5	6	7	8	9	10	11	12	13	14	15	16	17	18	19	20	21	22	23	24	25	26	27	28	29	30
30°	89	78	68	57	47	37	27	17	8																					
32°	90	79	69	60	50	41	31	22	13	4																				
34°	90	81	72	62	53	44	35	27	18	9	1																			
36°	91	82	73	65	56	48	39	31	23	14	6																			
38°	91	83	75	67	59	51	43	35	27	19	12	4																		
40°	92	84	76	68	61	53	46	38	31	23	16	9	2																	
42°	92	85	77	70	62	55	48	41	34	28	21	14	7																	
44°	93	85	78	71	64	57	51	44	37	31	24	18	12	5																
46°	93	86	79	72	65	59	53	46	40	34	28	22	16	10	4															
48°	93	87	80	73	67	60	54	48	42	36	31	25	19	14	8	3														
50°	93	87	81	74	68	62	56	50	44	39	33	28	22	17	12	7	2													
52°	94	88	81	75	69	63	58	52	46	41	36	30	25	20	15	10	6													
54°	94	88	82	76	70	65	59	54	48	43	38	33	28	23	18	14	9	5												
56°	94	88	82	77	71	66	61	55	50	45	40	35	31	26	21	17	12	8	4											
58°	94	89	83	77	72	67	62	57	52	47	42	38	33	28	24	20	15	11	7	3										
60°	94	89	84	78	73	68	63	58	53	49	44	40	35	31	27	22	18	14	10	6	2									
62°	94	89	84	79	74	69	64	60	55	50	46	41	37	33	29	25	21	17	13	9	6	2								
64°	95	90	85	79	75	70	66	61	56	52	48	43	39	35	31	27	23	20	16	12	9	5	2							
66°	95	90	85	80	76	71	66	62	58	53	49	45	41	37	33	29	26	22	18	15	11	8	5	1						
68°	95	90	85	81	76	72	67	63	59	55	51	47	43	39	35	31	28	24	21	17	14	11	8	4	1					
70°	95	90	86	81	77	72	68	64	60	56	52	48	44	40	37	33	30	26	23	20	17	13	10	7	4	1				
72°	95	91	86	82	78	73	69	65	61	57	53	49	46	42	39	35	32	28	25	22	19	16	13	10	7	4	1			
74°	95	91	86	82	78	74	70	66	62	58	54	51	47	44	40	37	34	30	27	24	21	18	15	12	9	7	4	1		
76°	96	91	87	83	78	74	70	67	63	59	55	52	48	45	42	38	35	32	29	26	23	20	17	14	12	9	6	4	1	
78°	96	91	87	83	79	75	71	67	64	60	57	53	50	46	43	40	37	34	31	28	25	22	19	16	14	11	9	6	4	1
80°	96	91	87	83	79	76	72	68	64	61	57	54	51	47	44	41	38	35	32	29	27	24	21	18	16	13	11	8	6	4
82°	96	91	87	83	79	76	72	69	65	62	58	55	52	49	46	43	40	37	34	31	28	25	22	20	18	15	13	11	8	6
84°	96	92	88	84	80	77	73	70	66	63	59	56	53	50	47	44	41	38	35	32	30	27	25	22	20	17	15	12	10	8
86°	96	92	88	84	80	77	73	70	66	63	60	57	54	51	48	45	42	39	37	34	31	29	26	24	21	19	17	14	12	10
88°	96	92	88	85	81	78	74	71	67	64	61	58	55	52	49	46	43	41	38	35	33	30	28	25	23	21	18	16	14	12
90°	96	92	88	85	81	78	74	71	68	64	61	58	56	53	50	47	44	42	39	37	34	32	29	27	24	22	20	18	16	14

Example:
Temperature of dry-bulb thermometer 76°
Temperature of wet-bulb thermometer 68°
The difference is 8°

Find 76° in the dry-bulb column and 8° in the difference column. Where these two columns meet, you read the relative humidity. In this case, it is 67 percent.

How Will Children Use or Apply What They Discover?

1. Can you find other instruments that will indicate or measure relative humidity?
2. How is relative humidity used by weather people to predict weather?
3. Why were you asked to fan the "wet-bulb" thermometer?

How Much Water Will Snow Make? (K–6)

What Do I Want Children to Discover?

When snow falls lightly on the earth, the crystals leave air spaces between them.
When snow melts, it becomes water.
When a substance changes from a solid state of matter to a liquid state, it absorbs heat.
Heat affects the rate of melting.
Water molecules occupy less volume as a liquid than as a solid.

What Will I Need?

Glass jar
Meter or centimeter stick
Crayon or pencil
Cup full of snow or crushed ice

Candle
Matches
Clock (with second hand)
Ring stand and ring

96 DISCOVERY SCIENCE RESOURCE ACTIVITIES

What Will We Discuss? Show the illustration below to start the discussion:
What can you tell about this picture?
Why is the man in the picture measuring the depth of the snow?
What will the snow change to?
When it melts and changes to water, how much water will this snow make?
Why does a soil conservationist want to know how much water snow will make?
What is he measuring that will help tell him how much water he is going to get from the snow?
What could you do to find out how much water the snow would make?

What Must I Know? This activity should be done in groups of two. If snow is not available, substitute crushed ice, but tell the class that snow varies from ice in the amount of water it contains.

What Will Children Do? PROCESSES

1. Obtain a jar and fill it with snow or crushed ice.
2. Mark the level of the snow with a crayon.

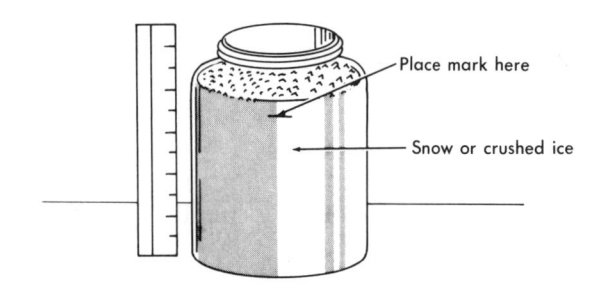

3. Let the snow or crushed ice melt.
4. Time the rate of melting in minutes and seconds, using the clock on the wall or your wristwatch.

Observing As the snow melts, what do you see collecting in the bottom of the jar?

Inferring What causes the snow to melt and change to water?

ENVIRONMENTAL SCIENCES 97

Hypothesizing How might you make the snow melt faster?
5. Fill another jar with snow or crushed ice.
6. Mark the level of snow or crushed ice.
7. Obtain a ring stand and ring.
8. Set the jar on the ring.
9. Obtain a candle and light it. Place it under the jar so the flame is about 5–8 cm. from the bottom of the jar.
10. Time the rate of melting in minutes and seconds as you did with the first jar.
11. When the snow in each jar finishes melting, record the time it took.
12. For each jar mark the level with a crayon.
13. Measure the water level in centimeters and record your findings.

Inferring What can you conclude about snow when it melts?
Observing and inferring Did heating the snow affect the amount of water produced? Why?

How Will Children Use or Apply What They Discover?
1. What happens to water when it freezes?
2. What do you think would happen if other substances such as dry ice were heated?

GEOLOGY

How Are Crystals Formed? (K–6)

What Do I Want Children to Discover?

Crystals are nonliving substances that grow into bodies of various shapes.
Crystals grow by adding on more layers of the same substance, keeping the same shape at all times.
Crystal size is determined by differences in the rate of crystallization.
If crystals are disturbed in the growing process, they will break apart into hundreds of microscopic pieces.
True solids are crystalline in form.
Crystalline form is important in determining some of the properties of substances.

What Will I Need?

Tablespoon
2 jars
2 jar lids
Salt
Water
2 small glasses
Sugar
2 pieces of clear silk thread
Copper sulfate
2 pencils
Plastic wrap
Magnifying glass or hand lens

What Will We Discuss?

What are crystals?
How could you grow a crystal?
What happens when a crystal is growing?
Why is a study of crystals important?

What Must I Know? This activity will involve one or two students.

What Will Children Do? PROCESSES

PART I
1. Obtain a tablespoon of salt, a jar lid, and a small glass. Mix a tablespoon of salt in the glass of water. Stir the water well. Let the solution stand for a few minutes until it becomes clear.

Observing   What happens to the salt?
2. Very gently pour some of the salt solution into the jar lid and let it stand for several days where the lid will not be disturbed.

Hypothesizing   What do you think will happen to the salt solution?
3. After several days have passed, look at the materials in the lid using your magnifying glass.

Communicating 4. Describe what you see.
Comparing 5. How are the materials in the lid different from your original salt solution?

Inferring   Why do you now have a solid when you started out with a liquid?
Hypothesizing   What name could you give to the formations in the lid?

What Must I Know? The salt dissolved in the water and when the salt water stood for several days, the water evaporated leaving salt crystals. Crystals are nonliving substances that are found in various geometrical shapes.

Salt crystals

PART II
1. Obtain a tablespoon of sugar, a jar lid, and a small glass of water. Be sure the tablespoon is clean. Mix a tablespoon of sugar in the glass of water. Stir the water well. Let the solution stand for a few minutes until it becomes clear.

Observing   What happens to the sugar?
Comparing   How is the sugar solution similar in appearance to the salt solution?
2. Obtain a lid and very gently pour some of the sugar solution into the lid and let it stand for several days.

Hypothesizing   What do you think will happen to the sugar solution?
3. After several days have passed, look at the materials in your lid using your magnifying glass.

Communicating 4. Describe what you see.
Comparing   How are the materials in this lid different from the materials in the lid containing the salt crystals? How are they alike?
Inferring   What happens to the sugar solution?

ENVIRONMENTAL SCIENCES

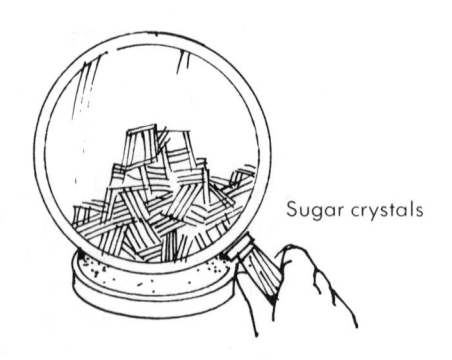

What Must I Know?   When the sugar water stood for several days, the water evaporated leaving sugar crystals.

PART III
1. Wash your hands carefully. Obtain two pieces of clear silk thread, two jars, copper sulfate, two pencils, plastic wrap, and water.
2. Fill the two jars three-fourths full of hot water and add copper sulfate until the water is saturated with it. Make sure you stir the water constantly while adding copper sulfate.
3. Obtain two seed crystals of copper sulfate and tie each one to one end of separate pieces of silk thread. (Seed crystals, which should be 1/8 inch to 1/4 inch in length, can be prepared in the same way that you just prepared sugar crystals.) Tie the free end of each piece of thread to separate pencils. Rest each pencil on a separate jar, allowing the crystals to fall into the copper sulfate solution. Place the jar where it will not be disturbed.

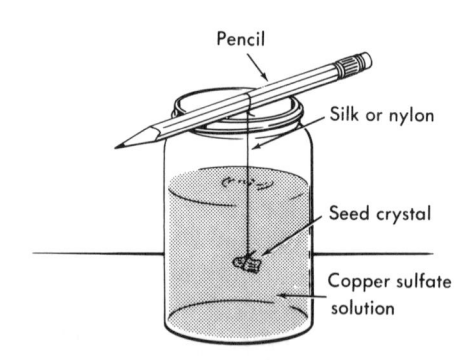

Hypothesizing   Why was it necessary for you to wash your hands?
Hypothesizing   What do you think the copper sulfate solution will do to the crystals?
4. Watch your crystals carefully for several days.

Observing   Record what happens to your crystals.

What Must I Know?   The copper sulfate solution causes the seed crystals to grow. Crystals grow by adding on more layers of the same substance, keeping the same shape at all times.

Hypothesizing	How could you grow larger crystals?
What Must I Know?	The slower crystals grow, the larger they become.
Hypothesizing	How could you slow down the growing process of the crystals?
What Must I Know?	Reducing the rate of evaporation causes the crystals to grow at a slower rate.
Hypothesizing	How could you slow down the rate of evaporation of the copper sulfate solution?

5. Remove one of the pencils. Obtain some plastic wrap, and cover the top of the jar from which you removed the pencil. Be sure to pierce a hole in the plastic wrap large enough for the suspended crystals to pass through when the pencil is returned to the top of the jar.

Comparing 6. Compare both jars closely over several days.
Observing How do the crystals formed in the two jars differ?
Inferring Explain why the crystals are different.

What Must I Know? The crystal in the closed jar will be larger since the plastic wrap slowed down the rate of evaporation, causing the crystal to grow at a slower rate. The open jar will have a smaller crystal since the faster rate of evaporation causes the crystal to grow at a faster rate.

Hypothesizing After the third day, what do you think would happen if you disturbed the crystals during their periods of crystallization?

Observing 7. Gently shake the jar without the plastic wrap and explain what happens.

What Must I Know? If crystals are disturbed in the growing process, they will break apart into hundreds of microscopic pieces.

Inferring Where are crystals found in nature?
Summarizing How are crystals grown?
Classifying Explain how crystalline form is important in determining the properties of substances.

Hypothesizing Why do some rocks have large crystals and some have small crystals?

What Must I Know? True solids are crystalline in form. Crystals grow by adding on more layers of the same substance, keeping the same crystalline form at all times. Crystalline form is important in determining some of the properties of substances. Differences in the rate of crystallization determine differences in crystal size.

How Will Children Use or Apply What They Discover?
1. What other experiments could you devise that would involve growing crystals?
2. How are crystals used in industry?
3. If there were no crystals on earth, how would people's way of living be affected?
4. How would you grow large crystals?

ENVIRONMENTAL SCIENCES

How Are Rocks Alike? (K–6)

What Do I Want Children to Discover?
Some rocks are heavy and some are light.
Different rocks have different colors.
Some rocks are smooth and some are rough.
Some rocks are hard and some are soft.

What Will I Need?
Knife
Penny
Glass
Newspaper
Hammer
Cloth
Magnifying glass
Sedimentary rocks
Conglomerates
Igneous rocks
Metamorphic rocks

What Will We Discuss?
Where could you find different kinds of rocks?
When you feel rocks, how do they differ?

What Must I Know?
This activity should be done in groups of two or more children.

What Will Children Do?

PROCESSES

1. Obtain the following materials: knife, penny, glass, newspaper, hammer, cloth, magnifying glass, and several types of rocks the teacher has available for you.
2. Place these materials on your newspaper.

Observing
Comparing
Comparing
Comparing

3. Observe the rocks closely.
   In what ways are the rocks alike?
   In what ways are the rocks different?
   When you feel the rocks, how do they differ?
   Compare two rocks of the same size.

Comparing
Inferring
Inferring

   How does their weight compare?
   Why do you think some rocks are rough and jagged?
   What do you think has happened to the rocks that are smooth and rounded?

Classifying

4. Place your rocks in groups.
   In what other ways could you group the rocks?

Designing an investigation

   How do you think you could tell the hardness or softness of a rock?
   (Scratch with knife, penny, fingernail, and so on.)

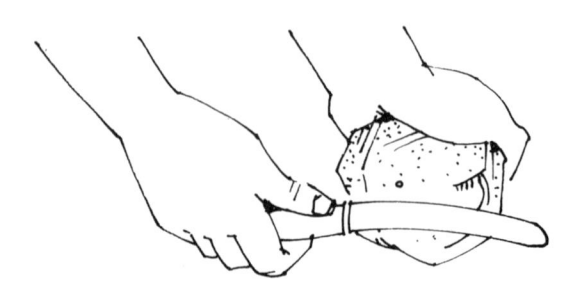

102 DISCOVERY SCIENCE RESOURCE ACTIVITIES

Hypothesizing

Designing an investigation

Designing an investigation

Inferring

Observing

Observing

Hypothesizing

5. Try some of your ideas on the rocks.
   If two rocks were the same size, how could you find out which rock was heavier?
   How could you tell whether a rock looked the same on the inside as it did on the outside? (Place in newspaper and hit with hammer.)
   How would you find out how rocks become smooth and rounded? (Place rocks in plastic jar of water and shake vigorously.)
   Why are some of the rocks made of many smaller rocks or pieces?
   Are the pieces of the rock rounded or jagged?
   Are the pieces dull or shiny in the rock?
   Why do you think they are like that?

How Will Children Use or Apply What They Discover?

1. In what ways are soft rocks used?
2. In what ways are hard rocks used?
3. How is concrete made?

How Do Limestone, Marble, and Granite Differ? (3–8)

What Do I Want Children to Discover?

A sedimentary rock can be changed by compression and compaction.
This change may cause lower rocks in a sedimentary bed to become harder.
Limestone and marble are chemically the same.

What Will I Need?

Pieces of granite   Vinegar
Pieces of limestone   Knife
Pieces of marble

What Will We Discuss?

How are limestone and marble alike?
How are limestone and marble different?
Why do you think these rocks could be different colors?

What Will Children Do?

PROCESSES

1. Obtain 3 or 4 pieces each of limestone, marble, and granite, 20 cc. of vinegar, and a knife.
2. Look at the rocks closely.

Designing an investigation

How can you tell which is limestone and which is marble?

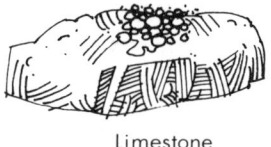

Limestone   Marble

Comparing

Hypothesizing

Hypothesizing

Classifying

Hypothesizing

How does the granite compare with the others?
In what way could you tell that the rocks are related?
Which of these would scratch the other rocks?

3. Scratch the different pieces across each other.
   Which are harder?
   What do you think will happen if you place a few drops of vinegar on your rocks?

ENVIRONMENTAL SCIENCES 103

Observing 4. Place a few drops on the pieces and record what happens.

What Must I Know? Explain to the class that geologists determine the similarity of substances by scratching them and by using chemical tests such as dropping acid on the rocks to see if they react chemically. They also have many other tests. Explain that limestone through heat and pressure in the earth is compacted into a harder substance called marble. Although its physical properties have changed, its chemical composition has remained the same. Marble may vary in color because of the various types of minerals that may be mixed with it.
Caution: Have children wash hands thoroughly after handling vinegar.

How Will Children Use or Apply What They Discover?
1. How do people use limestone, marble, and granite?
2. Which substances are the most common?
3. If you saw a substance you thought was salt, how would you prove it was salt?
4. What other ways do you think geologists identify substances? How could you find out?

How Does Erosion Affect the Soil? (3–6)

What Do I Want Children to Discover?
Soil consists of several layers.
Soil is made from rock.
There are many kinds of soil.
Erosion is the wasting away of soil.
Soil has organic material (material that is living or had been living) that enriches it.

What Will I Need?
Hammer
Rock, about the size of a tennis ball, which can be easily chipped
Quart jar, three-fourths filled with soil; lid
2 cans (preferably the size of soup cans): 1 three-fourths filled with soil; and 1 three-fourths filled with soil, dead grass, leaves, and peat moss
2 milk cartons, quart-size
Soil, approximately 8 cups
2 aluminum pie pans
Grass seed, 1 teaspoon
Scissors
Damp cloth large enough to cover a quart milk carton
Tap water, ½ gallon
2 blocks of wood, each 1½ x 3 inches
Measuring cup

What Will We Discuss?
You have all played with dirt (soil) or at least handled it in some way, such as washing it off your feet or hands.
Where does soil come from?
How could you make soil here in the classroom?

What Must I Know? This activity may be done in groups of two or more pupils.

What Will Children Do?   PROCESSES

PART I
1. Obtain a rock about the size of a tennis ball and two sheets of newspaper.

What Must I Know?   For safety reasons, have the children wrap a rock in newspaper before hitting it so the chips do not fly.

2. Place the covered rock on the table. Hold it in place with one hand and with the other hit it gently 5 or 6 times with the hammer. Unwrap the newspaper.

Observing   What do you observe?
Observing   Does the rock appear the same?

Observing   What do you see that looks like soil?
Inferring   Soil varies from one place to another. Can you suggest from this activity any reasons why?
Comparing   How does the soil on the desert or beach differ from the soil in the mountain?

What Must I Know?   Soil varies because it is made from different types of rocks, and its particle sizes may also vary. Some soils are made of coarse grains and others are composed of fine grains.

PART II
1. Obtain a quart jar three-fourths filled with soil and decayed plant material, one-half gallon of water, and a lid for the jar.

Hypothesizing   If you add water to this jar and cover it and shake it, how do you think the soil will settle?

2. Add water (about three cupfuls) to the jar until it is about two inches from the top. Shake the jar for about a minute. Then place the jar on the table and allow the soil to settle. Do not disturb the bottle.

Observing   What do you notice about the way the soil is settling?
Inferring   Why do certain particles of the soil settle to the bottom first?
Observing   In which layer is the *organic* material (material that is living or had been living) mainly found?
Inferring   What can you say about layers of soil?

PART III
1. Obtain two soup cans filled with different kinds of soil (like humus and sandy), about one-half gallon of water, and a measuring cup.

ENVIRONMENTAL SCIENCES

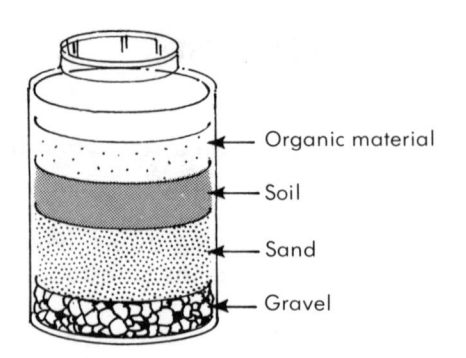

Hypothesizing
Comparing and observing
Comparing and observing
Comparing and observing
Interpreting

2. Pour about one cup of water into each can.
   What do you think will happen to the water in the soil of both cans? Which can seems to be able to hold moisture best?

   What difference do you notice in the soil in the two cans?

   Which has more organic material?

   Why is organic material good for the soil?

PART IV
1. Obtain two quart-size milk cartons, eight cups of soil, one-half gallon of water, measuring cup, a package of grass seed, two aluminum pie pans, two blocks of wood, damp cloth, and a pair of scissors.

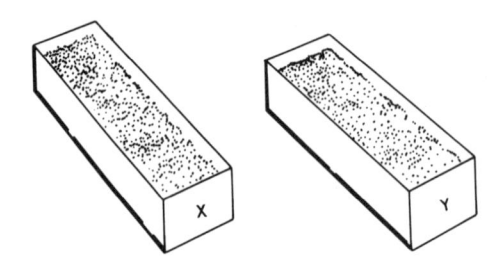

2. Using the scissors, cut out one of the long sides of both milk cartons. (See diagram above.)
3. Fill the milk cartons with soil, leaving about one-half inch from the top, and label the cartons X and Y.
4. In carton X, plant the grass seed just under the surface of the soil.
5. Water carton X and place the damp cloth over it to keep the moisture in. Continue to water the seeds until they have sprouted and are one inch high.
6. When carton X is ready, place one block of wood under one end of each carton. Carefully make 5 holes in each of the bottoms of the lower ends of carton X and Y, and place these ends into the aluminum pie pans. (See diagram.)

106 DISCOVERY SCIENCE RESOURCE ACTIVITIES

Grass — X   Y — No grass

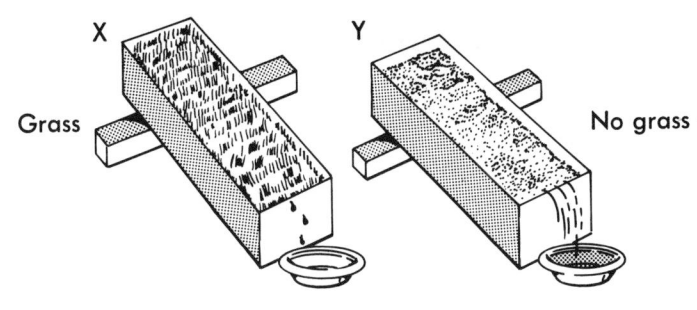

Aluminum pan

Measuring and observing
Collecting and organizing data
Inferring
Hypothesizing

Observing
Interpreting
Interpreting
Applying

7. Place these cartons in an area out of direct sunlight and wind.
8. Measure one cup of water and gently sprinkle this water over carton X. Do the same to carton Y.
   Repeat this each day for three days and write what you see.

   Why are the cartons set up in such a position?
   Which carton do you think will lose the most soil?
   After three days:
   Which carton has lost the most soil?
   Why does one carton lose less soil than the other?
   How can you prevent erosion (washing or wearing away) in soils?
   What, other than grass, can be planted to prevent erosion?
9. Draw a diagram to show what you would do to control erosion.

How Will Children Use or Apply What They Discover?

1. Make a "mountain" of pebbles, soil, and sand.
   What do you think will happen if you pour water down on it?
   Pour water over the mountain and observe what happens.
   What erodes first?
   What conclusions can you draw from this activity?
2. Take a walk around the schoolyard. What signs of erosion are there? What could be done to prevent this erosion?
3. How do you know there are many kinds of soil?
4. What are some of the ways by which erosion can be controlled?
5. Where is organic material mainly found in the soil?
6. In the experiment you did with the milk cartons, why did you not plant seeds in both cartons?
7. Why is erosion control important to farmers?
8. What are terraced rice fields? Why are they necessary and important?

What Is a Fault? (4–8)

What Do I Want Children to Discover?

Some land has been formed by sedimentation, causing layering.
When too much force is applied to the earth's layers, they crack.
The point where the earth's crust cracks and moves is called a *fault*.
A *normal fault* is where the earth's crust drops.
A *thrust fault* is where the earth's crust rises over an adjacent part of the earth.
Earthquakes may be caused by the earth's crust sliding along a fault.

What Will I Need?   Quart jar
Quart of water
Sand
Several types of soil—light, dark, and so on
2 paper cups
Balance
2 cigar box molds filled with layers of colored plaster
Knife to cut the plaster mold
3 food colors

What Will We Discuss?   If great force is applied to a rock or parts of the earth's structure, what will happen to the rock or the structure?
What is an earthquake?
What causes an earthquake?

What Must I Know?   This activity should be done in groups of two or more students. The molds should be made by mixing two or three pints of plaster of paris with different food coloring. The wet plaster of paris should be layered in the cigar boxes and allowed to dry partially before cutting as indicated below. Do not let the plaster of paris become too dry or it will be too hard to cut.

What Will Children Do?   PROCESSES

PART I
1. Obtain a quart jar, some sand, and several types of soil. Half fill the quart jar with water. Add sand to the jar until it is 1 inch thick in the bottom of the jar.

Observing
Hypothesizing

What happens to the sand?
What will happen if you pour soil onto part of the sand?

2. Add several other types of soil to the jar and observe.

Comparing
Inferring

How do the materials in the jar resemble parts of our earth?
Explain how you think parts of our earth have become layered.

3. Obtain a balance, a plastic cup half filled with water and another cup half filled with sand. Place the cup of sand on one side of the balance and the cup of water on the other side.

Hypothesizing

What ways can you balance the sand and water?

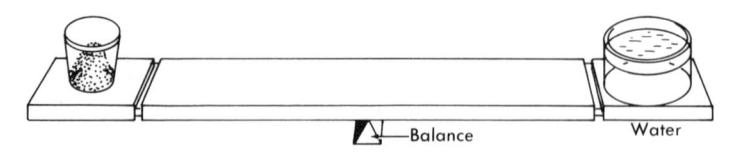

4. Use one of your methods to balance the sand and water.

Hypothesizing

Now that these are balanced, what will happen if you take some sand from one side of the balance and place it on the other side by the cup of water?

5. Do this and observe.

Inferring

How is what you did with the balance similar to some of the things that happen in the earth's crust?

What Must I Know?   The land surface of the continents is always being worn away. The particles formed from this wear often flow into streams and are carried to the sea. When the material gets to the ocean floor, it causes that part of the floor to become heavier and may cause the crust of the earth and the layers to bend. If they bend far enough, faults may appear. This is an

108   DISCOVERY SCIENCE RESOURCE ACTIVITIES

explanation for one type of fault, although it is a rare type.

Inferring

6. Rebalance sand and water and let stand undisturbed for several days. Why does the sand side go down?

PART II
1. Obtain a cigar box mold from your teacher and remove the plaster block. Using the knife, cut the block in two. Raise one of these blocks above the other as indicated in the diagram.

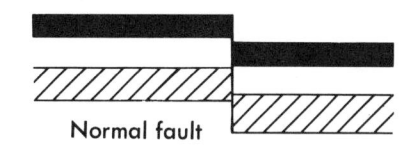

Normal fault

A place where the earth's crust and layers have broken similar to your cut is called a *fault*.

Comparing

How is the appearance of the block similar to the appearance of the earth in some places you have seen?

Summarizing

Explain how you think a rock structure could reach the condition similar to the one you have arranged in your model.

What Must I Know?

The rock structure could have formed a fault owing to stresses within the earth that drew the sections of rock apart. This stress could have caused one section to fall. This kind of fault is called a *normal fault*.

2. Obtain a 2 × 4 inch piece of wood that has been cut in two along a sloping line.

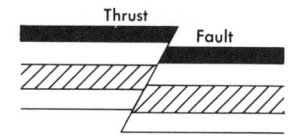

Thrust Fault

Comparing

How is this fault different from the normal fault?
What would you call this type of fault?

What Must I Know?

Explain that this type of fault is called a *thrust fault*. The fault occurs when compression pushes sections of rock closer together, forcing one section of rock to move or slide up.

Inferring
Summarizing

How could this structure have been formed in nature?
How would you define a thrust fault?

What Must I Know?

Other faults, such as the one that caused the San Francisco earthquake of 1906, may be caused mainly by horizontal movement of the earth. The San Andreas fault in California is of this type.

Hypothesizing

What connection is there between an earthquake and a fault?

What Must I Know?

Explain that earthquakes may be caused by the earth's crust sliding along a fault or by the forming of a fault.

How Will Children Use or Apply What They Discover?

1. What effects do faults have on our earth?
2. Could faults be prevented? How?

ENVIRONMENTAL SCIENCES

How Does a Geyser Work? (2–8)

What Do I Want Children to Discover?

Geysers are hot springs that throw up hot water and gases with explosive force from time to time.

Geysers are formed when ground water, heated by hot rocks or gases, gets so hot that it expands and releases dissolved gases in the water, which exert pressure.

The expansion of water forces the water to the surface through partially obstructed cracks in the earth.

Geysers are found in volcanic regions or areas where there used to be volcanoes.

What Will I Need?

Saucepan
Water
Pyrex funnel

3 bottle caps
Hot plate

What Will We Discuss?

What is a geyser?
How does a geyser work?
Where are geysers found?

What Must I Know?

This activity should involve one or two students.

What Will Children Do?

PROCESSES

1. Obtain a saucepan, water, a funnel, 3 bottle caps, and a hot plate. Fill the saucepan half full with water. Place the funnel in the saucepan, resting it on the 3 bottle caps. Set the saucepan on the hot plate and heat the water.

Hypothesizing
Observing

What will happen to the water?

2. As you observe the water, record what you see.

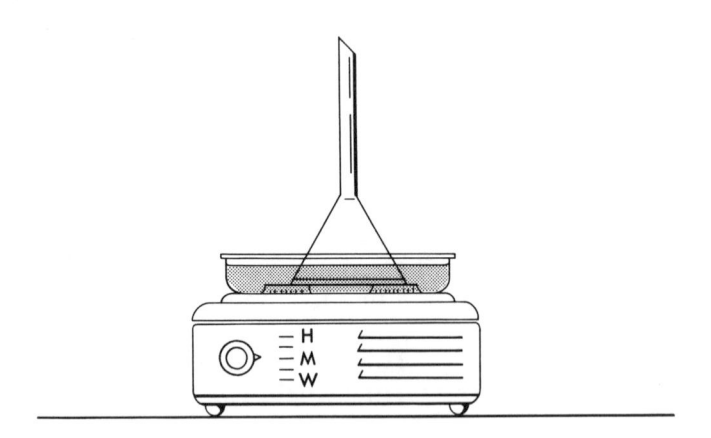

Observing
Inferring
Hypothesizing

What happens to the water when it is heated?
Why do you think this happens?
How does the funnel affect this experiment?

What Must I Know?

Water expands when heated. When the water at the bottom of the pan boils, it is forced by pressure out through the top of the funnel.

3. Remove the saucepan from the hot plate.

Hypothesizing

What will happen to your experiment if the source of heat is removed?

What Must I Know?	When the water is allowed to cool, pressure will be reduced, thus causing the water to remain in the saucepan.
Hypothesizing	How does water inside the earth become heated?
What Must I Know?	Ground water beneath the earth's surface is heated by hot rocks or gases.
Hypothesizing	What happens to the water inside the earth when it becomes heated?
Applying	Why does hot water inside the earth escape?
Hypothesizing	How does the water inside the earth escape?
	What is this type of geological feature called?
What Must I Know?	A geyser is an underground spring that releases hot water with explosive force from time to time. When ground water heats, it expands and releases dissolved gases in the water, which exert pressure. This forces the water to the surface through cracks in the earth, thereby forming a geyser
Summarizing	Explain how your experiment demonstrates what happens in nature when a geyser occurs.
Hypothesizing	How could you cause your geyser to erupt again?
Applying	How do geysers in our earth erupt again and again?
Hypothesizing	In what regions of the world are geysers found?
	Where are the most famous geysers located?
Designing an investigation	How would you find out?
What Must I Know?	Geysers in the earth erupt periodically as the ground water is heated and expands under pressure. Geysers are found only in volcanic regions or in areas where there used to be volcanoes. The most spectacular geysers are found in Yellowstone National Park. "Old Faithful," the best known geyser, erupts at fairly regular intervals of about one hour.
How Will Children Use or Apply What They Discover?	1. What other experiments could you devise that would demonstrate how a geyser works? 2. What would you do to make your geyser shoot higher? Why might it not be a good idea to do this? 3. Why are geysers not found everywhere? 4. In what ways are geysers helpful to people? 5. In what ways are geysers a problem?

What Are Fossils and Fossil Beds? (3–8)

What Do I Want Children to Discover?	A fossil is any remains or evidence of previous life. A fossil may have been buried in mud, covered by sand, volcanic ash, or other material, or frozen in ice or soil. Some types of fossils are actual remains found in ice, amber, asphalt pits, oil shale, coal, and other carbonaceous remains. Other fossils are petrified wood and casts, including tracks, molds, and coprolites (hardened feces). Fossil beds occur in areas containing sedimentary deposits. These are areas where soil has washed or blown over the organism.

ENVIRONMENTAL SCIENCES

What Will I Need? 2 ice trays Model of an animal or a cutout of
Fruit such as cherries and grapes   an animal
Water Several sheets of paper
Soil Actual fossils if available
Small cardboard box Pictures of fossils if available

What Must I Know? This activity should be done in groups of five.

What Will Children Do? PROCESSES

PART I
1. Obtain two ice trays, fruit, water, and soil.
2. Place some fruit in an ice tray and put the tray in the freezing compartment of a refrigerator.
3. Place soil and water in another ice tray and add some fruit to it. Put the tray in the freezing compartment of the refrigerator.
4. Place some of the same kind of fruit in the refrigerator on a shelf and in the classroom on a shelf.

Hypothesizing What do you think will happen to the fruit in the water in the ice tray?
Hypothesizing What do you think will happen to the fruit in the soil and water in the ice tray?
Hypothesizing What do you think will happen to the fruit on the shelf in the refrigerator?
Hypothesizing What do you think will happen to the fruit on the shelf in the classroom?
Hypothesizing How long do you think the fruit will last (be preserved) in each place?
Observing 5. Take your ice trays out each day and record what you see in them.

Communicating 6. Record information about the fruit in the refrigerator and on the shelf.
Observing What has happened to the fruit in each instance?
Observing How long did the fruit last in each instance?
Hypothesizing If an animal were to die in Alaska or in the Arctic and were covered by snow and ice, what do you think would happen to that animal? Some years ago, part of a mammoth (an animal that looks like an elephant) was found buried in the ice in Siberia.
Inferring What does this tell you about the area?
What do we call the remains of an animal or plant from an earlier geological period?

What Must I Know? Explain terms when necessary. Point out to the children that this is one way that fossils are formed.

PART II
1. Obtain soil and a small cardboard box.
2. Add water to the soil, making mud that is fairly thick.

112 DISCOVERY SCIENCE RESOURCE ACTIVITIES

Hypothesizing	Place it in the bottom of the small cardboard box. Smooth it out; press your hand in the mud so you get a good impression. Cover the mud with a layer of sand several inches deep. What do you think will happen to the impression of your hand? 3. After two or three days, carefully remove the sand.
Observing	What has happened to the impression of your hand?
Inferring	What would you call this impression?

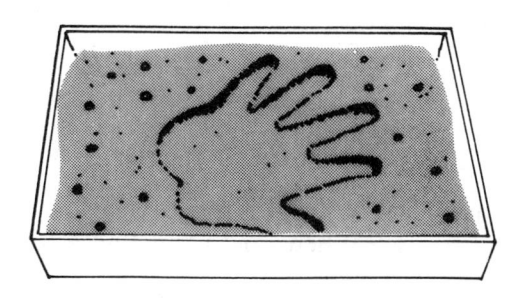

Inferring	What kinds of impressions similar to this help geologists find out about life in previous geological times?
Inferring	In what types of materials do you find imprints such as these?
Inferring	Where could you find imprints such as these?
What Must I Know?	Point out that this is another way in which fossils are formed. If possible, have some fossils and pictures of different kinds of fossils in the classroom. The children can examine and discuss them and discover more information.
	PART III 1. Obtain a model of an animal or a cutout of an animal and cover it with several sheets of paper. What have you made? What would each layer of paper be in nature?
Applying	What do you think would happen to the animal? What do you think a fossil bed is?
Inferring	Why do you think a fossil bed usually must have several layers of soil in it?
How Will Children Use or Apply What They Discover?	1. Where would you expect to find fossils? 2. Why are more fossils not found? 3. Explain why you could or could not expect to find fossils in the area in which you live. 4. What evidence is there that fossils are being formed today? 5. What information can you discover from fossils?

How Can a Fossil Be Made? (K–6)

What Do I Want Children to Discover?	A *fossil* is any remain, impression, or trace of an animal or plant of a former geological age. Fossils can be found in sedimentary rock. Sedimentary rock is formed from mud and silt.

ENVIRONMENTAL SCIENCES

Organisms whose fossils are uncovered lived and died in a period when the layers were laid down in which their remains are found.

Older layers of rocks have fossils that are unlike the animals and plants now living.

What Must I Know If possible, hold up some examples of fossils or show pictures of fossils. Show pictures of extinct animals. Ask the children how we know that these animals existed if they are no longer present on earth.

What Will I Need?

Pictures of fossils and extinct animals	Shells
Fossils	Vaseline
Plaster of paris	Cardboard
Assorted leaves	Water

What Will We Discuss? What is a fossil?
Where could you find a fossil?

What Will Children Do? PROCESSES

Designing an investigation

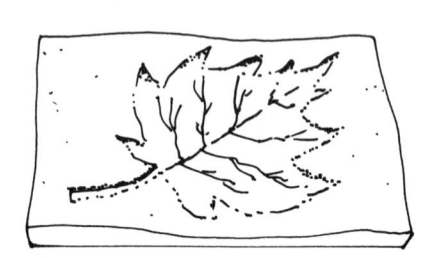

1. Obtain some plaster of paris, vaseline, a leaf or shell, and a piece of cardboard.
2. What could you do with these materials to make an imprint of a leaf or shell?
3. Mix a small amount of water with about 3 tablespoons of plaster of paris until the plaster is smooth and fairly thick.
4. Coat the leaf with vaseline and place the leaf on about ¼ inch of plaster. Press the leaf gently into the plaster. Let the plaster and leaf dry on the window sill.
5. Remove the leaf.

Comparing
What have you made?

What Must I Know? Point out that the plaster would be like small particles of dirt (sediment) dropped by a river and that it takes millions of years to make hard rock out of sediment.

Inferring
6. How do fossils enable man to tell the kinds of life on earth before written history?

Summarizing
Inferring
7. What evidence is there that life has changed in a million years? Why?

How Will Children Use or Apply What They Discover?
1. What other things could you use to make imprints?
2. Where do people get the oil they use in their cars?

114   ENVIRONMENTAL SCIENCES

ASTRONOMY

What Is the Shape of the Earth? (K–3)

What Do I Want Children to Discover?	The earth is round like a globe. The earth is very large.
What Will I Need?	Globe of the earth Several rubber balls of various sizes Pictures taken of the earth's surface from outer space
What Will We Discuss?	What shape do you think the earth is? How do you think you could find out?
What Must I Know?	This activity is to be done as a demonstration.
What Will Children Do?	PROCESSES

1. Obtain a world globe and several rubber balls of different sizes.
   Observing   What do you notice about each of the balls?
   Comparing   If the earth is round, what is there about the earth that is like the balls?

What Must I Know? Each ball has a different curve according to the size of the ball. A large ball would have a very slight curve.

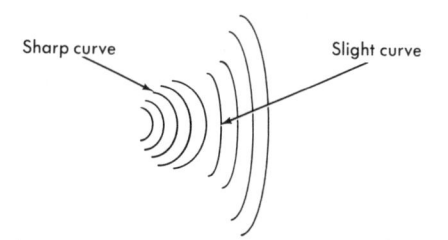

Sharp curve   Slight curve

Observing

2. Look out the window and observe the place where the sky and the earth meet.

Inferring   What do you think the horizon is?
Hypothesizing What could you do to see more of the earth's surface?
Hypothesizing If you were to see a ship sail into the distance, what part of it would you see last? Why?

What Must I Know? They would see the top of the mast last since the earth is curved and the ship would be moving over the earth's curvature.

Classifying   Would you see more or less of the earth's surface if you were flying in a plane?

Hypothesizing Why can a man in a space capsule take a picture of so much more of the earth than a man on a mountain?

ENVIRONMENTAL SCIENCES 115

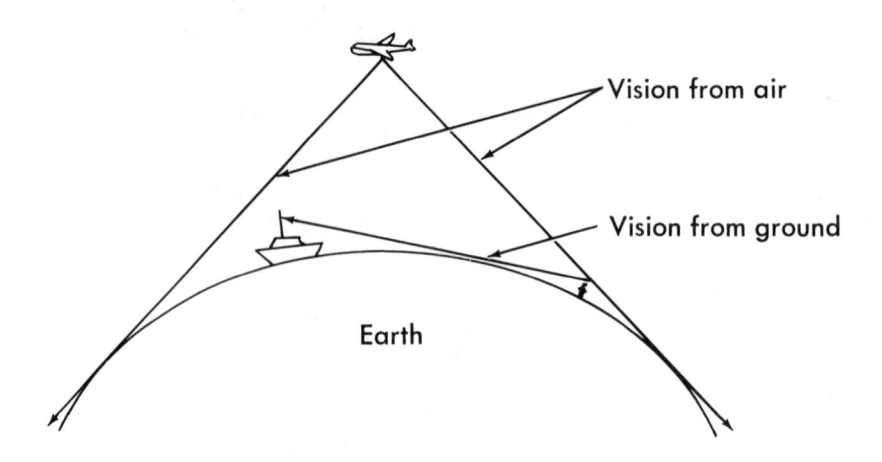

Diagram: Earth's curved surface showing "Vision from air" (from airplane) and "Vision from ground" (from ship), illustrating how curvature limits visibility.

Observing

3. Look at some pictures of the earth's surface taken from rockets.
   What shape is the earth's horizon?
4. Go to the second story of a building.
   Observe the different things you did not see on the ground floor.

Inferring

What do you see that might prove the earth is round?

How Will Children Use or Apply What They Discover?

1. If you were observing an eclipse of the moon, what could you find out about the shape of the earth?

Why Is There Day and Night? (K–3)

What Do I Want Children to Discover?

The earth rotates or turns around.
It rotates from west to east.
It takes 24 hours for the earth to make one complete turn or rotation.
The rotation of the earth explains why part of the 24-hour period is night and part is day.
The sun is always shining.

What Will I Need?

Strong flashlight or filmstrip projector
Knitting needle
Clay or Styrofoam ball

What Will We Discuss?

It is daytime here. Where would it be night?
When it is night here, where would it be day?
What could you do to find out about daytime and nighttime on the earth?

What Will Children Do?

PROCESSES

1. Obtain a strong flashlight or filmstrip projector, a knitting needle, and some clay. Make a clay ball as large as a baseball; Use it as a model of the earth. A Styrofoam ball may be used.

Comparing

In what way do you think the ball is like the earth?

2. Push the knitting needle through the clay or Styrofoam globe. Darken the room. Let the flashlight or filmstrip projector shine on the ball. The flashlight represents the sun.

Inferring

What side of the globe do you think is having night?

116 DISCOVERY SCIENCE RESOURCE ACTIVITIES

Inferring   What side of the globe do you think is having day?
Inferring   What tells you that the sun is always shining somewhere on the earth?

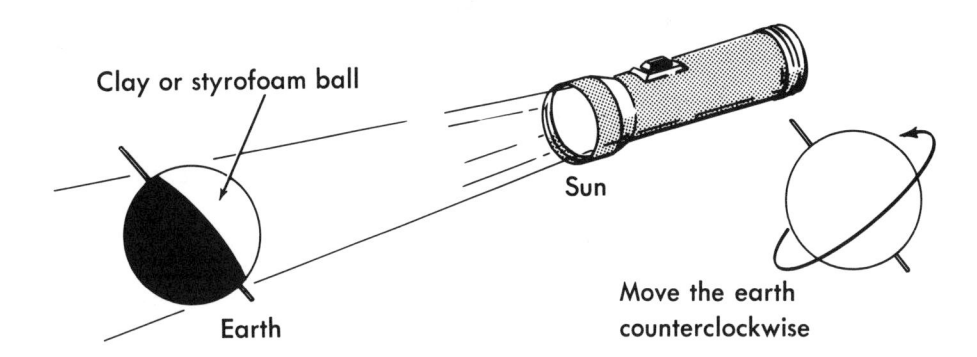

3. Stick a pin in the globe to represent the place where you live. Turn the globe slowly to the sunlight side.

Hypothesizing   Using the globe, how could you make night come to the place where you live?

What Must I Know?   The globe is turned slowly to show where night would begin to fall and where it would be midnight and sunrise. To show this, the globe must be turned counterclockwise.

Inferring   What time of day is it when your pin is on the same side as the sun?
Inferring   When your pin is away from the sun, what time of day would it be?

How Will Children Use or Apply What They Discover?
1. What would happen if the earth did not turn?
2. If the earth did not turn, which side would you rather be on? Why?

How Do the Planets Move? (4–8)

What Do I Want Children to Discover?
Planets move around the sun.
There are nine planets that move around the sun.
Planets vary in size and distance from the sun.
The planets farthest from the sun have the longest years and the longest paths to follow.

What Will I Need?
Lamp
Ruler
Clay or Styrofoam balls

What Will We Discuss?
On what planet do you live?
How does the earth move?
How do you think the movement of the earth corresponds to the orbit of the other planets.
How can you show the planets and how they move?

What Must I Know?
Some things cannot be seen, felt, or measured. Therefore, a scientific model must be formed. The pupils may select Styrofoam balls, purchased at the local dime store, to make the planet models. They can hang these from the inside of a cardboard box.

ENVIRONMENTAL SCIENCES   117

What Will Children Do?   PROCESSES

PART I
1. Obtain some clay or Styrofoam and shape it into balls so they vary in sizes as indicated on the following scales:

Planet	Small Scale Size in Diameter	Large Scale Size in Diameter
Mercury	1/16	1/4
Venus	2/16	5/8
Earth	2/16	5/8
Mars	3/32	3/8
Jupiter	1 5/16	6 3/4
Saturn	1 1/16	5 1/2
Uranus	1/2	2 1/4
Neptune	9/16	2 1/4
Pluto	7/16	1/4
Sun		5 feet

The scales of 1/16 or 1/4 inch are equal to about 4,000 miles. Make a ring of paper to place around Saturn.

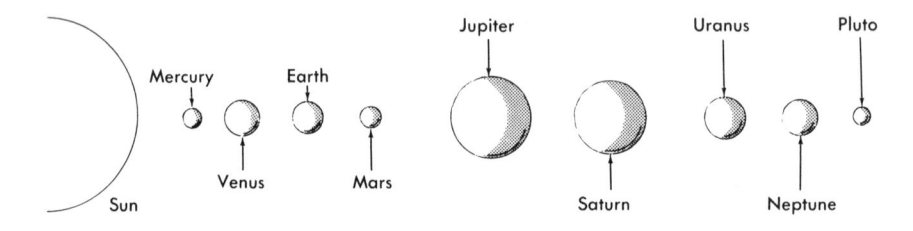

Inferring — Where does the earth get its light?
Inferring — Where do the other planets get their light?
Applying — How can you show that planets reflect their light from the sun?
Hypothesizing — Where should the sun be placed?
Hypothesizing — What planet should be placed next to the sun?

2. Attach the balls to paper clips and hang them from a tackboard. Write the names of planets on small paper and fasten the names below the planets.

Observing — How many planets are there?
Comparing — How do the planets differ in size?
Comparing — Which is the largest planet?
Comparing — Which two planets are the smallest?
Inferring — Why can't you have an accurate comparison of the planets with the sun?
— What is the name given to the sun and the planets?
Applying — Why is it called the solar system?

What Must I Know?   Pupils may use a reference book, or you may need to explain to some pupils that the word *solar* comes from the Latin word meaning sun. Distance *between* planets is difficult to simulate if the same scale of 1/16 or 1/4 inch = 4,000 miles is used. For instance, the earth's average distance from the sun is about 93 million miles. At 1/4 inch = 4,000 miles, you would have to place the earth about *485 feet* from the sun!

118   DISCOVERY SCIENCE RESOURCE ACTIVITIES

Observing   PART II
Observing   1. Work with your planet models and refer to resource materials to determine answers to the following questions:
Observing   Which planet has rings?
                   Which planet is closest to the sun?
                   Which planet is farthest from the sun?
Inferring   Which planet takes the longest to go around the sun?
Inferring   Which planet would have the longest year?
Inferring   Why would that planet have the longest year?
Applying   Which planet do you think would be the warmest?
Designing an investigation   How can you determine if all the planets move in the same direction?

How Will Children Use or Apply What They Discover?

1. What else could you do with your planet models to show how they move around the sun?
2. How could you construct an apparatus that would show all nine planets revolving around the sun?

What Must I Know?

The planets that children made could be fastened onto a wire that is attached between spools on dowel rods as shown in the diagram below. Another way is to attach the wire to corners of the ceiling in your classroom.

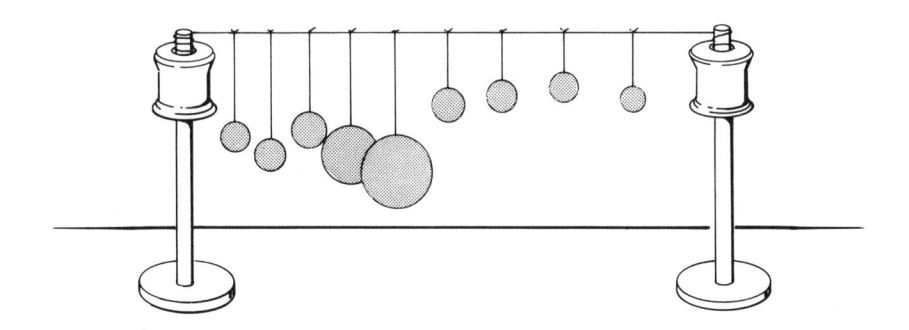

What Size is the Sun Compared to the Earth? (K–3)

What Do I Want Children to Discover?

The sun is many times larger than the earth.
Objects of similar size appear smaller when they are far away and larger when they are near.
Stars are very big in size, bright, and far away.

What Will I Need?

Basketball
Several radish seeds

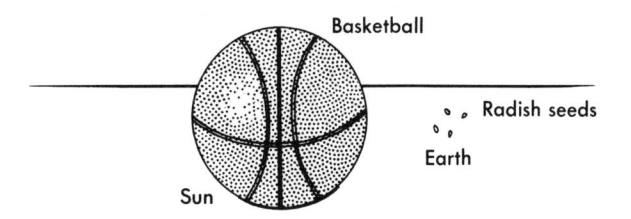

ENVIRONMENTAL SCIENCES   119

What Will Children Do?	PROCESSES
Comparing	1. Look at the basketball and the seeds. Which would you have represent the earth and which the sun? Why?
2. As you look at the stars on a clear night, how do they differ from each other?
What Must I Know	Some are brighter than others; some are different colors.
Observing	3. Darken your classroom. If this is not possible, go with your teacher into a darkened gymnasium, auditorium, or hallway, and have one of your classmates hold a flashlight at the opposite end of the room. He or she should walk slowly toward you.
How does the light change as it gets closer to you?
What Must I Know?	They should notice that the light gets brighter and bigger.
Inferring	Knowing this, why do you think some stars look different?
What Must I Know?	Some stars look closer to us than other stars because they are brighter or they are bigger.
How Will Children Use or Apply What They Discover?	1. If you had two flashlights giving off the same amount of light, what would you do to one to make it look dimmer than the other in a large, dark room?
2. Get two children of very different heights (a kindergartner and a sixth grader). Have the kindergartner stand 2 feet from the class on the playground and the sixth grader, 100 yards away. Compare their heights. Why do they appear as they do?

What Does the Sun Do for Us? (K–3)

What Do I Want Children to Discover?	The sun gives off energy in the form of heat and light.
The light of the sun can be brought to a point by using a lens.
What Will I Need?	Hand magnifying glass (1 for every 2 students)
Sheet of paper
What Will Children Do?	PROCESSES
1. Obtain a magnifying glass and a piece of paper.
2. Hold the magnifying glass over a piece of paper outside in the sunlight. Move the magnifying glass up and down above the piece of paper until the light comes to a point. Hold it there for a few seconds. *Caution:* Do *not* stare at point of light or put hands on focused point.

Observing	What happens to the paper?
What Must I Know?	The paper will begin to smoke and burn.
Hypothesizing	Why does the paper react as it does?
What Must I Know?	The paper burns because the magnifying glass concentrates the sun's heat rays into a small point of intense heat.
Observing	3. Try the same experiment with the light from a light bulb. What happens to the paper?
What Must I Know?	Nothing happens to the paper because the light is not intense enough.
Hypothesizing *Inferring*	Why does the paper react as it does this time? What do these activities tell you about the sun?
What Must I Know?	This shows that the sun gives off a great deal of heat and light.
How Will Children Use or Apply What They Discover?	1. If you wanted to melt some wax and did not have any matches, how would you do it? 2. On a cold day, why do you feel warm in sunlight but very cold when in a shadow?

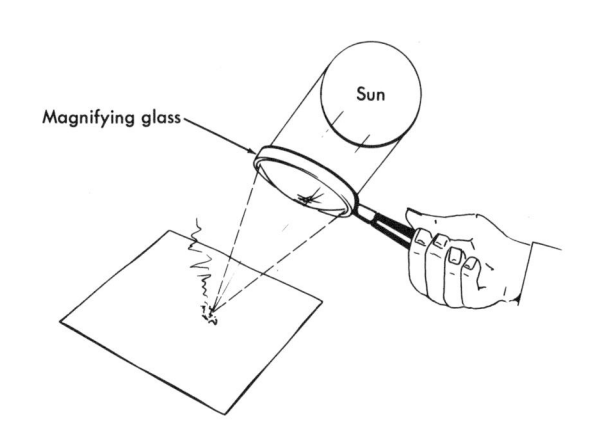

How Long Is a Year? (3–6)

What Do I Want Children to Discover?	The earth moves around the sun (revolves). It takes one year for the earth to make one trip around the sun. An earth year is 365¼ days. The earth rotates as it revolves around the sun. The earth moves around the sun in an elliptical path.

ENVIRONMENTAL SCIENCES

What Will I Need?	Globe Lamp Cardboard for each child Paper for each child 2 pins for each child String—15 inches for each child String—24 feet Masking tape Chalk Overhead projector Mirror Transparency of the planets in orbit Opaque circles to represent the sun and earth Planetarium if available
What Will We Discuss?	If the rotating of the earth explains the length of day, how can a globe and a lamp be used to show the length of a year? What kind of path does the earth make when it revolves around the sun?
What Must I Know?	Have a pupil use a globe and lamp to review how rotation causes day and night. This should be a demonstration activity.
What Will Children Do?	PROCESSES 1. Obtain a piece of paper, cardboard, 2 pins, string, and a pencil. 2. Try to draw a circle by sticking two pins 7 inches apart in the middle of the paper, which is resting on the cardboard. Form a loop from a piece of string 9 inches long. Slip the loop over the pins. Pull the loop tight with a pencil and, using the string as a guide, draw a line around the pins.
Comparing	How does the shape you made differ from a perfect circle? What might you call this shape?
What Must I Know?	If the children do not know, tell them it is called an ellipse.
	3. Use a longer string loop, masking tape, and chalk to make an ellipse on the floor. 4. Place a lamp in the center of the ellipse.
Inferring *Inferring* *Hypothesizing*	What does the lamp represent? What does the ellipse you drew around the sun represent? What could you use to represent the earth?
What Must I Know?	A child should walk on a line around the sun (the light) and should rotate as he or she follows the line.

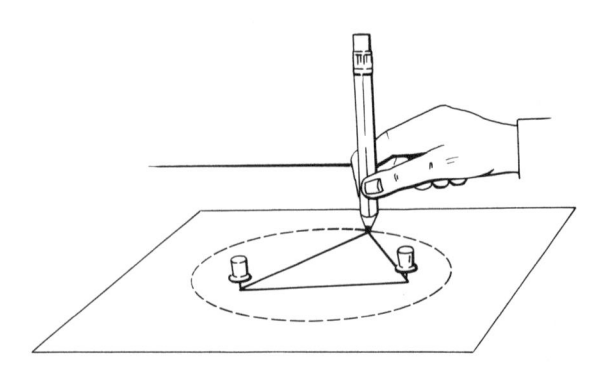

122 DISCOVERY SCIENCE RESOURCE ACTIVITIES

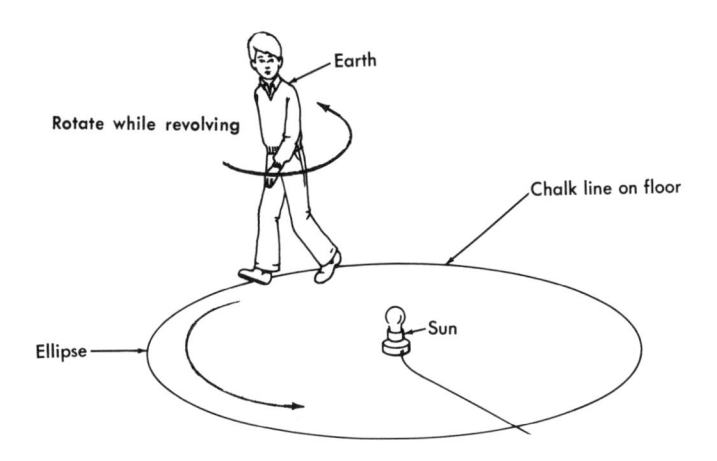

Diagram: A child walking around a sun (on the floor) along a chalk ellipse, labeled "Earth", "Rotate while revolving", "Chalk line on floor", "Ellipse", "Sun".

Applying	In what way should the earth move around the sun?
What Must I Know?	Children should take turns rotating as they revolve around the sun. You might tell them that rotation is like spinning; but in revolving, one object must go around another object.
Hypothesizing	What is the process of the earth moving around the sun called? When something revolves, what is it doing?
What Must I Know?	One trip around the sun is called a *revolution*.
Inferring	How many days make a year? How can you find out?
What Must I Know?	After they have checked the number of days in a year, the children might investigate why some of the statements say there are 365 days and others say 365¼ days.
Summarizing	6. Rotate like the earth. How long does it take the earth to rotate on its axis to make a day? 7. Demonstrate how the earth revolves around the sun. How long does it take for the earth to make one complete orbit around the sun? What is the name of the imaginary line on which the earth travels around the sun? How long is an earth year?
What Must I Know?	"Convert" the overhead projector into a planetarium by placing on the stage of the projector an opaque circle to represent the sun and a smaller opaque circle to represent the earth. Have a child show how the earth revolves around the sun by moving the earth correctly.
How Will Children Use or Apply What They Discover?	1. What else revolves around the sun? 2. How could you determine if other planets have the same length of year as the earth? 3. Which planet has the longest year? Why?

ENVIRONMENTAL SCIENCES

4. Which planet would have the shortest year?
   How could you demonstrate the revolution of the planets?
   What effect would the various lengths of years have on birthdays of people if all planets were inhabited?

What Must I Know? If a planetarium is available, use it as a visual aid. The overhead projector also may be used. Focus a transparency of the planets in orbit onto the ceiling and discuss their solar system.

What Causes the Seasons? (4–8)

What Do I Want Children to Discover?
The sun gives off light and heat.
The move sun rays that hit a section of the earth, the warmer that section will get.
When it is light on one side of the earth, it is dark on the other side of the earth.
The rotating of the earth causes night and day.
The earth makes one revolution around the sun in one year.

What Will I Need?
Flashlight or filmstrip projector   2 plastic or rubber balls
2 thermometers   Globe
Black paper

What Will We Discuss?
How do the four seasons differ?
Why does the continental United States have different seasons?
How could you use simple apparatus such as used in this activity to demonstrate night and day and to show the cause of the seasons?

What Must I Know? This investigation should not be crowded into a single period.

What Will Children Do? PROCESSES

PART I
1. Shine a flashlight as shown in diagram 1.

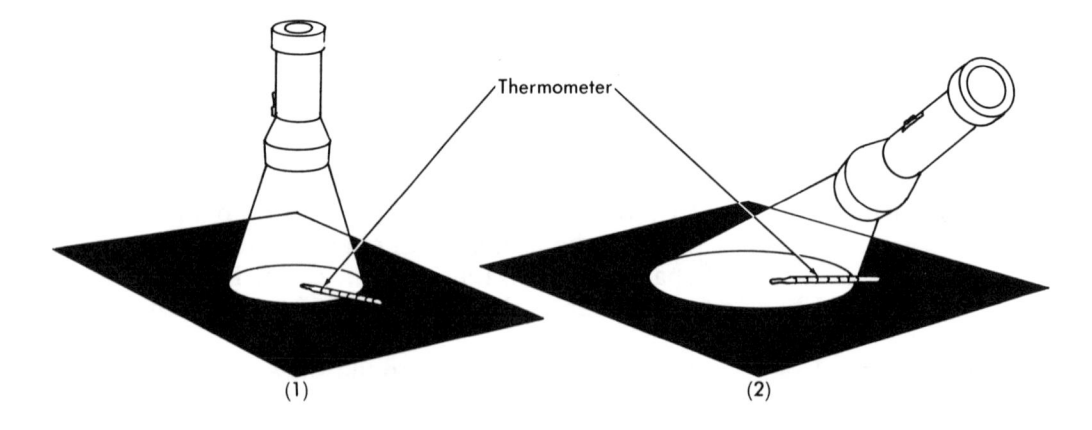

Observing   What do you notice about the way the light shines on the paper?
Observing   What kind of area is covered by the light as it shines on the paper?
Trace this area on the paper.

124   DISCOVERY SCIENCE RESOURCE ACTIVITIES

Hypothesizing If you shine the light as shown in diagram 2, what do you think will happen to the area covered? Trace this area. Compare the areas traced.
Hypothesizing In which way, direct or slanted, do you think the temperature would be greater? Why do you think so?
Designing an investigation How could you determine whether your answer is correct?

2. Take two flashlights or filmstrip projectors and two thermometers and shine them as in diagrams 1 and 2. Place a thermometer on the paper to see if you can detect a difference in the temperature.

Comparing How do the temperatures differ?
Inferring What do you think causes the variation?
Comparing How does the temperature vary with the seasons?

Graph your results as shown below.

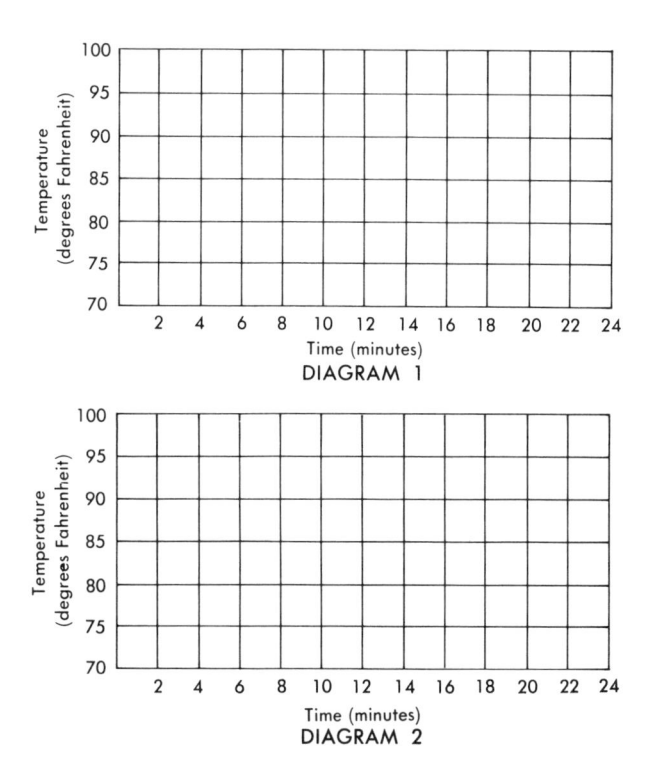

DIAGRAM 1

DIAGRAM 2

PART II

Hypothesizing How could you use a globe to show the cause of the seasons?

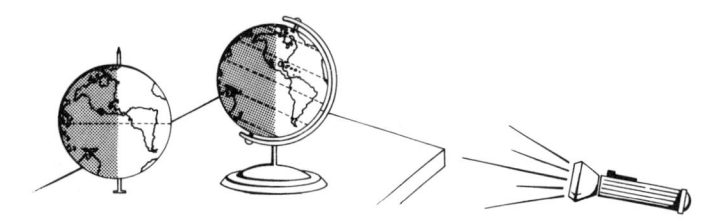

1. Obtain two plastic or rubber balls. Place each ball on a nail as shown in the diagram. A globe of the earth may be substituted for the second ball. Shine a flashlight beam directly on each globe.

Observing What do you notice about the way the light hits the two globes?
Hypothesizing What would you have to do to the globes to show what causes day and night?

ENVIRONMENTAL SCIENCES

Hypothesizing	If the earth were not inclined as in the second globe, how could you determine if there would be any seasons?
	2. Point the flashlight at the second globe, and move the globe around the flashlight.
Observing	What do you notice about the way the light strikes the globe as you move the globe, stopping at several places?
Inferring	What do you think the season would be at each point that you stop?
Hypothesizing	Why does the United States get more sunlight in summer than in winter?
Hypothesizing	Why does the sun not shine on the earth the same way every month of the year?
Observing	Which covers a larger portion of the earth, the slanted rays or the direct rays?
Applying	How can you determine which rays are cooler on the earth's surface—direct or slanting?
Summarizing	How long does it take for the earth to make one trip around the sun?
Observing	When it is winter in New York, what season is it in Argentina?
Inferring	How does the angle of the earth affect the seasons?

What Must I Know? Parts of the earth receive more heat from the sun at one time of the year than at another time because of the tilt of the axis. Place the following diagram on the board after the lesson and have the children point out the various seasons and explain them.

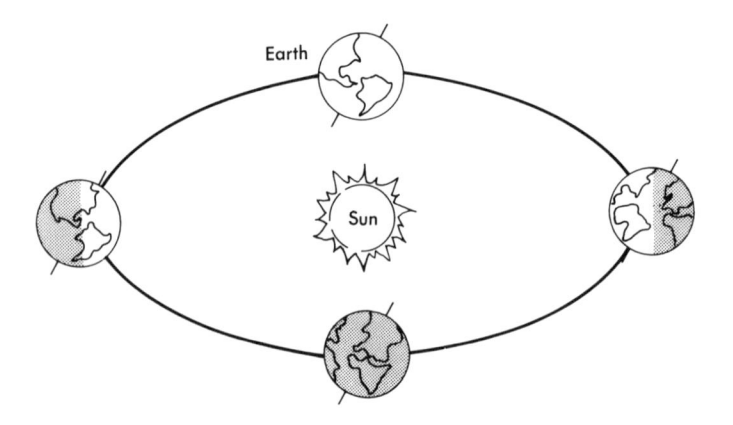

How Will Children Use or Apply What They Discover?
1. What other investigations can you show why the earth has seasons?
2. In what way would a knowledge of seasonal variations help you better understand the peoples of the world?
3. How do you explain portions of the earth being warmer in summer even though they are farther away from the sun than in winter?

Why Do Stars Appear Close or Far Apart? (K–4)

What Do I Want Children to Discover?
There are millions of stars, and they are tremendous distances from each other.
The earth's great distances from the stars make the stars appear closer together.

What Will I Need? 50 bottle caps or 50 marbles

What Will We Discuss?	How do the stars appear to you as you look into the sky? Explain why they look near to each other or far apart. Why do they look small? What can you do to show how things look at a distance?
What Will Children Do?	PROCESSES
Hypothesizing	1. Obtain and place 50 bottle caps in a cluster so no bottle cap is less than 1 inch from its nearest neighbor. Stand in front of the bottle caps, facing them. What do you think will happen as you move away from these objects?
Observing	2. Move away from the caps. How do the bottle caps appear as you move 5 steps away from them?
Observing	3. How do the bottle caps appear as you move 10 steps away from them?
Observing *Summarizing*	4. How do the bottle caps appear as you move 15 steps away from them? How do the bottle caps look as you move away from them?
Observing	5. Draw how the bottle caps look when you see them in front of you and then how they look when you take 15 steps away from them.
Designing an investigation	In what way could you go about finding how the stars look in the sky?
What Must I Know?	The more immature pupils will need more guidance. They may be asked to observe the night sky. The next day you and the pupils could discuss the results of their observation and investigation.
Inferring	How could you use this investigation with bottle caps and observation of the sky to explain why the stars look so close together?
Inferring	Why do you think stars look close together yet are so far apart?
Summarizing	What do you know now about how far away the stars are?
How Will Children Use or Apply What They Discover?	1. If you were to fill a Chinese checkerboard with marbles, would it make the shape of a star, or would it represent many "little" stars? Why? 2. If you were to look at cars at different distances, which would appear smaller, the near ones or those far away?

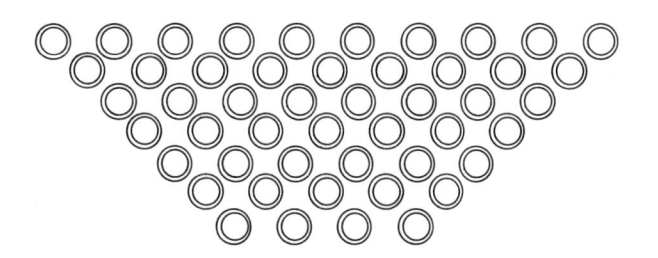

What Causes Some Stars to Be Different Colors? (4–8)

What Do I Want Children to Discover?	When objects are heated, they may change color. White-hot objects are hotter than red-hot objects. White stars are believed to be hotter than yellow stars, and yellow stars are hotter than red stars. A star is a giant mass of tremendously hot, glowing gases.

ENVIRONMENTAL SCIENCES 127

White stars have temperatures of 40,000° F at their surfaces; yellow stars, 10,000° F; and red stars, 3,000° F
Color is related to the age of a star.
Young stars are white.
Old stars are red.

What Will I Need? Pliers
Copper wire
Bunsen or alcohol burner

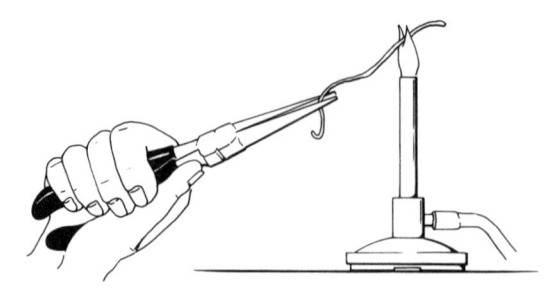

What Will We Discuss? If you saw two pieces of iron, both of which had been in a furnace, and one piece was red and the other was white, which one would you think was the hotter?
Why would one be hotter than the other?

What Must I Know Because of the equipment used and the possible danger of a child being burned, this activity should probably be done as a demonstration.

What Will Children Do? PROCESSES

Hypothesizing
1. With a pair of pliers hold a wire above a Bunsen burner.
   What do you think will happen to the wire as you heat it.

What Must I Know? The wire will change color, becoming red, then yellow, and finally white as the temperature increases.

Inferring What do you notice about the way the wire changes color?
Inferring What makes it change color?
Summarizing What are the different colors that the wire gives off in the process of being heated?
Inferring What color do you think is the hottest? The coldest?
Hypothesizing If you saw a red and a yellow star through a telescope, which of these do you think would be the hottest? Why?

What Must I Know? Red stars are cooler than yellow stars, and white stars are hotter than either red or yellow stars.

Explain from this demonstration how it is possible for an astronomer, a scientist who studies the stars, to tell how hot a star is without ever going to it.

What Must I Know? Explain that the color of the stars cannot be detected with the naked eye. The astronomer must use astronomical instruments in order to do this.

128 DISCOVERY SCIENCE RESOURCE ACTIVITIES

How Will Children Use or Apply What They Discover?

1. If you were going to heat some charcoal, which of the following types of light do you think it would give off first: red, yellow, or white?
2. What color is radiated from the hottest source in your home?
3. What other things might an astronomer study in the laboratory to help him or her better understand the stars?

Why Does the Moon Shine? (2–4)

What Do I Want Children to Discover?

Objects are seen when they give off their own light or when they reflect light from another source.

The moon does not give off its own light. Its light is reflected light from the sun.

What Will I Need?

Flashlight
Globe
Masking tape
Large ball

Small foil ball, about 1 inch in diameter, with attached string
Larger Styrofoam ball, about 3 inches in diameter, with attached string
Box with tight fitting lid (shoe box)

What Will We Discuss?

Place a ball on the table, darken the room, and ask:
What is on the table?
What do you need to be able to see the object?
Turn on the lights.
Why do you see the ball now?
Do you see it because it is giving off its own light or because it is reflecting light?
Look at the ceiling lights.
Why is it possible for you to see the lights?
How is this light different from the light you see when you look at the ball?
Darken the room.
What are two reasons why you may not see any lights in the room?

What Will Children Do?

Hypothesizing
Inferring

PROCESSES

How do you think the moon shines?
What is reflected light?

1. Obtain the following materials: box with tight fitting lid, foil made into a ball with attached string, flashlight, and masking tape.
2. Suspend the small ball on a string 1 inch long from inside the lid of the box as shown in the diagram. Insert flashlight in the end of the box and seal any space around it with masking tape. Make a small eyehole at the end of the box under the flashlight.

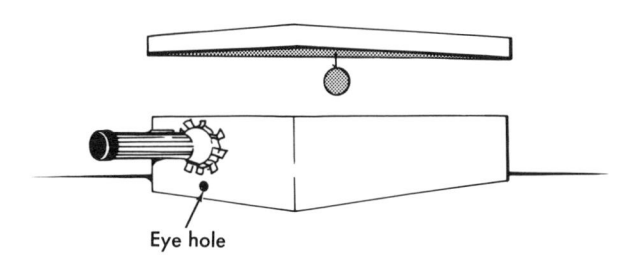

Eye hole

ENVIRONMENTAL SCIENCES 129

	Put on the lid with the ball suspended inside the box. Seal the edges around the lid.
Observing and inferring	What do you see when you look through the eyehole? Why?
	3. Turn on the flashlight.
Observing and inferring	What do you see when you look through the eyehole? Why?
Inferring	Do you see the ball because it reflects light or because it gives off light of its own?
Classifying	What two kinds of light do you see?
Inferring	What is the source of each kind of light?
	4. Look out the window.
Inferring	Why are you able to see some objects?
Inferring	What is the source of the light on the objects?
Inferring	Do the objects seen outside the window give off reflected light or light of their own?
Inferring	What does the sun give off?
Inferring	Why does the moon shine?
	5. Obtain a Styrofoam ball, 3 inches in diameter, with attached string. Use your box, flashlight, suspended foil ball, but add the larger Styrofoam ball suspended 2 inches down, as shown in the diagram. Seal the edges again. Seal the old eyehole and make a new eyehole as indicated in the drawing.

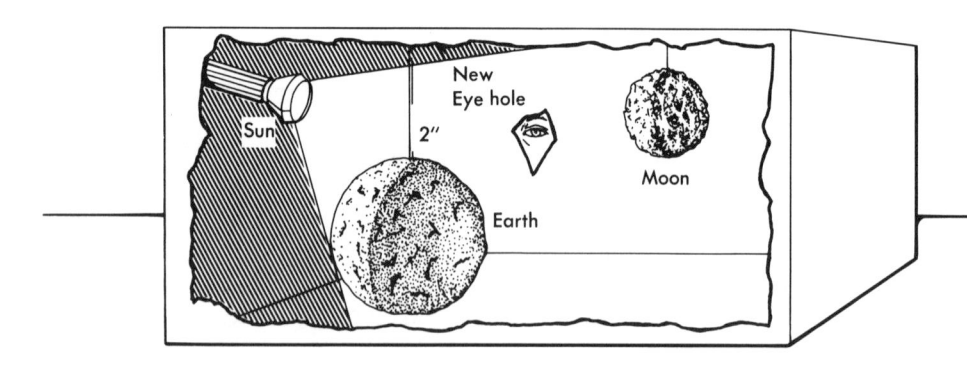

Formulating a model	If the small ball is the moon, what does the flashlight represent?
	6. Turn on the flashlight and look through the new eyehole.
Inferring	What does the large ball represent?
Inferring	7. Look at the ball representing the earth and tell which side is day and which side is night.
Inferring	On which side would you be if you could see the moon?
Inferring	How is it possible for you to see the moon if you are on the dark side of the earth?
Summarizing	Why does the moon shine?
How Will Children Use or Apply What They Discover?	1. If you lived on another planet, would you be able to see earth? 2. What are the positions of the sun, moon, and earth (a) when it is night for you, (b) when it is day for you?

130 DISCOVERY SCIENCE RESOURCE ACTIVITIES

Why Are There Phases of the Moon? (3-8)

What Do I Want Children to Discover?
Sometimes the moon appears fully round.
The moon seems to change shape.
Sometimes the moon seems to get smaller and smaller.
Sometimes the moon seems to get larger and larger.

What Will I Need?
Black construction paper
Soft white chalk
Globe
Small ball
Basketball
Flashlight or filmstrip projector

What Must I Know?
Before the experiment, consult the local newspaper to see when the moon's quarter will be visible during the day.

PROCESSES

What Will Children Do?

Observing

1. Obtain a large piece of black construction paper and some white chalk.
2. Take this home and observe the moon for the next five days. Draw the shape of the moon as you see it each night.
   In what way does the moon's shape seem to change?
3. Obtain a globe, small ball, and a flashlight or filmstrip projector. Using this equipment, make the following arrangement.
4. Place a pin on the night side of the earth as indicated in the diagram. The pin represents you.

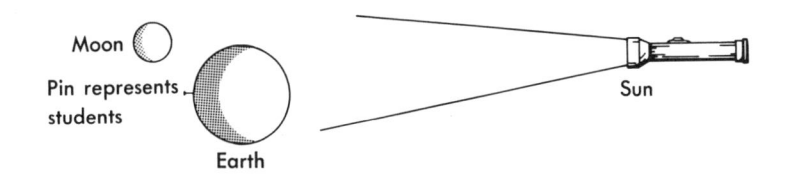

Inferring

Draw how much of a moon you would see if you were where the pin is.

Inferring
Inferring

5. Move the moon around the earth.
   On which side of the earth is the moon when you cannot see it?
   Where is the moon when it is full?
6. Make diagrams to help you explain the last three questions.
7. Look at the following diagram showing some phases of the moon.

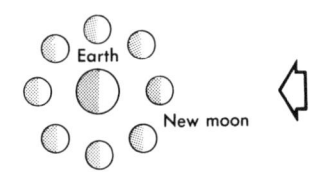

ENVIRONMENTAL SCIENCES 131

8. Prepare eight drawings showing how the moon would appear to you during the eight phases as indicated in the diagram.
9. Obtain a basketball and flashlight.
10. Choose two partners to help you. Have one partner hold the flashlight and shine it on the basketball being held by your second partner as he walks in a circle around you.

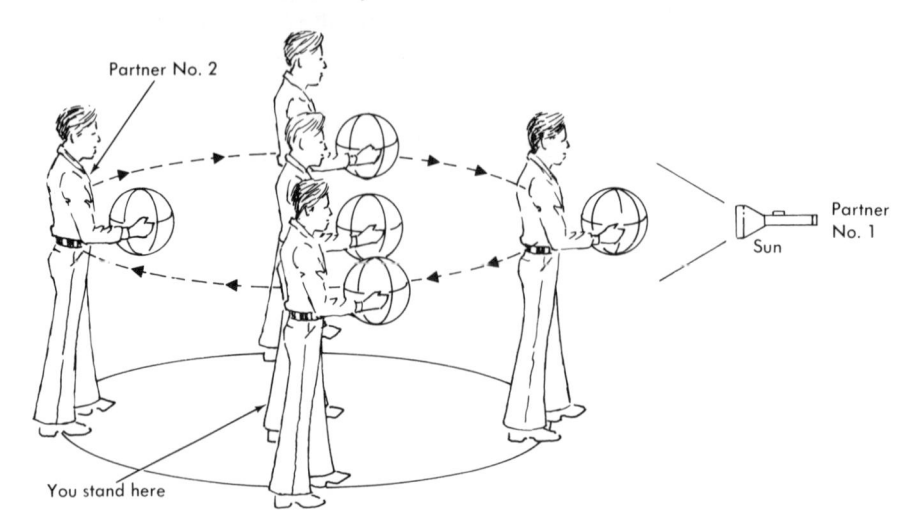

Inferring 11. As you observe the ball, diagram on a piece of paper how the light on the ball is similar to the phases of the moon.

Inferring In what position is the ball when it is covered by the shadow?
Inferring Where would the moon have to be when it is covered by a shadow?
Inferring When the ball shows no shadow, what phase of the moon would this represent?

Summarizing 12. Draw how the full moon looks from earth.
Summarizing What causes the phases of the moon?

How Will Children Use or Apply What They Discover?

1. If the moon is not out at night, on what side of the earth must it be located?
2. If the moon could remain still in the sky, how would it look every night?

What Causes The Tides? (4–8)

What Do I Want Children to Discover?

Gravitational attractions of the moon and sun on the earth cause tides.
The moon is smaller than the sun, but because it is closer to the earth, its tidal pull is greater than that of the sun.
Tides are highest when the moon and sun are pulling on the earth in a straight line. This occurs twice a month.
Low tides occur when the moon and sun are pulling at right angles to each other.
Gravity decreases with the increase of distance between two objects.

What Will I Need?

Horseshoe magnet   Paper clip
Ring stand   Styrofoam ball, 9 inches in diameter
String   Styrofoam ball, 2 inches in diameter
Book   Small round-shaped balloon

What Must I Know?   This activity should be done by groups of three or more students.

What Will Children Do?   PROCESSES

1. Obtain a ring stand, horseshoe magnet, some string, a paper clip, and a book.
2. Set up the equipment as shown in the next diagram.

Inferring
Observing
Assuming

What holds up the paper clip?
Are you able to see this force?
How do you know it is there if you cannot see it?

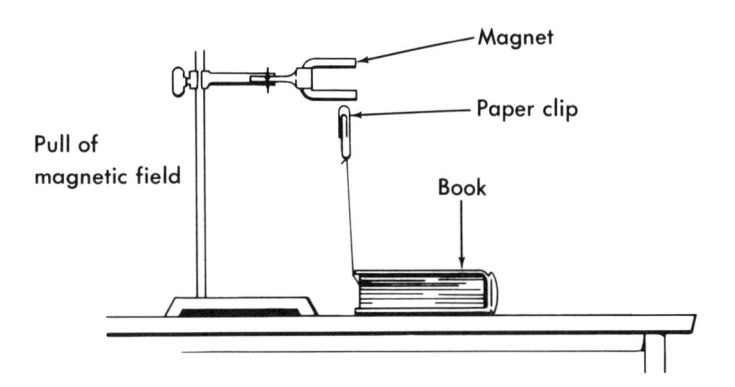

What Must I Know?   This is a magnetic force. It is shown here to illustrate what a force is and that a force may be invisible. Tides are not caused by magnetic force but gravitational force. The children should have done some activities involving gravity before they do this lesson.

Hypothesizing

Knowing this, what effect do you think the moon's gravitational force has on the water of the earth?

Hypothesizing

How will it pull the water?

3. Obtain two Styrofoam balls, 9 inches and 2 inches in diameter, and a small balloon from the scientific table.
4. Ask two partners to help you.
5. Blow up the balloon and tie the end closed. Have the two partners each hold one of the Styrofoam balls. You should hold the balloon in the position of the diagram below.

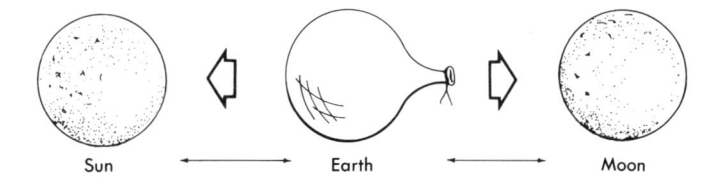

6. Pull the balloon with one hand toward the sun.
   Pull with the other hand toward the moon.

Inferring
Hypothesizing

What would the pull being exerted on the balloon represent?
What do you think will happen if the sun and moon are placed at right angles to the earty?

Hypothesizing

How will the gravitational forces vary?

7. Pull the balloon mostly toward the moon and exert much less force in the sun's direction.

ENVIRONMENTAL SCIENCES   133

Comparing From the way the balloon is being pulled, which has greater gravitational pull on the earth—the moon or the sun?

Hypothesizing Why do you think the moon has greater pull on the earth when it is so much smaller than the sun?

What Must I Know? The moon has greater effect because it is much closer to the earth than the sun is.

For summarization, draw the diagram below on the board and discuss it with the class.

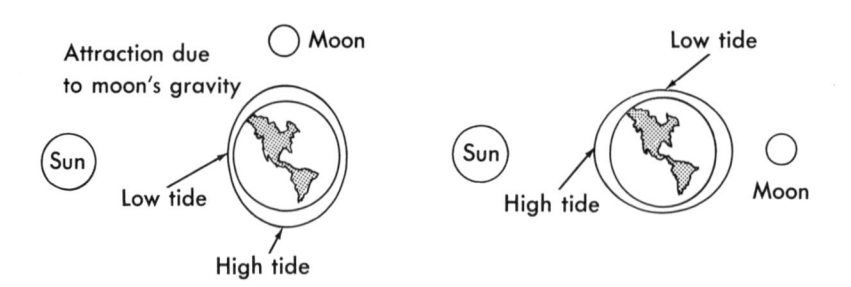

At the conclusion of the activity, discuss with the class the following concepts to be sure the students understand them:

Force is either a push or a pull exerted on an object. *Gravity* is a force you cannot see.

The greater the mass of an object, the heavier it is, and the more gravitational force it has.

The closer an object is to another, the greater the gravitational attraction there will be between them.

Mass is defined as the amount of matter a body contains.

How Will Children Use or Apply What They Discover?

1. Draw the positions of the moon, earth, and sun when there is a very high tide on part of the earth. How does the water around that part of the earth look?
2. When there is low tide at a place on the earth, how does the water look?
3. Why does the moon have a greater effect on the tide than the sun does?
4. What holds you down in your chair?
5. What effect do the gravitational forces of the moon and sun have on the world's continents?

What Is an Eclipse? (4–8)

What Do I Want Children to Discover?
The shadow of the moon on the earth causes a solar eclipse.
The shadow of the earth on the moon causes a lunar eclipse.
To see a solar eclipse, one has to be on the sunny side of the earth.
To see a lunar eclipse, one has to be on the night side of the earth.

What Will I Need?
(For each 3–5 students)
Flashlight, slide projector, or similar light source
Styrene (or similar) ball approximately 8 inches in diameter
Styrofoam (or similar) ball approximately 2 inches in diameter

What Will We Discuss?	What does the word *eclipse* mean? If something is eclipsed, what does it mean? What would it mean to say the sun is eclipsed?
What Will Children Do?	PROCESSES
Hypothesizing	1. Investigate the following questions, letting the flashlight represent the sun; the large ball, the earth; and the small ball, the moon. 2. How must the sun, earth, and moon be arranged for a solar eclipse to occur?
What Must I Know?	The moon must be between the earth and the sun.
Observing *Inferring*	3. Describe the shadow that falls upon the earth. When a solar eclipse occurs, would everyone on earth be able to see it? Explain your answer.
What Must I Know?	No, because the moon's shadow only touches a small part of the earth.
Inferring	Can a solar eclipse be seen at night? Explain.
What Must I Know?	No, it can only happen in the daytime when the moon can block out the sun's light.
Hypothesizing	How must the sun, moon, and earth be arranged for a lunar eclipse to occur?
What Must I Know?	The earth must be between the sun and moon for a shadow to fall upon the moon.
Hypothesizing	When is it possible to see a lunar eclipse?
What Must I Know?	Only at night.
How Will Children Use or Apply What They Discover?	1. The almanac indicates solar and lunar eclipses do not occur regularly each month as it seems they should. Use your equipment to see if you can discover an explanation to determine why this is so.
What Must I Know?	The children's activity should show that if the moon passes above or below the plane of the earth's orbit, the earth's shadow could miss the moon entirely, or the moon's shadow could miss the earth. In either case, the eclipse might be visible only from some point in space. The formulated hypothesis should be similar to the following: The plane of the moon's orbit is tilted away from the plane of the earth's orbit: eclipses can only occur when the earth, sun, and moon are in a straight line, and this does not happen each month.

ENVIRONMENTAL SCIENCES

SECTION 3

Discovery Activities for
PHYSICAL SCIENCES

STRUCTURE OF MATTER

What Is Matter? (K–3)

What Do I Want Children to Discover?
An object is made up of matter.
All matter has characteristics called *properties*.
Some properties of matter are color, size, shape, and texture.
Objects can be sorted by their properties.

What Will I Need?
Classroom objects such as books, desks, chairs, pencils, and chalkboard erasers
Box of assorted buttons

What Will We Discuss?
What can you tell us about these objects as I point to them?
How would you describe them to someone who had never seen them?

What Must I Know?
Accept statements related to object's *use*, but encourage students to concentrate upon *properties* by using questions such as:
What is the *color* of this object?
Is the object *smooth* or *rough*?
What is the *shape* of the object?
Is the object *large* or *small*?

After an appropriate amount of discussion, make a chart entitled "Properties of Objects." Encourage children to use the word *property* as they describe their selected object to be added to the properties chart. Reinforce the use of the word *property* by saying things such as, "Red and smooth are *properties* of this apple."

In a few weeks, as the list of property words increases, go over it with the class. Direct students to group property words under headings such as "size words," "color words," "shape words," "texture words."

What Will Children Do?
PROCESSES

PART I
1. One student is leader and picks an object in the room and whispers it to teacher.
2. Leader tells class in which part of the room (near radiator, front, back) the object is located. He or she gives clues about the object *in properties* without giving its name.
3. After each clue, the class tries to guess the object picked.

136 DISCOVERY SCIENCE RESOURCE ACTIVITIES

What Must I Know?	Encourage children to concentrate on clues (properties) instead of simply guessing wildly. It works best if you allow only one or two guesses after each clue.
	4. First student to guess the object is the next leader.
	PART II
	1. Obtain a handful of buttons from your teacher.
Observing	What are some of the *properties* of the buttons in front of you?
	2. Group all buttons that have the same properties together.
Summarizing	What are the properties you used to group your buttons?
	3. Regroup your buttons using different properties or combinations of properties.
Comparing	How do these piles of buttons differ from the ones you had first?
How Will Children Use or Apply What They Discover?	1. Regroup your buttons by using *opposite* properties such as rough-smooth, large-small, shiny-dull.
What Must I Know?	Help children to see that opposite properties are comparative rather than absolute. An object grouped as small in one pile may be large when placed with different objects. As an example, point out that your desk is larger than almost any object in the room, but is smaller than the room itself.

What Are Molecules? (K–8)

What Do I Want Children to Discover?	All matter is composed of tiny particles called *molecules*.
	Molecules are too small to be seen with the naked eye.
	Sometimes matter is made up of only one kind of molecule and scientists call this matter an *element*.
	Sometimes matter is made up of more than one kind of molecule and scientists call this matter *compounds*.
	Molecules are almost always in motion.
What Will I Need?	Piece of coal or charcoal Hammer
	Paper towel Shallow dish
	Ether, alcohol, or perfume
What Will We Discuss?	Have you ever heard of molecules?
	What do you know about molecules?
What Will Children Do?	PROCESSES
	PART I
	1. Obtain a piece of coal or charcoal (mostly carbon), a hammer, and a paper towel.
	Place the coal or charcoal on the paper towel and pound it with the hammer until you see fine coal dust.
Observing	How does the pounding change the coal?
Hypothesizing	Do you think you have made a new substance? Why do you think as you do?

PHYSICAL SCIENCES   137

Hypothesizing
Hypothesizing

2. What would you have to do to change the coal to a new material? If you keep pounding the dust into smaller and smaller pieces, what will you ultimately end up with?

What Must I Know?

Explain that all elements are composed of tiny invisible particles. These tiny particles are called molecules. *Important*: Do not convey to the children the idea that the dust from the coal is a single molecule. Molecules are too small to be seen by the naked eye and must be seen through a microscope. The dust particles are aggregations or collections of molecules. (See the diagram.)

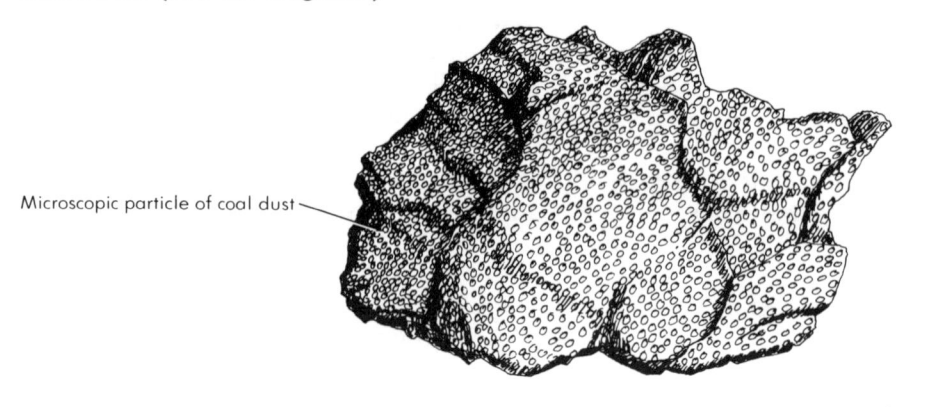

Microscopic particle of coal dust

PART II
1. Teacher will pour a liquid into a shallow dish at the front of the classroom.
2. Raise your hand when you first notice an odor.

Observing

From the sequence or order in which hands are raised, can you determine the direction in which the smell travelled?

Inferring

Why do you think this happened?

What Must I Know?

A reasonable assumption is that a little of the liquid evaporates and escapes into the air. It may be pointed out that the liquid must have been made up of tiny invisible particles and that the tiny particles called molecules must be in motion.

Designing an investigation

3. Can you think of some simple experiment to test the idea that molecules in liquids evaporate or go into the air at different rates?

What Must I Know?

If children cannot come up with an experiment, then suggest they smear ether, alcohol, water, and oil on the chalkboard. Solicit guesses or hypotheses about which liquids will disappear or evaporate at which rates and possibly why.

4. Test your experiment.

Applying

5. How can you speed up or slow down the liquid molecules' disappearing or evaporating?

How Will Children Use or Apply What They Discover?

1. Why do you think clothes dry faster on sunny days? Windy days?
2. Which would you smell first if a small dish were placed in front of your classroom and you were in the back of the room: vinegar, ether, alcohol, or perfume? Why did you pick the one you did? What were you thinking?

What Are Water Molecules and How Do They Affect Each Other? (K–8)

What Do I Want Children to Discover?

The deeper the water, the greater the pressure.
Water has cohesive force.
A *force* is defined as push or pull on an object.
Molecules of the same substance tend to stick to each other because they are attracted by an invisible force.
Each molecule of the substance pulls other atoms to it.
The force of attraction between molecules of the same kind is called *cohesive force*.

What Will I Need?

Quart milk carton
Water (enough to fill containers as desired)
Pencil or nail
Ruler
Glass or plastic tumbler
Medicine dropper
Pan or bowl
12 inch squares of wax paper

What Will We Discuss?

Why does a drop of water hold together as it runs down a windowpane?
Why are beads of water round, especially on a well-waxed automobile?
Why can some bugs walk on the top of water?
Why do you think drops of water from a medicine dropper are round?

What Will Children Do?

PROCESSES

PART I
1. Obtain a 12 inch square of wax paper. Using a medicine dropper place three or four drops of clean tap water on your wax paper.

Observing   How would you describe the shape of the water? What is its color?

2. Push the drops of water around with a pencil point.

Observing   What happens to the water when you push the pencil point into a water droplet?

Observing   What happens when you push several droplets near each other?
Hypothesizing   Why do you think this happens?

PART II
1. Obtain a glass or plastic tumbler and place it in a bowl or dish. Fill it completely full of water, until some water overflows.

Hypothesizing   Do you think you can add any more water to the glass tumbler?
Designing an investigation   Can you think of how you might test your hypothesis or guess?

PHYSICAL SCIENCES   139

2. Test your hypothesis or try this one:
   Using a medicine dropper, *slowly* drop water into the glass from about ½ inch above the water level of the glass. (See diagram.)

Measuring   How many drops of water can you add after the glass is "full"?
Observing   How would you describe the shape of the water above the rim of the glass?

Inferring   Why does the water rise above the rim of the glass?
Observing   At what point does the water run over the rim of the glass?
Inferring   Why do you think the water finally runs over the rim of the glass?

PART III

Hypothesizing   If the side of a milk carton were punctured with holes (one above another) and the carton filled with water, what do you think would happen to the water in it? How would the water pour out of the holes?

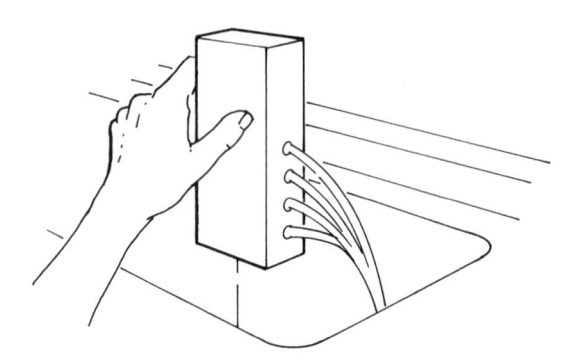

1. Obtain a clean milk carton that has the top cut out of it.
2. Puncture a hole with a pencil or nail from the bottom, about 1 - 1½ inches or 4 cm. Puncture three additional holes ½ inch apart above the preceding one. Put masking tape over holes. *Caution:* Do not make holes too large.
3. Over a sink, fill the container with water to within an inch of the top. Remove the masking tape.

Observing   What do you notice about the way the water comes out of the holes of the carton?
Inferring   Why do you think the water comes out of the holes like this?
Hypothesizing   If the carton were filled closer to the top with water, do you think there would be a difference in the way the water comes out?

Observing
Comparing

Inferring
Hypothesizing

4. Fill the carton until the water is closer to the top.
   What do you notice about the way the water comes out of the holes?
   Did you notice any difference in the water coming from the holes of the carton when there was less and when there was more water in it?
   What can you say about how water pressure varies with depth?
   What results do you think you'd get if you used a gallon or half gallon milk carton?
   Try it and record your findings.

PART IV

1. Puncture holes in the bottom of the carton about 1 cm. or 1 inch each apart as shown in the diagram. Put masking tape over holes. *Caution:* Do not make holes too large and make holes very close together.

Hypothesizing

   What do you think will happen when water is poured into this carton and the masking tape is removed?

Hypothesizing

   How many jets of water will you get coming out of the holes in the bottom of the carton?

2. Pour water into the carton.

Observing

   How many jets of water come out?

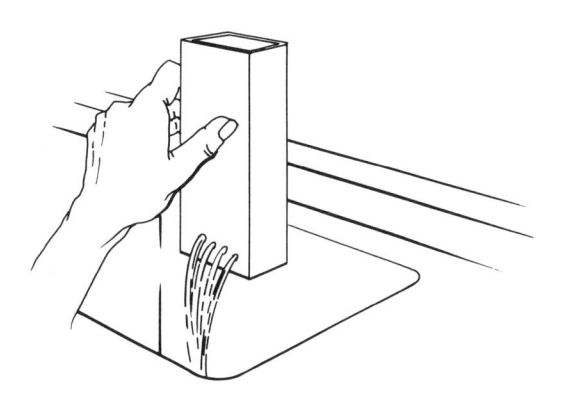

Designing an investigation

   What should you *do* to the water pouring out of the carton at the bottom so you could only get one jet of water without plugging any holes?

3. Test your hypotheses.
4. Try the above using gallon or half gallon cartons.

What Must I Know?

The children should pour water into the carton and pinch the jets of water together with their fingers just as though they were going to pinch someone. The jets will form one stream. If the water comes out in one jet, there must be some kind of force holding the water together. The force that holds similar molecules to each other is called *cohesive force*. Each molecule of water has cohesive force that pulls and holds other molecules of water to it. See the diagram that represents how molecules of water are held together to form a water droplet due to cohesive force. The pinching of the water brings the jets of water in contact, allowing cohesive force to hold together. This is true because the cohesive force between two substances increases as the distance between them decreases.

PHYSICAL SCIENCES 141

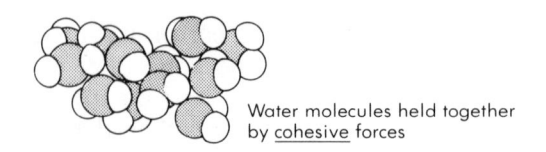

Water molecules held together by cohesive forces

How Will Children Use or Apply What They Discover?

1. Why do you think a dam must be built with very thick walls at the bottom and thinner walls at the top?
2. Why do your ears sometimes hurt when you dive deep in a swimming pool? What pushes in on your ears as you go deeper?
3. Why are the walls of a submarine so thick and strong?
4. What would happen to the water escaping from two of the holes of a can if you stopped one hole?
5. What will happen to the water coming out of the bottom hole as the water gets lower in the can?
6. Why do many towns have water storage tanks towering high above the city or built on a hill?

What Causes the Molecules of a Liquid to Move? (4–8)

What Do I Want Children to Discover

The molecules in liquids are constantly moving in a random pattern or Brownian movement.
This motion is caused by heat.

What Will I Need?

Gallon aquarium or wide-mouthed jar
Water
India ink
Microscope or microprojector

Microscope slide
Pen
Glass tubine
India ink

What Will We Discuss?

What would happen if you added a drop or two of ink to a bowl of water?
What would you do to find out?

What Will Children Do?

PROCESSES

PART I **Molecular Motion of Liquids**
1. Fill a gallon aquarium or wide-mouthed jar with water.
2. Dip a piece of glass tubing into a bottle of India ink. (India ink is used because it is an oil-based ink and tends to hold together longer than water-based inks.) Place your finger on top of the glass tubing and remove it from the ink bottle so that a column of ink, 2 or 3 inches in length, remains in the lower end of the tube. Wipe off the outside of the tube and, with your finger still in place, lower the tube *carefully* and slowly into the jar or aquarium. When the top of the column of ink inside the tube is level with the water surface, remove your finger for a moment and allow a *few* drops to flow downward without mixing with the water. Replace your finger on the tube and remove the tube carefully.

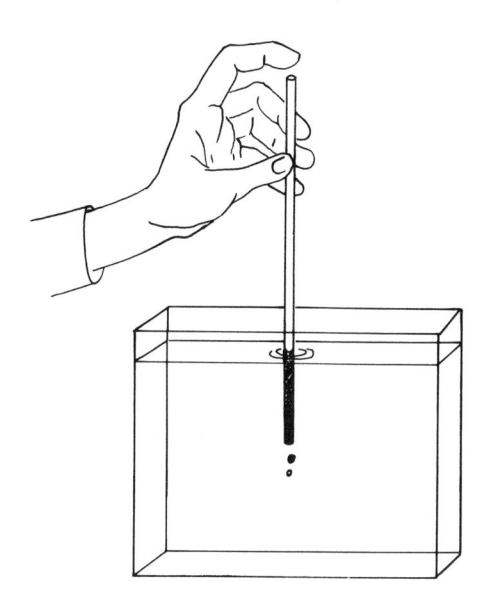

Observing	Do you see a few drops of ink suspended near the center of the jar?
	3. Watch the aquarium or jar for several minutes without moving or shaking it.
Hypothesizing	Why has the ink gradually moved to all parts of the water?
Observing	How long does it take for the color of the ink to be uniformly distributed throughout the aquarium or jar?

PART II The Movement of Water Molecules

Applying
1. Obtain a microscope or microprojector, a microscope slide, a pen, water, and India ink.
2. Place a drop of water on the microscope slide. Dip only the tip of your pen into the India ink. Place the tip of the pen into the drop of water on the microscope slide. Place as little ink in the water as possible.

Hypothesizing What do you think is happening to the ink and the water?

What Must I Know? Caution the children about being careful when focusing and handling the microscope. Check to make sure the children are seeing what is expected. If your children are not mature enough or skillful enough with the microscope, you can set the entire activity up on a *microprojector*. In this way, the entire class could view the same activity projected on a screen.

3. Carefully place the slide, with the drop of water and the ink, on the microscope stand. Focus the microscope on the drop. *Caution*: Do not crash the microscope lens into your slide.

Observing	4. Observe the ink in the water.
Observing	What are the particles of ink doing?
Observing	How are they moving?
Inferring	How is this motion caused?
Inferring	What evidence is there that the molecules of water may also be moving?

PHYSICAL SCIENCES   143

Brownian movement
of a molecule

What Must I Know? The motion the children see is Brownian movement, which means there is random movement of molecules.

What Are Atoms? (4–8)

What Do I Want Children to Discover?
Changing the size of an object does not change its physical characteristics.
All elements are composed of atoms.
An atom is very small.
Atoms are grouped in various ways to make molecules.
An atom is made up of electrons, protons, and neutrons.
Negatively charged bodies have more electrons than protons.
Electrons are negatively charged particles.
Protons are positively charged particles.
Neutrons have neither a positive nor a negative charge.

What Will I Need?
Wooden block or lump of clay
2 wire clothes hangers
Picture of solar system
Styrofoam ball about the size of a Ping-Pong ball
6 rubber jack balls or Styrofoam balls that size
Wire cutters

What Will We Discuss?
What do you know about atoms?
What do you think an element is?
What do you think an electron is?
What do you think protons and neutrons are?
How big do you think an atom is?
What do you know about molecules?

What Must I Know? Atoms are very small. The thickness of a human hair probably contains at least 500,000 atoms. An atom consists of fundamental particles called electrons, protons, and neutrons. Protons and neutrons are found in the center (or *nucleus*) of the atom and electrons revolve around the nucleus. The revolving electrons are grouped together in shells or orbits around the nucleus. The neutron has nearly the same mass as the proton and, as could be guessed from its name, is electrically neutral and carries no charge. The nucleus contains most of the weight or matter and is the most important part of the atom. Therefore, the nucleus is also the heaviest part of an atom. When an atom is neutral, it has an equal number of electrons and protons. If there are more electrons, the atom is negatively charged. All atoms have a tendency to balance the number of electrons and protons by drawing electrons or giving off extra ones and in the process become neutral.

What Will Children Do? PROCESSES

1. Obtain a wire clothes hanger, a block of wood or lump of clay, plasticine or Styrofoam or ping-pong balls, and 6 rubber jack balls. Assemble the materials as shown in the diagram.

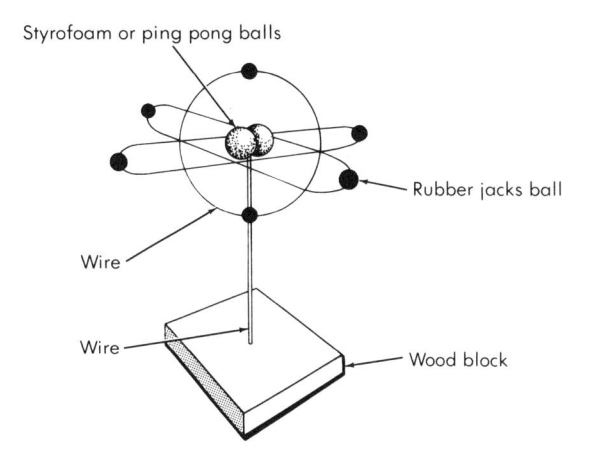

Inferring

2. In what ways is your model different from a real atom?

What Must I Know?

All the particles in the atom would be in motion. The orbits the electrons follow would not be so definite as those formed by the wire in the student model.

Hypothesizing

3. How could you improve the model shown in the diagram?
4. Look at a picture of our solar system.

Comparing

What do you notice about the solar system that can be said about an atom?

Comparing
Comparing

5. In what ways is the solar system different from an atom? How is it similar?

THERMAL ENERGY (HEAT)

What Is Heat? (K–8)

What Do I Want Children to Discover?

When an object is heated, its molecules move faster or vibrate more.
When an object is cooled, its molecules move more slowly.
Heat is the total energy an object has because of the motion of its molecules.

What Will I Need?

Small wooden board
12 baby-food jars
Tea bags
Pencils
Sandpaper
Sugar cubes
2 Pyrex or tin pans
Copper sulfate (obtainable from local drugstore)
Caution: Warn children not to taste copper sulfate as it is very poisonous.

PHYSICAL SCIENCES   145

What Will Children Do? PROCESSES

PART I
What do you think a board will feel like after you rub it very rapidly with sandpaper?

Hypothesizing

1. Obtain a board and a sheet of sandpaper.

Observing

2. Feel the board and the sandpaper. Are they warm?
3. Using the sandpaper, sand the board very rapidly.

Observing *Immediately* feel the sanded board and the sandpaper.
Inferring Why does the board feel the way it does? The sandpaper?
Comparing What do you notice about how the board felt before it was sanded compared to after it was sanded?

Inferring What did you do to the molecules in the board when you rubbed it quickly with sandpaper?

Designing an investigation

4. Can you think of some other things that can be rubbed together to show the same thing?

Try rubbing your hands together very rapidly for one half minute.

Observing What do you feel?
Hypothesizing Why do you think you felt what you did?

What Must I Know? When the board or children's hands were rubbed, molecules were agitated and therefore vibrated more, producing heat. The board, when touched, produced the sensation of being warmer, as did the hands when rubbed.

PART II
What caused the molecules to move on page 143?
How could we set up an experiment to test the effect of heat on movement of molecules in a liquid?

1. Fill three baby-food jars or plastic tumblers with water to within ½ inch of the top and let them stand until the water is room temperature.
2. *Slowly* lower a sugar cube, a lump of copper sulfate the size of a sugar cube, and a tea bag into the baby-food jars or tumblers. (See diagram.)

EXPERIMENT: Substances dissolving without stirring

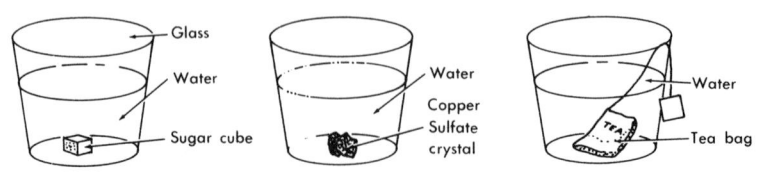

146 DISCOVERY SCIENCE RESOURCE ACTIVITIES

Make certain that the jars are in a spot where they will *not* be moved or jostled.
3. Set up the identical jars and materials as above but this time stir the jars until the materials dissolve, as shown in the diagram.

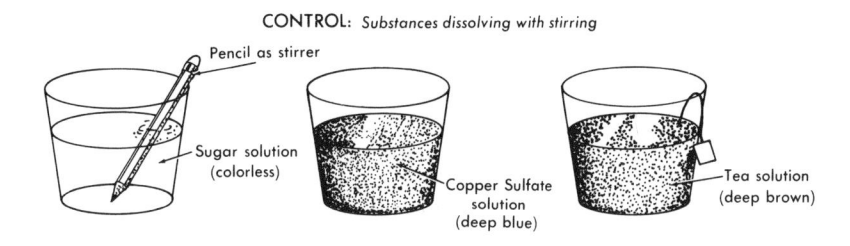

CONTROL: *Substances dissolving with stirring*

- Pencil as stirrer
- Sugar solution (colorless)
- Copper Sulfate solution (deep blue)
- Tea solution (deep brown)

Hypothesizing

This is called a *control* in science. Why do you think it is called this?
4. Taking observations on the hour, record how long it takes for the experimental jars to look like the control jars.

Hypothesizing
Inferring

Which materials do you think will dissolve first? Why?
Would the results be different if hot water were used? If cold water were used? Why?

Designing an investigation

How could we test this?
Try this:
Set up 2 more sets of jars with sugar, copper sulfate, and tea bags. Place one set in ice-cold water in a pan and the other in a pan of very hot water.

PART III

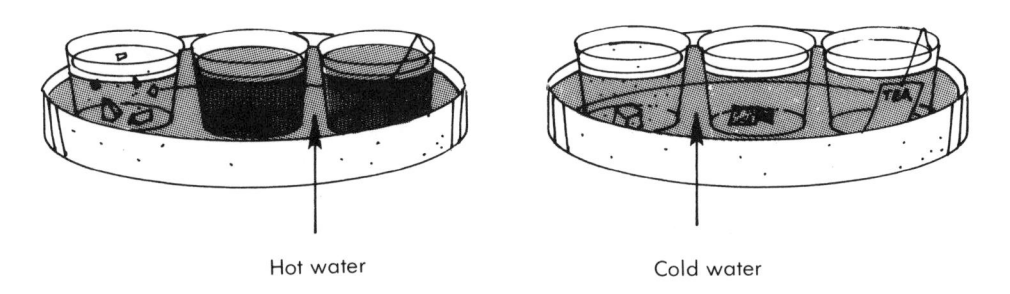

Hot water   Cold water

Hypothesizing

In which jars—in pans of hot or cold water—will the materials dissolve first?

Inferring

What does the hot water in the pan do to the molecules in the baby-food jars?

What Must I Know?

This is a review of the concept of the continuous movement of particles suspended in a liquid, called the Brownian motion. It also introduces several new concepts. Children will be helped to see that increasing the motion of molecules generates considerable heat. Conversely, matter that displays greater heat has greater movement of its molecules. In addition, the concept of a control is used as a standard against which scientists check their experimental work. If you think your students are ready, you can introduce the concept of *variables*. For instance, in Part II, the variable being tested is heat and its effect upon dissolving.

PHYSICAL SCIENCES

How Will Children Use or Apply What They Discover?

1. Why do you rub a match against the side of a match box?
2. Why don't matches catch fire sitting in a match box?
3. When you bend a wire back and forth several times, why does it get warm?
4. When you put two pencils together and rub them back and forth several times, what happens to your hands?
5. A man tried to strike a match against a piece of glass to light it. The match wouldn't light. Why?
6. If you feel the tires of your car before you take a trip and then just after you get out of the car, they will not feel the same.
   How do you think they will differ?
   How would you explain the difference?
7. A man was chopping wood with an axe. After chopping very hard for about 10 minutes, he felt the axe.
   How do you think the axe felt and why?

What Happens to Molecules of Solids When They Are Heated or Cooled? (4–8)

What Do I Want Children to Discover?

Heat is a form of energy.
Heat or thermal energy can be transferred.
Matter changes if heat or thermal energy is gained or lost:
  When heat or thermal energy is increased, the molecules move faster and farther apart (*expansion*).
  When heat or thermal energy is decreased, the molecules move slower and are closer together (*contraction*).

What Will I Need?

Candle
Metal pan
Matches
Nail
Forceps or tongs
Pair of pliers
Screw eye (The eye of this should be just *slightly* larger than the nail. If it is not, tighten with pair of pliers.)

What Will We Discuss?

What is heat?
What is energy?
What are molecules?
What do you think heat does to molecules?
What is a nail made of?
How does heat affect metal? What could you do to find out?

What Must I Know?

This activity should be done in groups of two students.

What Will Children Do?

PROCESSES

PART I
1. With the aid of your partner, obtain a candle, matches, a metal pan, forceps, nail, and screw eye.
2. Fix the candle so it stands in the center of the pan. To do this, light the candle wick and permit enough wax to drip onto the center of the pan (about the size of a quarter). Then blow out the candle and place it, wick end up, in the puddle of wax. Hold the candle steadily in the puddle until the wax hardens.

Observing	3. Try to fit the nail into the hole of the screw eye.
Observing	Does the nail fit the screw eye?
	How easily does the nail go into the screw eye?

Hypothesizing   What do you think will happen if you heat the nail and try to put it through the screw eye again?

What Must I Know?   The nail will have expanded so it will not enter the eye of the screw eye because the heat has caused the molecules to move faster and farther apart (expansion).

4. Light the candle.
5. With the forceps or tongs, pick up the nail. Hold the head of the nail over the hottest part of the flame. If you do not know where this is, ask the teacher.

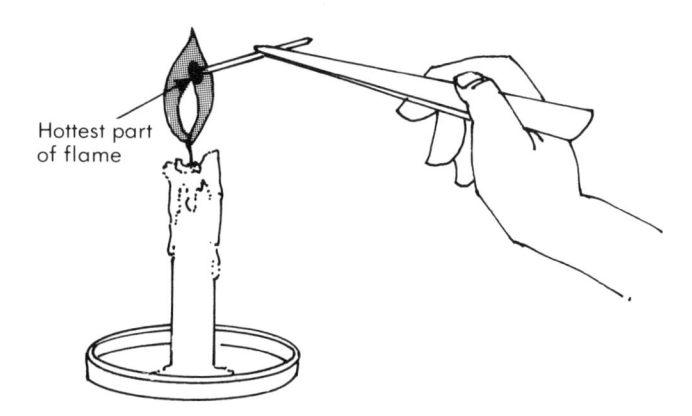

What Must I Know?   The candle flame is composed of two parts: a lower dark section and an upper bright part. The tip of the darker (inner) part is the hottest point of the flame. (See diagram.) Always have your students hold the object they are heating over the dark tip. Also, be prepared to explain the products of combustion if the children question the black deposit of carbon on the nail.

6. Pick up the screw eye and try to put the nail head through it. After you have done this, put the nail and screw eye in the metal pan—*remember* they are still hot.

Observing	What happened when you tried to put the nail head through the screw eye?
Inferring	Why do you think this happened?
Inferring	What happened to the molecules in the nail when you heated them?
Inferring	What did the heat do to them?
Inferring	Did the molecules move faster or slower?
Inferring	Did they gain or lose energy?

PHYSICAL SCIENCES

Inferring   Are the molecules in the heated nail closer together or farther apart than before heat was applied?

Inferring   How can you tell?

Explaining   Using the words *molecules, energy,* and *space between molecules,* try to explain what happens to a metal when it is heated.

How Will Children Use or Apply What They Discover?   Have children try the above using a screw eye that is slightly *smaller* than the nail, so the screw eye does *not* go over the nailhead. Put the nail in a freezer for 24 hours and then try to put the screw eye on. Does it now go over the nailhead? Why? Also try heating the *screw eye* and see if it will fit over the nailhead.

What Happens to Molecules of Liquids When They Are Heated or Cooled? (4–8)

What Do I Want Children to Discover?

Convection is the process whereby warm liquids or gases rise and cooler gases fall.

Warm liquids and gases expand and occupy more space. As a result, they have fewer molecules per volume than when they were cold. They are therefore less dense.

Warm liquids and gases rise because they are less dense than they would be if they were cold.

What Will I Need?

Food coloring
Glass container (quart size)
Ink or small paste bottle
2-hole rubber stopper or cork to fit small bottle
2 glass tubes or medicine droppers
Hot water
Cold water
Beaker
Coloring crystals—potassium permanganate crystals or food coloring are suggested
Paper towel

What Will Children Do?   PROCESSES

Hypothesizing   Knowing what you do about warm and cold gases in air, how do you think warm compared to cold bodies of *water* might behave?

1. Obtain a small ink or paste bottle, two glass tubes, a 2-hole rubber stopper or cork that will fit the bottle, food coloring, and a large glass container in which to put the bottle. Insert the glass tubes in the cork stopper or so one is higher than the other one as indicated in the diagram. *Caution*: Wet the cork and glass tubes before you try to insert them. Hold a paper towel folded several times around the glass tubes as you insert them. This is done to protect your hand in case the glass tubes break. Twist the glass tubes into the cork. *Do not use excessive* force inserting them. (See diagram.)

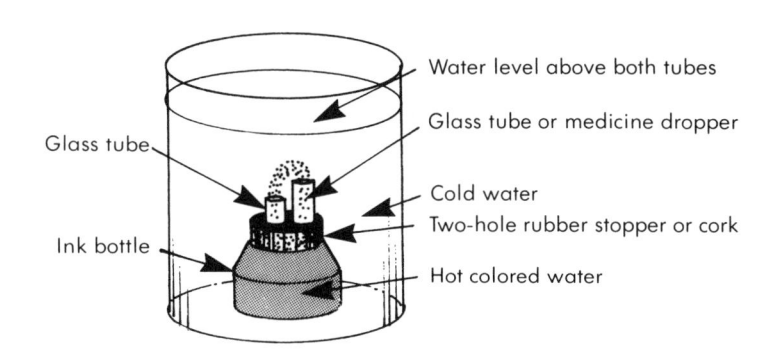

2. Put a few drops of food coloring in the small bottle. Fill it with *very hot* water and insert the cork. Fill the larger glass container with *very cold* water.

Hypothesizing — What do you think will happen if you lower the small bottle into the container of cold water?

3. Lower the small bottle into the cold water container.

Observing — What happens when the small bottle is dropped into the large container?

Inferring — Why does it happen?

The process of water and gases moving in this way is called *convection*.

Inferring — Why would it be possible for such currents to occur in the ocean?

4. Obtain a beaker and some colored crystals and fill the beaker with water. Place some of the *colored crystals* in the beaker in one corner. Place the beaker on the stand over a burner or alcohol lamp and heat the water as shown below:

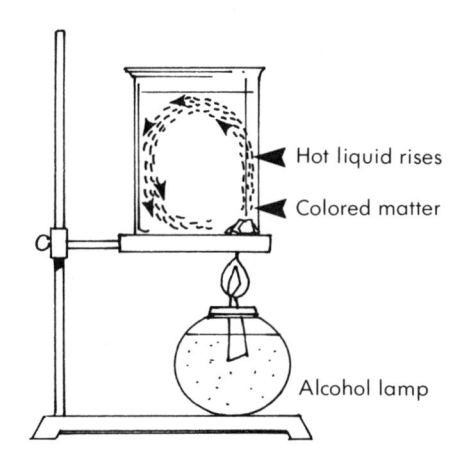

Hypothesizing — What do you think will happen to the crystals?
Observing — Describe what happens as the water is heated.
Inferring — Why does this happen?

5. Convection is defined as the transfer of heat by means of currents in the liquid or gas that is heated.

Summarizing — Explain what this definition means to you in your own words.

PHYSICAL SCIENCES 151

How Will Children Use or Apply What They Discover?

1. How would the temperature of the liquid affect the movement of the liquid molecules?
   How would you find out?
2. What other factors in addition to temperature affect the movement of liquid molecules?
3. How do other liquid molecules move?

What Happens to Molecules of Gases When They Are Heated or Cooled? (K–8)

What Do I Want Children to Discover?

Gases expand when heated.
Gases contract when cooled.
When gases are heated, the molecules move farther apart and exert greater pressure on the walls of the container.

What Will I Need?

3 balloons (same size) Radiator
String (5 feet long) Infrared lamp or large
Measuring tape   light bulb lamp
Gallon container filled with ice water

What Will We Discuss?

How could you use a balloon to determine if gas will expand or contract when filled with air and heated?
What happens to the molecules in an object when it is heated?
With a given rise in temperature, will gases or liquids expand the most? Why?

What Will Children Do?

PROCESSES

PART I

Hypothesizing

1. Obtain 3 balloons, a 5-foot piece of string, and a measuring tape. Blow up the balloons so they are about the same size and tie them closed. What do you think will happen to the air in a filled balloon if it is heated?
2. Measure with the measuring tape one of the balloons. Tie this balloon to the upper arm of a chair and place the chair about two feet from a heater.

Observing
Measuring

3. Observe the size and shape of the balloon as it is being heated.
4. At the end of 4 minutes, measure and record the balloon's diameter again. What change has occurred?

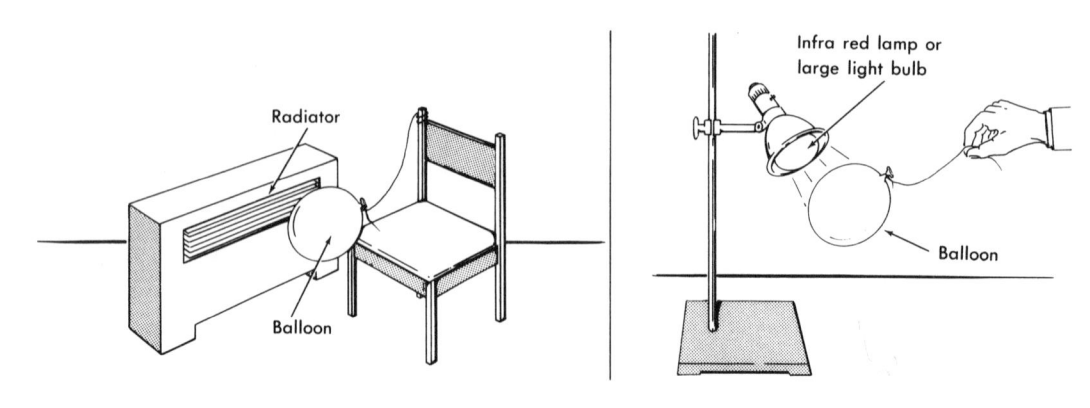

Hypothesizing	**PART II** What do you think will happen to the shape of a balloon if it is cooled?
Designing an investigation	What should you do to find out? 1. Measure a second balloon. Place it in ice cold water.

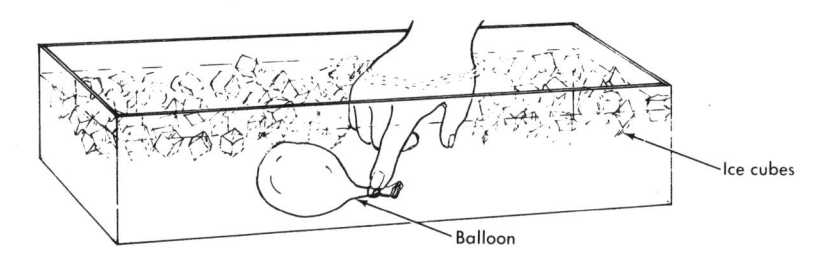

(Illustration: a hand placing a balloon in a tray of ice cubes, labeled "Ice cubes" and "Balloon")

Observing	2. Observe the size and shape of this balloon as it is being cooled.
	3. Leave the third balloon at room temperature (control or comparison).
Inferring	What is the purpose of leaving this balloon at room temperature?
Observing	Which of the three balloons expanded?
Applying	What do you think happened to the speed of the molecules inside the expanding balloons?
Observing	Which balloons contracted?
Applying	What do you think happened to the speed of the molecules in the cooled balloon?
Inferring	In which of the three balloons do you think the molecules are moving faster and hitting the sides with greater force?
Summarizing	What evidence do you have that gases expand when heated?
Summarizing	What evidence do you have that gases contract when cooled?
How Will Children Use or Apply What They Discover?	1. What would happen to a balloon if the air inside were overheated? 2. What might happen to a tire if the car were driven very fast down the highway on a hot summer day? 3. What might happen to a partly filled bottle brought into a warm room from the refrigerator?

How Is Heat Transmitted by Conduction and Radiation? (4–8)

What Do I Want Children to Discover?	A candle gives off radiant heat. Heat can be transmitted from one body to another by conduction and radiation. Light objects reflect radiant energy more than dark objects. Some surfaces conduct heat better than others.

What Will I Need?	Quart size tin can	4 x 4 inch square of asbestos
	Small can of *dull* black paint	Penny
	2 match sticks	9 thumb tacks
	Candle	Small paint brush
	4 x 4 inch square of aluminum foil	Piece of black paper
	Silver or stainless steel knife	Tripod stand
	4 inch length of copper tubing	Wood splint
	Bunsen or alcohol burner	

PHYSICAL SCIENCES

What Must I Know?	This activity may be done in groups.
What Will Children Do?	PROCESSES

PART I **Radiation**

Hypothesizing — What do you think will happen to two sticks attached with wax to the outside of a tin can when one-half of the inside of the can has been painted dull black, and a burning candle is placed inside the can? (See diagram.)

1. Obtain a one-quart tin can, two match sticks, a candle, a small can of dull black paint, and a small paint brush.
2. Paint one-half of the inside of the can with *dull* black paint; *leave* the other half of the inside natural metal.
3. Light a candle and let some of its wax drip on each side of the can as indicated in the diagram. Place the sticks in the wax while it is soft and hold them until the wax cools.
4. Place the candle inside the tin can as close as possible to the center of the can. Do not use a candle taller than where the sticks are attached to the can.
5. Light the candle with a wood splint.

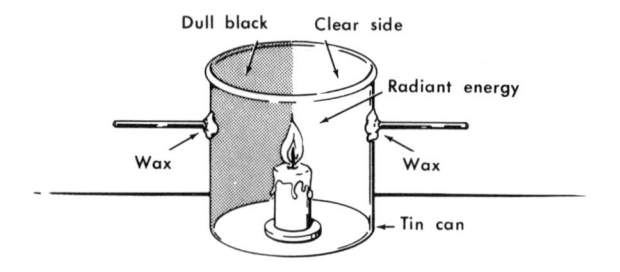

Hypothesizing	What do you think will happen to the sticks on the side of the can?
Observing	6. Observe and record what happens to the sticks.
Observing	Did this happen to each stick at the same time?
Inferring	Why do you think this happened?
Hypothesizing	What do you suspect about the inside surfaces of the can?
Hypothesizing	What happens to your eyes when you look at aluminum foil in sunlight?
Hypothesizing	What happens to your eyes when you look at a sheet of black paper in the sunlight?
	7. Obtain a piece of black paper and a piece of aluminum foil.
	8. Look at them in the sunlight.
Observing	How did the black paper and foil make your eyes feel as you looked at them in the sunlight?
Inferring	Why did each make your eyes feel differently?
What Must I Know?	Aluminum foil reflects radiant energy whereas black paper absorbs most of the radiant energy.
Inferring	Knowing what you do about how light (radiant) energy reacts on different surfaces, how would you explain why the sticks fell at different times from the can?

154 DISCOVERY SCIENCE RESOURCE ACTIVITIES

PART II Conduction

Hypothesizing

What do you think will happen to tacks that have been attached with wax to a strip of aluminum foil, a silver knife, and a copper tube, when the tips of these metals are heated? (See diagram.)

1. Obtain a 4 × 4 inch square of aluminum foil, a candle, a match, and nine tacks.
2. Roll the aluminum foil tightly.
3. Drip some wax from a candle onto three tacks and the aluminum foil rod so the tacks stick to the foil.
4. Obtain a Bunsen or alcohol burner, tripod stand, silver knife, and a 4 inch length of copper tubing.
5. Stick three tacks each to the knife and the tube as you did with the foil.
6. Light the burner.
7. Place foil, knife, and copper tubing on a tripod stand as indicated in the diagram. Heat the tips of each of these with a flame from a burner.

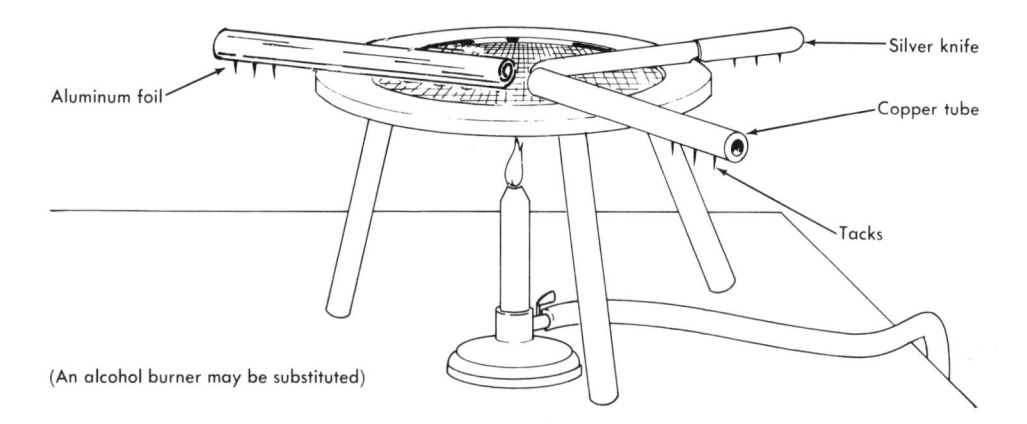

(An alcohol burner may be substituted)

Observing
Inferring
Inferring

Observe and record what happens.
Why didn't the tacks all fall at the same time?
From observing this activity, how do you think the heat affected the three metals?

PART III

Hypothesizing

If you were to place a penny on top of a piece of asbestos on a ring or tripod stand and place a flame below the asbestos, would the penny or asbestos feel warmer?

1. Obtain a ring stand, a piece of asbestos, a Bunsen or alcohol burner or candle, a match, and a penny.
2. Place the piece of asbestos on the ring of the ring stand.
3. Place the penny in the center of the piece of asbestos.
4. Light the burner or candle.
5. Place the burner or candle below the asbestos for a few minutes.
6. *Carefully* touch the penny, then the asbestos.
7. Remove the burner and turn it off.

Observing
Inferring
Interpreting

Which of these, the penny or the asbestos, feels warmer?
Why does one feel warmer than the other?
Since you know what happens to molecules when they are heated, what can you tell about the molecules in the penny compared to the asbestos?

PHYSICAL SCIENCES   155

How Will Children Use or Apply What They Discover?

1. When you stand in front of a fireplace and the front of you is warmed by the fire, how is the heat transferred?
2. How does heat or thermal energy come from the sun?
3. What colors are more likely to absorb heat?
4. Why do people generally wear lighter colored clothes in the summer?
5. In the can experiment, what kind of energy did the black surface absorb?
6. How was the heat transferred from the black surface to the wax?
7. Why is it desirable to have a copper-bottomed tea kettle?
8. Why wouldn't you want a copper handle on a frying pan?
9. What metals conduct heat well?
10. Why would asbestos be a good insulator against heat loss?
11. What advantage would there be in ordering a car with a white rather than a black top?
12. Why do many people in warmer climates paint their houses white?
13. Why would you prefer to put a hot dog on a *stick* rather than a wire to hold the hot dog above a camp fire?
14. Why do cooks sometimes use asbestos hot pads?
15. Why do astronauts wear shiny space suits?

What Is an Insulator? (4–8)

What Do I Want Children to Discover?

Water is a poor conductor of heat.
Wood, cork, glass, asbestos, and air are poor conductors of heat.
Heat from a burner rises.

What Will I Need?

Clamp
Steel wool
Test tube
Ice
Candle
Matches
Ring stand
Ring clamp
Asbestos (4 x 4 inches)
Wood
Glass
Glass rod
Metal rod (a brass curtain rod or aluminum foil foil rolled to make a rod can serve for this purpose)
Wax
Aluminum foil (4 x 4 inches)
Alcohol or Bunsen burner

What Will We Discuss?

Is water a good conductor of heat?
What could you do to find out?

What Will Children Do?

PROCESSES

PART I
1. Obtain a test tube, clamp, steel wool, ice, candle, candle holder, and matches. Set up the equipment as shown in the diagram.

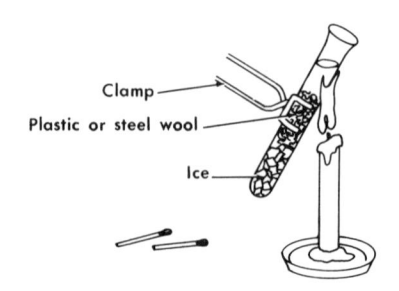

156 DISCOVERY SCIENCE RESOURCE ACTIVITIES

2. Heat the water *above* the ice cubes for several minutes until the water boils.
   What happens to the ice in the test tube?

Inferring From this, what can you conclude about water as a conductor of heat?
Inferring Why did you put steel wool in the lower part of the tube?

What Must I Know? Steel wool was placed in the tubes to hold the ice cubes down. Plastic wool used to clean pots can be substituted for steel wool.

PART II
1. Obtain the following items: aluminum foil, a Bunsen or alcohol burner, a ring stand, ring clamp, asbestos, and matches.

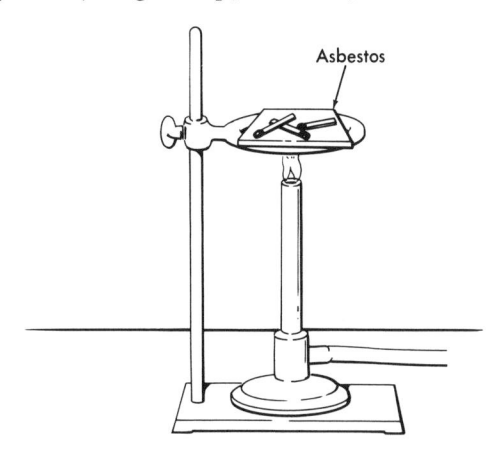

2. Set up the apparatus as indicated in the diagram. Place three matches on the asbestos.
3. Heat the lower surface of the asbestos.

Measuring 4. Time how long it takes for the matches to burst into flames.
5. Repeat the above procedure substituting aluminum foil for the asbestos.

Comparing What can you conclude about the ability of aluminum foil to conduct heat compared to asbestos?
Which of these would you call an insulator? Why?

PART III
1. Obtain a glass rod, a metal rod, a candle, a candle holder, wax, and matches. Place wax on each of the rods as shown in the diagram.

Hypothesizing What do you think will happen when you heat these rods as indicated in the diagram?

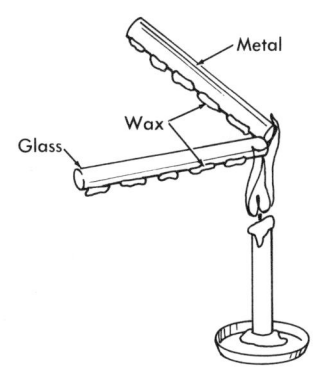

PHYSICAL SCIENCES 157

Observing
Comparing
Defining

2. Heat the rods gently over the candle.
   On which rod did the wax melt first?
   Which is the better conductor of heat: metal or glass?
   Define in your own words what a conductor and an insulator of heat are.

How Will Children Use or Apply What They Discover?

1. What are some materials you would use if you wanted to conduct heat from its source to another place?
2. Why can you safely hold your hand below a burning candle but not above its flame?
3. What materials would be good for making cups to hold hot drinks?
4. Where are insulators of heat used in your home?
5. How does house insulation help both heat the house in winter and cool it in the summer? Why is less fuel needed to heat (and cool) well-insulated houses? Why is foil-lined house insulation better than paper-lined insulation?

CHANGES IN STATES OF MATTER

How May Matter Be Changed? (K–8)

What Do I Want Children to Discover?
Matter may be changed chemically or physically.
If matter is changed chemically, its chemical makeup is altered.
Matter changed physically may be altered in its form, but its chemical makeup remains the same.

What Will I Need?
Small dish
Tablespoon
Prepared gelatin dessert
Butter
Water
Hot plate

Measuring cup
Candle
Matches
Quart container (pan)
Glass

What Must I Know?
Assemble the items you will need in the classroom. *Caution*: In the interest of safety, only *you* should handle the hot plate. Place all these materials on your demonstration area.

What Will We Discuss?
What kinds of things are there on the desk?
How do they vary?
In what ways could you cause these things to change?
What changes do you think would occur in these items?
What would change other than the form?
How can you find out?

What Must I Know?
The terms for matter should have been introduced in previous lessons.

What Will Children Do?
PROCESSES

1. Obtain a candle, some prepared gelatin dessert, and a match.
2. Light a candle.

Observing
Observe and record the changes you see.

Observing
Hypothesizing
and designing
an investigation

3. Observe the gelatin dessert.
   What is its form?
   How could you change its form?

4. Try to change the gelatin dessert's form.
5. Obtain some butter.
   What is the form of the butter?
   How can you change its form?

Observing
Hypothesizing

6. Try to change its form.

What Must I Know?

Set butter and gelatin dessert in a warm place or in a pan over the candle. Students should suggest that, after melting, the butter's form can be restored by cooling it.

Summarizing

What have you learned about how matter can be changed in this activity?

How Will Children Use or Apply What They Discover?

1. Which of the things above could easily be restored to the form they were originally?
2. What is the difference between a physical and a chemical change?
3. Observe the raw materials of gelatin dessert (powder and water) and butter (heavy cream) and describe the changes that went on from raw materials to end product.

What Effect Does Heat Have on the States of Matter? Part I—Solids (K–6)

What Do I Want Children to Discover?

There are many forms of sugar.
It is possible to obtain carbon from burning sugar.
Sugar may be broken down chemically.

What Will I Need?

Bunsen or alcohol burner or hot plate
Aluminum pie pan
Ring stand and ring
Teaspoon sugar or cube of sugar
Empty glass cup (tall)
Pot holder

What Will We Discuss?

Hold up a piece of sugar, and ask: What are some of the properties or characteristics of this piece of sugar?

What Must I Know?

They might say it is white, cubical in shape, small, made up of crystalline material, sweet, and so on. In its present form, sugar is a white solid. There are, however, ways of changing its appearance. One of the easiest ways is simply to crush the cube, producing sugar in smaller cyrstal form. These crystals can be crushed further to make a powdered sugar. Another way to change this cube's appearance is to dissolve it in a cup of water. No sugar can be seen, yet the solution will taste sweet. It is, nevertheless, sugar because some of its characteristics are identifiable.
In what ways can sugar be changed so it cannot be identified?

PHYSICAL SCIENCES 159

What Will Children Do?   PROCESSES

1. Obtain an aluminum pie pan and place it on top of an electric hot plate or ring stand. Regulate the burner so the pan is heated *slowly*.
2. Obtain one teaspoon of sugar and place it in the middle of the pan.

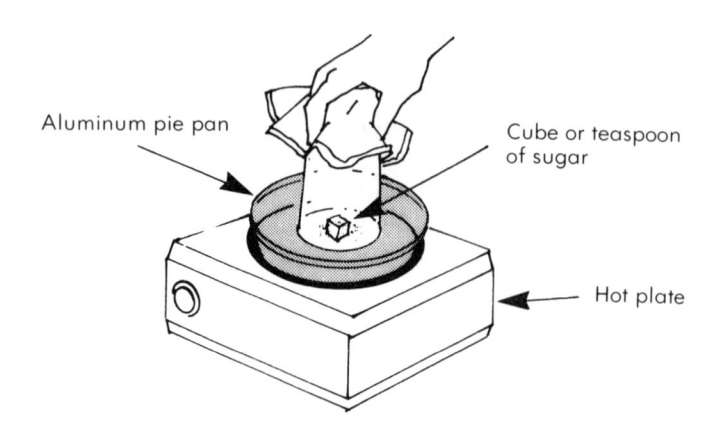

Hypothesizing
Observing
Observing

What do you think will happen when the sugar is heated?
3. Watch what happens to the sugar.
   What happens as the sugar begins to melt?
4. Obtain a tall, empty glass cup and hold it upside down over the bubbling sugar. Use a pot holder to do this.

Hypothesizing
Observing

What do you think will appear on the *inside* of the glass?
5. Observe the inside of the glass.
6. Touch the inside of the glass with your fingers.

Observing
Inferring

What do you feel?
What do you think it is? (water vapor)
7. After the sugar stops bubbling, describe what you see in the pan.

Inferring
Comparing

What do you think this material could be?
What does it look like?
Taste this material.

Observing

How does it taste?
Does it have the properties of sugar?

What Must I Know?

It is probably carbon. Sugar has carbon combined in its molecular structure.

How Will Children Use or Apply What They Discover?

1. From what you have learned about sugar, can you explain why a marshmallow turns black when roasted over a fire?
2. Why does sugar turn *brown* as it slowly heats up and melts? This brown liquid is caramel flavor.

What Effect Does Heat Have on the States of Matter? Part II—Liquids (4–8)

What Do I Want Children to Discover?

The temperature of water rises to the boiling point proportional to the amount of heat it absorbs.
At the boiling point, the temperature of water remains constant.

160   DISCOVERY SCIENCE RESOURCE ACTIVITIES

The heat added to water at the boiling point works to change the state of water to water vapor.

Whenever a state of matter is changed, for example, a liquid to a gas or a gas to a liquid, a considerable amount of energy must be added or given off in the process.

What Will I Need?

Beaker (500 ml.)
Thermometer (centigrade)
Stirring rod
Crushed ice
Bunsen or alcohol burner
Graduated cylinder
Ring stand
Ring clamp
Wire gauze
Stopwatch or wristwatch

What Will Children Do?

PROCESSES

1. Obtain a 500 ml. beaker, ring stand, ring clamp, wire gauze, thermometer, stirring rod, crushed ice to fill the beaker, a watch, and a Bunsen or alcohol burner.
2. Arrange the ring stand, ring, and wire gauze according to the diagram. Using the graduated cylinder, measure out 50 ml. of water and pour it in the beaker.

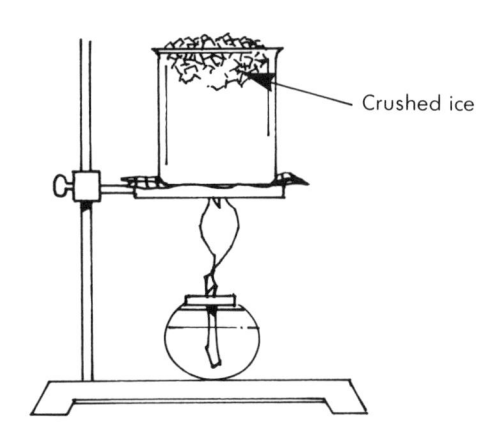

3. Fill the rest of the beaker to the top with crushed ice. Place the wire gauze on the ring.
4. Light and adjust the burner.
5. Adjust the height of the ring on the ring stand so the tip of the flame will just touch the wire gauze.
6. Place the burner under the beaker and time it with the stopwatch for 30 seconds.

Measuring

7. At the end of the 30-second interval, remove the burner. This will constitute one unit of heat. Stir continuously while heating, and as soon as the burner is removed, take the water temperature as quickly as possible. The data should be recorded in a manner similar to the sample data table.

No. of Heat Units	Temperature
0	(initial)
1	
2	
3	
etc.	

8. As soon as the temperature has been read and recorded, replace the burner and add another unit of heat, quickly taking the temperature again. Continue doing this, working as rapidly as possible, until all of the ice has melted and the temperature seems to have risen as far as it will go (until it becomes constant). Make a line graph of the data from the table. Use temperature and number of heat units as the coordinates. (Make the graph on graph paper.)

Inferring How many units of heat were added before the temperature began to rise?

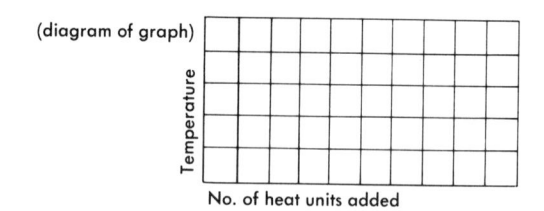

(diagram of graph)
Temperature
No. of heat units added

Inferring What is the significance of the point at which the temperature begins to rise?

Inferring What is the significance of the point at which the temperature seems to reach a maximum?

Inferring What happens to the heat supplied when no temperature change takes place?

How Will Children Use or Apply What They Discover?

1. How do you think your results would have varied if you had used sugar or salt water?
2. What would you think would be the results if you continue heating the water until it boils?
3. Why do you think you were asked to stir continuously while heating the water? What differences (if any) would you expect in the results if you did *not* stir continuously? Why?

AIR PRESSURE

What Is Air? (K–3)

What Do I Want Children to Discover?
Air is real.
Air is around us all the time.
Air is found inside solids and liquids.
Air takes up space and has weight.

What Will I Need?
Piece of cardboard
Commercial-sized mayonnaise jar or aquarium
Drinking jar
Food coloring

What Will We Discuss?
How do you know something is real?
What could you do to find out whether air is real?

What Will Children Do?   PROCESSES

Observing
1. Swing your hands back and forth.
   What can you feel?

Observing
Inferring
Observing
2. Swing a piece of cardboard.
   What do you feel now?
   What is the cardboard pushing against?
   What do you feel pushing against you when you ride your bicycle down a hill?

Hypothesizing
   What do you think will happen to a jar if it is turned upside down and placed under water?

3. Obtain a drinking glass. Turn the glass upside down and hold it in a large jar of water or an aquarium as shown (use food coloring to make water more visible):

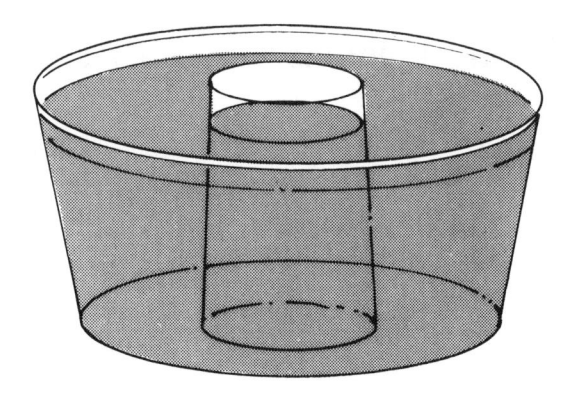

Observing
4. Turn the glass sideways.
   What happens to the inside of the glass?
   What are the bubbles that escape from the glass?

PHYSICAL SCIENCES

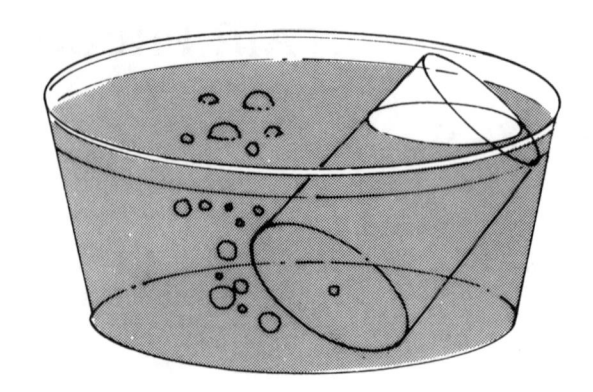

How Will Children Use or Apply What They Discover?

1. How can you keep water in a straw by holding it with your finger on the end like this?

2. If you fill a paper bag with air and then crush it, what happens and why?
3. Why does juice flow better from a tin can if you punch two holes instead of one?

What Shapes and Volumes May Air Occupy? (K–6)

What Do I Want Children to Discover?	A gas has no fixed shape. A gas has no distinct surface of its own. A change in shape or state is a physical change. Air or gas is elastic in that it can expand or contract to fill a space. Air can exert a force.
What Will I Need?	Plastic bag (quart size) Beach ball Balloon (oblong shape) Tire pump
What Will We Discuss?	What helps a kite to fly? Why does your hair blow in the wind? What do you breathe? Where do you find air? How do you know air is around you?

164   DISCOVERY SCIENCE RESOURCE ACTIVITIES

What form or shape does air have?
How can you find out?

What Must I Know? The materials described above are for a group of two or three children.

What Will Children Do? PROCESSES

PART I
1. Obtain a balloon, a plastic bag, a beach ball, and a tire pump.
2. Inflate the balloon by blowing into it.
   What is the shape of the balloon?
   What made it that shape?

Observing
Inferring or interpreting

3. Squeeze the balloon.
   What shape is it?
   Why does it take on different shapes when you squeeze it?

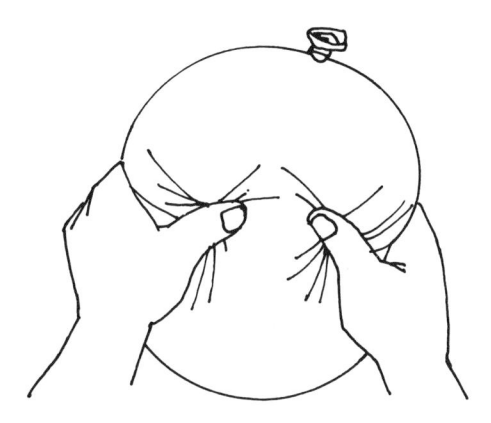

Observing
Inferring

4. Open the balloon.
   What happens to the air?
   What is the shape of the air now?

Observing
Inferring

PART II
1. Obtain a plastic bag and blow into it.
2. Is the shape of it the same or different from the shape of the balloon?
3. Release the bag.
   What happens to the shape of the bag?
   Why is the shape of the balloon similar to the shape of the plastic bag even though they are different?

Comparing

Inferring
Inferring

PART III
1. Obtain and inflate a beach ball.
   Is the shape of it the same or different from its shape before inflating?
   Why do you think the ball changed its shape?
   What can you say about the shape of the air in all these things?
   How do you think you could use a tire pump to show that air will fill any container?
2. Obtain a tire pump. Have your partner put his finger over the end of the pump.

Comparing
Inferring
Summarizing
Designing an investigation

PHYSICAL SCIENCES 165

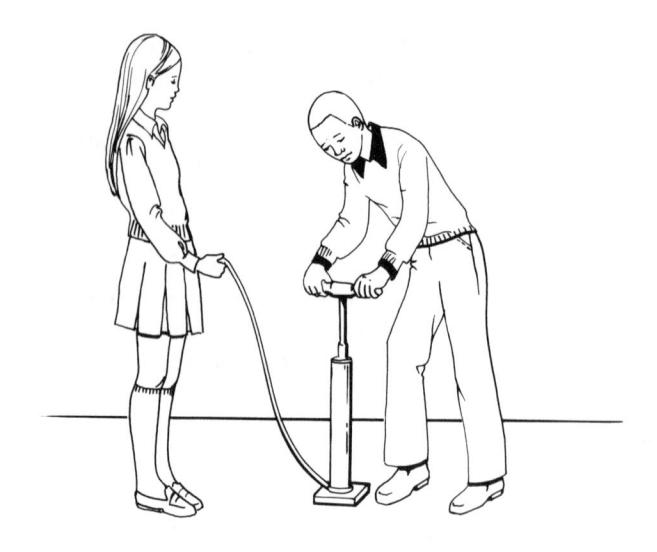

Observing	3. Push the plunger of the pump down. Was it easy or hard to push it down?
Observing *Inferring*	4. Keep the finger over the end, push the plunger down, and then let go of the plunger. What happens to it? What causes it to bounce back?
Comparing *Inferring* *Comparing* *Inferring*	5. Now remove the finger and push the plunger down again. Is it easy or hard to push? Why does it push differently now? How does this compare with the stretching of a rubber band or a balloon? How is it possible for the air to cause a balloon to become larger?
What Must I Know?	Explain that a *force* is a push or pull and then ask the children to determine if air can exert a force and to explain how they know that it can or cannot.
How Will Children Use or Apply What They Discover?	How can you use an inflated ball and an uninflated ball to show that air can fill a big space?

How Can Air Pressure Move Objects? (K–8)

What Do I Want Children to Discover?	Air pressure may be strong enough to crush a strong can. A partial vacuum is a space in which the atmospheric pressure has been lessened; in other words, the space contains fewer molecules of air than the air surrounding it.
What Will I Need?	Empty ditto fluid can with screw cap Water Marking ink Bunsen or alcohol burner or hot plate Cork
What Will We Discuss?	What are some things you know about air? What ways can you think of to crush a can?

What would happen to the can if you took out some air?
How could you remove some of the air from a can?

What Will Children Do?

What Must I Know?

PROCESSES

This activity should be done as a demonstration in the lower grades and may be done in groups in the upper grades. *Caution*: If children do the activity, it is best to use an alcohol burner instead of the Bunsen burner.

1. Obtain an empty ditto fluid can with its screw cap. *Rinse well*.
2. Add ¼ inch water to it.
3. Place it on a Bunsen or alcohol burner or hot plate for several minutes.
4. When the steam starts to rinse from the can, cork it (or screw on top) and *take it off the burner immediately. Use mittens to protect hands.* Why?
5. Mark the cork where it enters the can.

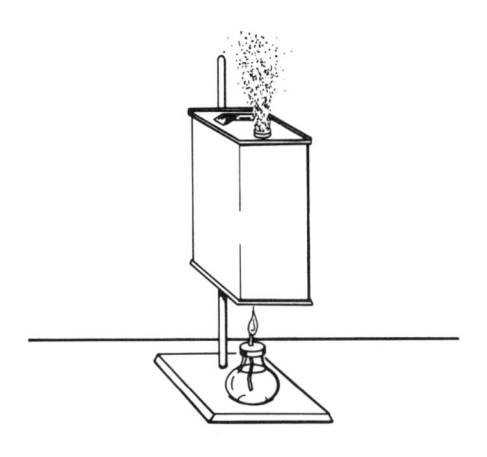

Inferring — Why did you put water in the can before heating it?
Inferring — What is happening to the air inside the can as it cools?
Hypothesizing — Now that the can is cooling, what do you think will happen to it?
Observing — What changes do you observe taking place beside the can?
Inferring — What is causing the sides of the can to be changed?
Observing — What happens to the cork?
Hypothesizing — How can you prove your answer?
Inferring — Why did this happen to the cork?
Inferring — What is now inside the can?
Hypothesizing — Why didn't the can cave in immediately.
Inferring — Why did you put the cork in the can?
Hypothesizing — What would have happened to the can if you had not put the cork in it?

What Must I Know?

Two variables affecting the outcome of this activity are (1) rapid boiling of water as seen by steam bellowing out of the opening and (2) tight fit of the cork or screw top to make air tight seal of the can.

How Will Children Use or Apply What They Discover?

1. How could you have made the can cave in faster?
2. How do some people use the ideas involved in this activity when they can fruit?
3. Why should you open a can of food before heating it?

PHYSICAL SCIENCES 167

What Must I Know? When the can is heated, the water in the can changes from water to water vapor. This warm water vapor expands into the can exerting a pressure causing some of the air in the can to escape. This process is fairly complete by the time the water has boiled for a few minutes. When the burner is removed and the can corked, the air inside the can begins to cool. As the air cools, some of the water vapor condenses back into water resulting in reduced pressure. The remaining air also contracts. Actually, a partial vacuum is formed by this process inside the can. Since there is less pressure pushing outward than there is pushing inward, the can caves in.

How Do the Effects of Moving Air Differ from Nonmoving Air? (4–8)

What Do I Want Children to Discover? The pressure of liquids or gases will be low if they are moving fast and will be high if they are moving slowly.
This principle is called Bernoulli's principle.

What Will I Need?
3 pieces of notebook paper
Pop bottle
Thread spool
Small card (3 × 3 inches)
Needle
Ping-Pong ball
Thistle tube or funnel

What Must I Know? Before doing this pupil inquiry activity, potential and kinetic energy should be explained.

What Will Children Do? PROCESSES

PART I
1. Obtain a piece of notebook paper.
2. Make a fold 1 inch wide along the long end of the paper. Make another fold at the other end as indicated in the diagram.
3. Place the paper on a flat surface.

Hypothesizing What do you think will happen if you blow *under* this folded paper?
4. Blow a stream of air *under* the paper.

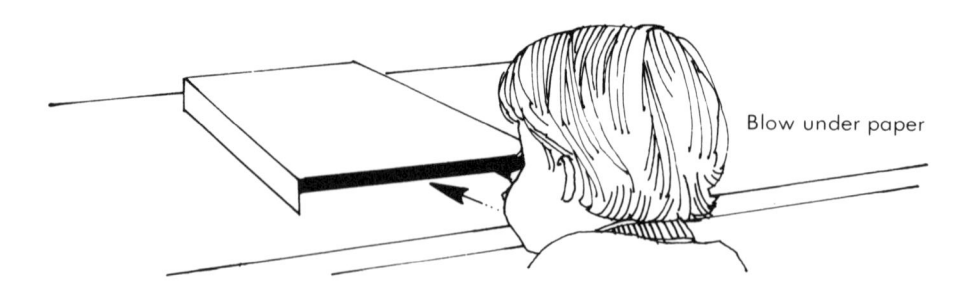

Blow under paper

Observing What do you notice about the way the paper moves? Describe how the air was circulating under the paper before you blew under it.
Comparing What do you know about the air pressure under the paper (when you blow under the paper) as compared with the air pressure exerted on top of the paper?

Hypothesizing

PART II

What do you think will happen to a wad of paper placed in the opening of a pop bottle if you blow *across* the bottle opening?
1. Obtain a small piece of paper and a pop bottle.
2. Wad the paper so it is about the size of a pea (¼ inch diameter).
3. Lay the pop bottle on its side.
4. Place a small wad of paper in the opening of the bottle, next to the edge of the opening. (See diagram.)
5. Blow across the opening in front of the bottle.

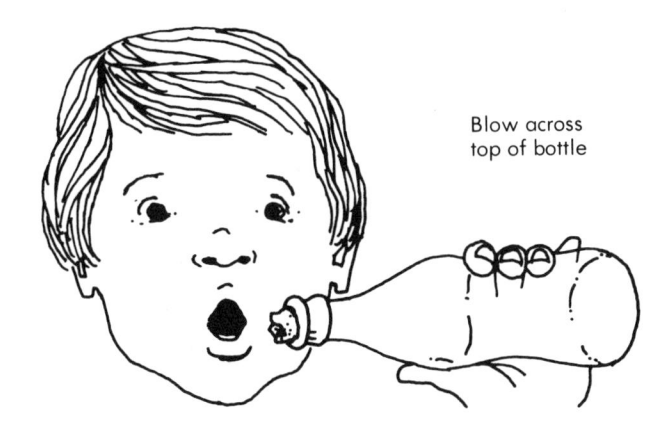

Blow across top of bottle

Observing
Inferring
Comparing

Hypothesizing

What happens to the wad of paper?
Why does the wad of paper do this?
What do you know about the air pressure *in* the bottle and the air pressure at the opening of the bottle when you blow across it?
What do you think will happen if you place a wad of paper in the opening of a pop bottle (as before) and blow directly into the bottle?
6. Blow directly into the bottle.

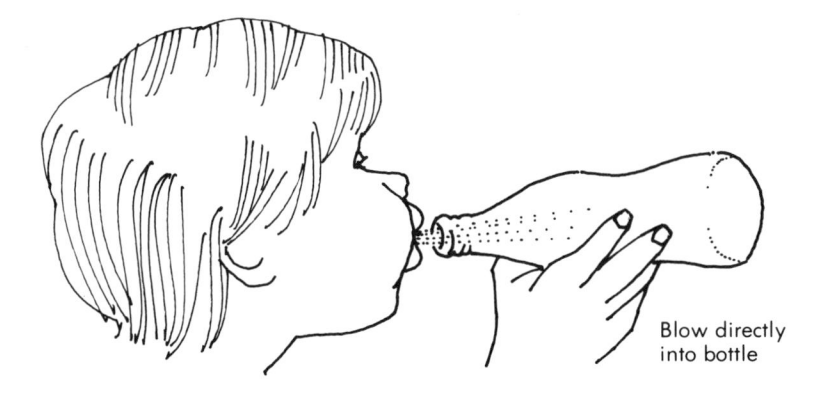

Blow directly into bottle

Observing
Inferring

7. Record your observations.
8. What do you conclude from your observations?

Hypothesizing

PART III

What will happen to a card with a needle thrust through its center if it is placed into a hole of a spool and a person blows into the hole of the spool as indicated in the diagram?
1. Obtain a spool, a small card (3 × 5 inches), and a needle.
2. Place a needle in the center of the card.
3. Stick the needle into the center of the hole of the spool. (See diagram.)
4. Hold the card, with your hand, against the bottom of the spool.

PHYSICAL SCIENCES   169

5. While blowing, let go of the card.

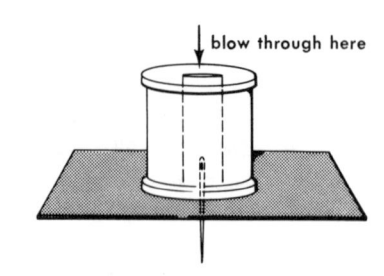

blow through here

Observing	What did you see the card do?
Inferring	Why does the card do this?
Inferring	What is holding the card?
Inferring	Why doesn't the air you blow through the hole make the card fall?
Inferring	Why do you need the pin in the middle of the paper?
What Must I Know?	Two variables affecting the outcome are (1) bottom of spool must be *very* smooth (sandpaper it if necessary) and (2) the student must get a deep breath and sustain a *long,* steady air column down the spool.

PART IV

Hypothesizing   What will happen to a Ping-Pong ball if it is placed in a large end of a thistle tube and you blow through the small end of the thistle tube?
1. Obtain a Ping-Pong ball and a thistle tube or funnel.
2. Place the Ping-Pong ball in the wide, larger opening of the thistle tube and blow through the other end with a *long,* steady breath.

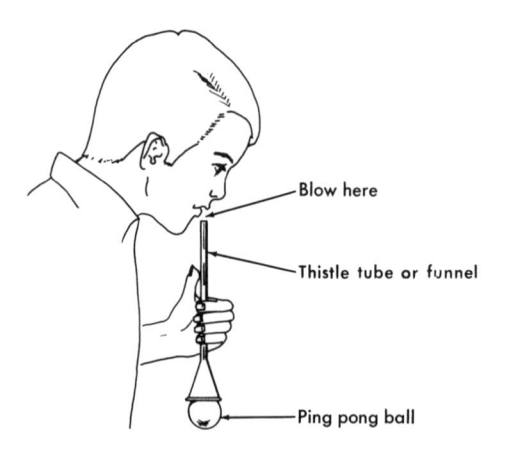

Blow here — *Thistle tube or funnel* — *Ping pong ball*

Observing	Record your observations.
Inferring	Why does the ball do what it does?
	Why does the ball rotate?

PART V

Hypothesizing   If you were to hold a piece of paper by each corner and blow across the top of the paper, what would happen to the paper?
1. Obtain a piece of paper.
2. Hold the lower left corner with your left hand and the lower right corner with your left hand. (See diagram.)

170   DISCOVERY SCIENCE RESOURCE ACTIVITIES

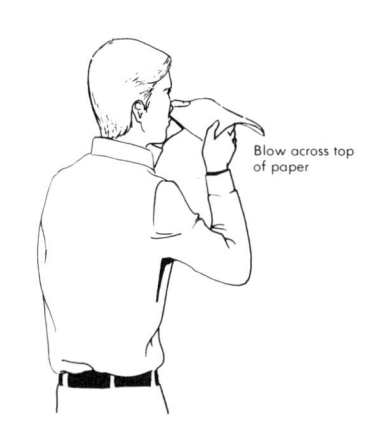

Observing
Inferring
Applying

3. Blow across the top of the paper.
   What happens to the paper?
   Why does the paper move in this direction?
   Why wouldn't it be wise to stand close to a moving train?

How Will Children Use or Apply What They Discover?

1. When you rapidly pass by another pupil's desk with a sheet of paper on it, what happens to the paper?
2. How would this principle of air pressure work when you fly a kite?
3. What happens to a girl's skirt if a car speeds close by her?
4. What would happen if the plane stopped moving in the air?
5. Why would this happen?

What Must I Know?

If a plane is moving fast enough, the reduced air pressure caused by air molecules flowing faster over the top of the wing surface provides "lift." It must keep moving to stay aloft. If it stopped in midair, it would glide down immediately.

6. In the drawing of the airplane wing below, is the air moving faster at A or B?
7. How do wing slopes vary and why?

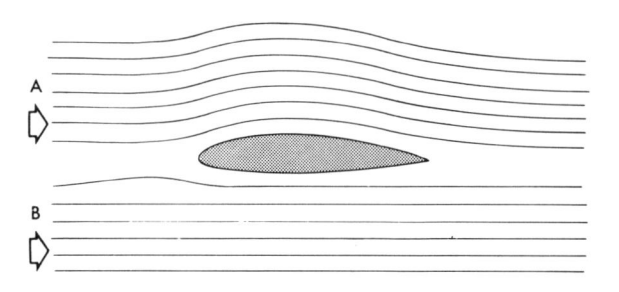

How Big Should You Make a Parachute? (K–8)

What Do I Want Children to Discover?

Air has pressure.
A larger surface will collect more air beneath it.
The more air beneath the surface of a parachute, the slower it will fall to the earth.
Large weights need larger parachutes.

What Will I Need? 3 pieces of plastic bag material
3 objects that weigh the same (something light like corks)
String or monofilament line

What Will We Discuss? Fan your hand from one side of your body to the other in front of you. What can you feel?
How does fanning affect the movement of air?
Cup your hands together and fan them from one side of your body to the other in front of you.
How does this affect the movement of air?

What Wll Children Do? PROCESSES

1. Obtain three pieces of plastic bag material and a weight for each.
2. Make three parachutes of different sizes but attach equal weights to each parachute as shown in the diagram. Make the string or monofilament line at least 1 foot long.

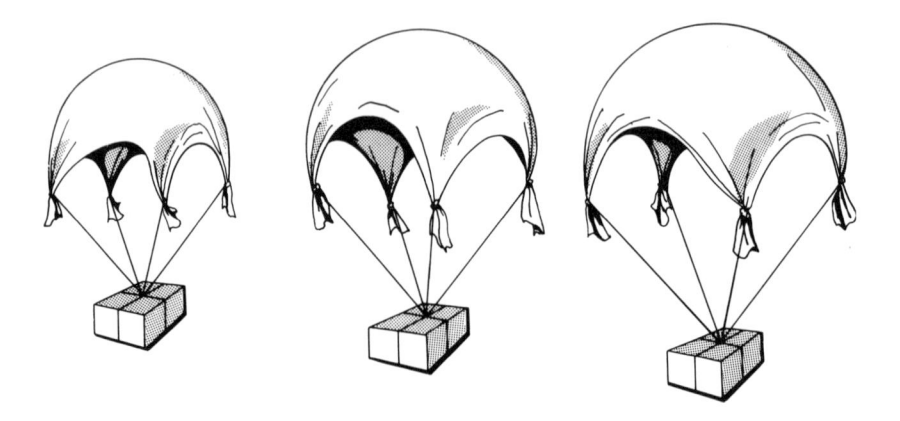

Observing
Comparing
Inferring
Applying
Inferring
Hypothesizing

3. Throw the parachutes as high into the air as possible and let them fall. If possible drop from second-floor window.
4. Record what happens.
   Which parachute falls the fastest?
   Why do you think one parachute falls faster than another?
   What are the parachutes catching as they fall?
   From this activity, what can you tell about the air?
   What do you think would happen if you used lighter weights on your parachutes?
5. Obtain some heavier weights and repeat the activity.
6. Record your observations.

Summarizing
Applying

   What general rule could you make about the size of a parachute?
   Could anything besides the size of the parachutes be a factor?

How Will Children Use or Apply What They

1. Do the activity again and change other factors.
2. How would you improve the observations and data you recorded to make them more accurate?

172 DISCOVERY SCIENCE RESOURCE ACTIVITIES

SOUND

What Is Sound and How Is It Produced and Conducted? (K–3)

What Do I Want Children to Discover?
When an object vibrates, sound may be produced.
Sound may be produced by vibrating a number of different objects.
Sound may be conducted by a number of different objects.

What Will I Need?
As many of the following things as possible should be placed on the desks of groups of four or more children:

Rubber band	6 empty pop bottles
Alarm clock	Aluminum foil
Bell	Toothpicks
Fork and spoon	Cotton
4 feet of string	Piece of thick glass
Aluminum foil pie pan	

What Will We Discuss?
How could you make a sound with a rubber band?

What Will Children Do?
PROCESSES

Designing an investigation
1. How could you make a rubber band produce a sound? How is the sound produced?

What Must I Know?
The children should stretch the rubber band and vibrate it. They should get the idea that the vibration causes the sound.

Hypothesizing
How many ways can you hear sound by placing your ear to the objects you have and causing a sound to occur?
2. Try these different ways.

Hypothesizing
What can you do to stop the noise once the sound is started?
3. Test your ideas.

Observing
Comparing
4. Determine what materials are better than others to produce sound. In what ways are these materials the same or different?

How Will Children Use or Apply What They Discover?
1. How would you produce a loud sound?
2. What would you do to make a room less noisy?
3. Why do drapes in a room make sounds softer?

How Does the Length of the Vibrating Body Affect Sound? (3–6)

What Do I Want Children to Discover?
Bodies in vibration make a sound.
The longer the vibrating body, the lower the tone.

PHYSICAL SCIENCES

What Will I Need?	Balsa wood strip 12 inches long 10 straight pins Piece of wood approximately 6 × 6 inches × 1 inch 3 tacks or nails Rubber band Hammer
What Will We Discuss?	What do you think would happen if you vibrated pins set to different depths in a strip of balsa wood? Would you get the same sound from each of the pins? If you think that different pins will give off different tones, which one would give off the highest tone?

PROCESSES

What Will Children Do?	PART I 1. Obtain a balsa strip and set pins in it to varying depths. (See the diagram below.)

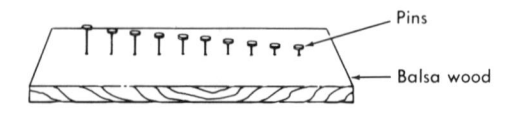

Pins — Balsa wood

Observing *Inferring* *Hypothesizing*	2. Determine if each vibrating pin gives off the same tone. What relationship is there between pin length and tone? Would nails stuck in balsa wood give the same results as the pins?
Hypothesizing	PART II 1. Look at the diagram below. Where would you pluck the rubber band to get the *highest* note?

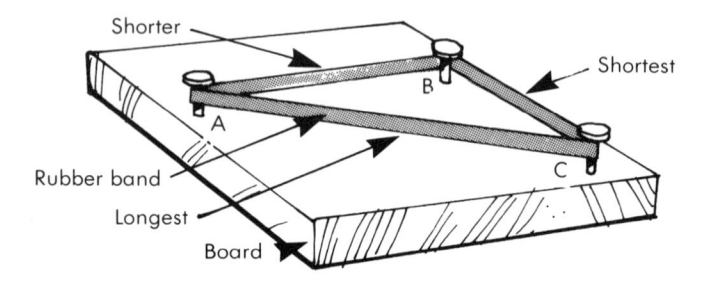

Shorter, Shortest, Rubber band, Longest, Board, A, B, C

Hypothesizing	Where would you pluck the rubber band to get the *lowest* note? 2. Obtain three tacks or nails, a rubber band, and a piece of wood. Pound the tacks or nails into the wood block as shown in the diagram. Place the rubber band around the tacks or nails. 3. Pluck the rubber band to see if your hypothesis was correct.
Comparing	4. How do the results of Part I compare with the results of Part II?
How Will Children Use or Apply What They Discover?	1. What would happen if you plucked rubber bands having the same length but *different thicknesses*? 2. What would happen to a tone if the vibrating length of the rubber band were kept the same, but *different amounts of tension* were applied? 3. How does sound travel from the rubber band to your ears?

How Does a Violin or Cello Work? (4-6)

What Do I Want Children to Discover?
Tension of string determines pitch.
If the tension is increased, the pitch is raised.
The length of the string determines the pitch.
A thick string will give a lower tone than a thin string if both are the same length.
The longer the string, the lower the tone.

What Will I Need?
Cigar box
Strings of equal and varying thicknesses—about 18 inches long (nylon fishing line may be used)
3 thumb tacks
Weights of equal and varying weight—small metal film containers filled with sand can serve this purpose
Small board to serve as a bridge—8 inches long

What Will We Discuss?
What are some things you know about sound?
If you were to stretch three strings of varying thicknesses across a cigar box and vibrate them by plucking, how would the pitch and tone of the sound vary?

What Will Children Do?
PROCESSES

1. Obtain a cigar box, thumb tacks, weights, and strings of varying thickness. Insert the thumb tacks at one end of the box. Tie strings around these tacks.
Tie the weight to the other end of the strings. Place the strings over the box.

Hypothesizing
What do you think will happen when you vibrate each string by plucking it?

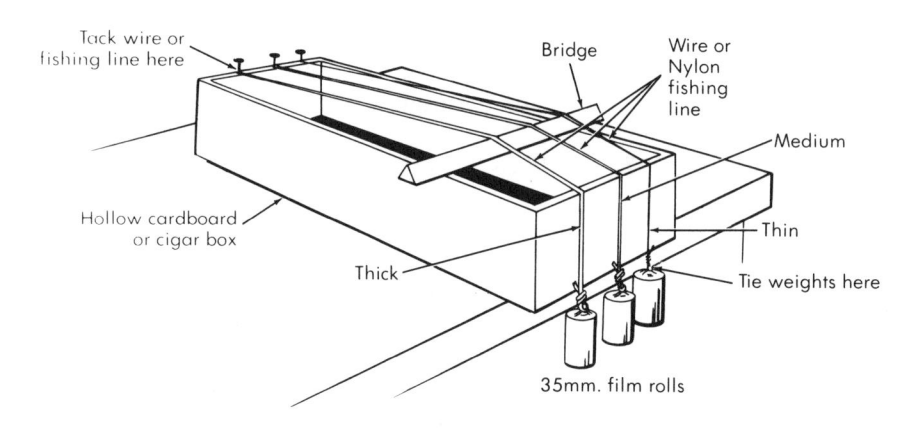

Comparing and inferring
2. Which string gives the highest tone. Why?

Comparing and inferring
3. Which string gives the lowest tone? Why?

Hypothesizing
What do you think would happen to the tone of the string if you were to take a weight off one of the thin strings and add a heavier weight to it?

4. Replace one of the weights with a heavier one.

Inferring
What does increased tension on the string do to the sound?

PHYSICAL SCIENCES 175

Hypothesizing	What other ways do you think you could arrange the strings to get different sounds? 5. Place a small triangular ruler under the strings and move it back and forth as you pluck them.
Classifying	What happened to the sound made by the strings?
How Will Children Use or Apply What They Discover?	1. What other things could you do to show how sounds can be changed from lower to higher pitch? 2. List some of the different sounds you hear every day and classify them from high to low. Why do you think they are high or low? 3. When you listen to a violin or cello, what can you say about how the sounds are produced in these instruments?

How Does the Length of an Air Column Affect Sound? (K–6)

What Do I Want Children to Discover?	The higher the pitch of a note, the more rapid the vibrations of the producing body. Pitch can be varied by adjusting the depth of an air column. The higher the water level, the shorter the air column, and the higher the pitch.
What Will I Need?	8 identical pop bottles Medium-sized beaker Soda straws Scissors
What Will We Discuss?	What would happen if you blew across pop bottles filled with varying amounts of water? Would a sound be produced? If sounds were produced, would they all be the same? If not, which would be the highest? the lowest?
What Will Children Do?	PROCESSES PART I
Hypothesizing	1. Fill eight pop bottles with varying amounts of water. What will happen if you blow across the lips of the bottles? 2. Blow across the bottles.

176   DISCOVERY SCIENCE RESOURCE ACTIVITIES

Observing	Do all bottles give off the same sound?
Observing	Which bottle gives off the highest note? the lowest note?
Hypothesizing	How could you make a musical scale out of the pop bottles?

3. Arrange the bottles to make a musical scale.
4. After you have made the musical scale, try to make a harmonizing chord. If you number the lowest note "1" and the highest note "8," what are the numbers of chords?

Inferring	5. What conclusions can you draw concerning the length of an air column and the sound produced?
Hypothesizing	What is the relationship between the length of an air column and a note produced in an open tube?

PART II
1. Give each child a soda straw and a pair of scissors.
2. Have children cut and pinch the straw to form a reed like this:

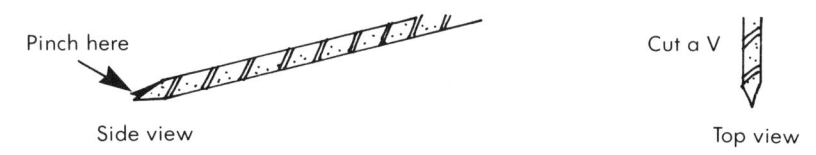

Pinch here   Cut a V

Side view   Top view

Hypothesizing	Why do we cut and pinch the straw?

3. Have children blow on the "V" cut into straw. (*Note*: They will need to experiment to get the proper lip vibration.)

Inferring	4. Now cut soda straws into different lengths to get different pitch.
Hypothesizing	What is the relationship between the length of the straws and the sound produced? How can the soda straws be used to play songs?

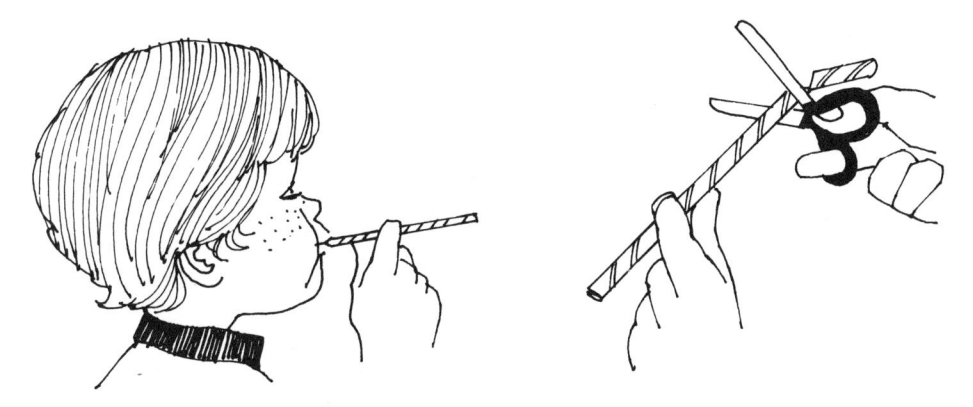

How Will Children Use or Apply What They Discover?	1. How would the results vary if you put the same amount of water in bottles of varying sizes?
	2. Does the thickness of the glass in the pop bottle affect the tone produced?
	3. Could you produce the same results using test tubes? How can the soda straws be used to play songs?
	4. Experiment to get straws calibrated in lengths in relation to octave. Then have the children play simple songs like "Mary Had a Little Lamb."
What Must I Know?	Once a scale is achieved, drop oil from a medicine dropper on top of the water in each bottle just enough to cover the top. This will prevent evaporation and change of pitch.

PHYSICAL SCIENCES 177

What Causes Sound to Be Louder? (K–6)

What Do I Want Children to Discover?
Sound is made when an object vibrates.
Loudness of a sound is caused by an object's vibrating with increased energy, but not an increased number of times per second.
The pitch is not changed by increased vibration.

What Will I Need?
Tin can with plastic lid
Piece of rubber large enough to fit over the can
Stick
Cork

What Will We Discuss?
What is pitch?
Is pitch affected by the loudness of sound?

What Will Children Do?

PROCESSES

1. Make a drum by fitting a piece of rubber over the opening of the can. An alternative is a plastic cover for sealing a coffee can. Place the cork on top of the drum.

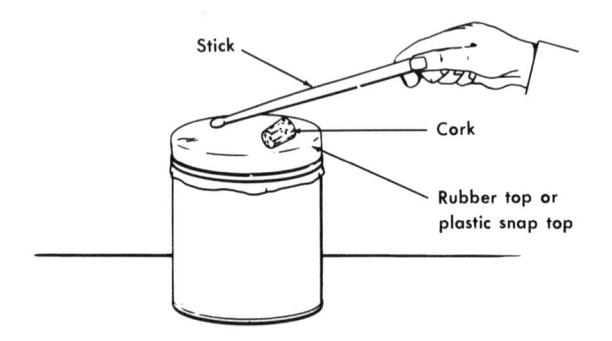

Hypothesizing
Observing
Hypothesizing
Inferring

What will happen to the cork if you hit the drum lightly?
2. Hit the drum hard. What happens to the cork?
3. What do you think will happen if the drum is hit much harder?
4. How does the pitch of the drum change by hitting it harder? Does a change in loudness occur? Why?

How Will Children Use or Apply What They Discover?

1. How would you use a piano to show what was demonstrated on the drum about pitch and loudness?
2. How can musicians play loud and soft music and still retain the pitch?
3. Explain how *you* make sound louder with your voice.

How Do Solids and Liquids Conduct Sounds? (4–6)

What Do I Want Children to Discover?
Sound can travel through solid substances.
Sound can travel through liquid substances.

What Will I Need?
2 paper cups
12 feet of strong cord or nylon fishing line
12 feet of steel wire

178 DISCOVERY SCIENCE RESOURCE ACTIVITIES

12 feet of copper wire
1 thick board about 12 × 4 inches × 1 inch
Wooden ruler
Bucket
Water
2 rocks
Buttons

What Will We Discuss? Have you ever heard people talking when you were in one room and they were in the room next to yours?
How do you suppose you could hear them through the wall?
You know that sound travels, but what substances will sound travel through?

What Will Children Do? PROCESSES

PART I
1. Obtain two paper cups and 12 feet of string or nylon fishing line.
2. With a pencil, punch a very small hole in the bottom of the paper cups just large enough to stick the string through.
3. Stick the ends of the string through each one of the paper cups. Tie a button to the ends of the string so the string will not be easily pulled from the cups.

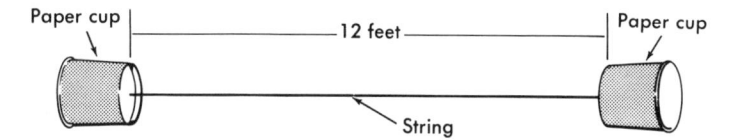

Hypothesizing

When you talk into one end of the cups, what will happen to the other cup? Why?
4. Talk into one cup while a student holds the other cup to his ear and listens.

Designing an investigation
Observing
Hypothesizing

Determine how sound can best be transferred from one cup to the other.
Record what you did to transmit the sound the best.
5. How will the sound be conducted if you use copper or steel wire? Try it.

Observing
Inferring and comparing
Hypothesizing

What happens when you use copper wire?
Is the sound carried better through copper wire than through string? Why or why not?
6. Why is it important for the string to be tight and not touching anything?

PART II
1. Obtain a small board and a pencil.
2. Hold a board to your ear. Scratch the other end with a pencil.

Observing

What happens?
3. Hold the board away from your ear and repeat the activity.

Applying

Does sound travel better through a solid or through air?

PHYSICAL SCIENCES

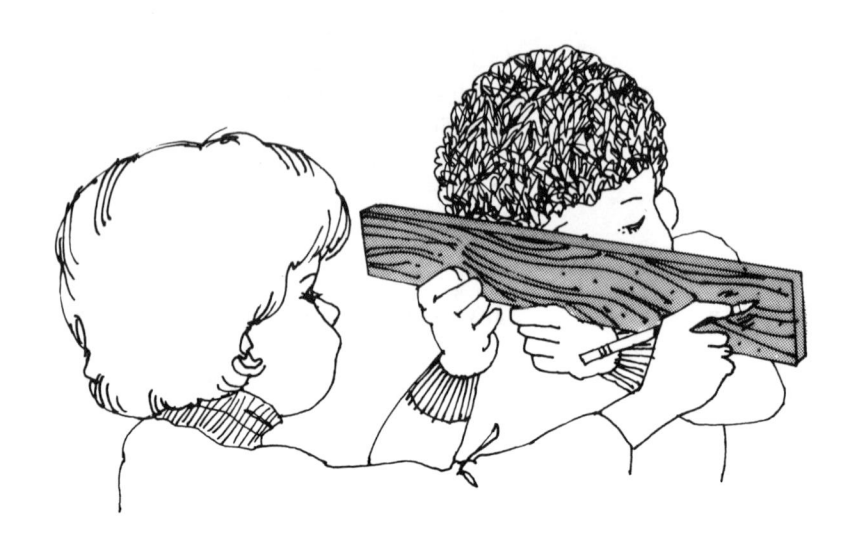

PART III
1. Obtain a wooden ruler. Hold it firmly with one hand against a desk. With the other hand pluck the overhanging part of the ruler, causing it to vibrate.

Hypothesizing
Designing an
investigation

2. What causes the sound to be produced?
   Produce a high-pitched sound by vibrating the stick.
   Produce a low-pitched sound by vibrating the stick.

Hypothesizing
Designing an
investigation

PART IV
How is sound carried in liquids?
How would you find out?
1. Obtain a large bucket full of water. Obtain two pieces of metal or two rocks and hit them together under water.

Inferring

2. Did you hear a sound when you hit them together? Why? What is your conclusion about the ability of a liquid to carry sound?

How Will Children Use or Apply What They Discover?

1. How far do you think sounds would travel between phones using copper wire, string, and steel wire?
   Design an experiment to see which conducts sound farther.
2. How would you use eight rulers to make a musical scale?
   Think about what you did to get a low pitch and a high pitch.
3. What is the purpose of making musical instruments out of wood?
4. How do you think liquids other than water conduct sounds?

180   DISCOVERY SCIENCE RESOURCE ACTIVITIES

How Can the Reflection of Sound Be Changed? (3–6)

What Do I Want Children to Discover?

When sound waves hit a hard surface, they may be thrown back.
Sound waves may be taken in and held in much the way a sponge holds water.
Some things absorb sound waves better than others.

What Will I Need?

2 large tin cans (about the size of a 2-pound coffee can)	About 1 square foot of paper
Nail	Aluminum foil
Hammer	Sheet of newspaper
About 1 square foot of cotton cloth	Shoebox with its lid
About 1 square foot of wool cloth	Alarm clock or small transistor radio
About 1 square foot of silk	Coat
	Sweater

What Will We Discuss?

What would happen to the sound of your voice if you yelled into a large can?
What would happen to the sound of your voice if you put holes in the end of the can and yelled into it?
What do you think would happen if you put something into the can before yelling into it, for example, a wool cloth?
What would you do to find answers to these questions?

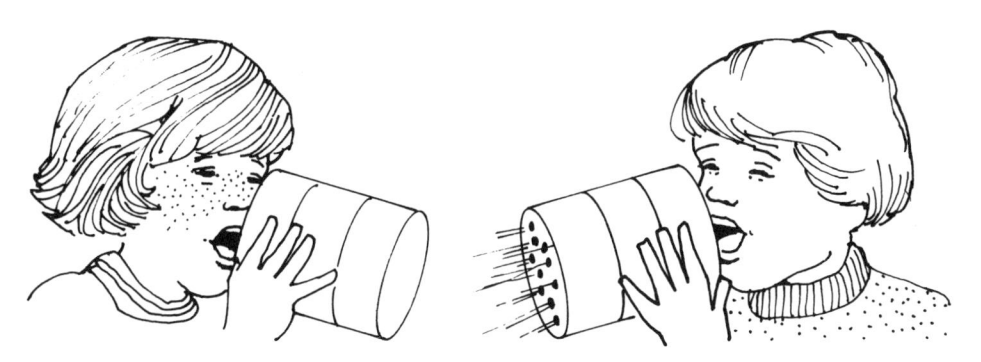

What Will Children Do?

PROCESSES

PART I

1. Obtain two large tin cans about the size of a two-pound coffee can (the larger cans are better), a nail, hammer, several pieces of cloth, newspaper, an alarm clock or small transistor radio, and aluminum foil.

Hypothesizing — What do you think will happen if you yell into one of these cans?

Observing — 2. Yell into one can and note what happens.

Inferring — What do you hear?

Inferring — What do you think happens to the sound waves when they hit the end of the can?

3. Take the other can and make six nail holes in the end of it.

Hypothesizing — What do you think will happen to the sound now if you yell into it?

Comparing — 4. Yell into the unpunctured can and then into the punctured can and note any differences.

Inferring — Why do you think the sounds coming from each can are not the same?

Hypothesizing — What happens to some of the sound waves in the punctured can?

PHYSICAL SCIENCES 181

Pieces of cotton cloth

PART II

1. Take a piece of cotton cloth and put it into the can without holes.

Hypothesizing — What do you think will happen to the sound when you yell into this can?

2. Yell into the can and note what happens.

Inferring — Why does the sound seem different?

Hypothesizing — What do you think will happen to the sound when you use other substances such as newspaper, wool, or aluminum foil?

3. Repeat steps 1 and 2 in Part II using a different substance each time, such as newspaper or wool, and note any differences in the sounds produced.

Comparing — What do you notice about the sounds produced when you use each of these substances?

4. Obtain an alarm clock or transistor radio and some wool cloth.

Hypothesizing — What do you think will happen to the sound of the alarm clock if it is wrapped in the wool cloth?

5. Turn the alarm clock on with the alarm ringing and wrap it in the wool cloth.

Observing — What happens to the sound of the alarm when the cloth is wrapped around the cloth?

6. Repeat steps 4 and 5 in Part II using a different material to wrap the clock in each time, such as cotton, silk, newspaper, a coat, and a sweater.

   Record your observations.

Inferring — Why are the sounds different for each of the articles?

7. Turn on the alarm and place the clock in the shoebox and cover the box with its top.

Inferring — Why doesn't the sound seem as loud?

Hypothesizing — What happens to the sound?

How Will Children Use or Apply What They Discover?

1. What kind of surface do you need for sound to reflect well?
2. What suggestions would you make for building an auditorium so there would be no reflected sound or echoes?
3. What things do you have in your classroom to help reduce noise or reflection of sound?

MECHANICS

Why Use an Inclined Plane? (K–8)

What Do I Want Children to Discover?

Inclined planes are used for moving objects that are too heavy to lift directly. The work done by moving an object up an inclined plane is equal to the weight of the object times the height of the plane.

Resistance × Height of the plane = Effort × Length of the plane

An inclined plane is one example of a simple machine.

What Will I Need?

Smooth board 4 feet × 6 inches
Support block 4 × 8 inches
Spring scale
Block with screw eye in one end or a rubber band wrapped around it to be pulled by a scale

What Will We Discuss?

What is an inclined plane?
Why use an inclined plane?
Where are there inclined planes on the school grounds?

What Will Children Do?

PROCESSES

1. Obtain a smooth board 4 feet × 6 inches, support block 4 × 8 inches, spring balance, and a block with a screw eye.
2. Take the 4 foot board and place the 4 × 8 inch block under one end so the end of the board is raised 4 inches. Place the block with the screw eye in it on the inclined board as shown in the diagram. Slip the hook of the spring scale through the eye of the block.

Hypothesizing

What force do you think will be required to pull the block?
Will it be greater or less than the weight of the block?
Why?

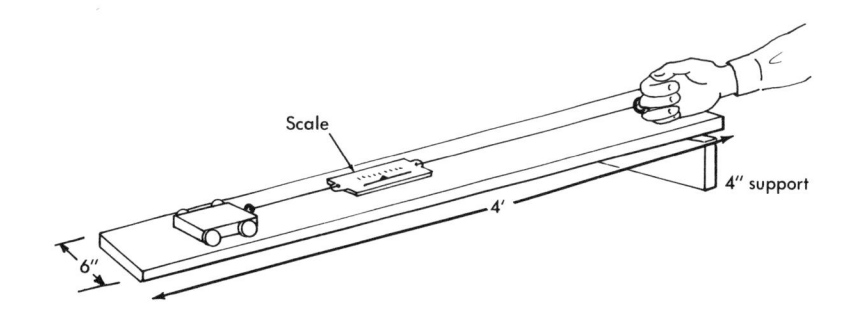

3. Slowly and evenly, pull the scale and block up the board.

PHYSICAL SCIENCES

Measuring
4. Record the amount of force needed to pull the weight up the board. Do this several times, and record your observations.
   Using the data obtained, determine the average force required to pull the weight.
5. Repeat the activity, but this time make the inclined plane steeper by changing the support block so its 8 inch dimension is under the end of the board.

Measuring
Comparing
Applying
6. Again, find the average force needed to pull the weight up the board. How do the two forces compare?
7. Lift the weight straight up, as shown in the diagram. Repeat this several times and find the average of the readings.

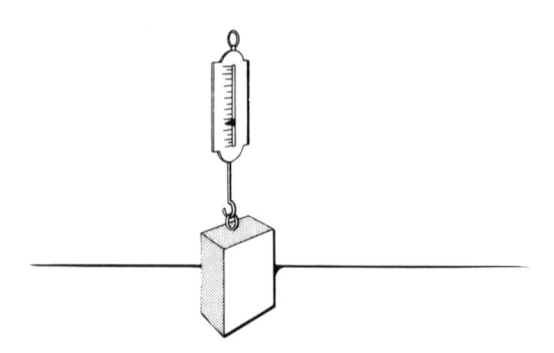

8. The following formula is used to calculate the force needed to move a weight up an inclined plane:

Resistance × Resistance distance = Effort × Effort distance

Inferring
Use this formula to calculate the force that should have been necessary to move the weight up the inclined plane.

Inferring
Why don't the experimental results and the calculated results agree exactly?

Hypothesizing
What can you say about the amount of force required as an inclined plane becomes steeper?

Hypothesizing
What is the advantage of having a long inclined plane rather than a short inclined plane if both planes are the same height?

How Will Children Use or Apply What They Discover?
1. Why don't roads go straight up and down mountains?
2. Which of the following examples is an inclined plane?
   a. Ramp
   b. Hill
   c. Gangplank
   d. Stairway
   e. Wedge
   f. Head of an axe
3. A man moved a 100 pound safe up an inclined plane 20 feet long and 2 feet high.
   How much effort did he have to use to move the safe?

Why Use a Jack? (4-8)

What Do I Want Children to Discover?
A screw is an inclined plane wrapped around a rod.
As with an inclined plane, force is gained at the expense of distance.
A large weight can be moved by a small force if the smaller force is applied over a greater distance.

What Will I Need?

Triangular pieces of paper	Model of a hill
Pencil	Board
Ring clamp	Nail
Hammer	Several screws
Screwdriver	Colored pencil or crayon
Tape measure	

What Will We Discuss?
Show the class several examples of screws and ask the following questions:
What are these called?
What purpose do they serve?
Where are they in the classroom?
What advantage do they have over nails?
What type of machine studied thus far resembles a screw?

What Must I Know?
A *screw* is a circular, inclined plane.

What Will Children Do?
PROCESSES

1. Obtain a small piece of paper and cut it in the shape of a triangle as shown in the next diagram.
   The paper will wind around the pencil. Color the edge of the paper so you can see it.

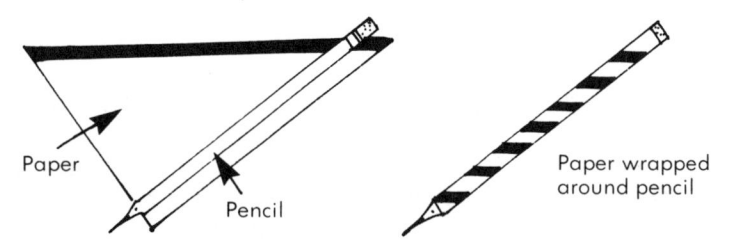

Observing — What kind of machine did the paper represent before you rolled it around the pencil?

Observing — What kind of machine did the paper represent after you rolled it around the pencil?

Comparing — How are the screw and the inclined plane related?

2. Obtain a ring stand clamp and insert a pencil as shown in the diagram below.

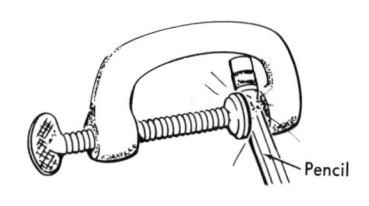

PHYSICAL SCIENCES

Hypothesizing What do you think will happen to the pencil when you move the screw inward?

Hypothesizing How much effort will have to be applied to break the pencil?

Jack

3. Look at the diagram of the jack.
Communicating Describe how the jack works.
Comparing How is the jack similar to a screw?
Inferring What is the purpose of using a jack on a car?
Inferring How is it possible for a man who weighs 150 pounds to lift a car weighing 3,000 pounds with a jack?

How Will Children Use or Apply What They Discover?

1. When are jacks used in a barber shop?
2. Where else are jacks used?
3. How many seconds would a man have to exert a force to raise a car a small distance?
4. What machine is involved in a spiral notebook?
5. If you were asked to push a heavy rock to the top of a hill, how would you move it up the hill?

What Is the Advantage of Using a Wheel and Axle? (K–8)

What Do I Want Children to Discover?

A *wheel* is a simple machine that aids in moving an object.
Every wheel has an axle. The wheel is used to turn the axle or the axle is used to turn the wheel.
The work obtained from a simple machine is equal to the work put into it less the work used in overcoming friction.
A small effort applied to a large wheel can be used to overcome a large resistance on a small wheel.
A wheel and an axle usually consist of a large wheel to which a small axle is firmly attached.
The mechanical advantage is equal to the radius of the wheel divided by the radius of the axle.

What Will I Need?

1 bicycle per class
Board
Hammer
Screw hook
Nail
Rubber bands
Balance weight

4 spools
5 or 6 round pencils
1 of the following:
   can opener,
   egg beater,
   or meat grinder

186 DISCOVERY SCIENCE RESOURCE ACTIVITIES

What Will Children Do?	PROCESSES
	PART I
Hypothesizing	1. In what way does the wheel help to move objects?
	2. Obtain a screw hook. Turn the hook into the end of a block of wood. Attach a rubber band to the hook (spring balance can be used) and measure the stretch of the rubber band as you drag the block on the floor. Use a wooden ruler and make a measurement just before and after the block begins to move.
Measuring	Record all your measurements.
Observing	3. With the rubber band on your finger, lift the block into the air and measure the stretch.
Observing	4. What change is made in the stretch of the rubber band?
	5. Now place two round pencils underneath the block and measure the stretch of the rubber band just before and after the block begins to move.

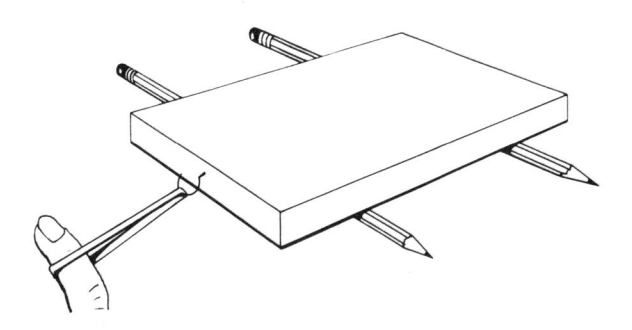

Observing	6. What happens to the stretch of the rubber band this time?
Comparing	7. What difference do the pencils make underneath the wood when you are moving it?
Comparing	8. How does your measurement change?
Inferring	9. What do you suppose is the purpose of measuring the movement of the block of wood?
Observing	10. Try the experiment again, only this time use four spools for the wheels and round pencils for the axles. Place the wood on the axle. Observe what happens as you push the block of wood very gently.

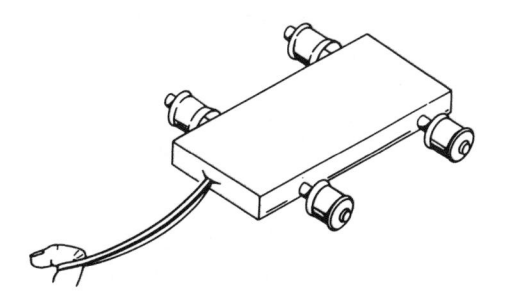

Measuring	Measure the stretch of the rubber band as you pull the block of wood.

PHYSICAL SCIENCES

Comparing 11. What difference is there in the stretch of the rubber band this time compared to moving the board without wheels?

PART II
1. Obtain a small wheel and axle or use a pencil sharpener, meat grinder, or can opener.
   Hypothesizing What is the advantage of using a wheel and an axle?
2. Hook a weight to the axle as shown in the diagram.

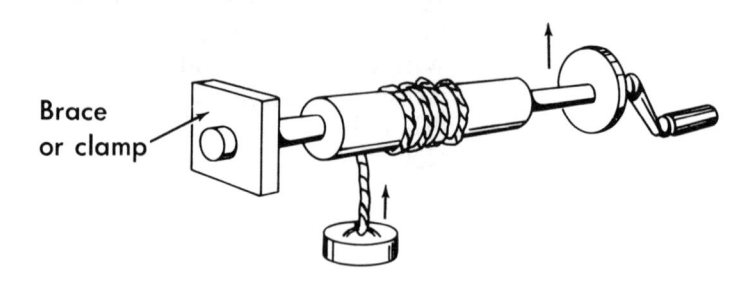

Hypothesizing What do you think will be gained if a large wheel is turned to move a small axle?
3. Turn the large wheel.
4. Count the number of turns you make to raise the weight 2 inches.

What Must I Know? A small force applied to a large wheel can be used to move a large resistance attached to the axle. This is done, however, at the expense of distance, since the large wheel has to be moved a great distance to raise the resistance a short way.

PART III
1. Observe a bicycle.
   Inferring Where on a bicycle is friction used to advantage?
   How is the bicycle wheel constructed to help reduce friction?

What Must I Know? The wheel produces less friction because there is less of its surface coming in contact with pavement than if a weight such as a person were pulled along a surface.

Observing 2. Where are the wheels and axles on a bicycle?
When you ride a bicycle, where do you apply the force?
Inferring Why do you apply the force to the small wheel?

What Must I Know? The effort is applied to the small wheel to gain speed. You move the small sprocket with a great force a short distance, and it, in turn, moves the large wheel a greater distance but with less force. Look at the diagrams of the following objects. Write below each of the diagrams whether they increase the ability to move heavier objects or increase the speed.

188 DISCOVERY SCIENCE RESOURCE ACTIVITIES

Pencil sharpener

Wheel & axle

Meat grinder

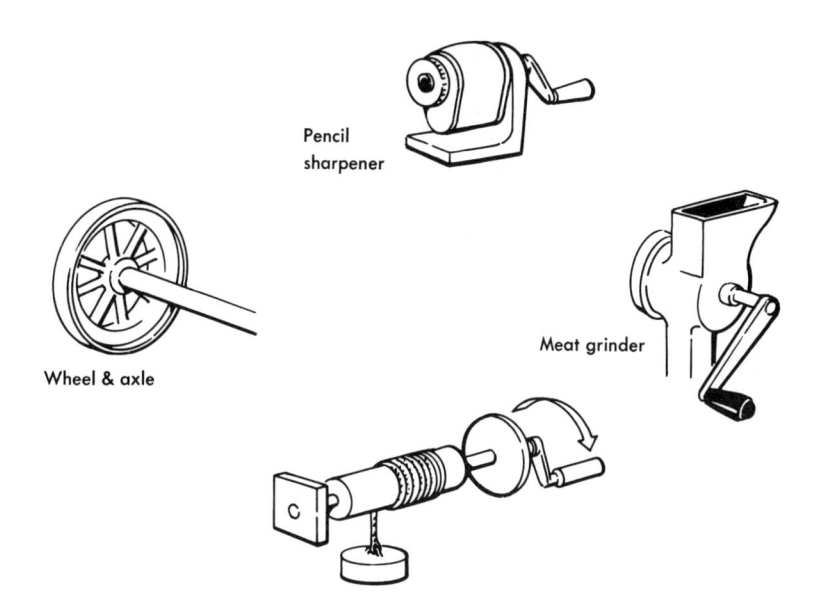

How Will Children Use or Apply What They Discover?

1. Pulling an object across the table produced a force.
   How can you tell whether you applied a greater amount of force by pulling the board without pencils under it or by using the pencils as axles?

What Must I Know?

A spring scale can be substituted for the rubber band. If you have a balance, you can determine how many pounds of force you need to pull the board across the table. If you use a rubber band you must calculate how far the rubber band stretches. The rubber band will not stretch as much the first time.

2. How are roller bearings and ball bearings used?
3. A boy wants to move a heavy desk drawer across his room to another shelf.
   How will he go about doing this with the least amount of effort and the greatest amount of speed?

Why Use a Lever? (4–8)

What Do I Want Children to Discover?

A *lever* is a simple machine.
A lever cannot work alone.
A lever consists of a bar that is free to turn on a pivot called the *fulcrum*.
By using a first-class lever, it is possible to increase a person's ability to lift heavier objects. This is called the *mechanical advantage*.
The mechanical advantage of a lever is determined by the formula:

$$\text{M.A.} = \frac{\text{Effort Arm}}{\text{Resistance Arm}}$$

PHYSICAL SCIENCES

The weight times the distance on one side of the fulcrum must equal the weight times the distance on the other side if the lever is balanced.
A first-class lever has the fulcrum between the resistance and the effort.

What Will I Need?   Ruler   Roll of heavy string or nylon fishing line
100 gram weight   Assorted weights of various sizes
20 gram weight   Platform with an arm for suspending objects

What Must I Know?   Define *resistance, force,* and *fulcrum* before beginning the activity.

What Will Children Do?   PROCESSES

1. Obtain some heavy string, a ruler, a 100 gram weight, a 20 gram weight, a ring stand, and a ring clamp.

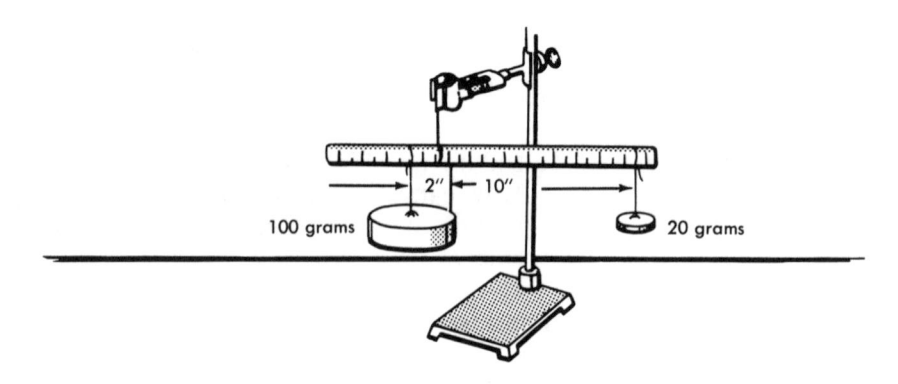

Hypothesizing

2. Assemble the apparatus as shown in the diagram.
   Where do you think you should attach the 100 gram weight and the 20 gram weight so the ruler will balance?
3. Attach the weights so the ruler is balanced.

Observing   How far is the 100 gram weight from the end of the ruler?
Observing   How far is the 20 gram weight from the end of the ruler?

4. Look at these 3 things: the string, which is suspending the ruler, the 20 gram weight, and the 100 gram weight.

Inferring   What is the relationship between the weight and distance on each side of the fulcrum?
Inferring   What are the advantages of using a first-class lever of this type?

5. Use the formula listed below to calculate the mechanical advantage (M.A.) of the lever.

$$\text{M.A.} = \frac{\text{Effort Arm}}{\text{Resistance Arm}}$$

What Must I Know?   At the completion of the activity, explain to the class that a *first-class lever* consists of a bar that is free to turn on a pivot point called the *fulcrum*. The weight moved is called the *resistance*. The force exerted on the other end of the lever is called the *effort*. Draw the diagram below on the board to illustrate this point. State that in a first-class lever, the fulcrum is always between the resistance and the effort. Have the children do some different problems as suggested by the formula:

$$\text{M.A.} = \frac{\text{Effort Arm}}{\text{Resistance Arm}}$$

Use metric measurements, if possible.

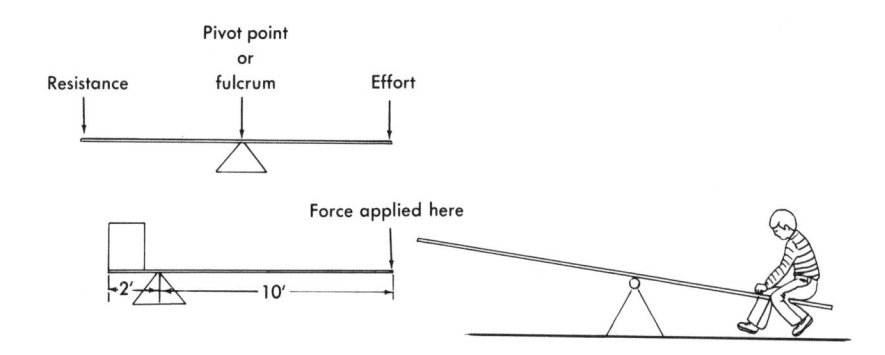

How Will Children Use or Apply What They Discover?	1. How is the M.A. affected when different weights are used? 2. What does an M.A. of 4 mean? 3. Where are first-class levers used?

How Does a Second-Class Lever Work? (4–6)

What Do I Want Children to Discover?	In a second-class lever, the weight is located between the effort and the fulcrum. The closer the resistance is to the fulcrum, the less the effort required to move the lever.
What Will I Need?	Board for a lever—a ruler will do Triangular block of wood Rock Pull-type scale Yard or metric stick
What Will We Discuss?	How is the lever in the diagram below different from a first-class lever?

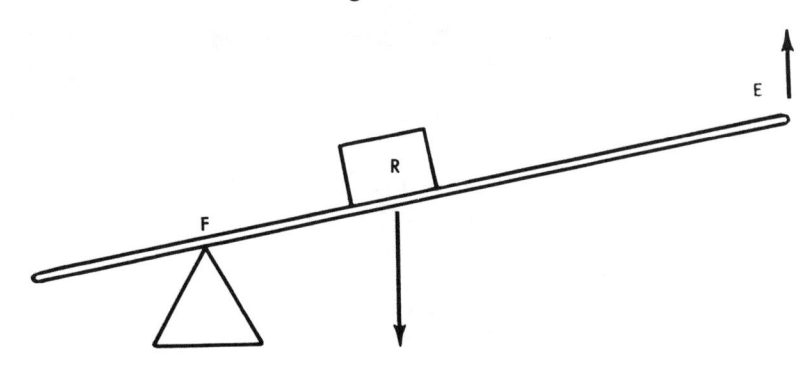

Where do you think the effort and the resistance are in the diagram?
You used a formula when working with the first-class lever in the last activity.
What do you think the mechanical advantage will be with this type of lever?

What Must I Know?	This lesson should follow the first-class lever activity.

PHYSICAL SCIENCES

What Will Children Do? PROCESSES

1. Obtain a lever, a block of wood, and a rock.
   Assemble your equipment as indicated in the next diagram.

Hypothesizing What would you do to determine the effort needed to move the rock?

2. Obtain a pull-type scale and attach it to the end of the lever farthest from the fulcrum and raise the rock by lifting the scale.

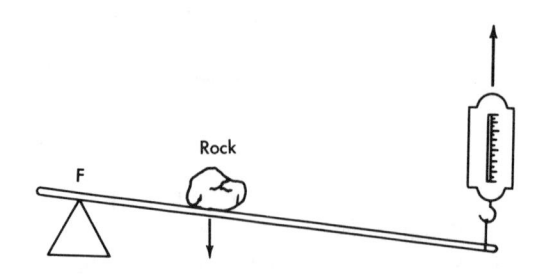

Observing
Hypothesizing

How is the scale affected when you raise the rock?
What do you think the distance of the rock from the fulcrum has to do with how much effort is needed to raise the rock?

Designing an investigation

What should you do to find out?

3. Test your ideas.

Hypothesizing

What do you think would happen if a lighter rock were used?
How would the amount of effort needed change?

How Will Children Use or Apply What They Discover?

1. How could a yardstick be used to obtain additional information in the above activity?
2. What are some examples of second-class levers?
3. How are second-class levers useful?

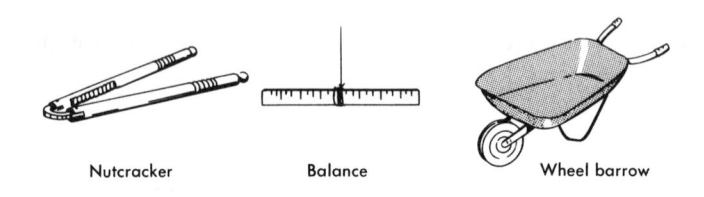

4. Which of the following are second-class levers and why?
   a. Crowbar
   b. Nutcracker
   c. Ice tongs
   d. Bottle opener
   e. Balance
   f. Teeter-totter
5. What advantage is there to having long rather than short handles on a wheelbarrow?
6. Where is it easiest to crack a nut with a nutcracker and why?

How Does a Third-Class Lever Work? (4–8)

What Do I Want Children to Discover?

In a third-class lever, the effort is always between the resistance and the fulcrum.

Third-class levers make it possible to multiply distance at the expense of force.

The mechanical advantage of a third-class lever is always less than one.

What Will I Need?

Ring stand
Ring clamp
Metre stick
Spring scale
String

200 gram weight
Scissors
Ice tongs
Ice cubes

What Will We Discuss?

How many types of levers have you learned about?
What are some examples of each type?
How many types of levers are there?

What Must I Know?

This activity should be done in groups of two.

What Will Children Do?

PROCESSES

1. Obtain a ring stand, ring clamp, metre stick, spring scale, 2 feet of string, 200 gram weight, and a pair of scissors.
2. Assemble the equipment as shown in the next diagram by fastening the end of the metre stick to the ring clamp. With the string at 10 cm., tie a loop of string around the metre stick at the 95 cm. mark. Slip the hook of the 200 gram weight over the bottom of the loop. Slip the hook of the spring scale under the metre stick at the 50 cm. mark.

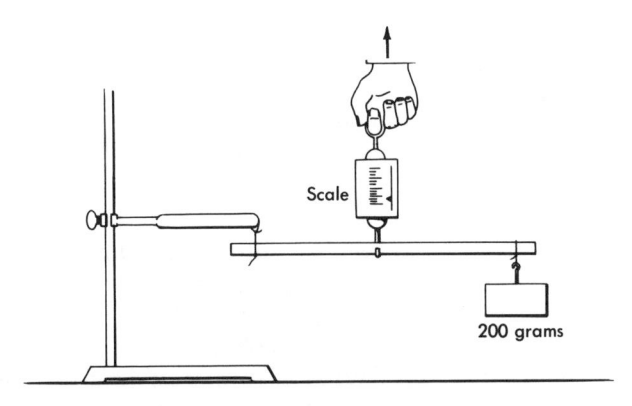

Inferring

What kind of a machine do you have?
How do you know?

Comparing

What is different about this machine compared to others you have studied? Refer to the diagram below for help.

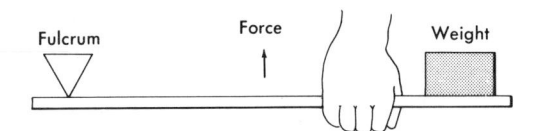

Hypothesizing

What effect will the arrangement have on the force necessary to lift a weight?

3. Using this arrangement and the scale, determine the effort necessary to support the weight as shown in the diagram.

PHYSICAL SCIENCES

Inferring

Inferring

Observing inferring

4. Do this two or three times by moving the position of the 200 gram weight. Note the lengths of the effort resistance arms in each case. (Be sure the spring balance remains between the fulcrum and the load.) What do you conclude about the effort required to lift a load with a lever of this type?

   What can you say about the mechanical advantage of this kind of lever?

5. Calculate the force that should be necessary to support the weight in each case you tested by using the lengths of resistance and the effort arms. To do this, use the following formula:

   Resistance x Resistance Arm = Effort x Effort Arm

6. Obtain some ice tongs and a piece of ice.
7. Pick up the piece of ice.
8. What type of lever are the ice tongs, and why?

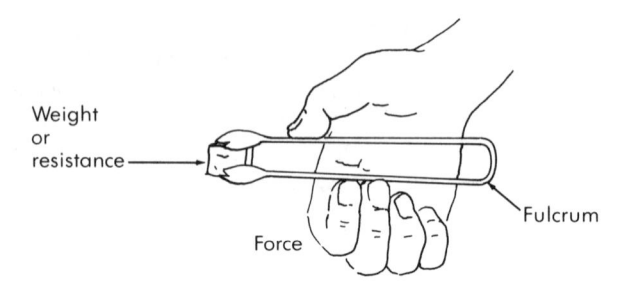

How Will Children Use or Apply What They Discover?

1. For what purpose is a third-class lever used?
2. Mark in front of each of the following what class lever each represents:
   a. ____ sugar tongs
   b. ____ tweezers
   c. ____ scissors
   d. ____ human forearm
   e. ____ crowbar
   f. ____ nutcracker
   g. ____ wheelbarrow
3. What examples of first-class levers do you find in school yards?
4. What machines may consist of two levers?
5. What advantage is there in using pliers?
6. What advantage is there in using a rake?
7. What kind of a lever would you have had if, in your experimental procedure, you had placed the spring scale beyond the weight?
8. A shovel is often used in two ways: to dig and to throw material. What class lever does the shovel represent when used to dig?
9. What class lever is represented in the action of throwing with your arm?
10. How could you change the experimental procedure and find the answers to the same questions? (Remember not to change it so you would no longer have a third-class lever.)

Why Use a Single Fixed Pulley? (4–8)

What Do I Want Children to Discover?

A single fixed pulley has no positive mechanical advantage, but it can be used to move an object in one direction while pulling in the opposite direction.

If a pulley is attached to a beam and does not move, it is called a *fixed pulley*.

The mechanical advantage (M.A.) of a pulley is computed by using the formula:

$$\text{M.A.} = \frac{\text{Resistance}}{\text{Effort}} \quad \text{or} \quad \text{M.A.} = \frac{\text{Number of strands holding up the resistance}}{\text{Number of strands holding up the effort}}$$

What Will I Need?

Single fixed pulley 50 gram weight
Thin cord or nylon fishing line 100 gram weight
Pull-type scale

What Will We Discuss?

What do you think will happen if you attach a weight and a scale to the ends of a pulley and attempt to move the weight?

How will the scale be affected when you raise the weight?

What Will Children Do?

PROCESSES

1. Obtain a single fixed pulley, a pull-type scale, and a 50 gram weight. When assembled, your equipment should be similar to the diagram.
2. Pull the scale, lift the weight, and record your observations.

Inferring

Why does the scale measure more force than the weight being lifted?

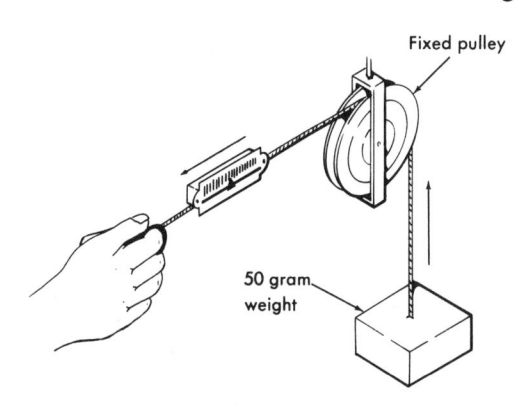

Hypothesizing
Inferring
Measuring

What do you think happens to the extra force?
Why should the activity be done more than once?

3. Complete the activity several times and record each measurement.
4. Compute the average measurement.

The formula listed below is used to compute mechanical advantage:

$$\text{Mechanical Advantage (M.A.)} = \frac{\text{Resistance weight}}{\text{Effort weight}}$$

Inferring

Where in the formula will you use the measurement recorded from the scale?

PHYSICAL SCIENCES 195

Gram weight | 50 | ? |

Applying — Where in the formula will you use the gram weight used in the activity?

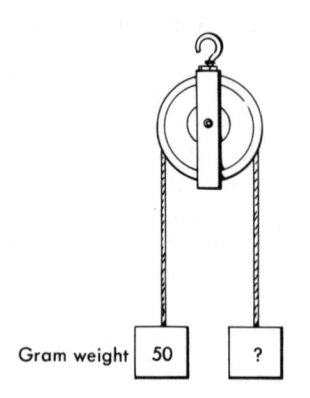

5. Compute the mechanical advantage of a single fixed pulley as used in your activity.

Applying — What can you tell about the M.A. of the pulley in the preceding diagram?

Hypothesizing — What would you have to do in the situation shown in the diagram below to keep the weight in place?

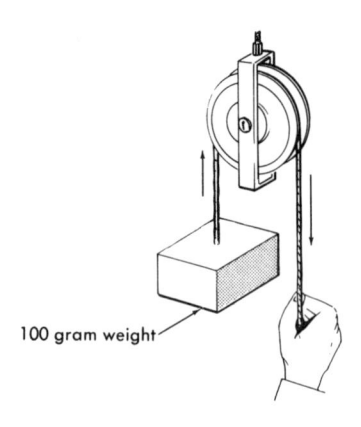

100 gram weight

Summarizing — What are the advantages in using the single fixed pulley?

How Will Children Use or Apply What They Discover?

1. How would you make a single fixed pulley so it produced very little friction?
2. Why is there an advantage to pulling *down* instead of up with a pulley arrangement?

Why Use a Movable Pulley? (4–8)

What Do I Want Children to Discover?

Pulleys that move with the resistance are called *movable pulleys*.

Movable pulley systems have a mechanical advantage greater than one.

The mechanical advantage of a movable pulley system is equal to the number of strands holding up the resistance.

196 DISCOVERY SCIENCE RESOURCE ACTIVITIES

What Will I Need?   Ring stand for attaching pulleys   50 gram weight
2 single pulleys   Yard or metric stick
Pull-type scale   String or nylon fishing line
100 gram weight

What Will Children Do?   PROCESSES

1. Obtain a ring stand and a clamp for attaching a pulley, a single pulley, a pull-type scale, and a 100 gram weight. Assemble your equipment as shown in the diagram.

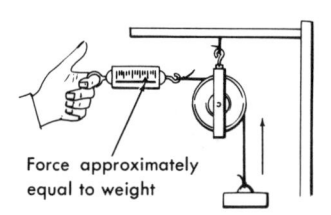

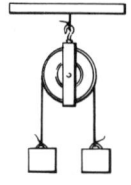

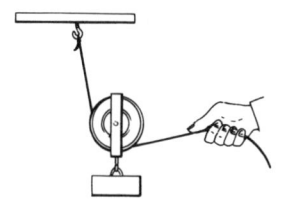

Hypothesizing   How much do you think you will have to pull on the scale to raise the 100 gram weight?
2. Pull on the scale and raise the weight.

Observing   How is the scale affected when you raise the weight?
Measuring   3. Repeat this activity several times and record each measurement.
Hypothesizing   What do you think will happen when you use two pulleys to raise the 100 gram weight as shown in the diagram below?
4. In addition to the equipment you have, obtain a single fixed pulley and a 50 gram weight. Assemble your equipment as shown in the diagram.

Observing   5. Pull the 50 gram weight and record your observations.
6. Remove the 50 gram weight and attach the scale.

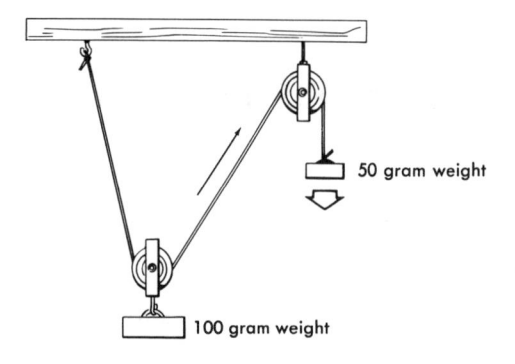

Your equipment should be constructed as shown in the diagram below.
Hypothesizing   How will the scale be affected when you raise the 100 gram weight?
7. Raise the weight by pulling on the scale.
Observing   What happens to the scale when you raise the weight?
Measuring   8. Repeat the activity several times and record each measurement.
Inferring   Why is there an advantage in using this type of pulley system?

PHYSICAL SCIENCES   197

Hypothesizing	9. Remove the scale and once again attach the 50 gram weight. How far do you think the 50 gram weight will move when it raises the 100 gram weight?
Hypothesizing	How far do you think the 100 gram weight will move when it is raised by the 50 gram weight?
	10. Obtain a yard or metric stick.
Observing	11. Move the 50 gram weight and measure how far both the weights move.
Measuring	12. Repeat this part of the activity several times and record your measurements.
Summarizing	What can you say about pulleys from the measurements you just recorded?
	13. Look at the measurements you recorded when 1 pulley was used and those you recorded when 2 pulleys were used. What does the information tell you about pulleys?
How Will Children Use or Apply What They Discover?	What kind of pulley system would be needed to raise a piano weighing 300 pounds? Draw a sketch of that pulley system.

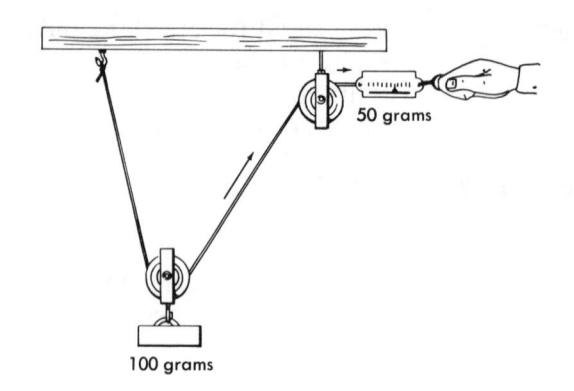

MAGNETISM AND ELECTRICITY

What Is a Magnet? (K–6)

What Do I Want Children to Discover?

A magnet has two poles. One end is called the *north,* and the other is called the *south*.
Like poles repel.
Unlike poles attract.
Around every magnet is an area called the *magnetic field* made up of magnetic lines of force.

What Will I Need?

2 round bar magnets
String
Steel needle
Cork
Glass or plastic pan
Water
2 rectangular bar magnets

What Must I Know?   Materials listed above are for a group of two or three children. Set up stations and equip each as indicated above.

What Will We Discuss?   Display a round bar magnet to the class and ask:
What is this called?
What is it made of?
How can it be used?
What are the properties or characteristics of a magnet?
What things can a magnet do?
What do you think will happen if two magnets are placed side by side?
How could you find out?

What Will Children Do?   PROCESSES

PART I
1. Obtain 2 round magnets. Place one magnet on the table.
   Place the second magnet near it.
Observing   Observe what happens.
2. Reverse one of the magnets.
Observing   Observe what happens.
   What happens when you put the second magnet beside the first one?
   What happens when you turn one magnet around?
   Why do you think one magnet rolls when the other comes near it?
   What did you notice when the magnets pulled together?
   What did you notice when the magnets pushed apart?
Inferring   How do you know from this that both ends of the magnet are not the same?
Inferring   What did you do to make the magnets push apart?
Inferring   What did you do to make the magnets pull together?

PART II
1. Obtain two rectangular or round bar magnets.
2. Tie a string around the middle of one of the magnets.

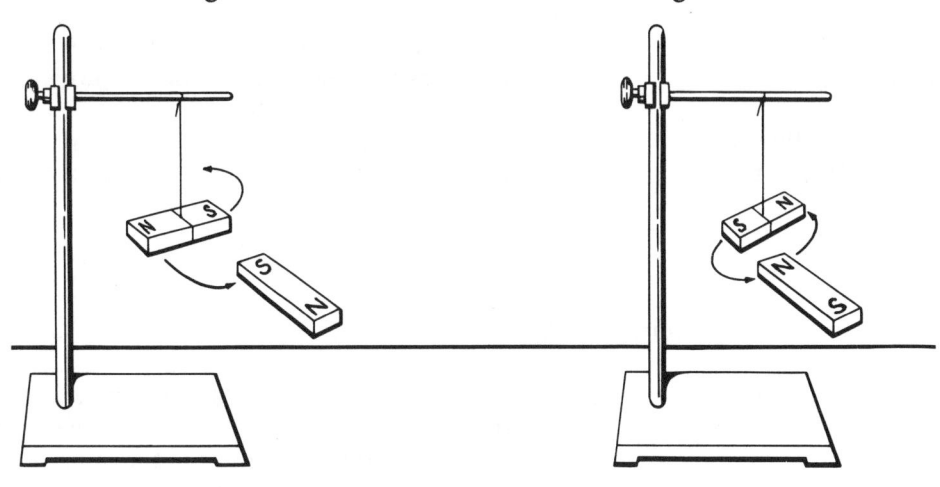

3. By holding the string, suspend the magnet in air.
Hypothesizing   What do you think will happen when another magnet is brought near the suspended one?
4. Bring another magnet near the suspended one.
Inferring   Why do you think the magnet moves?

PHYSICAL SCIENCES 199

Hypothesizing	What do you think will happen when you reverse the magnet in your hand?
Observing	5. Reverse the magnet and bring it near the suspended one.
Inferring	Why does the suspended magnet react differently when you approach it with the other end of the magnet in your hand?
Inferring	What causes the magnet to react in different ways?
Inferring	How do you know there is a force present when it cannot be seen?
Explaining	What is a force?

What Must I Know?   Point out that a *force* is a push or pull. This can be shown by pushing or pulling a child in a chair.

PART III
1. Obtain a steel needle, a magnet, and a pan with an inch or two of water in it.

Hypothesizing   What can you find out about the needle and the magnet?

2. Magnetize a needle by holding a magnet in one hand and stroking a needle downward several times. Lay the needle on the cork so the needle is in a horizontal position. Float it in the water you have placed in a pan.

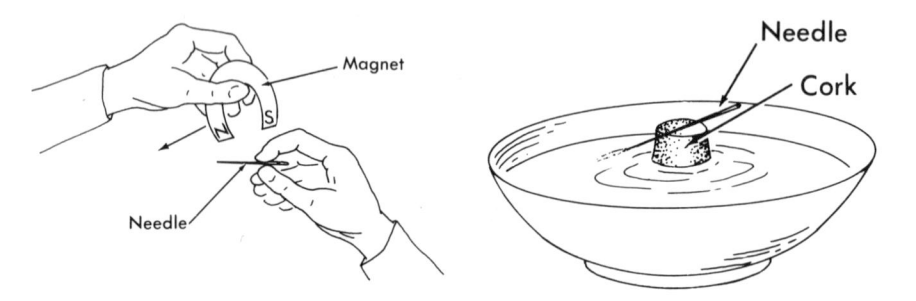

3. Bring a magnet near the cork and needle.

Inferring	Why do the cork and needle move when you bring a magnet near them?
Inferring	What happens to the needle when it is stroked with the magnet?
Summarizing	What causes the cork and needle to move?

How Will Children Use or Apply What They Discover?
1. How does a compass work?
2. How could you use a magnet to make a compass?

What Is a Magnetic Field? (K–3)

What Do I Want Children to Discover?   Around every magnet there is an area where the magnet can change the direction of iron filings. This is called the *magnetic field*.
Not every part of the magnetic field around a magnet is the same.

What Will I Need?   Bar magnet   String
Paper clip   3 books

What Will We Discuss?   What happens when a magnet is brought near a steel object?
Why doesn't the magnet have to touch the object to move it?
What causes the object to move when a magnet comes near?

200   DISCOVERY SCIENCE RESOURCE ACTIVITIES

What part of the magnet has the most pull?
How can you show there is a force around a magnet?

What Will Children Do? PROCESSES

1. Obtain a paper clip, some string, heavy books, and a magnet.
2. Tie the string around one end of the paper clip.
3. Put the other end of the string on the table and put a heavy book or two on it.
4. Hold up the string and paper clip. Place the magnet just above the paper clip and place another book on it. Be sure the clip and magnet do not touch as indicated in the diagram.

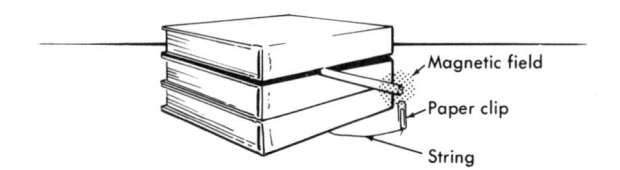

Observing 5. What happens to the clip when you let go of it?
Inferring Why does the paper clip stay suspended?
Inferring Why doesn't gravity pull the clip down again?
Inferring What force overcame gravity?

6. Bring another magnet close to the clip.
Observing What happens to the clip?
Inferring Why do you think this happens?
Inferring How did the second magnet affect the pull of the first magnet?

What Must I Know? The children should discover that around every magnet there is an area capable of attracting or repelling objects. This area is called the *magnetic field*.

How Will Children Use or Apply What They Discover?
1. Where is the field of force of a magnet?
2. How can you find out where the field is?

How Does a Magnetic Field Appear to Look? (3–8)

What Do I Want Children to Discover?
In a magnetic field there are magnetic lines of force.
The earth has a magnetic field.
The concentration of the lines of force around any part of the magnet determines the strength of the field at that point.
Magnetism will pass through most solid objects.

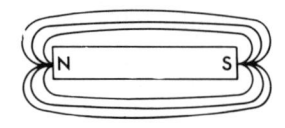

PHYSICAL SCIENCES   201

What Will I Need?   Bar magnet   Iron filings
                            Piece of cardboard or thick paper   Colored pencil or crayon

What Will We Discuss?   What do you call the areas of force around a magnet?
                            What parts of the magnet attract objects with the greatest pull?
                            Why doesn't a magnet need to touch a magnetic object to attract it?
                            What part of a magnet do you think has the greatest field of force around it?
                            What can you do to show where most of the force is located around a magnet?

What Must I Know?   Make a study sheet for the children to use in showing lines of force and the magnetic field similar to the diagram above. Have them label the poles, magnetic lines of force, and magnetic field.

What Will Children Do? PROCESSES

                            PART I
                            1. Obtain some cardboard or thick paper, some iron filings, a colored pencil or crayon, and a bar magnet.
                            2. Place the magnet on the table and put the paper or cardboard over it.
                            3. Sprinkle some iron filings on the cardboard.

Observing   How are the filings scattered around the cardboard?
Inferring   How far out are the filings affected by the magnet?
                            What do you notice about the way the filings arrange themselves?

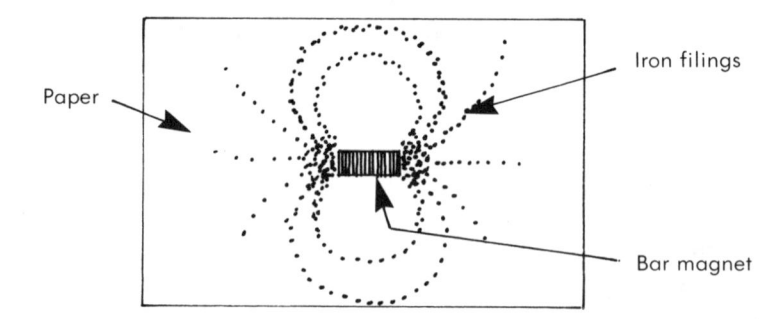

Observing   Are the filings in lines or are they solidly grouped?
Observing   Where is the greatest concentration of filings?
                            These lines are called *magnetic lines of force.*
Comparing   In what way is the pattern that these lines make similar to a map?
Inferring   Where is the greatest force located around a magnet and why?

What Must I Know?   The iron filings have become magnetized by induction. They organize themselves into little magnets that point north and south and that are arranged in lines. These are called magnetic lines of force. They run from the north to the south poles without crossing. The more lines of force there are in an area, the stronger the magnetic field. Since the ends of the magnet have the most lines, they have the greatest force.

                            How is the earth's magnetic field distributed?
                            What similarities can you think of concerning a magnet and the earth?

What Must I Know?

Make mimeographed lab sheets showing lines of earth's field of force and magnetic field similar to the diagram below and hand it out to the children to discuss.

Inferring
Designing an investigation
Hypothesizing
Assuming
Hypothesizing

In what direction does a compass point?
Why does a compass point north?
How can you show the lines of force of the earth's field?

How do you think the lines should be placed around the earth?
How do you know that the earth has a magnetic pole?
Where should the magnetic poles be placed?
How can you show this?

PART II

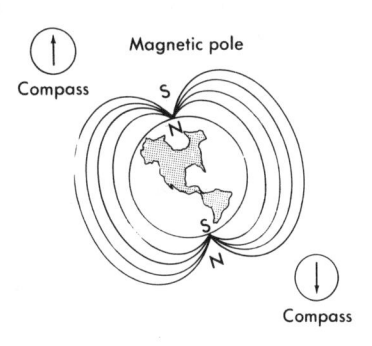

[Diagram: Earth with magnetic field lines, labeled "Magnetic pole", "Compass" at top and bottom, with N and S poles marked]

1. Obtain a lab sheet showing the earth.
2. Label the poles of the earth.
3. Color the magnetic field.
4. Label the magnetic lines of force.
5. Show the direction a compass will point on the lab sheet.

Summarizing
Inferring or interpreting
Summarizing

What pole of the magnet of a compass will really point north?
Why does that end of the compass needle point north?

Summarizing
Inferring
Summarizing

What can you say will always happen to the needle of a compass in reference to the poles of the earth?
What other things can you say about the magnetic field?
How do you know that magnetism can pass through solid substances?

6. Draw on a piece of paper the lines of force and the magnetic field of a bar or round magnet.

How Will Children Use or Apply What They Discover?

1. How does the magnetism of other planets vary from the earth's?
2. What else do you know of that has a north and a south pole?

What Is Static Electricity? (4–8)

What Do I Want Children to Discover?

All bodies are capable of producing electrical charges.
Conductors allow electrons to move, but insulators do not allow electrons to move easily.
Like charges repel; unlike charges attract.

PHYSICAL SCIENCES 203

What Will I Need? Lucite or resin rod or a hard rubber comb
Wool
Flour
Glass rod
Small pieces of paper
Large piece of paper
Balloon
Tap water
Piece of silk about the size of a small handkerchief

What Will We Discuss? What can you state about the reactions of poles of magnets toward one another?
What is the energy that we use to produce light and to operate many machines and household equipment?
What things can produce electricity?
How can you find out if all charges of electricity are the same?

What Will Children Do? PROCESSES

PART I
1. Obtain the following materials: a lucite or resin rod or a hard rubber comb, wool, flour, a glass rod, small pieces of paper, a large piece of paper, a balloon, tap water, and a piece of silk.
2. Take the resin rod (or hard rubber comb) and rub it with the wool cloth.

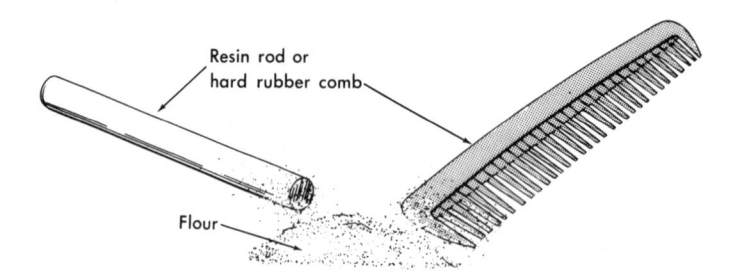

Hypothesizing

Observing
Hypothesizing

Observing

What do you think will happen when the rod is touched to the flour?
3. Touch the rod to some flour.
What happens to the flour?
Why do you think the flour is affected by the rod?
4. Clean the rod, rub it again, and touch it to small pieces of paper.
What does the rod do to the paper?

PART II
5. Rub the rod briskly with the wool cloth.
6. Turn on a water tap so a very slow stream of water comes out.

Hypothesizing What do you think will happen to the stream when the rod is moved close to it?
7. Move the rod close to the stream.

Observing What happens as the rod comes near?

204 DISCOVERY SCIENCE RESOURCE ACTIVITIES

Inferring   Why does the water react as it does?

Inferring   Why do you think it reacts as it does without being touched?

What Must I Know?   The students should note how close they have to bring the rod before it affects the stream of water. Develop the concept that there *is* an invisible field of electrical force around the rod that either pushes or attracts the water. This force cannot be seen, but it must be there because it affects the stream of water. Define *force* as a push or pull. In this case, the water is pushed or pulled without being touched by moving the rod toward and away from the water.

Designing an investigation   How can you find out if the rubbing of the cloth on the rod causes the electrical force?

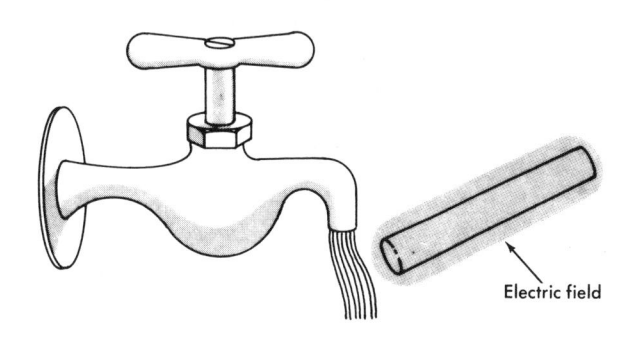

8. Rub the rod again with the cloth.
9. Now rub your hand over the rod.

Hypothesizing   What do you think will happen to the stream of water?

10. Repeat the procedure by approaching the slow stream of water with the rod.

Observing   What effect does the rod have on the water this time?

Inferring   Why doesn't the rod have the same effect?

Inferring   What happens to the charge that the wool cloth induces in the rod?

Inferring   Why do you think the charge fails to last?

What Must I Know?   When the resin rod is rubbed with wool or fur, electrons are rubbed off these materials onto the rod. The rod, however, is an insulator, so the electron movement is slight. The rod becomes negatively charged since each electron produces a small amount of negative charge. When a hand is rubbed over the rod, the rod becomes discharged because the electrons leave the rod and enter the hand. The rod is then neutral.

Explain the difference between a *conductor* and an *insulator*.

PART III

Summarizing   1. After your discussion concerning conductors and insulators, would you say the rod is a conductor or an insulator?

Inferring   Why do you think so?

2. Obtain two balloons.
3. Inflate the balloons.
4. Tie a string to each balloon and suspend it from a bar as shown in the next diagram.

PHYSICAL SCIENCES

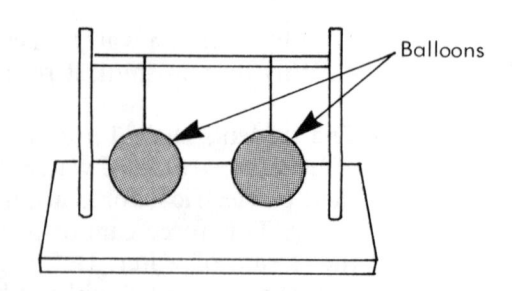

	5. Rub each balloon with the wool cloth.
Observing	What do the balloons do?
Inferring	Why do they repel each other?
Summarizing	Do you think the balloons are conductors or insulators?
Hypothesizing	What do you think will happen if a charged resin rod is brought near the balloons?
	6. Rub the resin rod with wool and place it near the balloons.
Observing	In which direction do the balloons move?
Inferring	Why do you think they were repelled by the rod?

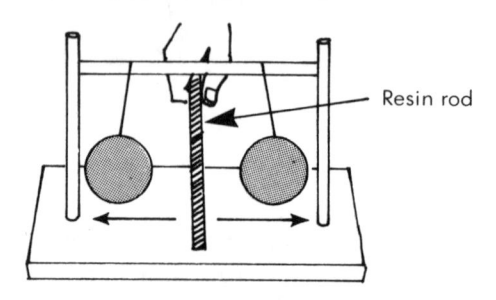

Assuming	Do you think the balloons have a like or unlike charge? Why?
Hypothesizing	What do you think will happen to the balloons if you touch them with a glass rod?
What Must I Know?	These balloons were charged in the same way; therefore, each must have the same charge. When they do have the same charge, they repel each other because like charges repel.

7. Rub the glass rod with the piece of silk.
8. Place it near the balloons.

Observing	What happens as it comes near the balloons?
Comparing	How does the glass rod affect the balloons in comparison to the resin rod?

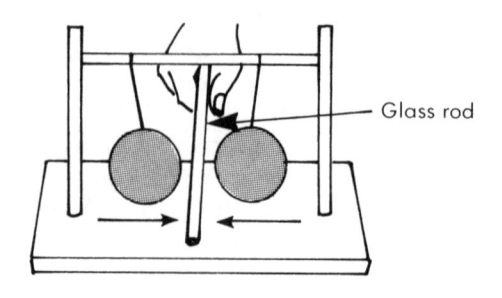

206   DISCOVERY SCIENCE RESOURCE ACTIVITIES

Comparing	What can you say about the charge on the resin rod compared to the glass rod?
	PART IV 1. Rub one of the inflated balloons against the piece of wool. 2. Place it next to a wall. (See next diagram.)
Hypothesizing	What do you think will happen to the balloon?
What Must I Know?	The glass rod will have a positive charge since electrons were rubbed off the rod onto the silk. It will attract the balloon because the balloon was negatively charged by the resin rod, and unlike charges attract.
Inferring	Why doesn't the balloon fall?
Inferring	Is the force that pulls the balloon to the wall greater or less than the gravitational force pulling the balloon down to earth?

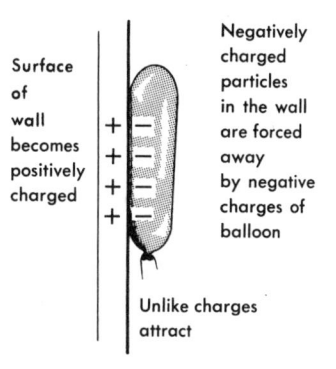

Inferring	What happened to the negatively charged particles in the wall when the balloon came near?
Summarizing	What can you say about charging matter after following the above steps?
Summarizing	What is a conductor?
Summarizing	What is an insulator?
What Must I Know?	When you rub the balloon, it becomes negatively charged. When it is placed next to the wall, its negative charge forces the electrons in the wall away from the surface, leaving the surface positively charged. The balloon sticks because the unlike charges attract. The balloon is negative and the wall surface is positive, as is indicated in the diagram.
How Will Children Use or Apply What They Discover?	1. What is electricity? 2. How can you use a magnet to make electricity?

How Can You Make Electricity by Magnetism? (4–8)

What Do I Want Children to Discover?	Around a magnet there are magnetic lines of force. If you break the magnetic lines of force, you can make electricity. A *force* is defined as a push or a pull.
What Will I Need?	Copper wire (about 3 yards) Compass Bar magnet

PHYSICAL SCIENCES 207

What Will We Discuss? How is electricity used?
How does electricity get to your home for you to use?
What happens when you slide your feet across a wool rug?
What can you produce when you rub a glass rod with wool?
What is the area of force around a magnet called?
What is a force?
How can you use a magnet to produce electricity?

What Will Children Do? PROCESSES

1. Obtain a length of wire (about 3 yards), a bar magnet, and a compass.
2. Take the wire and wrap it 20 to 30 turns around the compass as indicated in the diagram.

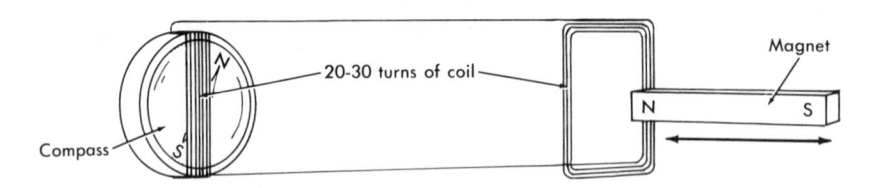

Inferring
Inferring
Inferring
Designing an investigation
Observing

3. Loop the other end of the wire several times as shown in the diagram.
What happens when electricity goes through a wire?
What do you think the area around the wire could be called?
What has the electricity produced?
How do you think magnetism could be used to produce electricity?

Observing
Inferring
Applying
Hypothesizing
Hypothesizing

4. Take the bar magnet and plunge it back and forth inside the loops of wire. Instruct your partner to watch what happens to the compass.
What happens to the compass?
Why do you think the compass needle does what it does?
What attracts the compass needle?
What do you think causes the needle to be deflected?
Where do you think the magnetism was produced to cause the compass needle to move?

Inferring or interpreting

If there is magnetism produced in the wire around the compass, what do you think the plunging of the magnet through the loops of wire has to do with it?

Inferring or interpreting
Summarizing
Summarizing
Summarizing
Summarizing

When is electricity produced in the wire?

What is the force of a magnet called?
What does a magnet do to a magnetizable object?
What does a magnet do to a nonmagnetizable object?
Explain how magnetism can be used to produce an electrical current.

What Must I Know? Around every magnet there is an area that can push or pull objects such as iron filings. This area is thought to consist of lines of force. When these lines of force are broken by plunging the magnet back and forth through a coil of wire, electricity is made in the wire. Electricity is defined as a flow of electrons along the wire, making an electrical current. Whenever there is an electrical current produced, there will be a magnetic field around the wire. This magnetic field causes the magnet (compass in this activity) to move. Using magnets to produce electricity is the principle involved in making electricity in a dynamo. Make certain that the compass is far enough away from the magnet to avoid direct magnetic influence.

208 DISCOVERY SCIENCE RESOURCE ACTIVITIES

How Will Children Use or Apply What They Discover? How can you use electricity to make a magnet?

How Can You Make an Electromagnet? (4–8)

What Do I Want Children to Discover?

When electricity passes along a wire, it produces a magnetic field around the wire that acts like a magnet.
A magnetic field can make iron temporarily magnetic.
The more current flows through a wire in a unit of time, the more magnetism is generated around the wire.
If a circuit is broken, electricity will not flow.

What Will I Need?

Insulated copper wire
Steel nail
Dry cell battery
Teaspoon of iron filings
Paper clips

What Will We Discuss?

How is magnetism made by electricity?
By using a wire that is carrying a current, how could you make a large magnetic field?
If you wanted to magnetize a nail, how would you do it?

What Must I Know?

The supplies listed above are for two or three students.

What Will Children Do?

PROCESSES

1. Obtain a dry cell battery, a steel nail, a piece of copper insulated wire, some iron filings, and a paper clip.
2. Wrap the wire around the nail several times as shown in the diagram.

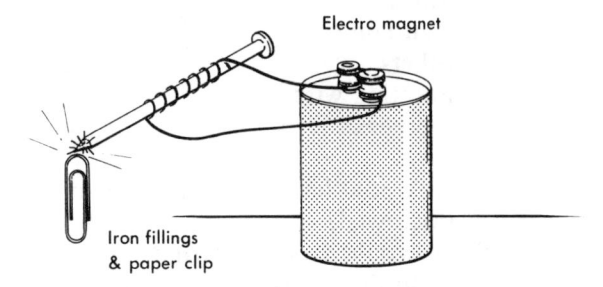

Electro magnet

Iron fillings & paper clip

3. Scrape the insulation off two ends of the wire. Connect one end of it to one terminal of the dry cell and the other end to the other terminal of the dry cell. *Caution:* Avoid leaving both terminals attached for more than a few seconds as intense heat builds up.

Hypothesizing

What do you think will happen to some iron filings if you place them near the nail?

4. Place them near the nail.
5. Place a paper clip on the nail.

Observing — What happens to the filings and paper clip?
Inferring — Why do the iron filings stay on the nail?
Inferring — What has been produced around the wire?

PHYSICAL SCIENCES 209

Inferring	What has the nail become?
Hypothesizing	What do you think will happen if you disconnect one of the terminals?
	6. Disconnect one of the terminals.
Observing	What happens to the iron filings?
Inferring	Why do they fall when you disconnect the wire?
Applying	What must you do with the circuit to produce electricity?
Summarizing	What can you say about the production of magnetism around a wire when electricity goes through it?
Summarizing	What would you call the magnet you made by passing electricity through a conductor?
Designing an investigation	How do you think you could increase the magnetism in the nail?
Hypothesizing	What do you think would happen if you wrapped more wire around the nail?
Hypothesizing	Will the magnetism increase or decrease? Why?
Assuming	Is the magnet you produced a temporary or a permanent magnet? Why?
Inferring	How do you know?
How Will Children Use or Apply What They Discover?	1. In what other ways can you use a battery and wire to make a circuit? 2. How could you make a parallel or series circuit? 3. By what other means could the magnetic field around the nail be increased?

What Are Parallel and Series Circuits? (4–8)

What Do I Want Children to Discover?	For the electrons to move in a circuit, there must be a path that is unbroken to and from the source of electrical energy. If one lamp burns out in a series circuit, the circuit is broken. In a parallel circuit, one lamp can burn out, but the rest of the circuit will still function.
What Will I Need?	2 batteries 4 small lamps 4 sockets Connecting wires 2 switches
What Will We Discuss?	What would happen if one light on a string of Christmas tree lights were unscrewed? What would you do to find out? Why don't all strings of Christmas tree lights behave the same?
What Will Children Do?	PROCESSES 1. Obtain a battery, 2 small lamps, a switch, 2 sockets, and connecting wires. 2. Connect these things so that the lights work.
Hypothesizing	What do you need to make the lights work?

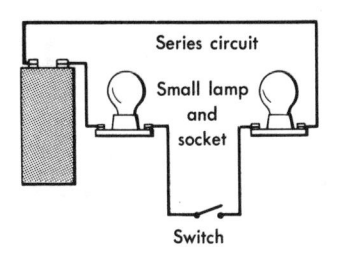

Series circuit diagram: battery connected to two small lamps and sockets with a switch.

What Must I Know? The diagram of the series circuit is for your information. It should not be shown to the children until they have done the activity.

Hypothesizing What purpose does the switch serve?
Hypothesizing What do you think will happen when you unscrew one of the lights?

3. Unscrew one of the lights.

Inferring Why did the other light go out?
Hypothesizing What can you do to make the lights go on again?

4. Using the same equipment, rearrange it so if one light goes out, the other will burn.

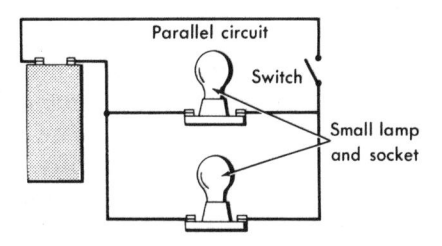

Parallel circuit diagram: battery connected to two small lamps and sockets with a switch.

What Must I Know? The diagram of a parallel circuit is available for your information. It should not be shown to the children until after they finish this activity.

5. Unscrew one of the lights. If you wired it differently than the first time, one of the lights should still burn even though you unscrewed the other.

Inferring Why?
Comparing What is the difference between the two types of circuits you have constructed?

What Must I Know? In a parallel circuit, there may be more than two paths for the current to take to complete its circuit. If one of the circuits is broken, the current can still use the other circuit as indicated in the preceding diagram.

How Will Children Use or Apply What They Discover?
1. What kind of circuits do you have in your home?
2. How could you find out what kind of Christmas tree lights you have?
3. Examine a flashlight. What kind of a circuit does it have?

PHYSICAL SCIENCES

LIGHT

How Does Light Appear to Travel? (3-8)

What Do I Want Children to Discover? Light appears to travel in a straight line.

What Will I Need? Round box such as oats come in   Candle
Waxed paper   Matches
Rubber band

What Will We Discuss? You may help pupils by demonstrating this simple activity and by raising the following questions:
What do you know about light?
How does it seem to travel?
How does a camera work?
In what direction does light travel?

What Will Children Do? PROCESSES

What Must I Know? This activity should be done in groups of two. One child will perform the activity for the other pupil and vice versa.

1. Obtain an oats box, waxed paper, rubber band, candle, and matches. Puncture a small hole in the end of the box with your pencil. Cover the other end of the box with waxed paper and secure the paper with a rubber band. Place the candle in front of the box and light the candle. Darken the room. One student should move the small-holed end back and forth in front of the candle while the other student watches the waxed papered end.

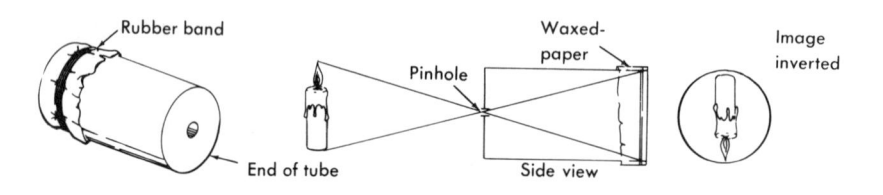

Observing What appears on the waxed paper?
Observing What does the image look like on the waxed paper?
Inferring Why does the image appear this way?
Hypothesizing Why does the student move the punctured end back and forth?
Inferring From this activity, what would you conclude about how light travels?
Inferring How do you think a picture of an object appears on the film in the back of a camera?

How Will Children Use or Apply What They Discover?
1. What would happen to the image on the waxed paper if you moved the box 2 or 3 feet from the candle?
2. What would happen to the image if you blew the candle flame out? Why?

What Must I Know?   After the children have completed the above activity, place the diagram on the board and have the children draw the image of the candle. Discuss how the light travels through the hole.

How Is Light Changed When It Passes from Air to Water? (3–8)

What Do I Want Children to Discover?
A substance that is curved and transparent can be used as a lens.
Light may be refracted (bent) when it passes through water or glass.

What Will I Need?

Quart jar filled with 16 ounces of water and 8 ounces of cooking oil	Flashlight
	Straw
Pint jar or small aquarium (only 1 is needed for a class)	Black paper
	½ teaspoon powdered milk
Water	Milk
Ruler	Flashlight
Coin	Sheet of black paper or piece of cardboard
Shallow pan	

What Will We Discuss?
What is a lens?
How are lenses used?
How do light rays affect the appearance of an object in water?
How can the direction of light rays be changed?
How can light rays be bent?

What Must I Know?   This activity should be done in groups of two.

What Will Children Do?   PROCESSES

PART I

Hypothesizing   How may water serve as a lens?
Hypothesizing   How do you think a ruler would look if you placed it in a jar of water?
1. Obtain a jar of water and a ruler.
2. Place the ruler in the jar.

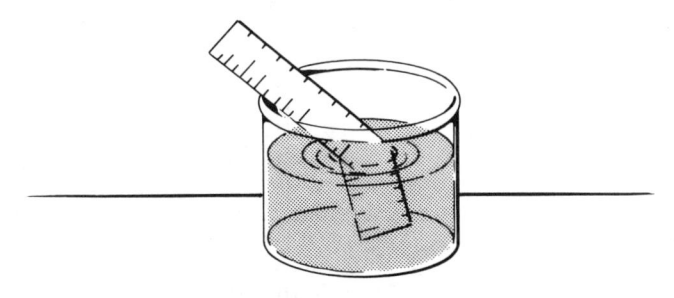

Observing
3. Observe the ruler.
   How has the ruler changed in appearance?

PART II
1. Obtain a pan, a small coin, and a jar of water.
   Put the coin in the bottom of a pan. Have a student back away from the pan until the coin disappears out of his or her line of sight.

Hypothesizing   How could it be possible for the student to see the coin again without moving?

PHYSICAL SCIENCES   213

Designing an experiment
Hypothesizing
Applying

Inferring
Inferring

2. Another pupil should gradually fill the pan with water until the pupil observing the pan sees the coin.
  Why is it easier to see the coin after water is added than before?
  What must the water do to the light rays coming from the coin to your eyes?
  How is the light bent?
  What conclusions may be drawn from the activity with the coin and ruler?

What Must I Know?

After the activity you might insert the following diagram and discuss it.

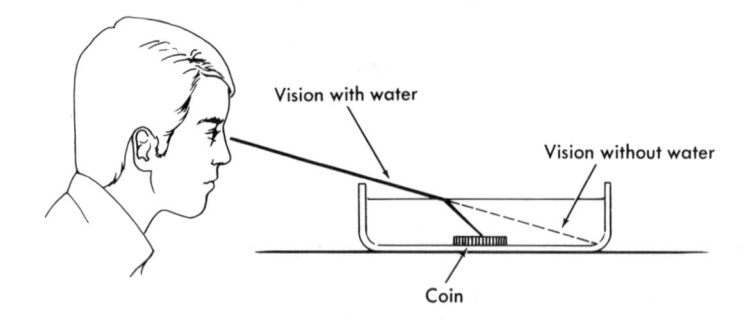

PART III
1. Obtain a glass jar or square aquarium filled with water, a flashlight, a piece of black paper, and a teaspoon of milk.
2. Add just enough milk to the jar or aquarium so a light beam from a flashlight is visible when passing through the milk.
3. Make a small hole in a piece of black paper.
4. Turn the flashlight on and shine a beam of light through the hole in the black paper into the milky water as shown in the diagram.

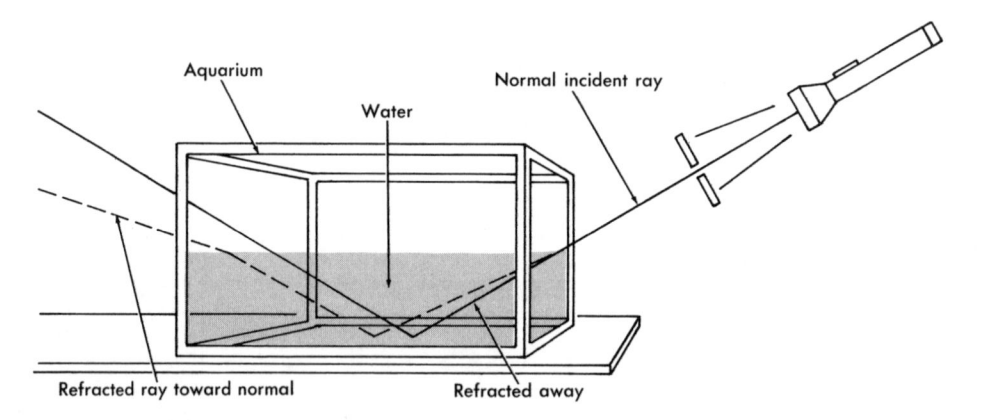

Observing

How is the beam of light refracted (bent) when it enters the water?

5. Have another pupil hold the jar or aquarium off the desk and shine the light through the hole in the paper onto the solution from above as before.

Observing

How does the light beam leaving the bottom of the aquarium or jar look?

Comparing

How does this differ from the way the light behaved when entering the solution?

214 DISCOVERY SCIENCE RESOURCE ACTIVITIES

What Must I Know? Air is said to be less optically dense than water. This means that when a light beam goes from some less optically dense medium into something more optically dense, it will bend. Oil is optically more dense than water. Do not confuse optical density with the density of a substance. Remember oil is really less physically dense than water because it will float on water.

Hypothesizing Draw how you think light rays would look when passed through a jar of water containing a layer of oil.

6. Obtain from your teacher a jar of water with oil and determine whether your ideas are correct.

What Must I Know? When the activity is completed, ask the class to draw on the chalkboard what happens as the light passes through plain water with milk. They should make a diagram something like the one below.

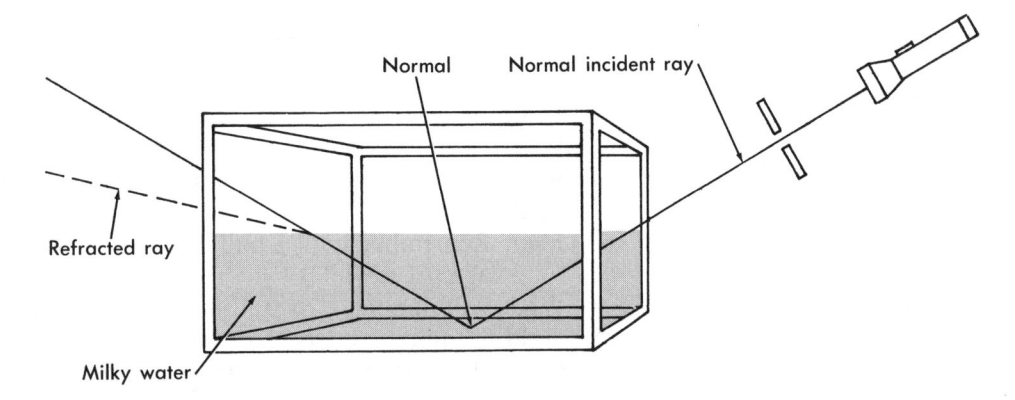

[Diagram: A rectangular container with milky water, showing a flashlight emitting a "Normal incident ray" entering the container, with the "Normal" line perpendicular to the surface, and a "Refracted ray" exiting through the milky water.]

Discuss how light bends.

Observing How is the light refracted when it leaves the solution?

What Must I Know? Draw the last two diagrams above on the board after the lesson and explain that when a light ray passes obliquely from one medium into another of greater optical density, it is refracted toward the normal. The normal is defined as a perpendicular line to the plane at a given point.

How Will Children Use or Apply What They Discover?
1. Would colored water change the way light rays are reflected from the ruler?
   What would you do to find out?
2. What other substances could you use to show that light rays may be altered?
3. What would happen if you used a clear plastic glass and rubbing alcohol or vinegar instead of water?

How Is Light Reflected? (4–8)

What Do I Want Children to Discover? When light is reflected from a mirror, it is reflected at the same angle as the angle of light hitting the mirror. A physicist would say that the angle of incidence equals the angle of reflection.

PHYSICAL SCIENCES

What Will I Need? Rubber ball
Mirror

What Will We Discuss? How is light refracted?
How is light reflected?
What are some ways that light is reflected?

What Will Children Do? PROCESSES

Observing
1. Obtain a rubber ball and bounce it at an angle against the wall.
   How does the ball bounce away from the wall?
2. Continue to bounce the ball against the wall, hitting the wall at various angles.

Observing
Hypothesizing
   At what angles does the ball bounce back from the wall?
   What do you think will happen to light if you shine it onto a reflecting surface in a manner similar to the way you threw the ball?

Comparing
   How does the way light reflects off a wall resemble the way a ball bounces off a wall?
3. Hold a mirror so you can see yourself.
   Where did you have to hold the mirror?
4. How did the light coming from your face reflect so you could see your face?
   Hint: Remember how a ball bounces when you throw it straight against a wall?

Hypothesizing
   What will happen if you hold the mirror at an angle?
5. Hold the mirror in front of yourself.
   Move the mirror so you can see another person or another part of the room.
6. Diagram on a piece of paper your location compared to the mirror.
   Indicate with arrows how the light comes from the mirror to you.
7. Now hold the mirror at different angles.

Observing and inferring
   How is light reflected when you hold the mirror at different angles?

How Will Children Use or Apply What They Discover?
1. What things besides mirrors may be used to change the direction of light?
2. How would you make a periscope from mirrors? Tell how it would work.

216 DISCOVERY SCIENCE RESOURCE ACTIVITIES

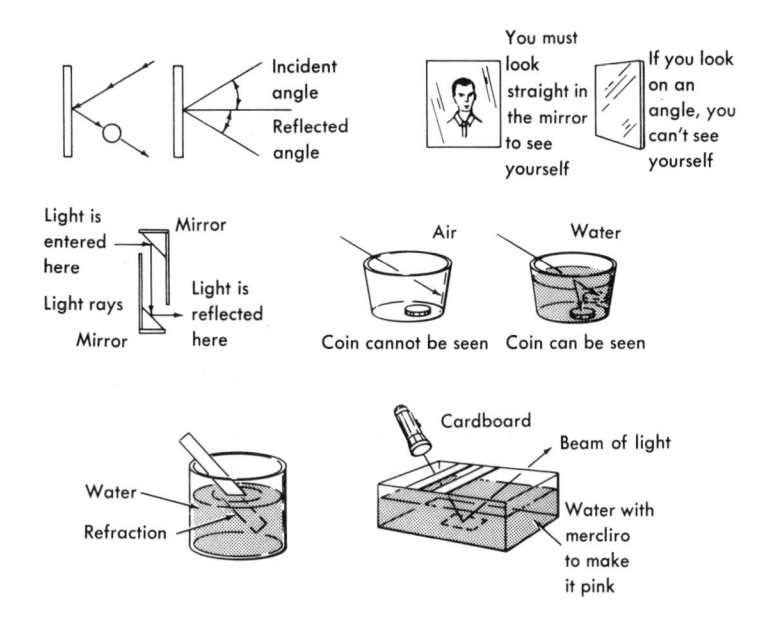

What Must I Know? To summarize what the children have discovered about light, draw the above diagram on posterboard by using a felt pen. Hold the charts up and ask the children to explain what is taking place.

What Does a Prism Do to Light? (4–8)

What Do I Want Children to Discover?	White light, when passed through a prism, disperses to form a continuous spectrum similar to a rainbow. White light is a mixture of many colors of light. Each color in the spectrum has a different wave length.
What Will I Need?	A prism
What Will We Discuss?	What is a prism? What does a prism do?
What Must I Know?	This activity should be done in groups of two or more children.
What Will Children Do?	PROCESSES

PART I
1. Obtain a prism.

Hypothesizing
    What do you think will happen to the light rays after they pass through the prism?
2. Place the prism in the path of a strong beam of light as indicated in the diagram.

PHYSICAL SCIENCES 217

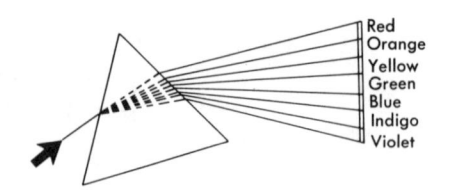

Observing	What does the prism do to the light rays when they pass through it?
Observing	What colors do you see?
Observing	Which color seems to have bent the most?
Observing	Which color seems to have bent the least?
Inferring	What do you know about the way the different colors of light are refracted (bent) by the prism?
Inferring	What is white light made of?
What Must I Know?	The children should see that white light is produced by the combination of several wave lengths of light. Draw a prism on the board and have the children show how the spectrum is formed. Their drawing should be something like the previous diagram.

PART II

Hypothesizing	What do you think will happen if you look through the prism at your partner?
Experimenting	1. Look through the AB side of the prism at your partner.

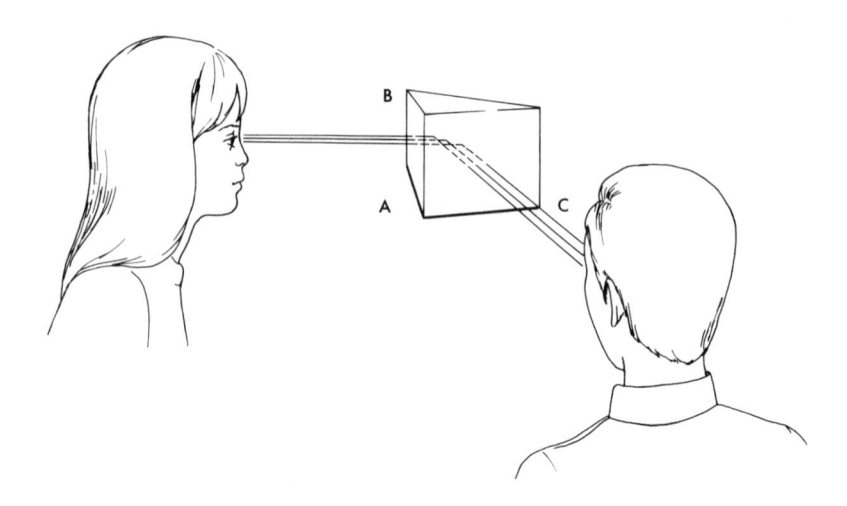

2. Record your observations.

Inferring	Why is it possible to see what your partner is doing without looking directly at him or her?
Inferring	What happens to the light entering the prism that makes it possible for you to see your partner?
Inferring	What does the prism do to the light rays?
Comparing	What is the difference between a prism and a mirror in the way that each affects light?

What Must I Know?

A prism is used in expensive optical equipment instead of mirrors because prisms absorb less light. At the conclusion of this activity, place a diagram of a prism on the board and have the children draw how light passes through it. If they do not understand how a prism can be used in a periscope, draw and discuss the diagram below.

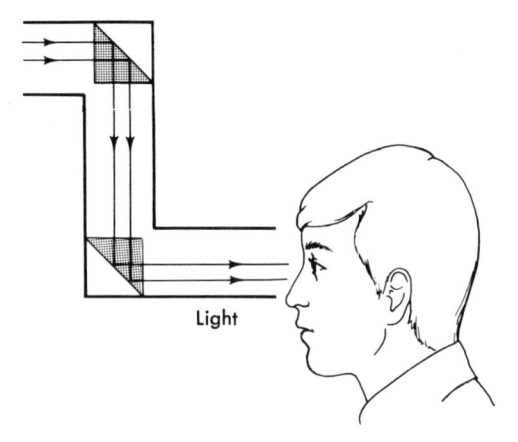

How Will Children Use or Apply What They Discover?

1. What happens to X rays when they pass through a prism?
2. What would happen if you passed light through two prisms?
3. Why are prisms used in expensive optical equipment instead of mirrors?

How Do Convex and Concave Lenses Affect Light Passing Through Them? (4–8)

What Do I Want Children to Discover?

When light is passed from a dense to a less dense medium or vice versa, it may be refracted (bent).
A convex lens may magnify close objects and invert objects far from the lens.
The thicker the lens, the more the light rays will be bent.
Convex lenses converge light rays.
Concave lenses diverge light rays.
Concave lenses make objects look smaller.

What Will I Need?

Convex lens   Paper and pencil
Concave lens   Cardboard box and scissors
Piece of plain glass   Flashlight (or slide projector)

What Will Children Do?   PROCESSES

Hypothesizing

In what ways could you find out if a lens can change the direction of light?

1. Obtain a convex lens, a concave lens, a piece of plain glass, a cardboard box, a pair of scissors, paper and pencil, and a strong light source such as a flashlight or slide projector. Take the cardboard box

PHYSICAL SCIENCES   219

and cut the top and one end as shown in the diagram. Cut a slit for the light to pass through as indicated in the diagram. Place a projector or strong light source in front of the slit. (A good flashlight may be substituted for the projector.) This apparatus will be used with the lenses and glass to find out how they work.

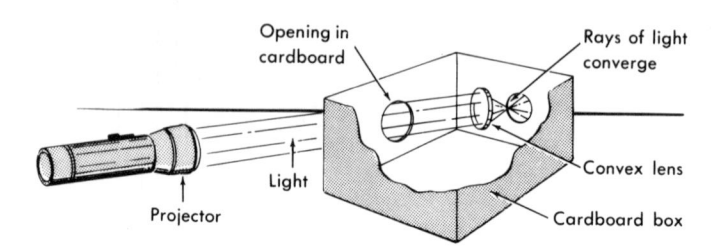

Observing

2. Before using the cardboard box, examine the two lenses and the piece of glass very carefully. Hold them to your eye. Look at the glass through them. Have someone look through the other side.

Comparing

3. Compare what you see through each of the three lenses.
   How do the objects differ?

Observing
Inferring
Hypothesizing

4. Take the convex lens and move it slowly away from your eye.
   What happens as you move the lens away?
   Why do you think this happens?
   What could you do to find out the reason for what happens?

What Must I Know?

The image becomes inverted. This happens because as the lens is moved away from the eye, it reaches a point where the distance is greater than the focal length of the lens, and the image becomes inverted as a result. (The focal length is the distance from a lens or a mirror to the point where rays of light are brought together to form an image.) When a student first looks at another student through a convex lens, the student appears right-side up. As the student moves the lens away from his eye so that it is at a greater distance than the focal length of the lens, the student he is looking at becomes inverted as shown in the diagram.

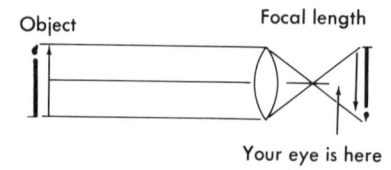

5. Take the concave lens now and place it near your eye and move it slowly away like you did the convex lens.

Observing

What happens as you move the lens back and forth in front of your eye?

Comparing

What do you see in the two lenses that differ from what you saw with the plain glass?

Hypothesizing

What do you think will happen when you shine light through the lenses and flat piece of glass onto a surface?

6. Hold the plain piece of glass inside your box as indicated by the diagram.

Observing
Observing

What happens to the light?
What effect, if any, does the box have on the lens?

220 DISCOVERY SCIENCE RESOURCE ACTIVITIES

Collecting data	7. Draw a side view of the lens light when it passes through the glass onto the cardboard. 8. Repeat this step but substitute the concave and convex lenses for the plain glass.
What Must I Know?	In a convex lens the edges are always thinner than the center. When light passes through a convex lens, it converges as shown in the diagram.

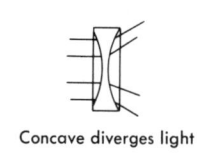

Concave diverges light

The edges of a concave lens are always thicker than the center, and light is diverged by this type of lens as shown in the diagram.

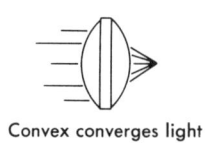

Convex converges light

	9. Observe your lenses again.
Comparing	How does the shape of the concave lens differ from that of the convex lens?
Comparing	In what ways does the shape of the plain lens differ from the convex and concave lenses?
Comparing	In what ways does the light passing through the convex lens differ from the light passing through the concave lens?
Inferring	What evidence do you have to support the statement that a converging lens may cause light to approach a single point?
What Must I Know?	Draw the two previous diagrams on the board and discuss them.
How Will Children Use or Apply What They Discover?	1. What proof is there that light can be refracted (bent) by lenses? 2. If you wanted to start a fire and had no matches, which lens could you use and why? 3. How might fires be started by old bottles lying in dry grass? 4. What kind of lenses do you have in your eyes? 5. Why do some people have to wear glasses?

Why Do You Need Two Eyes? (2–6)

What Do I Want Children to Discover?	To judge the third dimension adequately (depth and distance), you need two eyes. Two eyes are needed to see well, especially to see how far away things are and how high or low they are.
What Will I Need?	Table or desk lower than waist high Pop bottle Nickel or object similar in size and thickness

PHYSICAL SCIENCES

What Will Children Do?   PROCESSES

Hypothesizing

What do you suppose will happen if you try to flip a coin standing on end out of a bottle using only one eye?

Organizing

1. Obtain the following materials: a pop bottle and a nickel from the teacher (or your own). Be sure to work on a table or desk that you have to look *down* upon so it is below your eye level.

Observing

2. Place the coin in the pop bottle on the desk; walk 10 to 15 feet away from the table in any direction. Facing the table, cover one eye with your right hand. With the left hand held waist high, walk toward the table at a normal pace. When you reach the bottle, flip the coin without hesitation with your free hand. Do not just push the coin off the pop bottle, but flip it with your finger. (See diagram.)

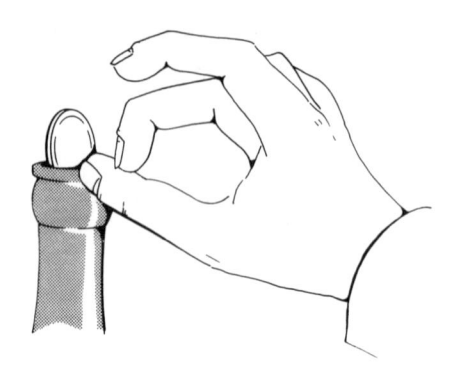

Observing

What happens to the coin?

What Must I Know?

Most people will not flip the coin out of the bottle because they cannot locate it easily. One cannot judge depth and distance well with only one eye.

3. Repeat the activity again. Follow Step 2 very carefully, only this time cover your eye with your left hand and use your right hand to flip the coin.

Observing   What happens to the coin this time?
Inferring   Does changing hands make any difference?
Comparing   How does this differ from the first time?
Hypothesizing   What would happen if you repeated the activity again, only this time using both eyes?

4. Repeat it and use both eyes.

Observing   What happens to the coin this time?
Inferring   Why do you think using both eyes is better? Explain your answer.
Inferring

5. What effect does repeating this activity have on how accurately you can flip the coin?

How Will Children Use or Apply What They Discover?

1. What do you suppose would happen if the room were darkened a little while doing this activity? Explain your answer.
2. Why does a shooter usually aim a rifle with one eye closed?
3. What are optical illusions?

SECTION 4

LESS STRUCTURED DISCOVERY ACTIVITIES

Less Structured Activities (Preschool)

Outlined below are some sample preschool physical activities. They generally follow the suggestion of Piaget that children perform actions on objects so they develop physical knowledge. This section is followed by activities having to do with learning the names of colors and with the idea that objects may be grouped (classified) in several ways. The next section involves children in making several things and in noting their changes and what causes them. This section is followed by preschool-primary activities, many of which are appropriate for upper preschool and lower primary grades.

Rolling Things

A. Spools

Materials Spools of all sizes, balls of various sizes, strings, rubber bands of various thicknesses

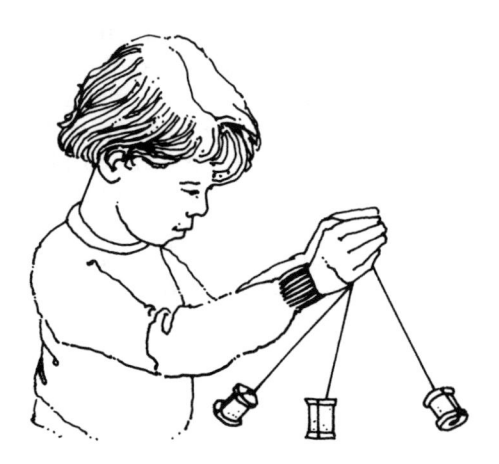

Opening Questions What kind of game can you plan with these materials?
What other things can you do with the spools?

Some Possible Activities

Have a spool race by pushing small and large spools to see which ones will roll the farthest. Arrange the spools in different ways and roll balls against them to see how they scatter. See who can make the highest stack without it falling. Make a spool necklace. Paint the spools differnt colors, tie a string around them, and swing them. Let them go to see how they fly, depending on how they are released. Make a spool wall. Drop the spools in an aquarium or gallon jar and see how deep they drop into the water.

B. Balls

Materials

Balls of different sizes including Ping-Pong, golf, tennis, and larger ones; straws; boards to make inclined planes

Opening Questions:

What things can you do with these balls?

Some Possible Activities

Find out which balls roll the easiest across the floor. What happens when they are kicked? Which ones will roll down an inclined plane the farthest? Find out which balls balance best. Throw the balls against the wall at different angles and find out how they bounce off the wall. For example, how should the children throw the ball so it will come back to them? Float the balls in water and find out which ones float and which do not. Also, notice how deep they sink in the water. Line up the balls and roll a ball down an inclined plane so it hits the end of the line. Then roll two balls down so they hit the line one after another. Place all but one of the balls in a close group. Roll another ball into the group and see how the balls scatter. Play croquet with different balls. Play roll and hit the person with a ball. Construct a tetherball.

C. Marbles

Materials

Marbles of different sizes; inclined plane; 2 boards or 2 meter sticks

Opening Questions   What can you do with these marbles?

Some Possible Activities   The children can do any of the above activities suggested for balls. Place a board on top of the marbles and move them around. Transport something on the boards this way across a room. Place two boards parallel to each other. Leave enough distance for the marbles to move between them. Place marbles in the row between them. Shoot other marbles so they hit one end of the row. Invite students to suggest some marble games.

D. Roller Skates/Skateboards

Materials   Boards (boards for inclined planes and to put on top of a skate/skateboard); oil can; newspaper

Opening Questions   What can you find out about skates/skateboards?
What kind of skate/skateboard race can we have?
How many bricks or cans with rocks can you move with skates/skateboards?

Some Possible Activities   Invite the children to find out how far a skate/skateboard will go when let go down an inclined plane. Have a contest where they see how many cans or bricks they can move across the room without one falling off.

Invite them to place a board on a skate/skateboard and see how they can balance it so the skate/skateboard will be able to carry a lot. Have the children go outside and find out what surface the skate/skateboard moves on the best and the worst. Have them play hit the skate/skateboard, where another child pushes a skate/skateboard out in a circle and the other children try to hit it with their skates/skateboards. Invite students to turn their skates/skateboards upsidedown and slide boards and other things over the wheels. They should also spin the wheels to find out how they move. Give a skate/skateboard to the children when the wheels do not move very well and ask what they could do to get the skates/skateboards to move better. Later, give them an oil can and some newspaper and ask them what they could do with these.

Blocks

Materials   Blocks of different sizes

Opening Questions   What can you build with these blocks?

Some Possible Activities   The children can build towers, bridges, or enclosures for animals. Sort blocks on the basis of shape or color.

Wheels and Things That Roll

Materials Rollers, small round wheels, buttons, toy cars, small round rocks, oranges, apples, thimbles, boards to make inclined planes, milk bottle paper caps or some cut from poster board, thumb tacks, match boxes

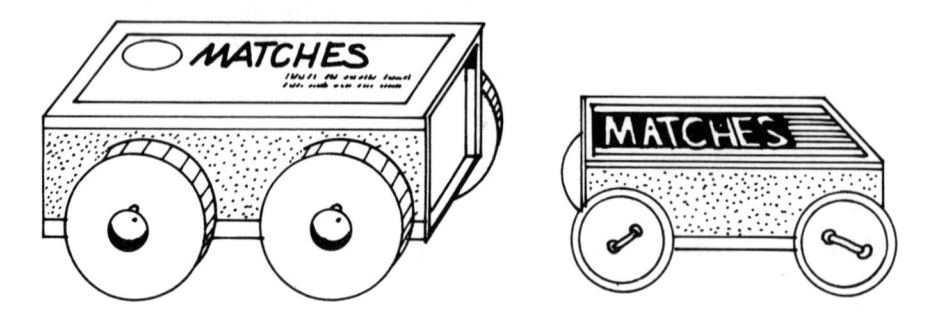

Opening Questions What can you do with these things?
What kind of game can you play?
How can you make a toy car using the match boxes and other things?
Which of the things you see are wheels? Which are not wheels?
How are wheels different from the other things?

Some Possible Activities The children could try seeing how far different things would roll on the floor, down an inclined plane. They could also make toy cars with the match boxes with the bottle caps or buttons tacked to the sides. The children may also be invited to make toy cars out of a square small board where axles are made from clothes hangers. These are nailed to the board and bent at the ends after the button or bottle cap wheels are attached.

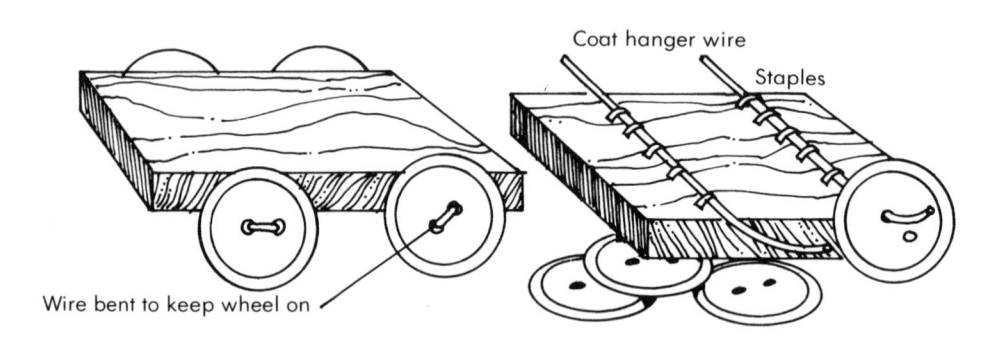

Water

A. Brushing with Water

Materials Sponges, paint brushes, dish cloth. This should be done on a hot day, outside the classroom.

226 DISCOVERY SCIENCE RESOURCE ACTIVITIES

Opening Questions

What will happen to water if you brush it on different things outside?
How can you find out?
Where do you think the water will disappear first? Why?

Some Possible Activities

Invite the children to take their paint brush, dip it in water, and brush it over several places to see what happens. Have them play a game to see whose water will disappear first. Have them feel the places where the water disappears rapidly and compare it with places where it doesn't seem to disappear fast, for example, on hot sidewalks and in the shade. Have them repeat the activity but use sponges and washrags instead of brushes. Have them place wet sponges on different places and determine which ones dry first.

B. Hanging Wet Things on a Line

Materials

Paper towels, different pieces of cloth (some that are thin and some that are thick like a towel), sponges, twine to hold the cloth, clothespins

Opening Questions

How can we make these wet?
How can we dry them?
How can we use the twine and clothespins to dry them?
Where is the best place to put the clothesline? Why?
Which things do you think will dry first?

Some Possible Activities

Ask the children to make the clothesline. Have them dip various things in water, drain them, and place them on the clothesline with clothespins.

Color

A. Name the Color

Materials Several different colored objects

Opening Questions What do you notice about these things?
What colors are they?

Some Possible Activities Give the children several objects with different colors and ask them to identify and learn the names of their colors. After doing this, have them find and name things in the room that are of the same color.

B. Group by Color

Materials Several different colored objects

Opening Questions How can you group these things?

Some Possible Activities Give the children several objects and ask them to group them by color. Ask them to find other objects in the room that they could place in the same group.

C. Group by Color and Shape

Materials Several different colored objects of different sizes having different shapes; for example, red, yellow, and green squares, circles, and rectangles.

Opening Questions What different ways can you group these things?

Some Possible Activities Give the children several different objects that vary in color and shape. Ask them to group together those objects that are of the same color and shape.

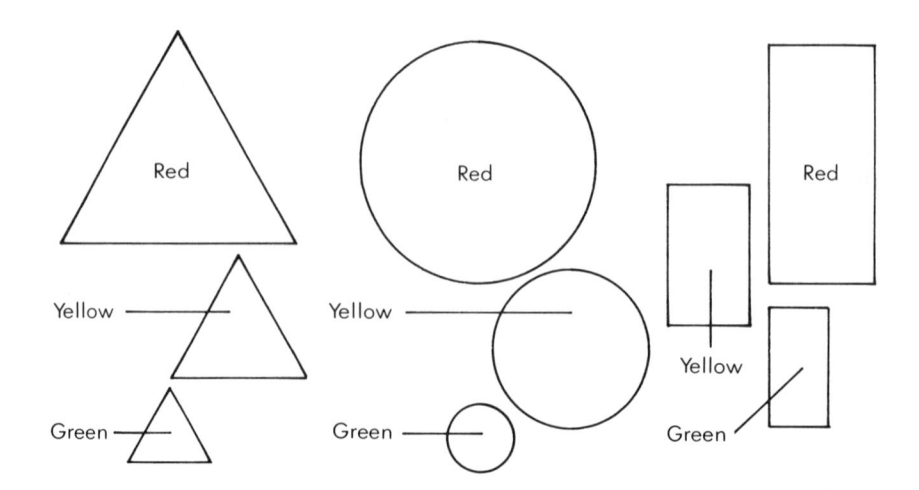

228 DISCOVERY SCIENCE RESOURCE ACTIVITIES

LESS STRUCTURED ACTIVITIES (PRESCHOOL-PRIMARY GRADES)

Making Things

Making different types of foods helps children see how things can be changed and helps them develop a better understanding of how their *actions* can cause an effect.

The children should prepare and mix the ingredients as much as possible. Make a series of experience charts using diagrams to illustrate the steps they need to follow in preparing them. For example, a chart for popcorn is shown below:

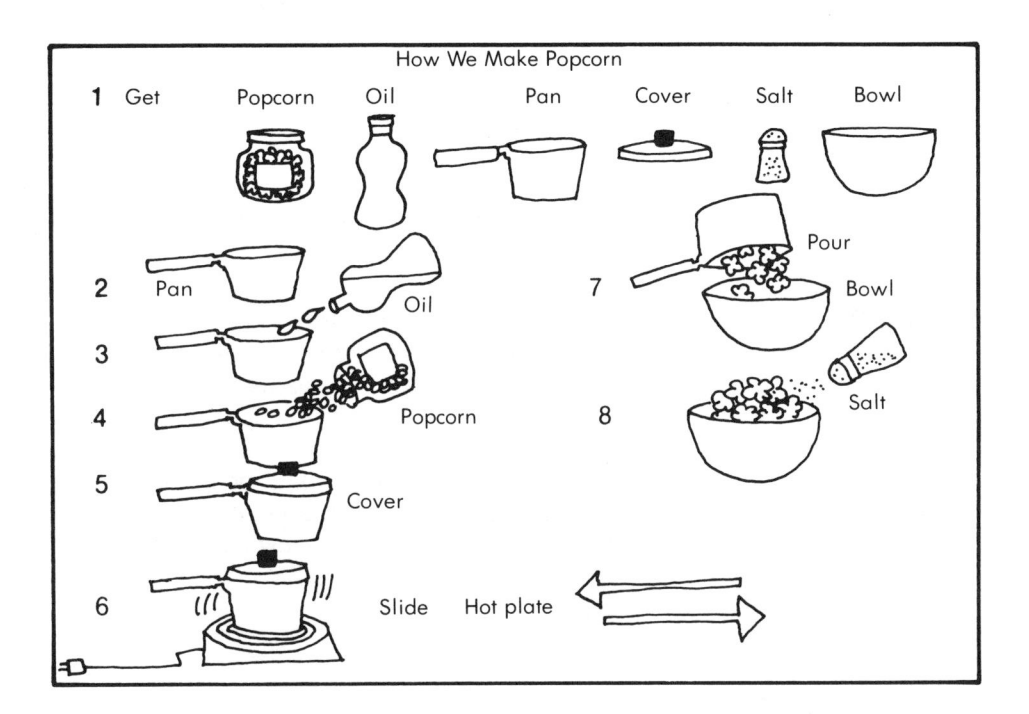

A. Making Popcorn

Materials Popcorn, pan with a cover, cooking oil, heat source. (*Important:* Do NOT use an open-coil electric hotplate.)

Opening Questions What can we do to make popcorn?

Some Possible Activities Place the popcorn in a pan with a little oil and move it back and forth over the heat source. Invite the children to listen for evidence that the corn is popping; ask them when they think the corn is done and ask how the corn has changed. Have the children draw how the popcorn has changed.

B. Making Bread

Materials — Things needed to make bread. See recipe book for directions.

Opening Questions — How can we make bread?

Some Possible Activities — Make bread. Bake some for different lengths of time. Invite children to compare the different effects. (*Hint:* Use an electric slow cooker and breads can be made in the classroom in 1-2 hours.)

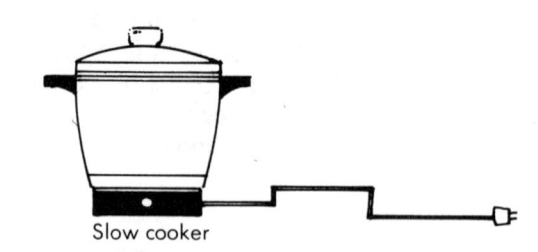

Slow cooker

C. Making Ice Cream

Materials — See cookbook, for example, *Better Homes and Gardens,* on how to do this.

Opening Questions
What is your favorite food?
How many of you like ice cream?
How can we make ice cream?

Some Possible Activities — Invite the children to make different kinds of ice cream. They should mix the different ingredients and note what different things they add. You might give them nuts, pieces of candy, coconut, dried fruit, chocolate, caramel, and so on that they can add as they wish.

D. Making Popsicles

Materials — Fruit juices, straws or popsicle sticks to stick in the ice trays

Opening Questions
How many of you like popsicles?
How can we make some popsicles?

Some Possible Activities — Provide the children with different juices and tell them they can make the popsicles any way they want. Invite them to try to make different shapes and colors, to add small pieces of fruit, for example, pineapple, if they would like to try it. Let some of the popsicles melt and ask the children what they think will happen if the melted popsicles are put back in the refrigerator or freezer again.

E. Making Rice

Materials Rice, bowl with water, cooking pan, hot plate or stove. (If possible, obtain some Indian Rice to soak. It really changes in appearance.)

Opening Questions How many of you have eaten rice?
What does rice look like before it is cooked?
What will happen to rice if you soak it?
How can we make some rice to eat?

Some Possible Activities Invite the children to feel the rice and note how various kinds differ in appearance. Have them soak the rice and note whether any floats. They should also note what happens to the rice and water as they are soaked. Cook the rice and give some to the children from time to time to taste. They should note how the taste and solidity of the rice change with cooking.

Identifying Things

A. Draw the Hidden Object

Materials Paper bag and several different shaped objects, for example, cube of sugar, button, match box, triangular piece of cut cardboard

Opening Questions How well can you tell what is in the bag without looking at it?

Some Possible Activities Have students put their hands in a bag and feel different objects. They should then say what they think an object is and draw it. After they have done this, they should place their hands back in the bag to select and pull out the object to see if they were right.

B. Sort and Label Materials

Set out materials such as the following and invite the children to sort and label them as to whether the materials are hard or soft:

Materials

Hard Materials	*Soft Materials*
paper clips	sponges
marbles	silk
sticks	absorbent cotton
washers	string
nuts and bolts	clay
pennies	velvet

Note: Help the children learn names of materials used and assist them with classification if needed. Collages, hard and soft books, and other activities can be used as follow-up.

C. Play Follow-the-Leader

Using ten objects that have a clear contrast of one property, such as hard-soft as in number B above, play "follow-the-leader" like this:

One child is designated leader and picks one object.
The leader states one property (softness).
Each player picks one of the objects with the specified property until all the objects with the same property are picked.
Each child assumes the leader role, and different properties are used.
Note: Try these variations of the same theme of classification games:

1. *Advanced follow-the-leader:* Leader picks object that has two properties such as soft and round, hard and square, and red and flat.
2. *Grab-bag game:* Leader reaches into bag of objects and tells class how it feels before removing it. Child is then to find an object in the bag that feels the same as the leader's choice.
3. *Hands-behind-the-back game:* Children have hands behind their backs. Put a *hard* object in each child's right hand and a *soft* object in his left hand. Ask for all *hard* objects to be put on table by saying, "One of your objects is hard and one is soft. Put the *hard* one on the table." Ask that all *soft* objects be put on table.

Tying Knots

Materials String and rope, buckets filled with objects

Opening Questions What kind of knots can you make?
Who can draw a knot with string?
Who can draw a knot with rope?

Who can copy a picture of this knot?

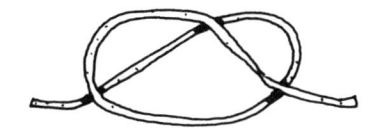

Which of these will make a knot?

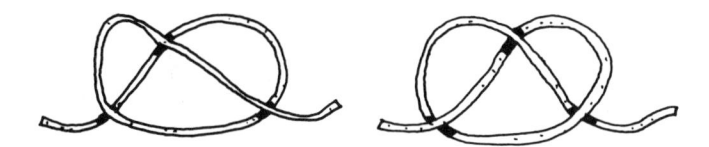

Which knot in this picture is a false knot?

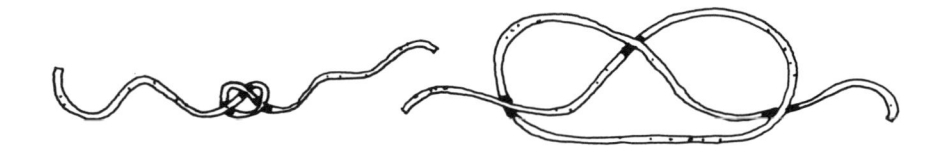

Which knot is a tight knot?
Which knot is a loose one? Why do you think so?
How can you find out?

Some Possible Activities

Invite the children to tie different kinds of single knots and to show you how they make them. Have them tie a rope to a bucket and lift things over a bar that serves as a beam or use a single pulley. As them to draw pictures of the knots they made. Have them look for knots in their classroom and school. Students who have trouble making knots may also be invited to make tracings of single knots.

Making Things with Animals

A. INVESTIGATE ANIMAL EXPRESSIONS

Invite the children to cut out animal faces from magazines. Show how the animals look when they are mad, when they are happy, and when they are hungry.

B. EXAMINE A BABY

Have the children investigate and examine pictures of a baby giraffe and then measure the neck and legs. Have them look at a picture of a giraffe.

Ask: "How long are the giraffe's legs?" "How long is the neck?" "What do giraffes eat?"

C. PASTE PICTURES OF PETS

Make a pet chart like the one below:

PETS

Cats	Dogs	Other Pets

Have the children take different pictures of pets and place them on the chart.

D. INVENT YOUR OWN ANIMAL

Have the children invent their own animal and make a name that describes it.

E. MAKE AN ANIMAL CALENDAR

Have the children paste a picture and the name of an animal on a calendar for each day. The children should suggest the animal to be placed on it. Each child should have a chance to draw one for a day on the calendar.

F. TRACE THE PATH OF AN EARTHWORM

Materials   Crayons, paper, earthworm

Opening Questions How can you make a map of how an earthworm moves?

Some Possible Activities Give students crayons, paper, and an earthworm and have them follow the earthworm's path with a crayon. They might compare how earthworms move with how mealworms or caterpillars move.

G. MAKE A BIRD MOBILE

Invite the children to draw or make some paper birds or cut out pictures of birds from magazines and hang them from a mobile.

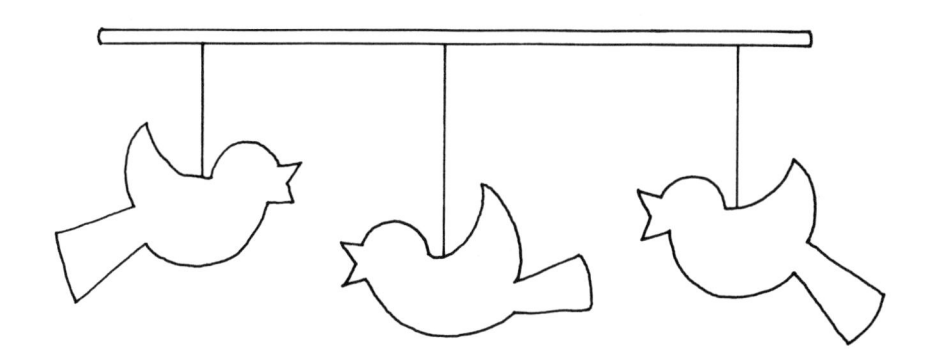

Maps

A. MAKE A MAP

Help the children make a map of their classroom, school, or community. Invite the students to identify important places on the map.

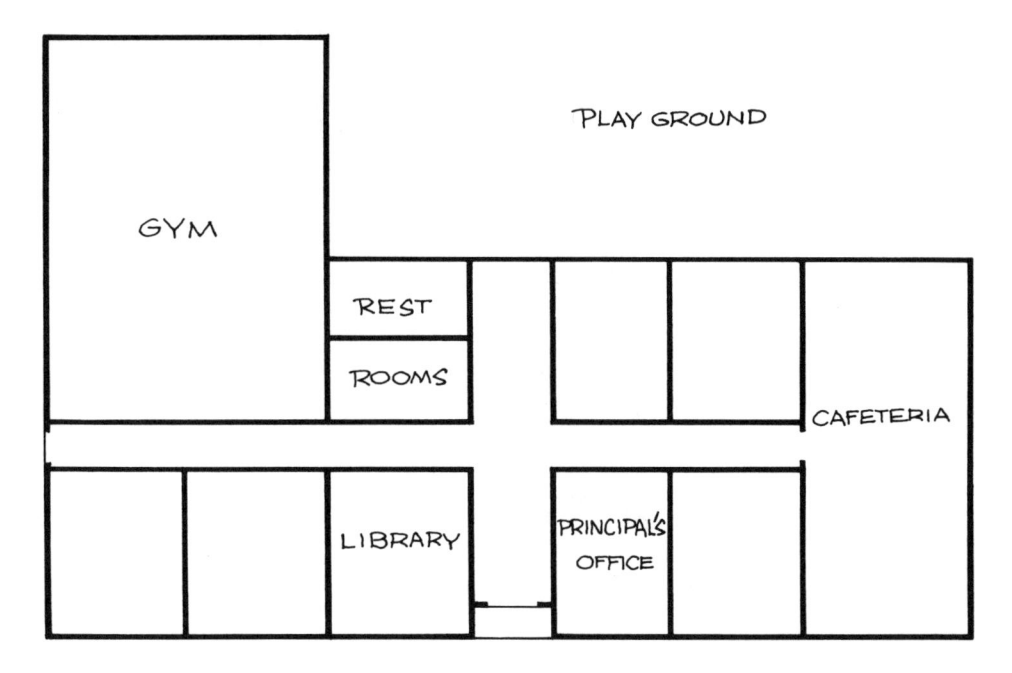

LESS STRUCTURED 235

B. PLACE ANIMALS AND PLANTS ON A MAP

Invite the children to take a walk around the school, community, or a zoo. Have them make a map and draw on it where they saw different animals and plants.

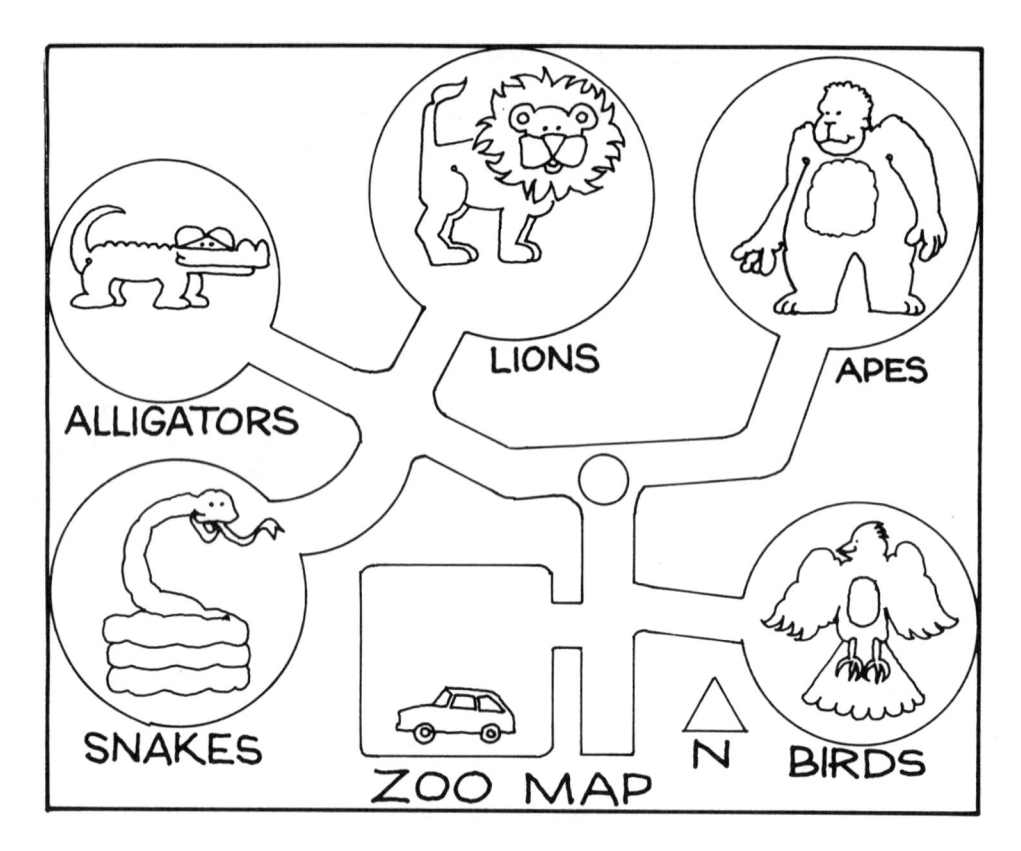

C. MAKE A THREE-DIMENSIONAL MAP

Invite the children to make a three-dimensional map showing lakes, mountains, forests, fields, rivers, towns, and so on.

D. MAKE A POLLUTION MAP

Help the children draw a map with places around their school or community where there is pollution. Use concrete examples, for example, waste paper, garbage, places where there are a lot of people smoking, and so on.

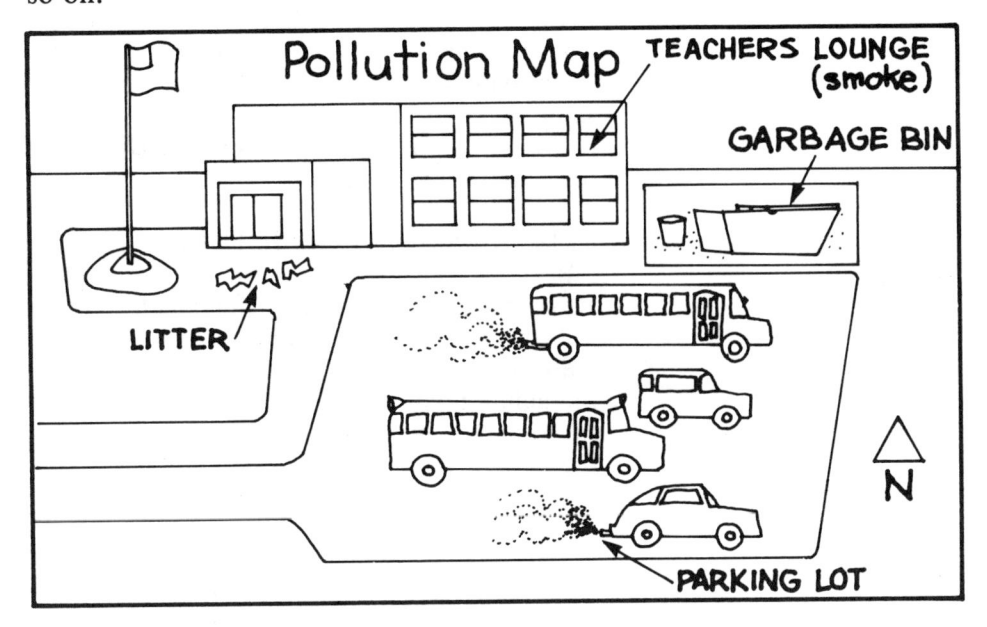

E. MAKE A PLANT MAP

Help the children draw a map of and learn the names of different plants that grow around the school.

Doing Things with Plants

A. HUG AND FEEL A TREE

LESS STRUCTURED 237

Have the children hug a tree trunk, feel its surface, and describe how it feels. Smell the bark. Have the children draw and give a name for their favorite tree or cut pictures out of magazines.

B. PRESS PLANTS

Invite the children to collect parts of plants, for example, leaves and flowers. *Caution:* Stress collecting *fallen* plant parts only. Do not pick from living things. Have them press them between newspapers. Place some books or something heavy on the newspapers. After several days, remove the weights and newspaper. Discuss how drying helps to preserve the plants and food.

C. MAKE SPLATTER PICTURES OF LEAVES

Have the children collect different types of leaves and bring them to class. Tell them to: Place the leaves on colored paper. Dip brushes in poster paint and splatter paint over the leaves to make a picture outline. Have the children compare the different types of leaves and what they had to do to make good splatter pictures. For example, how did the thickness of the paint affect the quality of the picture.

LESS STRUCTURED ACTIVITIES (GRADES 4–6)

Water Drops

Materials   Waxed paper, paper towel, napkins, typing paper, plastic wrap, eye dropper, food coloring

Opening Questions   What will happen when you drop droplets of water on these different kinds of paper and plastic?
How can you find out?
What paper will hold the water the best?
What paper or plastic will water run off of the easiest?

Paper napkin　　　Waxed paper　　　Plastic wrap

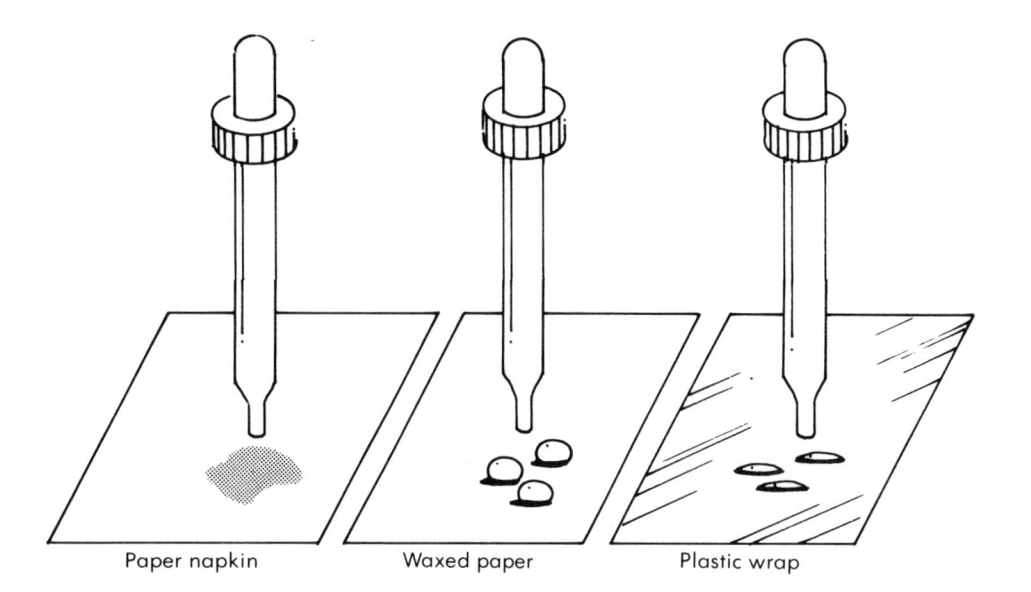

Some Possible Activities

Have the students find which paper and plastic absorbs the water the best and the least. Have them play Water Droplet Chase. Use red food coloring to make some red drops and blue food coloring to make some blue drops. Drop the water into separate droplets distant from each other on wax paper or plastic wrap. Place one red drop and several blue drops on the paper. Invite the students to capture all the blue drops, one at a time, with the red drops. Have the students make drop slides of the same lengths and inclination. They can vary the material they use for the slide. Two students should compete with each other to see which slides the drops will move down the fastest.

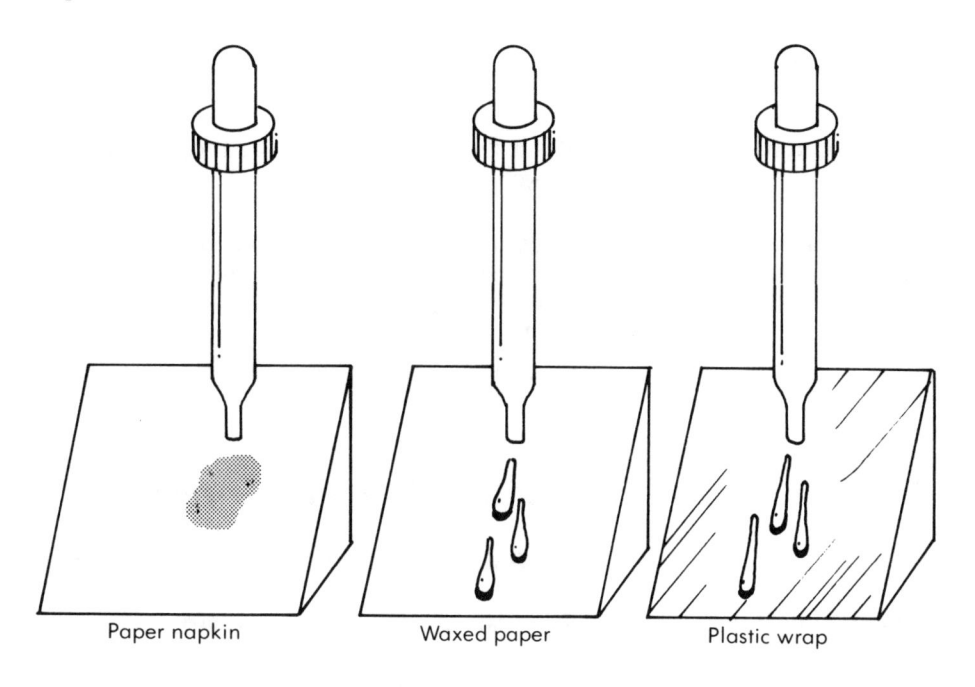

Paper napkin　　　Waxed paper　　　Plastic wrap

LESS STRUCTURED

What Do Chicks Like to Eat?

Materials Baby chicks, different kinds of food

Opening Questions How can we find out what chicks like to eat?

Some Possible Activities Let the children determine if chicks have a preference for different foods by feeding them different kinds of food at the same time and see what they eat all of first. The children could also determine what food chickens will or will not eat.

Making Soap Films

Materials Water, wire, liquid soap, container. For soapy water, use 5 to 10 long squirts of soap in it.

Opening Questions What does the shape of the loop have to do with the kind of bubbles you make?

Some Possible Activities Encourage students to make all kinds of different shaped loops. Have them try to find what kind of loop makes the largest bubbles and the smallest. They should also determine the best mixture for making soapy bubbles. Try to see that they control the variables, for example, the amount of soap, when experimenting.

Who Can Lift the Most with a Tongue Depressor?

Materials Tongue depressor, rice or other small seeds, balance, small paper cups

Opening Questions Who can lift the most seeds with a tongue depressor?

Some Possible Activities Have the students compete in using their tongue depressors to see who can lift the most seeds and place them in containers. Later, they might be invited to modify their depressors to be able to lift more seeds.

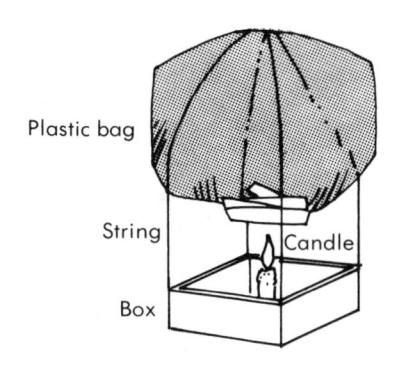

Make a Hot Air Balloon

Materials	Different sizes of plastic bags, small candle, string, scissors, small light paper or cardboard box to hold the candle in, transparent tape
Opening Questions	How can you make a hot air balloon from these materials?
Some Possible Activities	Suggest that students consider carefully how the weight of the box will affect how the balloon works. They might also like to make their own balloon out of a piece of plastic. They can wrap the ends around a ring. Invite students to innovate as much as possible.

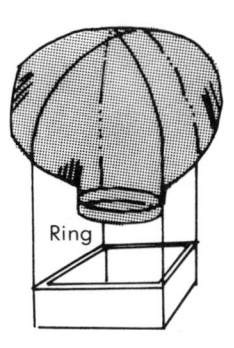

LESS STRUCTURED ACTIVITIES (GRADES 6-8)

FUN PRACTICE USING METRICS

A. MAKE METRIC COOKIES

Materials — Use a recipe from a cookbook but convert ingredients to metric.

Some Possible Activities   Discuss whether the children had any problems cooking metrically.

B. Have a Metric Broad Jump or Hop

Materials Metric tapes or metric sticks

Opening Questions How far can you hop?
How far can you broad jump?

Some Possible Activities Have the students jump in groups of five and determine metrically the average jump and/or hop of their groups.

C. Have a Balloon-Distance Race

Materials Balloons, metric tape or metre stick

Opening Questions Which team can get their balloons to go the farthest?

Some Possible Activities Go outside and divide the class into groups of five. Each student is to blow their balloons up as much as they dare. One student in each group releases his or her balloon. The second student then goes to where that balloon landed and releases his or her balloon. This continues until all the children in the team have had a turn. The distance is then measured metrically to determine how far their balloons went from the starting point. The team whose balloons went the greatest distance wins.

Play Deaden the Sound

Materials A small radio, several different size boxes, each of which can fit over one or more of the others and over the radio, cloth, paper, insulating material, cotton balls

Opening Questions How can we deaden the sound of this radio using these materials?

Some Possible Activities If possible, have two radios with the same volume and invite two groups of students, in a stipulated time, to have a "deadening the sound" race. Later, discuss how sound can go through objects and what kinds of things deaden sound well.

What Do Things Look Like Under Sun Lamps (Ultraviolet Lamps)?

Materials White cloth, any kind of rocks that will give off a florescence under ultraviolet light

Opening Questions What do things look like under ultraviolet lamps?

LESS STRUCTURED

Some Possible Activities

Have the children look at white cloth in normal light and then under ultraviolet light. Invite them to look at all kinds of things. If you can get some florescent paints or rocks, have them look at these as well. *Caution:* Students should not look into these lamps as they might burn the retina of the eye. They should also be warned not to have the light shining on their skin as they could get sunburned in only a few minutes.

Flying Things

A. Make a Toy Helicopter and Spin It

Materials

Small thin pieces of wood, candy sticks, and wood glue

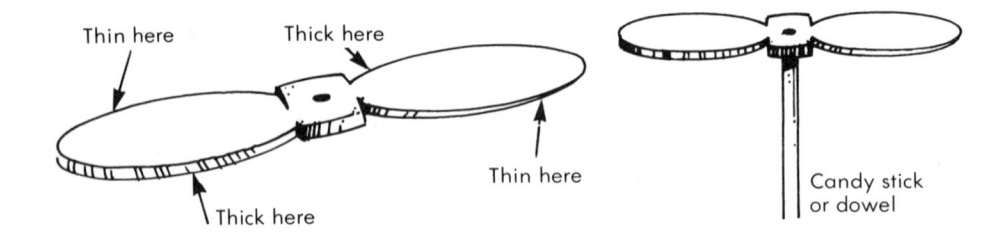

Opening Questions

Who can make a helicopter to stay up the longest?
Who can make a helicopter go the farthest?

Some Possible Activities

Invite students to make a helicopter. Have them make a propeller from a small piece of wood about 14 cm. long, 1.5 cm. wide, and 1 cm. or less thick. It is suggested that the propeller initially be made of wood and be cut with a knife or prepared in advance in a wood shop. It should be sandpapered and the tips rounded to make a good propeller. Make a small hole in the center of the propeller with a point of a knife or a small drill so it will just fit over a candy stick or a small dowel as shown in the figure. Place some wood glue around this hole and allow it to dry for 24 hours or more.

When dry, pick up the helicopter and roll it rapidly several times between the palms of the hands. When the propeller is spinning rapidly, let it spin away from the hands. If this is done correctly, it should spin in the air for several metres. It may be caught by other students or allowed to fall, preferably on a surface that will cushion its fall, like a lawn.

Invite students to study what factors influence how well the helicopter flies, what they need to do to make
a better helicopter, and how they can make it more appealing to the eye. For example, ask how they would make one from plastic and cardboard, how the weight of the materials they use affects the flying of the helicopter, and so on.

Challenge them to try to construct a super helicopter from several kinds of materials.

B. Paper Airplanes

Materials
Different kinds of paper, for example, typing and construction paper, poster board, plastic backed paper, and so on

Opening Questions
How can you make a paper airplane out of these things?
Which kind of paper will make the best airplane?
What will an airplane have to do to be good?
After they have made their airplanes, ask:
How do you feel about your airplanes?
State:
If someone is having trouble with an airplane, would you please help him or her?
Discuss some things they might try to make their airplanes go farther.
Later ask:
What have you discovered about your plane? What seems to affect how the plane flies?

Some Possible Activities
Invite students to set a distance goal and try to reach it by modifying their planes or making new ones until they reach it. Discuss how the size of the wings and shape of the nose and tail affect how the plane flies. Have them time how long their plane stays up and determine what they can do to increase the time.

Observe some birds or films of them and discuss how the birds differ and which ones soar the best and why.

Invite the children to see how good their spatial relations are by having each student sail his or her plane, one at a time, while another student tries to hit it in midair with his or her plane. After this, discuss what can be done to prevent air collisions. Ask: "What can you learn from birds that might help you make better airplanes? What factors seem to affect how your airplane flies? How do you think your airplanes would fly with the wind or against the wind? Why? What could you do to find out? What could we do to make our planes more attractive? How could we display them?"

Invite students to make gliders and test how they fly.

C. Kites

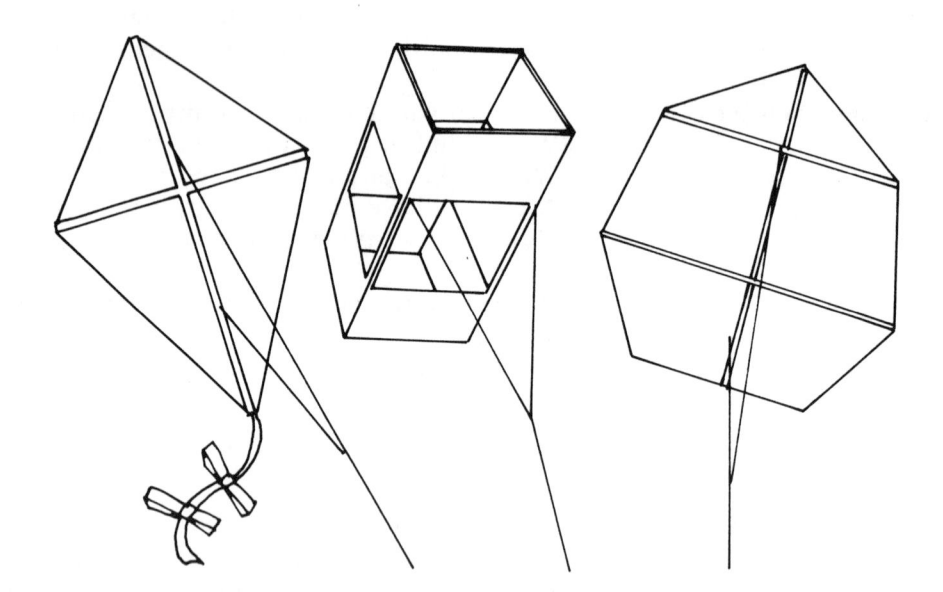

Materials	Plastic such as that used by dry cleaners and paper to cover the kite, small pieces of wood to form the supports, string, transparent tape or glue, cloth for the tail
Opening Questions	How can we make some kites? What will we need? How should they be constructed? What shape should they be?
Some Possible Activities	Encourage the children to plan in small groups how they are going to make their kites and then construct them. After they have done this, you might bring in some books on kites. Discuss the role of the tail and how it helps to stabilize the kite. Have them experiment with how long the tail should be by flying their kites on windy and calm days. If there is a local kite store, invite the children to visit it. Discuss some of the dangers of flying kites near power lines. Point out that they should *never use thin wire instead of string to fly a kite because of the danger involved if it hits a power line.* Invite them to make several kinds of kites and find out how different cultures use them, for example, how the Japanese use them to celebrate certain holidays.

What Will Happen to Ice Cubes Placed in Alcohol and Water?

246 DISCOVERY SCIENCE RESOURCE ACTIVITIES

Materials	2 #300 ml. beakers — one ½ filled with water, and the other ½ filled with alcohol, ice cubes
Opening Questions	What do you think will happen if an ice cube is placed in water? What will happen if it is placed in alcohol?
Some Possible Activities	Place the ice cubes in water and alcohol. Invite the students to weigh equal volumes of alcohol and water and to compare which has a greater density. They then might do an additional activity where they compare how a hard-boiled egg sinks in water but floats when salt is added to the water.

How Can You Make Something Move Up and Down without Touching It? (Cartesian Diver)

Materials	Small, plastic, transparent bottle filled with water and capped, eye dropper

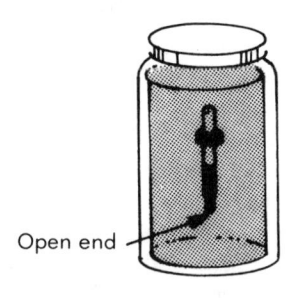

Open end

Opening Questions	How can I make the eye dropper go up and down without touching it?
Some Possible Activities	You should adjust the amount of water in the eye dropper so it only sinks about half way in the bottle. Pick up the bottle and tell the students you have special powers. You can make the eye dropper go up or down *at your will.* Press it. It will move down. Stop pressing it and it should move up.

What Can You Find Out About Isopods?

Materials	Isopods, metric ruler, straw or stirring stick
Opening Questions	What can you find out about isopods?
Some Possible Activities	Invite students to measure the isopods and determine how they vary in size. Find out if the isopods prefer a dark or a light place, a warm or a cold place. Determine how they move and how they can smell or see. Have an isopod race.

LESS STRUCTURED

SECTION 5

PIAGETIAN TYPES OF DISCOVERY ACTIVITIES

Outlined below are a few special Piagetian types of activities to help you see how Piaget's theory may be applied to the different elementary school levels. These activities are outlined under specific operational cognitive abilities such as classification and conservation to show you how to take an operation and devise activities to involve children in these processes. Many of the other activities in this Discovery Resource Activities section of the text are also Piagetian in design but are not organized around specific operations as these are. To get more ideas for activities, look at the Piagetian interviews in chapter 2.[1] These interviews may also be given as activities. You should realize, however, that perhaps one half or more of your students may not attain the tasks correctly. If this happens, the children who did not achieve them need further involvement with similar experiences. The children who do not achieve the tasks should *not* be told they failed. Piaget states that the children themselves will know when they get the tasks correct. He believes, for example, that appropriate reinforcements for physical knowledge can come only from the physical objects themselves.

These activities are not included specifically to teach some operation but to demonstrate how children might be involved in physical experiences relative to their approximate development.

Each child will get out of the activity what he or she is cognitively ready to assimilate. The suggested questions are provided to illustrate how you *might* interact with children to determine what they are focusing on and how they reason. Practice in giving these activities should sensitize you to listening better to children and learning how to intervene with questions to cause them to think about what they are doing. Learning this style of teaching should help you to develop better the children's thinking and science knowledge.

Chapter 2 also describes activities involving class inclusion, conservation, ordering, and reversibility.

PIAGETIAN ACTIVITIES (PRIMARY GRADES)

See all the other preschool-primary grade activities. Those requiring students to act on objects are all Piagetian types of activities.

---

1. See Arthur A. Carin and Robert B. Sund, *Teaching Science Through Discovery,* 4th ed. (Columbus: Charles E. Merrill, 1980).

Class Inclusion: Do they know that subclasses are included in a major class? (Ages 6–7)

1. Show several pictures of plants and animals.

ASK:

How many plants are there?
How many animals are there?
Are there more animals than plants?
Are there more living things than animals?

2. Invite students to collect pictures of animals that move fast and slow, for example, a fly or rabbit and a turtle or a snail.
Try to get more examples of fast animals than slow ones. Place the pictures of the fast and slow ones on the tackboard.

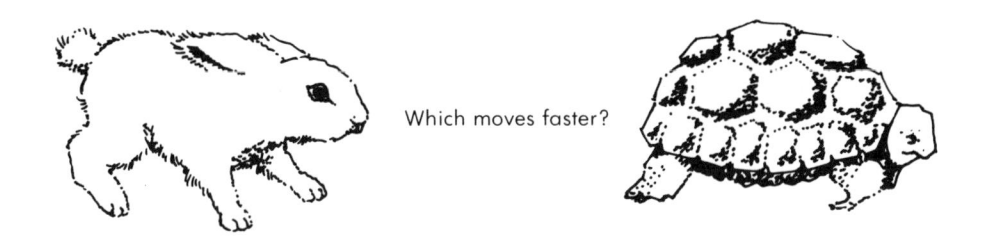

ASK:

What are all the pictures of?
How many slow animals are there?
Are there more fast animals than slow animals?

DISCUSSION:

Class inclusion is a very important operational ability. It is a good indicator that a student is developing representational thought, which is so essential in using symbols such as letters of the alphabet. A child that has difficulty with class inclusion probably has problems with reading.

Spatial Relations (Ages 6–7)

1. Give students pieces of straw and ask them to construct the diamond shape as best they can. Their construction should be accurate in construction, not cuboidal as indicated below.

2. Ask children to duplicate the following:

DISCUSSION:

If they do not duplicate objects to the correct shape or size, they do not have good geometrical spatial conceptualization.

Also have students read words with letter combinations (words) such as "park," "bath," "dad," "quiet," "man" and "woman," and so on. If they do not perform well on these tasks and the letter discrimination, we suggest you involve them with activities found in the Elementary Science Unit: Attribute Games and Problems, Webster Division, McGraw-Hill, 1974, or Material Objects Unit SCIS II, Rand McNally, 1976. Both of these units involve activities to help students discriminate better and develop class inclusion.

Ordering: Placing objects in order (Ages 6–8)

Give the children ten cards showing different animals. Each drawing of an animal should increase in size over the previous one. Tell them to: Place the animals in order. Start with the smallest. Number the animals in order. Have the children check their answers with the other children. Note if they seem to order mainly by trial and error or have some organized procedure for doing this. If the students do this well, you may want to give them four more pictures that fit in between these ten animal sizes. Have them place these four where they think they belong.

DISCUSSION:

If they do this well, they probably are able to order relatively well.

Associativity: Realize that it doesn't matter how you arrange things. The number or area will remain the same. (Ages 6-8)

1. Place ten counters, blocks or buttons, in a straight line and have students count them. Then move them to form a circle.

ASK:

Are there more, less, or the same number of counters now as when they were in a straight line?
How would you prove you are right?
Note that this activity is also related to conservation of substance and number, but here you are trying to find out if students know that reorganizing the counters doesn't change its number.

2. Invite students to count counters in two directions, for example, from left to right and then right to left, to see if they get the same number. Have them count two groups of objects, for example, three and two, and then count all of them to see what number they get. Then have them count first the group of two and then three to see what they get.

DISCUSSION:

If they have associativity, they will realize that three and two equals five objects and that two and three equals five objects.

One-to-One Correspondence (Ages 6–8)

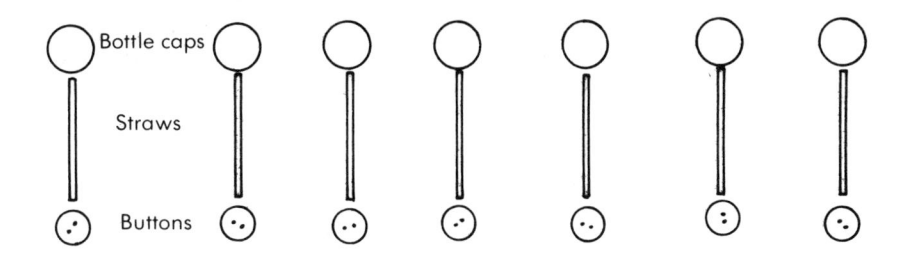

Obtain five bottle caps, buttons, straws, or any other type of marker that you want to use (for example, coins). Have the students line up the buttons in a row and then do the same thing with the bottle caps directly across from the buttons.

ASK:

Are there more, less, or the same number of buttons as bottle caps?
Then move the buttons so they are spread out but do not move the bottle caps.

ASK:

Are there now more, less, or the same number of buttons as bottle caps? Why?
If the children think there are more buttons than bottle caps,

ASK:

Please count them. Now what do you think?
If they still do not realize that each button corresponds with each bottle cap, have them connect each pair by placing a straw between them.

ASK:

Are there more, less, or the same number of buttons as bottle caps now?

DISCUSSION:

If students still do not conceptualize one-to-one correspondence, just smile and have them place the materials in a box to be collected. Repeat this activity several times using different markers until the children do correspond.

Coordinating Systems, Horizontal and Vertical (Ages 6–12)

This is an exercise in reproducing and estimating the length of a line. Give the children a meter, compass, string, small triangle that has one angle similar to the one shown, rulers and paperstrips.

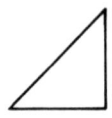

ASK:

What is the length of the line?

Draw a picture just like this one.

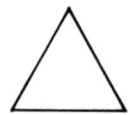

Remove the picture from the students' vision. Tell them that they may refer to it if need be.

DISCUSSION:

Children of 6-7	usually use no measurement.
7-8	measure the length of the lines.
9-10	superimpose △ to measure angle.
10-12	begin to use measurement to accurately reproduce the angle.

Failure to be able to coordinate the horizontal and vertical as presented here would present children with problems in geometry and in understanding certain science concepts, particularly in geology and astronomy.

Conservation of Length (Ages 7–8)

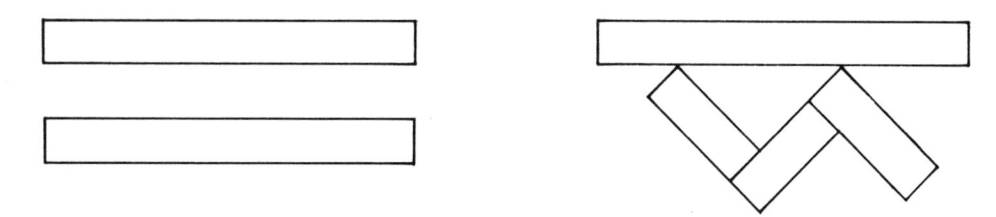

Take two strips of paper.

ASK:

Are these strips just as long as each other?
Cut one of the strips and combine them so as not to make a straight line as indicated above. Tell the students that you have a rabbit that is going to move along the two paper paths.

ASK:

Would the rabbit make just as many hops on each path or would it make more or fewer hops on one of the paths?
Why do you think so?
If the children think the uncut paper is longer, they do not conserve length and will have difficulty in understanding units and measurement.

Conservation of Length (Ages 7–8)

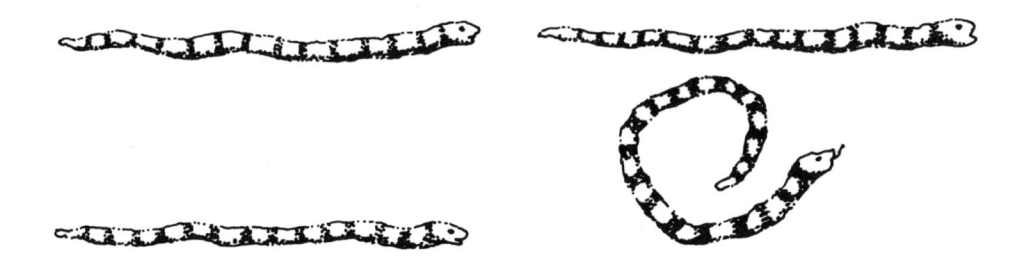

Draw the following diagrams of the snakes.

ASK:

What do you notice about their lengths in diagram 1?
In diagram 2, is the coiled snake longer, shorter, or the same length as the other snake?

Take a rope and lay it out flat. Then twirl it.

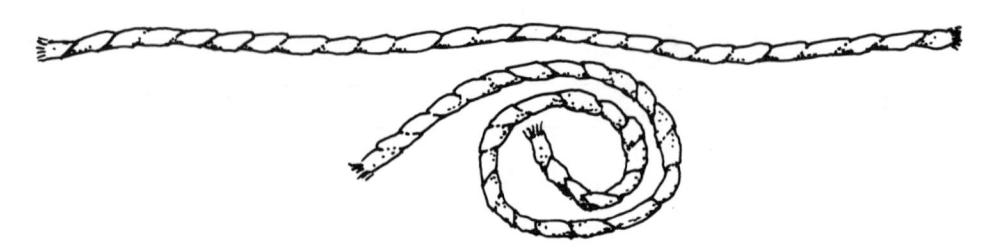

ASK:

Is the rope now longer, shorter, or the same length as when I curled it?

DISCUSSION:

You might invite students to measure its length, but even if they measure it and do not conserve length, they will still think the curled rope is shorter.

Conservation of Area (Ages 7–8)

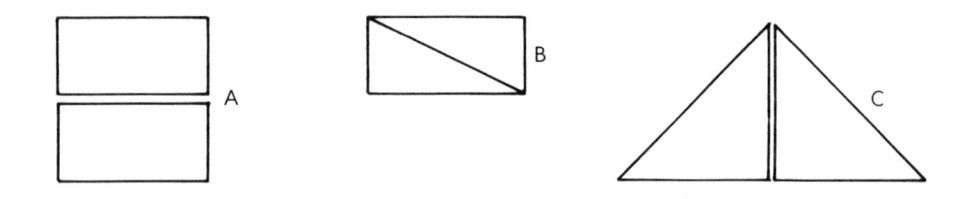

Cut a piece of paper into two rectangles.

ASK:

Do these two pieces of paper cover the same amount of table?
Cut another piece of paper of the same size diagonally as shown in B and arrange each triangle as shown in C.

ASK:

Do the cut pieces of paper in C cover as much as the paper in A?
Why do you think your answer is correct?
How could you prove your answer is right?

DISCUSSION:

If the students suggest that C covers as much as A, this indicates they conserve area. They should then suggest that if the two pieces of paper were combined together as in A, they would be the same. This indicates that they are capable of *reversing* and establishing *logical necessity*. This also means that they reason; that since nothing has been taken away, the paper covers as much. Reversibility and logical necessity are intrinsically involved in conservation tasks.

254   DISCOVERY SCIENCE RESOURCE ACTIVITIES

Ascending a Class Hierarchy (Ages 7-8)

Prepare ten pictures of animals. Include some birds, fish, and mammals.

ASK:
*Please group these animals any way you want.
How did you group them? Why did you group them that way?
Which of these groups were fish?
Which of these groups were birds?
Which of these groups were mammals?
Is there some way we can place all of them in one group?
What would the group be? Why?
Are birds animals?
Are fish animals?
Are hairy animals (mammals) animals?*

DISCUSSION:

If the children realize on their own that all of these things are animals and that the subgroups of birds, fish, and mammals can be grouped under animals, they are able to ascend a classification hierarchy.

Time — Understanding Sequence and Duration (Ages 7-8)

Time requires the coordination of motions. Set up the apparatus as shown in the diagram.

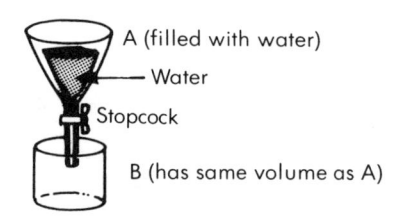

A (filled with water)
Water
Stopcock
B (has same volume as A)

Give a sheet with several sketches of the apparatus to the children but show no water in either the top or bottom container.
Have the children note, in the demonstration, the water level in A.
Let a little water flow from A to B.

ASK:

Please draw where the water is now in A and B.
Repeat this six or seven times.

ASK:

Please number your drawings in order in the margin.
You determine whether the order is correct.

ASK:

Please cut off the numbers indicating the order.
Please cut the paper into strips so that each separate drawing is on its own strip.
Please shuffle these and then arrange them in their proper order.
When water A was at (pick a certain level), where was B?
Which drawing did you make at B that equals the one in A?
Did the time it took for the water to leave A equal the time it took to fill B?
Does the liquid take as much time to go from this level of A (point to one level change) as it does to go from here to here in B?

DISCUSSION

Time is a relatively complex thing for primary children to learn. To comprehend it, they have to understand that with time, motion is involved. They also have to understand that in time, things follow a sequence, have a duration, occur in a succession, and are simultaneous. When water goes from A to B, all of these things occur.

To read time on a clock, children, furthermore, must be able to order, know numbers, and know what units are. They also must understand that they may be repetitive and follow in succession in a linear as well as a circular manner as in seconds, minutes, and hours on a clock. Teachers may be fooled into thinking some young children understand time if they can read a digital clock. This may not be the case. All the children may be doing is mouthing a sequence of numbers without really understanding their relationship to the duration of time. After all, 4:30 has quite a different meaning from 430, although the same numbers are used.

Spatial Relations (Ages 7 – 8)

256 DISCOVERY SCIENCE RESOURCE ACTIVITIES

Ask the children to draw a mountain and place trees on it.

DISCUSSION:

If they have good spatial relations, they will draw the trees perpendicular to the mountain.

Constructing a Set Containing a Single Element (Ages 7–9)

Show six triangles. Let triangles be all red or green, with one of them yellow. On the back of the yellow one, make an "x". Show the children both sides of the triangles. Then place all of the triangles color side up with no markings.

ASK:

Which one of these objects is entirely different from the others?
What makes it different?
How could we group all of these objects?

DISCUSSION:

If students can identify the triangle with the "x" on the back as being unequally different, they are able to establish a set as having a single element.

Making *All* and *Some* Relationships — Realizing That Some Objects, (Those in the Subset) Are Also Included in the Group Referring to All of Them (the Set) (Ages 7–8)

Cut triangular, circular, and rectangular shapes out of the colored paper.

ASK:

Are all of the squares red?
What color are all of the circles?
What color are the triangles?
Are all of the triangles red triangles?
Invite the students to group all of the triangles together.

ASK:

Are all of these things triangles?
Are some of these triangles green?
Are all of these triangles green?

DISCUSSION:

Some children in this age group have difficulty differentiating between *some* and *all* because they do not class include well. The advent of this ability indicates that the children are beginning to develop the class-inclusion operation. They still may not, however, understand that all dogs are also animals.

Reordering (Ages 8–10)

Cut ten straws so they vary from short to tall. Prepare ten pictures of trees ordered in a similar way.
Ask the children to order the straws from short to tall and place the trees in the opposite order (tall to short next to them). One study found that only about 10 percent of second graders could do this.

Spatial Reasoning (Age 9)

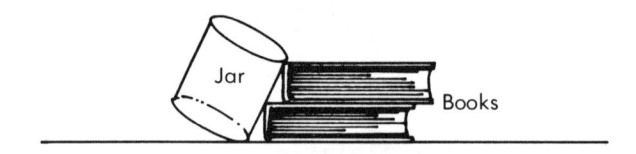

Show a tipped bottle and tell the children the bottle is supposed to be one-half filled with water.

ASK:

Please draw how you think the water will look in the jar.
After they have finished their drawing, take a bottle and fill it one-half full of water. Have them check their drawing with what they saw.

DISCUSSION:

Children do not have a good concept of coordinates. Therefore, they will draw the water oriented to the sides or bottom of the jar rather than to the table it is sitting on.
  Reordering means to be able to order in different ways, forward as well as backward. This activity requires children to order in each way as well as to do one-to-one correspondence. For example, for every large tree, there is a small straw.

Unit Repetition or Iteration (Ages 7–10)

In this exercise, students measure a large area by using a small unit over and over again.
Cut a rectangle as shown in A. Then cut a triangle as shown with one side 2 cm. long.

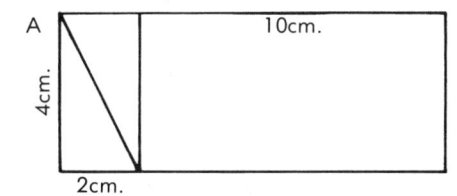

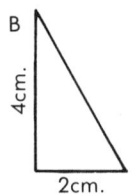

ASK:

How would you use triangle B to determine the area in A?
Why do you think your response is correct?

DISCUSSION:

If students achieve the task, this shows they can use units to determine area by superimposition. In this case, they superimpose the small triangle on the rectangle and then total the number of triangles used to state the area in triangles. More advanced students may be able to determine the area mathematically.

Ordering by Weight (Ages 9–10)

Try to obtain several (six or more) different pieces of metal of the same volume or take medicine vials of the same volume and fill them with different kinds of materials, for example, salt, sand, dirt, water, baking soda, rice, flour, and so on.

ASK:

Please place these things in order by weight.
Later have them weigh the objects and order them.

ASK:

How good were your estimations?

DISCUSSION:

Children may have difficulty doing this for as long as two years after they are able to order by length or height.

Concept of a Null Class (Ages 9–11)

Cut 12 triangular, circular, and rectangular shapes from colored paper. Draw and paste pictures of plants, animals, or houses on 9 of them. Leave the other 3 papers blank.

ASK:

Please group these things any way you wish.
They should now place them in only two groups: blank and nonblank.

DISCUSSION:

Children, however, up to age 11 have difficulty realizing the existence of a null set. This may be attributed to their concrete thinking. A null set requires abstract reasoning.

Descending a Classification Hierarchy (Ages 9–11)

Insure that the students know the characteristics of mammals. Prepare ten pictures of mammals, birds, and other animals. Include several dogs as well as other mammals and ducks as well as other birds.

ASK:

Please group these animals any way you like. What groups did you get?
How many mammals did you get?
How many birds did you get?
Is there any way you can divide your mammal group? Why?
Is there any way you can change you bird group?
What group of animals do dogs belong to?
What group of animals do ducks belong to?
What group do mammals belong to?
What group do birds belong to?

Ask the students to mix all of the pictures again, make a few groups, and use these groups to try to make more subgroups.

ASK:

How did you group your animals?
Why did you group them that way?

DISCUSSION:

If students go from animals to mammals and birds and then to dogs and ducks, they have indicated they can descend a classification hierarchy.

Conservation of Weight (Ages 9–12)

Obtain some clay. Have students prepare two round balls that weigh the same. They can check their weight by using a balance.

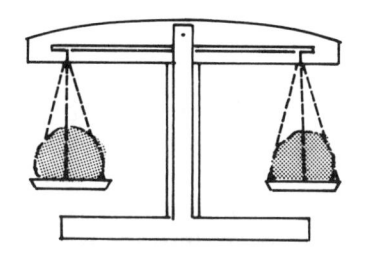

ASK:

Please make one of your clay balls into a hamburger shape.
Will your clay now weigh more, less, or the same amount as before?
How could you tell?
Have the students weigh their clay and find out.

ASK:

What did you find out?
Why do you think it weighs the same?
Is there some rule you can give about changing things and their weight?

DISCUSSION:

If they state that spreading things out changes the thickness but also increases the area covered, and that there is no loss in weight, they are giving a compensation type of justification. This means that the weight of the increased area compensates for the loss in weight in the thick area. If they state that when you roll the ball up again, it will weigh the same, they are demonstrating reversibility. This means they can reverse their thought processes. Both reversibility and compensatory reasoning characterize concrete-operational thought.

Conservation of Displacement Volume (Ages 11 and Beyond)

Obtain a graduate or use a jar. Fill it three-fourths full of water. Take a cube of clay and wrap a string around it so it can be lowered into the water. Place a rubber band around the graduate to estimate where the water will be when the clay is lowered into it. Lower the clay very slowly.

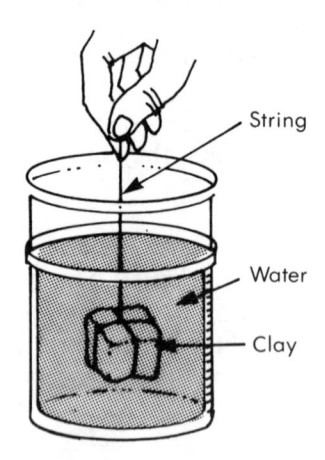

ASK:

How good was your estimate?
Move your rubber band so the top of it marks where the water is. Now take your clay out of the water. Cut it in half. Tie each half with string. Estimate where you think the water will be now when you lower these two halves into the water. Use a marking pencil to mark where you think it will be. Do not move your rubber band. Lower your two pieces of clay into the water slowly.

ASK:

What did you discover?
Can you give a rule for what you discovered?

DISCUSSION:

If the children explain that the volume of the two halves of clay is the same as the whole piece and that they displace the same amount of water, they are conserving displacement volume. It is the volume here and what it displaces that is important and not the weight.

Law of Buoyancy — Flotation (Ages 11 and Beyond)

An object will float if the weight of its volume is less than an equal volume of water. The object will float above the water line when its weight displaces an equal amount of weight of water.

262 DISCOVERY SCIENCE RESOURCE ACTIVITIES

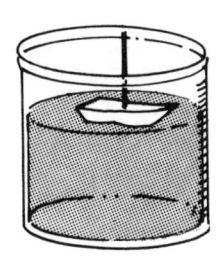

Tell the students that 1 ml. of pure water weighs 1 gram. Have them make a small clay boat or make one out of a small milk carton and weigh the boat. Tell the students you have a rectangular barge that weighs 500 grams and a volume of 1000 ml.

ASK:

How much water would it displace?
How far would it sink into the water? Why?

DISCUSSION:

If they suggest that it would sink about halfway in the water, they probably understand the concept of buoyancy and flotation. A further check would be to give them problems where odd numbers of weights and volumes are used for the barge.
They should then estimate how many grams and milliliters of water their boat will displace. Have them: obtain a large graduate or calibrated beaker and fill it three-fourths full with water. Determine the amount of water in the container and then place the boat in it.

ASK:

How far does the ship sink in the water?
Add a 10 gram weight and determine how high the water moves.

ASK:

How high would it move with a 20 gram weight? Why?

Conservation of Internal Volume (Ages 10–12)

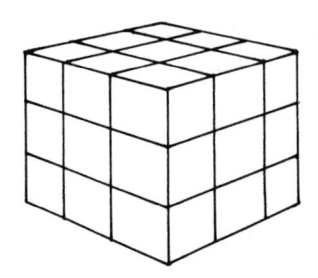

Present students with 27 small cubes arranged to form a large cube. Tell the students that each cube represents a hollow room and all of the cubes have open doors between them. Inside the hollow rooms there is a butterfly that flies from room to room. These rooms can be rearranged by the owner since they are modules.

One day the owner has to move the modules to a different lot. She has to arrange the modules in a different way.

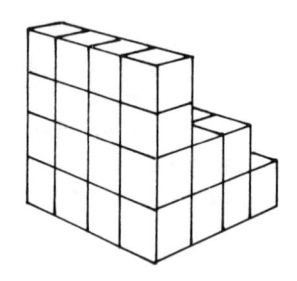

ASK:

Is there just as much, more, or less space inside now for the butterfly to fly? Why?
How would you prove it?
How could you use mathematics to prove it?
If they indicate that no rooms have been taken away or added, therefore, there is the same amount of interior, they are using logical necessity to justify their answer. A more sophisticated response showing higher cognitive abilities would be to demonstrate that the number of rooms are the same.

Spatial Relations (Ages 11–12)

The child realizes that the angle at which light or an object hits a surface or another object will be reflected at the same angle. In scientific terms: the angle of incidence equals the angle of reflection.

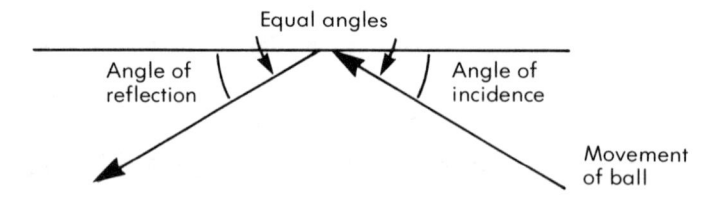

Give students a marble or Ping-Pong ball. Invite them to hit it against a wall.

ASK:

What kind of rule can you discover about how the ball bounces back?

DISCUSSION:

If they come up with an explanation that the ball seems to bounce from the wall as it goes in, they probably understand the rule.

Continuous Divisibility (Related to Concept of Infinity) (Ages 11–12)

Ask the students to divide a circle as many times as possible and see if they keep at it for awhile.

ASK:

How long could you keep on dividing the circle?

DISCUSSION:

If they come up with the idea that this could go on and on and on, they have grasped the basic concept of infinity and realize that some things, as in nature, can be continually divided, for example, the measurement of temperature, time, motion, and change. Consider whether the students understand the continuous possibility of divisibility.

ASK:

How long could you go on dividing a rod or line?

Spatial Relations (Age 11 and Beyond)

Show one surface of a cube.

□

ASK:

How many edges can't you see?

DISCUSSION:

Most students have difficulty perceiving the object from different viewpoints. Many adults have difficulty with this problem, too, and suggest numbers other than eight.

SECTION 6

Discovery Activities for
"SPECIAL" CHILDREN

Below are a few discovery activities to help you to work with children in your class who are "special." No doubt you either now have or soon will have such children in your class. There are over 8 million youngsters in our schools today (one in ten!) with some form of handicap. Public Law 94-142 allows for mainstreaming handicapped students into the regular classroom whenever practical. The children's handicaps may be sensory, mental, emotional, physical, or social. Whatever the handicap, it interferes with a child's ability to learn.

Discovery science activities can assist you in providing success and a sense of achievement to handicapped children who seldom enjoy such success in school. It is not easy to accomplish this task. However, by becoming aware of the kinds of "specialness" *each* child possesses and possible ways of helping the child function within these limitations to the best of his or her ability, you will begin to individualize your science program.

Labels often get in the way of looking at individuals. We believe "special" individuals differ significantly in what they need to succeed in the world. They are individuals, as Norris Haring says, "with *special needs,* a phrase that is becoming more and more popular as a description of these members of our society."[1]

Discovery science activities are presented for children who have these handicaps or disabilities and are more likely to be in mainstream classes like yours:
1. Sensory handicapped—hearing or vision impairment
2. Mentally retarded
3. Visual perception problems
4. Emotionally handicapped

Although other handicaps and disabilities are prevalent and not unimportant, our activities are limited here to the above four categories of children most frequently encountered by classroom teachers. For more about these special children, refer to chapters 8 and 10.

These activities are not meant to be exhaustive but represent ways you can try to meet the special needs of your students in science. As you practice using them, you will sensitize yourself to getting to know these students better and finding ways to provide successful science/learning activities for them. You probably will discover ways of modifying the discovery science activities in the later sections of part five for this purpose. Learning to be more sensitive to children with "special needs" will help you respond the same way with all of your students. The unexpected gain to you of focusing upon "special" children will be to see all your students as special.

---

1. Norris G. Haring, Ed., *Behavior of Exceptional Children, An Introduction to Special Education,* 2nd ed. (Columbus, Ohio: Charles E. Merrill Publishing Co., 1978), p. 1.

SENSORY HANDICAPPED CHILDREN

How Can Blind or Visually Impaired Children Learn about Magnets? (K–8)

Materials Assorted magnets, common objects attracted and not attracted by magnets (paper clips, rubber bands, buttons, plastic and metal zippers, pencils, paper, wire, and so on, 2 shallow boxes. (*Important Note:* Avoid sharp or pointed objects.)

Opening Questions *What are magnets?*
What things do they pick up?

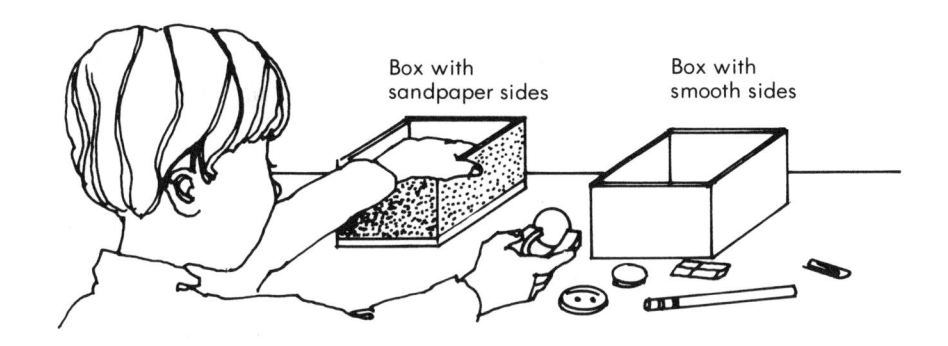

Some Possible Activities Have the children handle magnets and describe the shapes (bar, disc-shaped, horseshoe, U-shaped, cylindrical, and so on)

ASK:

How will you know if a magnet picks up (attracts) an object?

They will readily discern by touching the magnet that something was attracted as it "sticks" to the magnet. Ask them to name the objects on the table and then test to "see" (find out) if they are attracted by the magnet. They can sort objects tested by the magnet into two shallow boxes. One with smooth sides can be called "Objects attracted by magnets." Sandpaper glued to the other box can facilitate *tactile* sorting in this box called "Objects not attracted by magnets." Once they understand the sorting system, they can verify the contents of both boxes by themselves and even test new objects with magnets.

In What Ways Can the Blind or Visually Impaired Identify Objects in the Environment? (K–8)

Materials Masks to cover eyes, pairs of noise makers (rattles, party horns, "clickers," and so on)

Opening Questions *Can you find your partner if you cannot see him or her? How?*

Some Possible Activities

Take a group of sighted and blind or visually impaired children outside your classroom on a relatively open (free of trees, shrubs, or other obstacles) lawn area. Use other students or adults to keep the children from moving outside the area as they engage in the activity. Play a game in which the children assume the roles of limited-vision animals. Sighted children wear masks on their eyes. One child is a predator, the other prey. Each prey has one of a variety of paired noisemakers (two clickers, party horns, and so on). At a signal, preys try to find their partners who have the same noisemakers. Predators in the meantime try to capture the noisy prey.

After the fun game, have the children all sit quietly and listen to the environmental sounds.

ASK:
Which sounds can you identify?
Which sounds are made by the same source?
In which direction do you hear the various sounds?
Which sound do you like the best? Why?
Which sound do you like the least? Why?
How do you think a particular sound was made?

For more information about this and other life science activities for the visually impaired student, see Larry Malone and Linda DeLucchi, "Life Science for Visually Impaired Students," *Science and Children,* 16, no. 5 (February 1979): 29–31.

What Are Some Ways for Blind or Visually Impaired Students to Find Out About Their Bodies? (K–8)

Materials — Stethoscopes, braille-faced clocks

Opening Questions — *Does you heart beat faster when you lie down or stand up or run?*

Some Possible Activities

After raising the question with blind or visually impaired children, give simple instructions on how to use the equipment and carry out the activity. Invent the term *variable* and explain that the variable they will investigate is body position and how it affects their heart rate. Have the children learn to listen to their heartbeats through the stethoscope and count the beats on the braille-faced clock. For younger children, an adult or older child can help them with the numbers.

After they have completed taking and recording their heart rates in lying and standing positions, discuss this and help them to see the effect of body position on heart rate. You can extend the activity by asking further questions.

ASK:

What other variables could be investigated in this activity?
What effect would these things have on heart rate: age, amount of movement, time of day, drinking soda pop, smoking, and so on?

Encourage the children to explore the variables without your giving them directions on how to do it. You might also introduce animals and see if the children can use them to compare and do further exploration.

How Can Blind Students "See" and Compare Varying Polluted Water? (4–8)

Materials
4 jars of water containing different pollutants, light sensor (available on Federal Quota from the American Printing House for the Blind, P.O. Box 6085, Louisville, Kentucky 40206), light source (sunlight, filmstrip projector, and so on)

Opening Questions
How can we (blind students) find out (by using our hearing) which jars contain the most polluted water?

Some Possible Activities
Prepare four jars of water with varying amounts of pollutants (soil, debris, egg shells, and so on). Introduce and demonstrate to the students the *light sensor device* produced by the American Printing House for the Blind (APH). This device produces an *auditory* signal of varying pitch and volume as a result of its exposure to the intensity of light. Set up the four jars of varying pollutants with a light source behind it in this way:

Have students examine each jar at close range by pointing the light sensor directly at each jar, as shown above. A beeping sound is emitted, which becomes higher and more frequent with the greater amount of light coming into the sensor. Students will discover that the less pollutants in each jar, the greater amount of light coming through the jar, and therefore the more shrill and rapid the beep from the sensor. More pollutants result in much less light coming through the jar to the sensor and then a slower and lower pitched beep.

Note: For an excellent expanded description of the use of the light sensor with blind students, see Frank L. Franks and LaRhea Sanford, "Using the Light Sensor to Introduce Laboratory Science," *Science and Children* 13, no. 6 (March 1976): 48–49.

MENTALLY RETARDED CHILDREN

How Can Mentally Retarded Children Learn to Develop a Thermic Sense (Sense of Temperature)? (K–8)

Materials — Several metal bowls, water of varying temperatures

Opening Questions — *How do hot things feel?*
How do cold things feel?

Some Possible Activities — Prepare several metal bowls with varying temperatures of water from ice cold to very warm. *Caution:* Do not have the hot water hot enough to scald or injure any child. Let the water set in the bowls for a few minutes and then have the children feel the *outside* of the bowls.

ASK:

Which bowl feels cold?
Which one feels warm?
Which one feels hot?

If a child does not know the difference, repeat it.

Say:
This bowl feels cold.
Does it make your hand cold?
This bowl is hot.
Is your hand hot?
Where else have you felt hot and cold things?
Bring this activity to their immediate lives by relating to holding a glass of iced drink, a cup of hot soup, and so on.

Point out the dangers of hot and cold.

ASK:

Why should we use this potholder if we are holding something hot from the oven or stove?
Why should you wear a coat or gloves when it is very cold outside?
Where are very hot things in our homes?
Have pictures of oven, stove, radiators, and so on.

ASK:

Which things are very cold in our school?
Take the children to the cafeteria and have them tell or show you (or you show them) the refrigerator, freezer, and so on.

How Can Mentally Retarded Children Learn Sense of Weight? (K–8)

Materials — Small blocks of wood of the same size but different woods such as balsa (model airplane wood), oak, pine, mahogany, and so on

Opening Questions — *Which of these blocks do you think would be the heaviest? Lightest?*

Some Possible Activities — Ask the children what it means when people say something is heavy. Have them use whatever words will help them to develop the concept as long as the words do not connote misconceptions. They might say, "It's harder to lift." If they have difficulty with this concept, help them to develop it. Do the same with the idea of something lighter in weight. Now give them the blocks.

ASK:

Do you think they all weigh the same?
Which one might be the heaviest? Lightest?

Have the children feel the blocks and place them in order from heaviest to lightest.

Label the heaviest block with an H and use an L for the lightest one. Ask the children what things in the classroom are heavy and light. Place an H and L on the objects selected (heavy: desks, cabinets, teacher; light: paper, pencils, paper clips; and so on.) Explain why it is dangerous to lift very heavy things.

How Can Mentally Retarded Children Learn to Discriminate Tastes? (K–8)

Materials Box of cotton swabs and a bottle of solutions of common liquids that are salty, sweet, sour, bitter, acid, neutral

Opening Questions *How many of you would like to play a game?*
Are you a good detective?

Some Possible Activities Tell the children they are going to play a detective game to try to find out which things are in the bottles you have. Caution them never to taste anything they don't know about. Ask why they should not do this and get the point across about the dangers of poisons. Tell them that all of the things in the bottle are not poisonous and are things they taste everyday.

Have all children use a different swab and explain why they should (germs, colds, other diseases, and so on). Have all children get a sample of something sweet (syrup).

ASK:

What kind of taste is this?

Have them agree that it is *sweet* and if possible have them identify the source (syrup). Toss the cotton swab away and give them a second one. This time use a sour solution. Repeat the procedure in identification and invent the word *sour* orally and, if appropriate for the group, in writing on the chalkboard. Repeat this procedure for all of the solutions.

Ask the children what kinds of foods they eat that are salty, sweet, sour, bitter, acid, or neutral. Have them cut out pictures from magazines for each category. Discuss their lunch in school and visit the cafeteria to observe the foods and which category each food is in.

Note: For older or less retarded children, you can show them that different places on the tongue react more strongly to certain tastes. Touch solutions to these four sensation areas of the tongue:

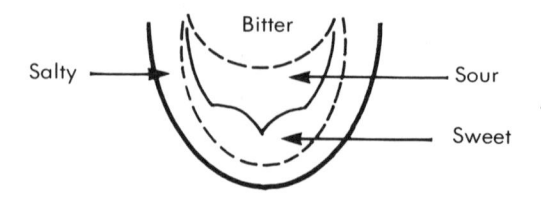

How Can Mentally Retarded Children Learn to Recognize Common Odors? (K–8)

Materials — Common odors in jars: onion, perfume, alcohol, pepper, cinnamon, peppermint, and so on

Opening Questions — *Who can tell us what this odor (smell) is?*

Some Possible Activities — Have the children smell a familiar odor (peppermint) by bringing the jar with the odor at least one foot below their noses and raising it slowly until they can smell it. (This avoids overwhelming the child with the odor and with some odors that might injure the child's sensitive nose.) *Note:* At first, for some mentally retarded children, it is best to help the children learn to recognize various odors by presenting the smell with the appropriate label, having them see the material, and then asking them to discriminate among various odors while blindfolded.

Label the odors either before or after identification, depending upon the children's level. Use words both orally and written for the names of odors as appropriate. Have the children identify odors in their homes, school, and outdoors. Have them cut pictures from magazines for common odors and label them: gasoline, flowers, paint, smoke, and so on. Have the children identify odors they like and dislike. Stress that some odors are dangerous, such as gas and smoke.

CHILDREN WITH VISUAL PERCEPTION PROBLEMS[2]

Observing Properties of Leaves (K–3)

Materials — Variety of leaves (maple, oak, elm, birch, and so on)

Opening Questions — *What do you notice about the shape of this leaf?*

---

2. The authors are indebted to the following article and others in the whole *Science and Children* issue devoted to "Science for the Handicapped": Marlene Thier, "Utilizing Science Experiences for Developing Perception Skills," *Science and Children* 13, no. 6 (March 1976): 39–40.

Have each child look at a maple leaf.

ASK:

What is this?
Where do you think it came from?
How many points does it have?
What color is it?
How many large lines (veins) are there coming from the stem?

Let the child experience the leaf through sensory activities, that is, feeling with hand, against cheek, smelling it, crushing it, and so on.
What does the smell make you think of?
How else would you describe the leaf?
Ask the children to think of other properties. Invent the word *property* for the children to refer to the leaf's attributes. Introduce another species of leaf.

ASK:

How are the leaves alike? Different?
What properties are the same?
What properties are different?

Note: This activity can stimulate children to become sensitive in their visual perceptions of objects in their environment. Care should be taken not to rush the activity.

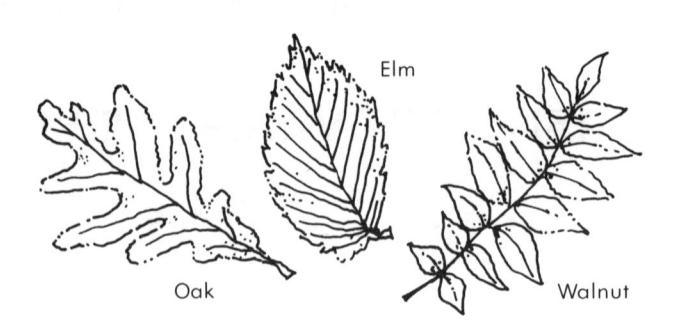

Comparing Properties of Shells or Buttons and Classifying Them (K–3)

Materials Assortment of shells or buttons

274 DISCOVERY SCIENCE RESOURCE ACTIVITIES

Some Possible Activities

Give each child a handful of shells or buttons.

ASK:

How are these things alike?
How are they different?
Group them together by the same property.
Which properties might you use?

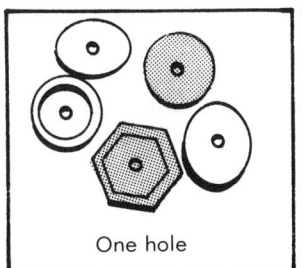

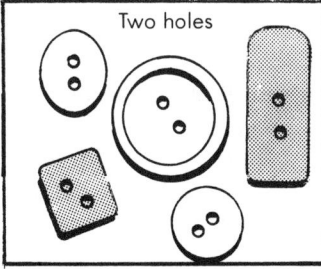

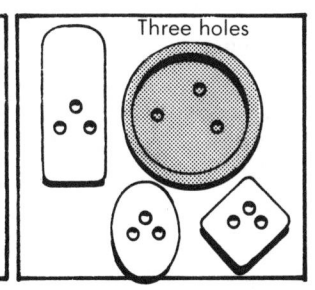

[One hole] [Two holes] [Three holes]

Let the children group them.

ASK:

How can you group the buttons using a different property?

Note: In this activity the child not only makes visual discriminations, but acts upon them.

Using Plants to Teach Visual Sequencing (K–3)

Materials Milk cartons, soil, pea seeds, chart paper

Some Possible Activities Have each child plant a pea plant in a milk carton. Make certain the children keep the soil moist, and have a time each day when they observe and record their observations. Mark on your chart any changes that take place each day. As soon as germination takes place and plants break through the soil, set up a chart for the children to record the growth of each of their plants. They can measure plant height using gummed paper to show the various stages of growth over a six-week period, like this:

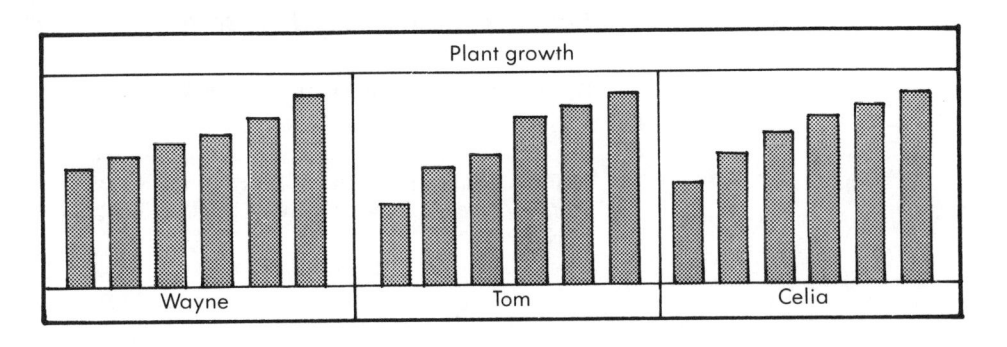

Plant growth — Wayne, Tom, Celia

"SPECIAL" CHILDREN 275

When working with younger children, plant an additional seed each week so they can see plants ranging in growth from one to six weeks. This reinforces their chart and helps them with visual sequencing. They begin to observe a natural phenomenon and learn to record small changes over a period of time and in a sequenced progression—something they need to know.

"Mr. O" and Relative Position and Motion (K–6)[3]

Materials Mr. O for each child, white pipe cleaners, gummed white dots, blocks

Some Possible Activities Children with perceptual problems usually have poor directionality concepts. "Mr. O" from the SCIIS Relative Position and Motion unit can help these children with learning position in space, relative position of the child in his or her environment, directionality, and figure–ground relationships.

Here is Mr. O. He sees things only from his point of view.

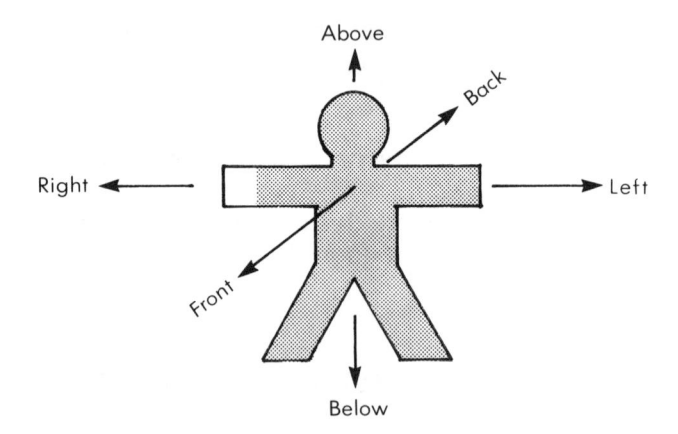

Cut out a Mr. O for each child. For younger children, after introducing Mr. O, play a game to familiarize them with his parts and invent words for directions in relation to him, as shown on the Mr. O sketch above. Younger children can also hang Mr. O around their necks at this point and you can point these things out to them:

Mr. O's right hand is white.
Put a white pipe cleaner around your right hand.
Mr. O has three white buttons on the front of him.
Put three white gummed paper dots on the front of you.

Now ask the children to place a block to the right of Mr. O.

---

3. For a detailed description of Mr. O, see Robert Karplus et al., *Relative Position and Motion (Level 4),* Teacher's Guide SCIIS (Chicago: Rand McNally & Co., 1978), pp. 29-39.

ASK:

Where is the block in relation to Mr. O?
Where is the block in relation to you?
Is it near or far?

Do the same with the left side, in front of, in back of, above, below, and so on using only one variable at a time. Gradually build to more than one variable.

Once the child begins to understand this use of Mr. O, take Mr. O from around the child's neck and turn Mr. O to face him or her.

ASK:

Where is Mr. O's hand now in relation to yours?

Place the block to the right, left, front, and back of Mr. O, and ask the child to report the position relative first to Mr. O and then to himself or herself.

Note: Children become aware of changes needed in describing directionality from a nonego-centered frame. They begin to develop direction giving through awareness of relative position in space and figure-ground relationships. Children with visual perception handicaps have great difficulty with this task and need the systematic help shown here.

Outside-the-Classroom Walk to Develop Visual Scrutiny and Analysis (K–6)

Materials Small envelopes or plastic bags, paper, pencils

Some Possible Activities Select a site outside your classroom where you and your students can take a walk. Before going, instruct the children to observe, record, or collect the following (task cards—3" x 5" index cards—can be used to write down what the children will look for):

A sample of five different colors of any *natural* object that has fallen to the ground (caution children not to pick anything from living organisms)
Places (to be listed on their recording sheets) where they saw:
   a. 3 different colors on the same plant
   b. 5 different shades of any one color (green, for instance) along the path
   c. 6 different textures on living organisms
   d. as many different colors as they can find
Samples of evidence that animals have inhabited the environment
Samples of dead insects
Samples of evidence that people have been in the area
Samples of different kinds of seeds in the area
Other samples that are applicable to your outdoor site

Have the children place their samples in small envelopes, plastic bags, or other suitable containers. With younger children or children who have severe visual perception handicaps, it is best to use one of the activities at a time, so they focus on one variable in their environment and filter out distractions. The activities also are progressive, moving from observation of many different plants (looking at plants and finding colors) to finding the same variable on only one plant (how many different colors on one plant).

Later, in the classroom discussions, help the children describe their samples and share them with their classmates. Further activities in pasting samples on paper, writing descriptive words for each object, and talking about their findings all aid children with visual perception handicaps in developing skills they will need for further exploration of their environments and for reading, writing, spelling, and so on.

Emotionally Handicapped Children

Learning About Our Environment by Touching

Materials Paper, crayons, chalk, soft pencils, tin foil

Opening Questions How can our fingertips give us different kinds of information than our eyes?

Some Possible Activities Direct contact and the understanding and mastery of everyday living experiences under a sensitive teacher's guidance can produce an extensive and exciting learning environment for the emotionally handicapped child. One such activity can be a tactile experience. Take your students (with assistance from parents) on a walk around the school. Have the children select surfaces and have them do rubbings of those surfaces using the materials listed above. They can do rubbings, for instance, in urban areas of sidewalks, manhole covers, grates, signs, and fences. The rubbings can be used to create texture panels and are also effective when they are individually matted and mounted. You might also attempt to get your students to talk about how the objects felt, for example, whether they were rough, smooth, soft, hard, wet, or dry.

You can find many more activities for emotionally handicapped children in this practical book: *An Outdoor Education Guide for Urban Teachers of the Emotionally Handicapped* (Proceedings), presented by the State University of New York State Education Department Division for Handicapped Children and the Division of Health, Physical Education and Recreation, in co-sponsorship with State University College of Arts and Science at Plattsburgh and Clinton, Essex, Warren, and Washington Counties BOCES, Special Study Institute, Funded Through: PL 91-230, June 1974.

Learning About Our Environment by Listening and Moving

Materials A walking trip in the community

Opening Questions *What people-made sights and sounds can you identify?*
How can you use your body to reproduce the sights and sounds?

Some Possible Activities Sitting or working in a confined space (a desk and chair, for instance) can make for static learning experiences. This is especially true for emotionally handicapped children. They need to stretch and expand their bodies and minds, probably more than other children. These children can also begin to feel the same freedom of clear movement outside as they would in a gymnasium. Take them into the community and ask them to identify these people-made sights and sounds:

taxi cabs	ambulances
cars	fire engines
fire alarms	construction machines
buses	trucks
airplanes	motorcycles
helicopters	air hammers

ASK:

What are the sounds of each vehicle?
How can you show the intensity and rhythm of each one with your body?
How is the fire engine sound different from the ambulance sound?
Show us the differences with your movements.
Would you move fast, slow, or jerky if you sounded like an airplane? A dump truck?
How are car horn sounds different? Make the sounds to show us.
How do various sounds make you feel? Happy? Sad? Show us by your movements.
Imitate with your body a vehicle starting and stopping.

Hearing – Handicapped Children

There are many benefits for hearing handicapped children in the regular classroom with "normal" children, if they are about the same chronological and mental age, and if there is an attempt to individualize instruction.

All of the discovery science activities described for other handicapped or disabled children are applicable for the hearing handicapped, as are the discovery activities for "normal" children, when you use these minimal adaptations of your regular classroom procedures:

1. Seat the child where he can see your lip movements easily. Avoid seating him facing bright lights or windows.
2. Speak naturally, in complete grammatical sentences. Do not over-emphasize lip movements or slow your rate of speech. Do not speak too loudly, especially if the child is wearing a hearing aid.
3. Avoid visual distractions such as excessive make-up and jewelry that would draw attention away from your lips.
4. Do not stand with your back to a window or bright light source. This throws your face in a shadow and makes speech reading difficult.
5. Try not to move around the room while speaking or to talk while writing on the board. If possible, use an overhead projector, which allows you to speak and write while keeping eye contact with the children.
6. During class discussions encourage the hearing handicapped child to face the speaker. Allow him to move around the room if necessary to get a better view.
7. In some cases, a manual interpreter will be assigned to the child. Allow the interpreter and child to select the most favorable seating arrangements. The manual interpreter should interpret everything said in the classroom as precisely as possible. The interpreter may also be asked to interpret the child's oral or signed responses to the teacher and class. Interpreters are not tutors or classroom aides but rather professional personnel who are facilitators of classroom communication.

8. When possible, write assignments and directions on the chalkboard or distribute mimeographed directions to the class. If assignments are given orally, a hearing student may be asked to take notes for the hearing handicapped child.
9. Ask the handicapped child to repeat or explain class material to make sure he has understood it. Embarrassed by his handicap, a hearing impaired child might learn to nod affirmatively when asked if he understood, even though he may not have understood the instructions at all.
10. If the child has a hearing aid, familiarize yourself with its operation and ask the child or his special teacher to demonstrate it to the class. The child should assume responsibility for the care of his aid.
11. Maintain close contact with the other professional personnel who have responsibility for the child's education. If possible, regularly exchange visits with the special class teacher or therapist to observe the child in his other educational settings.[4]

---

4. Harin, *Behavior of Exceptional Children*, pp. 318-19.

APPENDIX A
SUPPLIES, EQUIPMENT, AND MATERIALS FROM COMMUNITY SOURCES

This is only a partial list of places in the community that are possible sources of items for a science program in the elementary school. Other sources that should not be overlooked are local factories, the janitor of the school, the school cafeteria, radio and television repair shops, florists' shops, the other teachers in the school, the junior and senior high school science teachers, and so on. The materials are there; it just takes a little looking.

There are times, though, when in spite of the most careful searching, certain pieces of equipment or supplies are not obtainable from local sources; also there are many things that schools should buy from scientific supply houses. A partial list of some of the selected, reliable, scientific supply houses serving elementary schools is given in Appendix B.

DIME STORE

balloons
balls
candles
compasses (magnetic)
cotton (absorbent)
dyes
flashlights
glues and paste
inks
magnifying glasses
marbles
matches
mechanical toys
mirrors
mouse traps
scissors
sponges
thermometers

DRUGSTORE

acids (HCL, etc.)
adhesive tape
alcohol (rubbing)
bottles
canned heat
carbon tetrachloride
castor oil
cigar boxes
cold cream
corks
cotton
forceps
heat-resistant nursing bottles
hydrogen peroxide
iodine
limewater
medicine droppers
mercury
pipe cleaners
rubber stoppers
soda bicarbonate
spatulas
straws
sulfur

ELECTRICAL APPLIANCE SHOP

bell wire
burned-out fuses and light bulbs
dry cells
electric fans
electric hot plates
flashlights
flashlight bulbs
friction tape
magnets (from oil appliances)
old radios
soldering iron
sun lamp
worm out extension cords, electrical appliances

FABRIC SHOP

cardboard tubes
cheesecloth
flannel
knitting needles
leather
needles
netting
silk thread
spools
scraps of different kinds of materials

FARM OR DAIRY

birds' nest
bottles
clay
containers
dry ice
gravel
hay or straw
humus
insects
leaves
lodestone
loam
rocks
sand
seeds

FIRE DEPARTMENT

samples of material used to extinguish various types of fire
water pumping equipment

GARDEN SUPPLY STORE

bulbs (crocus, tulips, etc.)
fertilizers
flower pots
garden hose
garden twine
growing plants
labels
lime
seed catalogs
seeds
sprinkling cans
spray guns
trowels and other garden tools

GAS STATION

batteries
ball bearings
cans
copper tubing
gasoline
gears
gear transmissions
grease
inner tubes
jacks
maps
old wet-cell batteries
pulleys
tools
valves from tires
wheels

GROCERY STORE

ammonia
baking soda
borax
candles
carbon tetrachloride (carbona)
cellophane
clothespins
cornstarch
corrugated cardboard boxes
fruits
matches
paper bags
paraffin
plastic wrapping
salt
sponges
sugar
tinfoil
vegetables
vinegar
wax
waxed paper

HARDWARE STORE

brace and bits
cement
chisels
clocks
dry-cell batteries
electric push buttons, lamps, and sockets
extension cords
files
flashlights
fruit jars
glass cutters
glass funnels
glass friction rods
glass tubing
hammers
hard rubber rods
insulated copper wire
lamp chimneys
metal and metal scraps
nails
nuts and bolts
paints and varnishes
plaster of paris
pulleys
sandpaper
saws
scales
scrap lumber
screening
screwdrivers
screws
steel wool
thermometers (indoor and out door)
tin snips
toy electric motors
turpentine
wheelbarrow
window glass (broken pieces will do)
wire
yardsticks

MACHINE SHOP

ball bearings
iron filings
iron rods
magnets
nuts and bolts
screws
scrap metals
wire

MEDICAL AND DENTAL OFFICES AND HOSPITALS

all kinds of chemicals
corks
flasks
funnels
glass tubing
hard lenses
litmus paper
microscopes
models, such as teeth
rubber sheeting
rubber tubing
rubber stoppers
test tubes
test tube holders
thermometers
tongue depressors

MUSIC SHOP

broken string and drum heads
musical instruments
pitch pipes
tuning forks

PET SHOP

air pumps
animals
animal cages
aquariums
ant houses
birds
cages
fish
insects
nets (butterfly, fish, etc.)
plastic tubing
strainers
terrariums

RESTAURANT, DINER, OR FAST FOODS

bones (chicken, etc.)
bottles
cans (coffee, 5 gallons)
drums (ice cream)
dry ice
five gallon cans (oil)
food coloring
gallon jars (wide-mouthed, pickles, mayonnaise, etc.)
gallon jugs (vinegar)
pie tins

SUPPLIES, EQUIPMENT AND MATERIALS FROM COMMUNITY SOURCES

APPENDIX B

SELECTED SOURCES OF SCIENTIFIC EQUIPMENT, SUPPLIES, MODELS, LIVING THINGS, KITS, AND COLLECTIONS

American Basic Science
　Club, Inc.
501 East Crockett St.
San Antonio, Tex. 78202

American Optical
　Instrument Div.
Eggert and Sugar Roads
Buffalo, N.Y. 14215

Atomic Accessories, Inc.
811 West Merrick Rd.
Valley Stream, N.Y. 11580

Atomic Corp. of America
14725 Arminita St.
Panorama City, Calif. 91402

Baird-Atomic, Inc.
33 University Rd.
Cambridge, Mass. 02138

Barnett Instrument Co.
Kraft St.
Clarksville, Tenn. 37040

Bausch & Lomn, Inc.
85737 Bausch St.
Rochester, N.Y. 14602

Bioscope Manufacturing Co.
Box 1492
Tulsa, Okla. 74101

Cambosco Scientific Co.
37 Antwerp St.
Boston, Mass. 02135

Carolina Biological Supply
　Co.
Burlington, N.C. 27215

Cenco Scientific Company
2600 South Kostner Ave.
Chicago, Ill. 60623

　3232 Eleventh Ave.
　Birmingham, Ala. 35201

　3241 East Jackson
　Phoenix, Ariz. 85034

　6446 Telegraph Rd.
　Los Angeles, Calif. 90022

　1040 Martin Ave.
　Santa Clara, Calif. 95052

　160 Washington St.
　Somerville, Mass. 02143

　237 Sheffield St.
　Mountainside, N.J. 07092

　6910 East Twelfth St.
　Tulsa, Okla. 74115

　6610 Stillwell St.
　Houston, Tex. 77017

Central Scientific Co.
1700 Irving Park Rd.
Chicago, Ill. 60613

Clay-Adams Co.
141 E. 25th St.
New York, N.Y. 10010

Corning Glass Works
Building 8, 4th Floor
Corning, N.Y. 14830

Creative Playthings
P.O. Box 1100
Princeton, N.J. 08540

W. H. Curtin & Co.
Box 14
New Orleans, La. 70101

Denoyer-Geppert Co.
5235-5259 Ravenswood
　Ave.
Chicago, Ill. 60640

Dumville Manufacturing
　Co.
Box 5595
Washington, D.C. 20016

Eckert Mineral Research, Inc.
110 East Main St.
Florence, Colo. 81226

Edmunt Scientific Corp.
101 E. Gloucester Pike
Barrington, N.J. 08007

Educational Services, Inc.
108 Water St.
Watertown, Mass. 02172

Farquhar Transparent Globes
5007 Warrington Ave.
Philadelphia, Pa. 19143

Fisher Scientific Co.
620 Fisher Building
Pittsburgh, Pa. 15219

General Biological Supply
   House
8200 South Hoyne Ave.
Chicago, Ill. 60620

General Electric Co.
1001 Broad St.
Utica, N.Y. 13501

A. C. Gilbert Co.
Erector Square
New Haven, Conn.

Hubbard Scientific Company
Box 105
Northbrook, Ill. 60062

Ideal School Supply Company
11004 S. Lavergne Ave.
Oak Lawn, Ill. 60453

Irving Science Labs
2052 Hillside Ave.
New Hyde Park, N.Y. 11040

Jewel Aquarium Company
5005 W. Armitage Ave.
Chicago, Ill. 60639

Kimtec, Inc.
3625 Westheimer
Houston, Tex. 77027

Laboratory Furniture Co.
Old Country Rd.
Mineola, N.Y. 11501

Labosco, Inc.
Lombard, Ill. 60148

Lafayette Radio
165-08 Liberty Ave.
Jamaica, N.Y. 11433

Arthur S. LaPine & Co.
6001 South Knox Ave.
Chicago, Ill. 60629

Living Science Labs
1605 Jericho Tpke.
New Hyde Park, N.Y. 10040

Macalaster Scientific Corp.
253 Norfolk Ave.
Cambridge, Mass. 02139

Models of Industry
2804 Tenth St.
Berkeley, Calif. 91501

New York Scientific Supply Co.
28 W. 30th St.
New York, N.Y. 10001

A. J. Nystrom and Co.
3333 Elston Ave.
Chicago, Ill. 60618

Ohaus Scale Corporation
1050 Commerce Ave.
Union, N.J. 07033

F. A. Owens Publishing Co.
Dansville, N.Y. 11437

APPENDIX C

NONCOMMERICAL SOURCES AND CONTAINERS FOR ORGANISMS

ORGANISMS	NONCOMMERCIAL SOURCE	CULTURE CONTAINERS
POND SNAILS	Fresh water ponds, creeks	Aquaria, gallon glass jars
LAND SNAILS	Mature hardwood forests: on rocks, fallen logs, damp foliage	Terraria, large battery jars
DAPHNIA	Freshwater ponds: at water's edge, and associated with algae.	Gallon glass or plastic jars
ISOPODS AND CRICKETS	Under rocks, bricks, and boards that have lain on ground for some time; between grass and base of brick buildings.	Glass or plastic terraria, plastic sweater boxes. (Provide vents in cover.)
MEALWORM BEETLES	Corn cribs, around granaries	Gallon glass jars with cheese cloth
FRUIT FLIES	Trap with bananas or apple slices. (Place fruit in a jar with a funnel for a top.)	Tall baby food jars, plastic vials. (Punch hole in jar lids, cover with masking tape and then prick tiny holes in tape with a pin.)
WINGLESS PEA APHIDS*	Search on garden vegetables, e.g., English peas	On pea plants potted in plastic pots, milk cartons. (Keep aphids in a large terrarium so they cannot wander to other plants in the school.)
GUPPIES	Persons who raise guppies as a hobby. (Usually glad to reduce population when they clean tanks.)	Aquaria, large battery jars
CHAMELEONS*	Dense foliage along river banks or railroad tracks. (Catch with net or large tea strainer.)	Prepare cage from broken aquaria. (Broken glass can be replaced by taping cloth screening along sides.)
FROGS*	Along edges of ponds, ditches, creeks. (Catch with large scoop net.)	Large plastic ice chest. (Set near a sink so a constant water supply is at hand.)
CHLAMYDOMONAS AND EUGLENA	Freshwater pond	Gallon glass jars, aquaria, battery jars
ELODEA (ANACHARIS)*	Ponds, creeks: usually along edge or in shallows	Aquaria, large battery jars
EELGRASS*	Wading zone of brackish water	Aquaria, large battery jars
DUCKWEED	Edge of ponds or fresh water swamps	Aquaria, large battery jars
COLEUS AND GERANIUM	Persons who raise them. (Start by rooting cuttings in 1 part sand, 1 part vermiculite in plastic bags; keep moist.)	Clay pots, milk cartons, tin cans

*These species are difficult to obtain from their natural habitats. Unless you have a convenient source, it is better to buy them commercially. Try a local aquarium or pet shop.

Source: Carolyn H. Hampton and Carol D. Hampton, "The Establishment of a Life Science Center." Reproduced with permission by *Science and Children* 15, no. 7 (April 1978): 9. Copyright 1978 by The National Science Teachers Association, 1742 Connecticut Avenue, N.W., Washington, D.C. 20009.

APPENDIX D

REQUIREMENTS FOR VARIOUS ANIMALS

FOOD AND WATER	RABBITS	GUINEA PIGS	HAMSTERS	MICE	RATS
Daily					
pellets	rabbit pellets: keep dish half full		large dog pellets: one or two		
or					
grain		corn, wheat, or oats:		canary seeds or oats:	
green or leafy vegetables, lettuce, cabbage and celery tops	keep dish half full 4-5 leaves	2 leaves	1½ tablespoon 1 leaf	2 teaspoons ⅛-¼ leaf	3-4 teaspoons ¼ leaf
or					
grass, plantain, lambs' quarters, clover, alfalfa	2 handfuls	1 handful	½ handful	—	—
or					
hay, if water is also given					
carrits	2 medium	1 medium			
Twice a week					
apple (medium)	½ apple	¼ apple	⅛ apple	½ core and seeds	1 core
iodized salt (if not contained in pellets)	or salt block	sprinkle over lettuce or greens			
corn, canned or fresh, once or twice a week	½ ear	¼ ear	1 tablespoon ⅓ ear	¼ tablespoon or end of ear	½ tablespoon or end of ear
water	should always be available		necessary only if lettuce or greens are not provided		

Source: Grace K. Pratt, *How to ... Care for Living Things in the Classroom* (Washington, D.C.: National Science Teachers Association, 1965), p.9.

FOOD AND WATER, PLANTS (FOR FISH)	WATER TURTLES	LAND TURTLES	SMALL TURTLES
Daily			
worms or night crawlers	1 or 2	1 or 2	¼ inch of tiny earthworm
or			
tubifex or blood worms			enough to cover ½ area of a dime
and/or			
raw chopped beef or meat and fish-flavored dog or cat food	½ teaspoon	½ teaspoon	
fresh fruit and vegetables		¼ leaf lettuce or 6-10 berries or 1-2 slices peach, apple, tomato, melon or 1 tablespoon corn, peas, beans	
dry ant eggs, insects, or other commercial turtle food			1 small pinch
water	always available at room temperature; should be ample for swimming and submersion large enough for shell		half to ¾ of container

FOOD AND WATER, PLANTS	GOLDFISH	GUPPIES
Daily		
dry commercial food	1 small pinch	1 very small pinch; medium size food for adults; fine size food for babies
Twice a week		
shrimp—dry—or another kind of dry fish food	4 shrimp pellets, or 1 small pinch	dry shrimp food or other dry food; 1 very small pinch
Two or three times a week tubifex worms	enough to cover ½ area of a dime allow one gallon per inch of fish	enough to cover ⅛ area of a dime allow ¼—½ gallon per adult fish
Add enough "conditioned" water to keep tank at required level	add water of same temperature as that in tank —at least 65 °F	add water of same temperature as that in tank—70—80 °F
Plants		
cabomba, anacharis, etc.	should always be available	

	NEWTS	FROGS
Daily		
small earthworms or mealworms	1-2 worms	2-3 worms
or		
tubifex worms	enough to cover ½ area of a dime	enough to cover ¾ area of a dime
or		
raw chopped beef	enough to cover a dime	enough to cover a dime
water	should always be available at same temperature as that in tank or room temperature	